Jicarilla River

Ragen Mountains

Vellexa Temy

Apathy Range

Tho

Belmoth

Lake Hyalin

Sulmen *

Rebel Mountains

M a g

Rampën

Vanern

Vanker Mountains

Saeten

N

The Birthright Chronicles

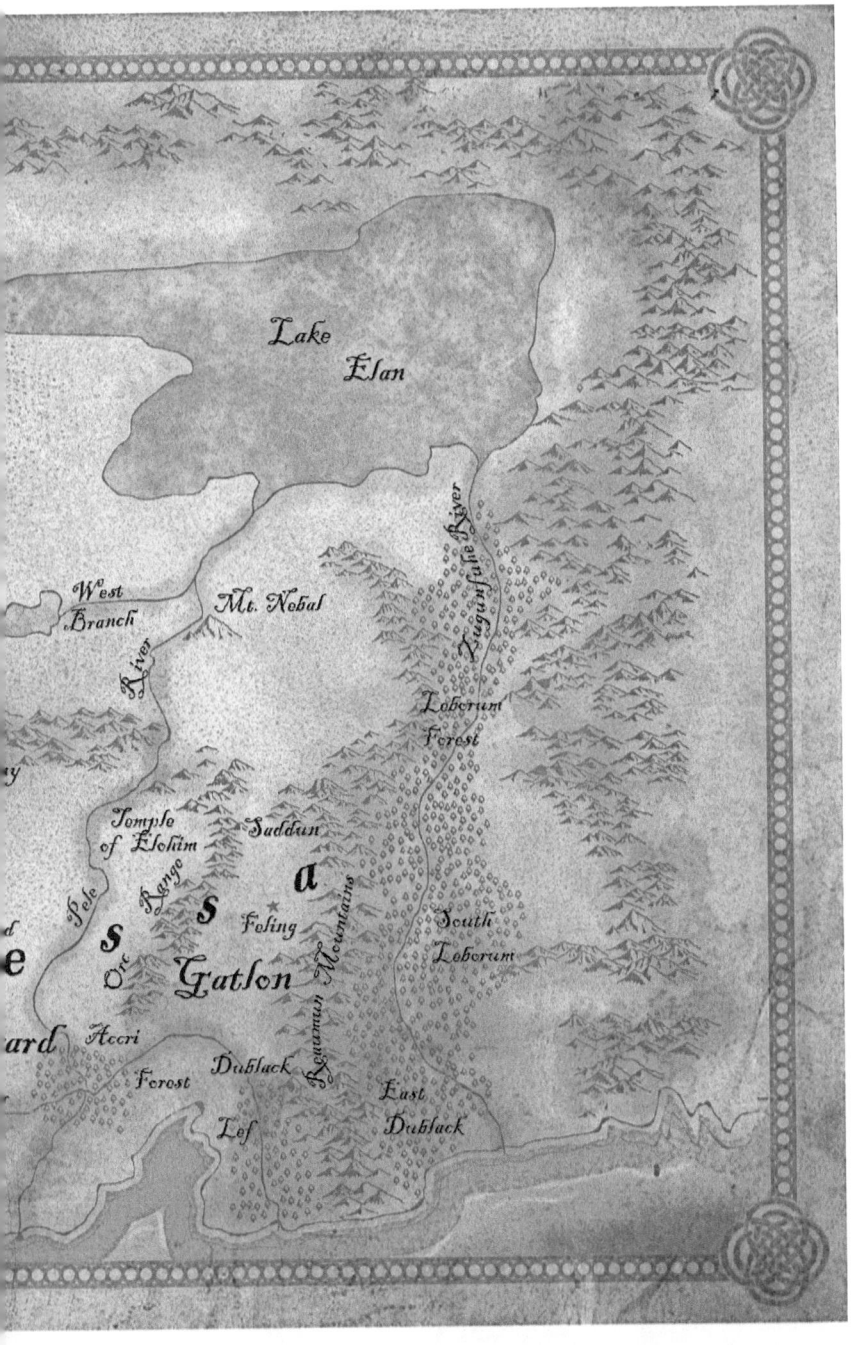

The Wizard's Tower

Peter Last

Published by:
Bluewater Publications
www.BluewaterPublications.com

Credits

➤ Robert Rausch artist with Gas Studio of Tuscumbia, AL
  for his extraordinary work on the book's cover.

➤ Scott Campbell created illustration on the front cover

➤ David Walker graphic artist that designed the map

➤ Sheri Dee Developmental Editor

Acknowledgements

I would like to express my sincere gratitude to everyone who helped make this book a reality. I would specifically like to thank the following individuals who made this book possible through their constant help, suggestions, and snide comments.

- ❖ My mom and dad for bearing through twelve years of this, even when my dad wishes I would get a 'real job' over the summer!

- ❖ My sister Rachel for her constant advice on revisions. Even though she and I disagree on some aspects of writing, she still continues to make my work better.

- ❖ My family for pretending to be interested in the story line and all the 'mind benders' in the plot, even though I secretly think they don't care as much as they let on.

- ❖ Ben for his suggested improvements to the story. Even though I haven't seen you in over a year, your contributions continue to affect my work!

- ❖ Ben Broyles, for believing my work was good enough to publish, even before he read it. Also for his invaluable help with promotional filming and marketing assistance.

- ❖ My fiancée for continuing to stick with me through this, even when date night gets postponed so I can do 'book stuff'.

- ❖ Tyler Yasaka for his fantastic work with my website.

- ❖ Sheri Dee for her fantastic editorial and proofreading skills; also, for all the marketing guidance.

- ❖ Dean, Katie, Tammy, and many others who have helped with the review and editing of the book.

❖ All my fans who read the first book and continue to inquire about the future of the series. I couldn't do what I do without you guys.

❖ Finally, and most importantly, God for giving me the ability and opportunity to do this. This book is all for you.

Prologue

Wellter was the lead for this mission. He would have gladly been the operative, but the commander had some sort of in with these wizards. This was unexpected, though not a shock. The commander was a powerful magician and well respected, although not much was known about his past. A strong association with the world of magic was a given, but a history riddled with dark magic was also assumed. Whatever the case, no one doubted that his allegiance was with Elohim now.

The current mission was typical for the group. The plan was to use the commander's contacts to relieve a particularly mighty wizard of his magic. The problem was that the contacts were also wizards and had only agreed to help the commander if they split the power among themselves. The scheme had grown from there. The commander would drain the wizard of his magic. When the three wizards working with the commander closed in, Jothnial would move in and distract them long enough for the commander to transfer the power to Scrogg. Wellter and Jared would be held in reserve in case something went wrong, and something was likely to go wrong. When wizards were involved, it usually did.

Wellter glanced back to where Jothnial and Jared were playing Lex Tanna. The commander and Scrogg were the only two who had already been deployed to play their parts in the scheme. The commander was nowhere to be seen, but for the past hour Scrogg had been moving about the market that Wellter's window overlooked. It was getting close to "go time," and Wellter's nerves were beginning to fray. He looked at Scrogg again and scanned the area around him. Without looking away, he snapped his fingers at Jared and Jothnial and motioned them over.

"What's up, Wellter?" Jared said. Since he was the backup, any change in plan would likely involve him.

1

"Do you see the bald man about fifteen feet to the north of Scrogg?" Wellter asked. "That man's been tailing Scrogg for the past half an hour. Fifty to one he's a magician."

"So what do you want me to do?" Jared asked. Although he already knew, he wanted to make sure everyone was on the same page.

"Take care of him," Wellter answered.

"And if you're wrong about him?" Jared asked.

"That's a chance that we'll have to take," Wellter said. "Don't do anything lethal to him, of course, but take him out of the picture."

"Will do," Jared said. With a blast of wind he disappeared from the room. Wellter and Jothnial looked into the square and, though there was no wind that day, saw the cloth walls of a stall jump forward from a breeze. Moments later, Jared stepped out from behind the booth and started making his way toward the bald man that Wellter had identified.

"He's not very good at that, is he?" Jothnial commented.

"Teleporting?" Wellter asked. "No, he's definitely an attack magic guy. Stealth and subterfuge have never been his strong suit."

"And you asked him to take care of the bald man?" Jothnial asked. "Don't you think he'll cause a scene?"

"I said it wasn't his strong suit, not that he couldn't do it," Wellter said. "He'll do fine. Just make sure that *you* do your job."

"Speaking of which, is that the commander?"

"Yes, it is," Wellter said. The man that he was with would be the mark, the wizard that that they were targeting. "He's ahead of schedule, but that's fine."

2

"Where are the others?" Jothnial asked, scanning the crowd for the commander's compatriots.

"I wouldn't expect them until after the transfer has occurred," Wellter explained. "Just be prepared to get down there and distract them without letting on that you are a magician."

"You can count on me," Jothnial said.

Wellter turned his attention back to his commander and the man that he was with. From the way that they were interacting, it was almost as if the two were friends. Perhaps they had been in the past. Whatever their history was, it was certainly helping in the current situation. Everything was going according to plan, but Wellter was still unsure of how the commander planned on siphoning the target's power. That was something that he had been mysteriously quiet on. Apparently the other wizards had come up with a way to do it, one that the commander seemed to think would work. His confidence was enough for Wellter.

The commander and his companion were about in the center of the market area when things were set in motion. Gripping the hilt of his sword with one hand, he wrapped his free arm around his companion's shoulders. It was no more than a very powerful twitch, but Wellter could tell that the transfer of power had begun. The commander's friend began to struggle, but it was too late. In the moments that it took for the transfer to take place, the target seemed to shrink in size and an aura, unnoticed by Wellter until it was gone, disappeared. In seconds he was reduced to a shell of what he had been before and collapsed to the ground. Physically there was nothing wrong with him, but the sudden absence of power had rocked him to his core.

Wellter turned to Jothnial, only to notice the elf was already gone. He was definitely good; Wellter hadn't noticed a thing. He looked back out the window and saw Jothnial step out from behind a stall. But where were the other three wizards the commander had mentioned? There they were now, entering the market on the opposite side from Jothnial. Wellter steeled himself for the worst. It was times like these that plans went wrong.

He saw the plan begin to fall apart before his very eyes. Jared, unaware of what was going on, was still on a collision path with the bald magician. Jothnial vanished and teleported across the market to where the commander three contacts had just entered. The obvious goal would be to appear in such a way that they would not notice, but something went wrong. The power transfer had been a large one and was certain to create a disturbance in the surrounding area; Wellter could already begin to feel the effects, and he was much farther removed from the anomaly than Jothnial. Whether due to conditions out of his control or just his own incompetence, Jothnial materialized directly in front of the commander's three compatriots. The looks on their faces gave away what they were thinking; the appearance of another magician at this location at this time was no coincidence. They looked toward the commander who had already begun the spell for the second power transfer. At this point it was still possible for the plan to work, albeit a bit sloppily; however, Wellter was unprepared for what happened next.

Jared finally reached the bald magician and attempted to put him down with a spell, but the target was prepared. A simple ward shot the spell skyward where it exploded. For a few moments nothing happened as the people stood, too shocked at what had just happened to move. Then pandemonium broke out among the market stalls as magic began to fly in all directions. Evidently not only had the commander's friends planned on double crossing him, they had brought an army to back them up. The commander spotted Scrogg across the market and knew he would never reach him in time due to the bedlam. His fingers began to twitch with the creation of a new spell.

"Don't do it," Wellter said to the empty room.

The commander flicked a wrist toward Scrogg, then pulled his sword from its sheath just in time to block a slash from a weapon that had seemingly materialized out of nowhere. A ward deflected a fireball into a stall, causing it to go up in flames. Things were going from bad to worse very quickly, and Wellter knew that there was only one reasonable course of action. In the blink of an eye, he teleported out of the room and was behind Jothnial. All three of the wizards that he was supposed to be distracting were hammering away at his hastily constructed protection spell; it wouldn't last much longer. Grabbing a fistful of Jothnial's shirt, Wellter teleported both of them to where the commander was fighting off a half dozen attackers.

"Get us over to Jared and Scrogg!" Wellter yelled to Jothnial. He grabbed hold of the commander's belt just in time.

The three magicians materialized in the shallow crater one of Jared's effective but flashy spells had created. Scrogg had already constructed a dome shield large enough for the five magicians to fit under, and it was taking fire from every corner of the market place. It was a barrier designed to keep out magical attack while allowing physical objects through. Though not an ideal solution in this situation, it would work.

"Scrogg and I will maintain the shield," the commander yelled. He was clearly in charge again. "Jared, blast anyone who is stupid enough to come inside. Wellter and Jothnial, get us out of here!"

Wellter grabbed the backs of the commander's and Scrogg's shirts while Jothnial took hold of Jared's and Wellter's belts. Together the two magicians worked to teleport out of the area. There were clearly some magicians whose job it was to keep them from escaping, and they were making it difficult indeed. Every direction seemed to be blocked by the ethereal powers of the other magicians; Wellter tried to push through, but was unable. Then, so suddenly that it shocked Wellter himself, the group disappeared.

Wellter had always thought that it was a strange sensation to teleport. It was impossible to describe with words the feeling of dissolving from one place and whizzing through space to arrive at another location. The transfer was always instantaneous, but it did not feel as such. There was always a length of time to mentally prepare for what would be on the other side, but this time, Wellter did not know their destination. Clearly it was Jothnial who had gotten them out alive.

The trip was much shorter than Wellter had imagined, and he materialized in knee-deep water, almost falling forward into it. There was little light in this place, but the stench gave it away instantly.

"Good going, guys," Scrogg said sarcastically. "The sewer was exactly where I wanted to end up."

"Well, at least we're not getting attacked from all sides at the moment," Wellter shot back.

"Be quiet, both of you," the commander's voice said out of the darkness. "Jothnial and Wellter, can you get us out of here?"

"No problem," Wellter answered rather irritably. The next spell was not his best. They vanished in a flash, one that ignited the fumes in the sewer, shooting flames out of every outlet and collapsing a section about a hundred yards long.

******

"Based on the fact that no one is saying much, I'm going to assume that our plan failed," the commander said. All of the magicians had bathed, but the smell of the sewers still hung in the air.

"I never received the power transfer, if that's what you're asking," Scrogg said, turning away from the window out of which he had been looking. Its bars cast shadows from the setting sun across the floor. The headquarters of a secret magician organization being inside a jail cell may have puzzled some people, but as the commander said, "If you don't want someone to find something, put it in the last place they'll expect to find it." A jail was certainly the last place anyone would look for this organization.

"I don't get it," Jothnial said. "If you didn't transfer to Scrogg, wouldn't you still have the power?"

"Because the commander siphoned the power, he was the target when the double cross happened," Wellter explained. "He got rid of the power like any sensible person would have done."

"He would have had to do a long range transfer," Jared said. "But they're only theoretical."

"Oh, they work alright," the commander said. "The only problem was, apparently it didn't go where I intended."

"But if you don't have the power anymore," Scrogg said, "and I don't have it either…"

"Someone or something did receive the transfer, though who or what is still a mystery," Wellter explained. Of all of the magicians, he had the broadest spectrum of knowledge.

"Which is why this is far from over," the commander said. "Someone out there has the power that I transferred, and with as many magicians and wizards as were in that market today, the probability of it being in one of their hands is quite high."

"That means we have to track them all down and deal with them," Jared said.

"Only if you want to spend a whole lot of time chasing impossible trails and dead ends with the hopes of turning something up," the commander said. "The three wizards that I made the deal with are the ones that we need to worry about. They're the only ones who know the extent of the power which is at stake. If we simply sit back for a while, they will eventually find out who has acquired it. All we have to do is keep tabs on them so that when they turn up something, we can swoop in and take it from them."

"So, we just sit and wait?" Wellter asked. He knew the commander better than most, and even he was surprised at this.

"No," the commander said. "We may not know where the power is, but I do know that none of the three wizards will know how to extract it when they do find it. That is why I was the one to siphon the power today. This means they will need magicians who have the ability to perform the transfer. If we can take care of them, it will at least slow the process down. In any case, we will keep our ears open for news. Whenever the vessel for the power is uncovered, we will finish what we started today."

One

A cold wind blew the rain into Senndra's face, making her pull her cloak even tighter around her body. The rain had started two days ago and had not let up at all since it had arrived, leading some people to think that it was of unnatural origin. Magical or not, the rain had turned the dirt of the path into mud, forcing Senndra to focus her entire attention on the ground in front of her so that she did not slide down the slick mountainside. The path leveled out just long enough to allow a large stream of water to cross it. Senndra jumped over it, splashing mud on her pants and cloak, but she didn't care; she just wanted to get to her dorm room. She had started down the hill when the rain seemed to have let up slightly; however, it began to pour again, this time with a vengeance. All Senndra wanted was the warm fire in her room.

The dorm came into view, and Senndra quickened her step. She almost lost her balance as she slipped and slid down the path, coming to a jarring stop against the door of her room. Fumbling with the latch, she managed to raise it, push the door inward, and tumble inside. Rita lay on the floor in front of the fire, her head resting on the back of a dragon that lounged behind her. This was her dragon, Sowpa, who had hatched only three weeks before and was already the size of a large dog. Sowpa's scales were a shiny blue color, and a row of bumps ran down her back and tail. She stretched one of her front legs out in her sleep and extended the claws momentarily before sheathing them again. These claws were sharp enough to shred flesh, bone, and even some dragon scales.

Senndra changed into dry clothes and spread the wet ones out in front of the hearth. She tossed a few more logs on the fire before stretching out on the floor beside her friend. As she watched Rita and Sowpa sleeping, her thoughts turned to her own dragon. When she had returned to the academy a little more than half a year ago, he had been slightly smaller than Sowpa was now; however, he had not stayed that size for very long. He had grown rapidly until reaching his current size: from his nose to the tip of his tail, he measured around ninety feet long, and his wingspan stretched one hundred and eighty feet; he would not get any larger than this. His growth had been watched closely and with much speculation. Due to the character traits of the only other known brown dragon, many assumed that Feddir would be substandard, unable to grow scales or breathe fire. Others conjectured that because dragon color had no known bearing on character traits, Feddir would be just like any other dragon. The debate had continued, sometimes in a heated fashion, but Senndra had dismissed all of it. What was the point in arguing this? Time would tell which side was correct, and indeed it had. Ten days ago, Feddir's first scales had begun to force their way through his skin. His breath had also continued to grow hotter and, with the appearance of his scales, everyone agreed that it was only a matter of time before he could breathe fire as well.

Senndra sat down and stared at the flames. As she continued to think about her dragon, her eyelids drooped, and finally she nodded off. Sleep, however, was not the reprieve that it normally was. As she slipped into the land of unconsciousness, she found herself floating in her room. Looking down, she could see herself sleeping. She felt an unknown force begin to pull her, and rafters flew by as she passed through the roof and was flung out into the open sky. The force that was drawing her stopped with a jerk, and she found herself floating upright as though standing on thin air, suspended about a hundred feet above the ground. The force abruptly started to pull her again, this time toward the north. The mountains rushed beneath her until they dropped away to a plain which quickly turned into marshlands. In the distance, Senndra could see a city positioned in the swamp, and instinctively she knew that it was Vollexa Temp. Dark clouds surrounded the city, and a stench worse than that of the swamp assaulted Senndra's nostrils. As Senndra had passed over the marshland, she had not noticed how quickly she was traveling; however, now it was obvious that she was traveling at breakneck speed. She began to descend as she neared the city, and her destination became evident; if she did not stop, she would smash headlong into the tower in the middle of the city. The tower seemed to be the source of power that was pulling her, and her speed increased as she approached it. She reached the tower and passed through a window, a mere slit in the stone wall. A large circular room was on the other side of the window, and her speed decreased rapidly as she entered, bringing her to a halt in the middle of the room, hovering about ten feet above the floor.

The room was well furnished and appeared to be comfortable for whoever lived in it. Indeed it was obvious that someone lived there; a bed was in the center of the room directly below her, and off to one side was a table with dishes that still had some food on them. On the other side of the room a desk and some bookshelves stood near a wall. The shelves contained dozens of books, but Senndra could not make out any of the titles from where she was. The desk had a handful of books piled up on it along with some paper, quills, and ink. Several chairs were scattered throughout the room, and a bench rested near the foot of the bed. Off to one side were facilities for bathing. Pictures and embroidered wall hangings helped make the room look more inviting; however, little could be done to counteract the trapped feeling of the room which came from having only a few, very small windows.

Senndra could see no doors, physical or magical, anywhere in the room; however, almost immediately after she had completed her quick search of the perimeter, a man appeared through the wall. Behind him Senndra now saw a faint glimmer that she had missed on her previous inspection. The man appeared to be an elf, though from her vantage point, Senndra could not positively identify his race. He walked to the bench by the bed and lounged on it, waiting for something. Senndra did not have to wait long to find out for what he waited; a smooth, oily voice came out of the darkness. It did not come from any one direction, but seemed to come from all directions at once. Immediately Senndra knew that it was coming from the very walls of the tower and that this was the voice of Molkekk, bane of Magessa.

"Regulus, the time has come," Molkekk's voice said to the man on the bench. "Gather the full force of my army and launch a full scale invasion on Magessa."

"I had anticipated your command, my lord," Regulus said. "Therefore, I have already begun to muster your army. The dragons have already been sent to Magessa to take care of an academy for training dragon riders. The rumor is that more than half of Magessa's dragons reside in this location, so a decisive victory there will give us a distinct advantage in the war to come. As for the bulk of the army, almost all of your goblins have arrived. Messages have been sent out to all of the peoples that are under our control; however, only a few nomadic tribes of elves have arrived. I anticipate that most of our reinforcements will be here within a week."

"Excellent," Molkekk's voice said. "When they arrive we will immediately begin our offensive. Do you have a battle plan for the conquest of the nation?"

"Indeed, sir," Regulus answered. "The plan, which is already in progress, is to split the army into three sections. One of these will attack the dragon riding academy in Belvárd. We will give them just enough time to begin to respond to the attack and then, when their troops are on the move, we will use the other two sections of our army to attack Saddun and Belmoth, the two gateways into their country. News of the secondary attacks will take time to reach the capitols, and when it does, they will have great difficulty finding many troops to send to aid the cities. All in all, they should not be very hard to defeat."

"The cities should not be very hard to defeat?" Molkekk said in an angry voice. "Have you so soon forgotten the defeat at Saddun? A few thousand untested soldiers kept the entire might of the dwarf army at bay long enough for reinforcements to arrive. By now, there will be even more soldiers at each city."

"Even in the unlikely incident that we are defeated at one city, we will almost certainly overrun the other," Regulus said in an even tone. "The dwarf army which seemed like an unstoppable force was defeated; therefore, I have increased the number of our soldiers. Each of our attack forces will have half a million soldiers as well as siege equipment of every variety. With these massive forces, they should not be able to withstand either attack much less both of them. As our soldiers arrive here, I will send them to reinforce our armies, so that no matter how many of our men the enemy kills, there will always be more to take their place. Added to that is the fact that we will have the sea on our side."

"Very well, proceed with the attack," Molkekk's voice said. "But make sure that you do not fail me."

"No sir, I will not fail you," Regulus said. He bowed to the floor, but Senndra was already floating away.

She passed through one of the room's window slits and began to pick up speed as she traveled back toward Magessa. This time she was so close to the ground that the soles of her boots brushed the tops of the short swamp vegetation. The mountains of the Apathy Range drew nearer, but even so, Senndra's altitude remained the same. All at once she was upon the foot of the mountains, and her speed slowed slightly as she plunged into an opening in the rock, a bare fissure in the side of a cliff. She continued to move forward at breakneck speed, the complete darkness of the tunnel making it impossible to determine how far she traveled or how long the journey through the mountain lasted. By the time she exited the tunnel, she was exhausted. She was conscious enough to realize that it opened into a cave set high on a cliff. When she left the cave, her forward momentum ceased and she began to rise until she recognized the slopes of the mountain that the academy was built upon. Her eyes were so heavy by now that she could no longer fight the urge to shut them. Once her eyes closed, she sank into a deep sleep.

******

Josiah tossed and turned on his bunk. Sweat drenched his body, yet he did not awaken. In his dream he stood atop the wall of Saddun with a sword in either hand. He glanced back and saw a group of old people and young children. All around him lay thousands of young men, apparently slain in the battle and directly in front of him was a large army of dwarves. The dwarves were moving toward him, but at a leisurely pace, apparently not in any hurry to reach him. He caught sight of crossbowmen in their ranks and cursed silently. Bolts from the crossbows filled the air as they flew straight toward him. They slammed into him, piercing armor and flesh wherever they contacted, sending flares of pain through his body. Doing his best to shut the pain from his mind, he struggled to stand up. The dwarves charged him with vigor now, bearing down on their seemingly helpless foe. With pain coursing through his body, Josiah stood his ground and raised both of his swords. Several bolts had pierced his legs, rendering him immobile, so he waited for the dwarves to reach him. The moment they came within his sword range, he started swinging, laying out three dwarves with

14

his first stroke. His second swipe was blocked by the shield of a dwarf who returned the blow, burying his ax deep into Josiah's side. Josiah gasped in pain, slumped forward, and fell to the ground. The dwarves stampeded over his body, their iron-shod boots cutting into his flesh and crushing his bones. He could hear the shrieks of those he had tried to protect as the dwarves reached them and began to kill indiscriminately.

Josiah bolted up in bed. His breath was coming in short gasps, and his heart was pounding. Slowly his breathing and heartbeat returned to normal, and he lay back in the bed. He stared at the bunk above his and wondered if his dream meant anything. Already it was fading from his memory, and he wondered whether he would be able to remember it the next morning. He tried for half an hour to get back to sleep, yet it eluded him. Finally he gave up, rose from his bed, and stepped out of the barrack and into the open air. It was cool outside so Josiah ducked back inside for his cloak. Then he walked to the center of the city were a stream cut the city in half, north and south. He walked onto the bridge that spanned the water and sat down in the middle with his legs hanging over the edge.

The night was clear, and hundreds of stars were visible in the sky. Josiah lay on his back and tried to find images among the pinpoints of light. He had found this to be one of the most relaxing things in the world and often employed it in an attempt to distract himself from memories of his battle with the dwarves. Normally it was an effective method of distraction, but tonight there was no diversion from his thoughts. Eventually he gave up and closed his eyes.

Sleep overtook him almost immediately, and he dreamed again. He stood on the battlefield of Saddun again, but this time the battle was over. Dead from both armies littered the ground, and there was nothing living for as far as he could see. Slowly he began to make his way toward one of the remaining buildings of the city, moving carefully so as not to step on any bodies. The structure was smoking and it was obvious that it had burned in the

15

recent past. As Josiah walked by, a large section of roof collapsed inward expelling a cloud of smoke and soot. The building was just another evidence of the ravages of the enemy army that had occupied the city, or so Josiah thought until he saw the entrance. The doors had been nailed shut and fastened with massive lengths of chain. They were not locked, and Josiah wasted no time in ripping them loose from the doors. Next were the nails. They were harder, and Josiah strained at them for several minutes until they began to give way. Slowly the doors creaked farther and farther open until, with no warning, they swung completely open. Josiah went down hard but scrambled to his feet and away from the doors as an avalanche spilled from between them. Charred bodies of all races, ages, sizes, and genders tumbled out of the building, barely recognizable through their burns. A mixture of feelings, anger, sadness, and hate burst from his lips in an earsplitting bellow.

Josiah sat up so quickly that he almost fell off of the bridge. He quickly glanced around the city, but none of the death and destruction of his dream met his eyes. Instead he saw the orderly buildings of Saddun. A bell rang to indicate the changing of guards. To the east, the sky was beginning to turn pink as the sun prepared to rise above the mountains.

Josiah shook his head to clear away the vision of his dream and slowly stood to his feet. He walked back to his barrack and began to prepare for the day ahead of him. First he showered in the facilities behind the building. The water was cold, but he didn't mind. When he had finished, he put on his uniform and strapped on the weapons that went with it. Next he looked at the soldiers that slept in his barrack.

"No one should still be asleep at this time," he said out loud. With both hands he grasped the cord of a bell that hung just inside the door and began to swing it as hard as he could. A harsh clanging filled the building, pulling the cadets from their sleep. Quickly they scrambled out of bed and dressed. This whole process took less than two minutes, at which time the entire population of the barrack stood at attention in four rows between the bunk beds. Josiah looked over them and suddenly had an idea.

"Get those sleepy looks off of your faces," he shouted, "we're going to be running before breakfast, so get moving double time."

Josiah led the cadets out the door of the building and into what had only minutes before been the beginnings of a beautiful day. Now, however, clouds blocked the sun and threatened rain at any moment. The four rows of cadets wound their way through the city until they had reached the south wall. They followed the wall to the west end of the city and turned north, cutting through the buildings until they arrived at the mess hall. Just as Josiah stepped inside, rain began to come down outside. In less than a minute it was pouring, and Josiah watched as his men passed into the mess hall in perfect order, paying no attention to the rain. It took almost fifteen minutes for all of them to get into the hall and sit at their tables. Those on kitchen patrol quickly set the tables and served the food, while the other cadets talked. Josiah walked to a window of the hall and stared out at the rain. It was coming down in torrents now, and the few cadets that were still straggling into the hall were soaking wet.

Josiah turned from the window to go to his table when the window behind him exploded in a shower of glass and rain. Josiah threw his hands over his head and ducked as the glass shards rained down around him. Finally he was able to stand up, and he turned to examine the broken window as several people rushed to make sure he was not hurt. A small tree was lodged in the window frame, having been blown over by the wind. Josiah grasped a branch and pushed with all of his might. He was quickly joined by several other cadets, and together they pushed the tree out of the mess hall window. Already other people were bringing materials with which to patch the hole for the time being. In practically no time, the window was boarded up, and two cadets were sweeping up the leaves and broken glass while another one mopped up the rain that had formed a large puddle on the floor. Josiah sat at a table and took a draught of water to help calm his nerves. His heart was beginning to slow to its normal rate, but his nerves were still on edge. He took a few deep breaths; it was unlike him to not be able to control his feelings. Glancing at the boarded up window, he wondered if it was the storm that made him uneasy or if something more sinister lingered in the air.

******

Senndra jerked awake at the sound of boots scraping across the floor. She sat up and saw immediately that Rita was not where she had been when Senndra had fallen asleep. Senndra threw a quick glance around the room and spotted her standing in front of the closet. Rita turned around when Senndra groaned and stood to her feet.

"Good morning, sleepyhead," she said in a cheerful voice.

"It's morning?" Senndra asked.

"I don't know," Rita answered. "It's still pouring down rain, so I can't tell anything right now."

"Where's Sowpa?" Senndra asked, suddenly realizing that the dragon was nowhere to be found.

"She was acting weird, so I let her outside," Rita answered.

"Acting strange how?" Senndra asked.

"I don't really know how to explain it," Rita said. "It wasn't like anything that I have ever seen. Her scales started shifting, and her wings unfolded. She kept making noises like she was trying to growl, but couldn't for some reason."

"Hmm, that isn't like anything that I have ever heard of," Senndra said. "I wonder…" She was interrupted by a gasp from Rita.

"There is danger of some sort," Rita said in a panicked voice. "Sowpa's feelings are rank with fear."

"Don't worry about it," Senndra advised. "She probably just ran into an especially large snake or something. Feddir used to scare me like that all the time until he became familiar with the world around him. Now, if Feddir starts to feel fear, then we need to start worrying." Without warning, fear and excitement simultaneously flowed across the mental link that attached Senndra to Feddir. Senndra's eyes widened at the strength of the feeling, but what surprised her more was when these feelings turned to ones of anger and hatred. Quickly she grabbed her weapons and began to strap them on.

"Feddir also has feelings that seem to indicate danger," Senndra told Rita over her shoulder. "Get dressed and come with me." Even before she had finished talking, the campus bell that was reserved specifically for emergencies shattered the silence. Rita needed no more encouragement, and in less than a minute she was armed. Together the two girls cautiously stepped outside and were met with the most terrible sight that either had ever seen. Dragons of every color circled the academy, battling above them. Balls of fire flashed through the air, sometimes contacting dragons and sometimes lighting a building or group of trees on fire. Griffins were also interspersed throughout the fighting, though their effect was not quite as magnificent as that of the dragons. They dashed in and out of the dragons, slashing wings whenever they could and occasionally attacking a wounded dragon. Half a dozen of them grouped together and attacked a dragon head-on. Three caught fire before they ever reached their target, and the other three practically exploded in a cloud of feathers as the dragon's razor-sharp claws wreaked havoc on them.

Senndra grabbed Rita's arm and dragged her away from the dorm and down the mountain. A dragon hit the mountain side in front of them and slid over a cliff. The friends left the path and plunged downhill by a more direct route. A roar sounded behind them, and Senndra glanced over her shoulder to see a black dragon bearing down on them. She broke into an all-out run, but only a few steps later, her foot hit a loose stone. She held onto Rita, trying to regain her balance, but only succeeded in dragging her friend down with her. The two girls bounced and slid down the slope into a thick stand of trees. Bushes and briars scratched them painfully while slowing them to stop. They lay still for several long seconds; finally Senndra crawled over to where Rita lay.

"I think he's gone," she said in a low voice. Rita nodded and started to get to her feet, but stopped suddenly. The ground above them shook with the weight of a large body landing on it, and the girls dropped into the underbrush again. Everything was still for several seconds, and the girls held their breaths, hoping that the dragon would not hear them. The ground started to shake again, making it obvious that the dragon was stalking down the slope and into the trees. Grunts, groans, and the snapping of trees and underbrush marked the progress of the dragon; it was heading straight toward Senndra and Rita. They slowly began to slither down the slope on their bellies, trying to make as little noise as possible, but it was no use. The dragon's keen ears isolated the sounds and began to move more quickly. The companions rose to their feet and broke into a run. Branches scratched their faces, and the underbrush tripped them constantly, but they crashed forward at breakneck speed. Suddenly they burst from the trees and found themselves slipping on loose rock. Twenty feet in front of them, the slope turned into a cliff. The girls turned around and looked at the trees. The ground continued to shake, a grim testament of the beast that was approaching. The friends backed up until their heels were inches from the cliff, and they clung to each other as they waited. The tops of the trees rustled, and suddenly the dragon burst from them. He came to a halt when he saw the humans, clearly surprised to see them facing him; however, he soon regained his bravado and began to slowly stomp toward them.

As Senndra and Rita cowered in each other's arms, they were able to discern shapes twisting into and out of the clouds that hung over the mountain. One of the shapes began to solidify, and it appeared as if it were approaching them. The girls' hope began to rise, but the shape banked to the left and disappeared below the ridgeline. Once again, the approaching dragon was all that filled their sight. What could have almost been called a grin appeared on his face, and he let loose a ball of fire in their direction. They screamed and ducked, and the fireball flew over their heads. The dragon blew another fireball at them, and they screamed and ducked again. The dragon was less than ten feet away from the girls, and they tried to back up, but their feet found only empty space. Staggering forward to avoid falling from the cliff, they sprawled onto the ground in front of the dragon. The dragon shot his head forward and snapped his teeth at them. As he drew his neck back for another strike, they crawled backward. Senndra's hand touched empty space, and she stopped crawling. There was no place to go.

The dragon shot his head forward, his gaping jaw ready to snap shut on its meal. Senndra saw the teeth and throat approaching. A gust of wind from behind blew her forward, and talons appeared out of nowhere, reaching inside the dragon's mouth and ripping upwards. Blood flew from the gashes on his face, and he toppled backwards. Senndra and Rita scrambled to their feet and, following the cliff edge, skirted the dragon and clambered up the hill away from it. When they were a good distance from it, Senndra turned back and saw that it was still lying on the ground. Another dragon stood beside it, its jaws dripping with blood. Senndra recognized the dragon and slid down the hill toward it.

"Feddir!" she yelled as she hit his scales. She knew that she was going to have bruises from that move but didn't care at the moment. She threw her arms as far around his neck as they would go and squeezed as hard as she could. Across their mental link, Feddir projected images of the mayhem and destruction that he had seen. Senndra projected an image of herself and Rita riding on him, and he lowered his belly to the ground in response. Senndra turned and saw that Rita was making her way down the slope toward them.

"Get on Feddir," Senndra called. She climbed onto Feddir's back. "He is going to take us up to the academy, so we can see what the situation is like." Feddir reared slightly and projected a feeling of utter fear, but Senndra blocked it from her mind.

"I don't care what's up there or how many of them there are," she said as Rita climbed up behind her. "We are part of the academy, so we are going to go see what the situation is like and whether we can help or not."

Fear still clouded Feddir's mental projection, but he sent a feeling of submission. He stood to his feet and with a thrust from his back legs leaped into the air and spread his wings. The massive leathery sails caught the wind, and he flapped them three times to gain altitude. He circled upward and angled toward the mountain, keeping plenty of distance between it and himself. Spots of flickering light were scattered across the landscape, and above them dragons circled in the air. No fighting was apparent, indicating that the vicious battle had been short-lived. Feddir approached the mountain cautiously but was not attacked by the dragons. He landed near the mess hall, one of the only buildings left standing. Senndra and Rita dismounted Feddir and joined the growing group of people in front of the building. They forced their way through the crowd looking for familiar faces, but finding none. No one appeared to be in charge, and to Senndra it looked like the crowd was on the verge of panic. The feeling was beginning to rise in her, causing her throat to constrict when suddenly those around her became silent. She turned around to see that an officer had gotten their attention.

"Don't panic," were the first words out of the man's mouth. "The attack has been completely extinguished. Where it came from and why is still unknown; however, we are safe for the time being. Nevertheless, an evacuation is being commenced to move all of you to a safe location. Please step inside the mess hall so that we can count you and make arrangements for those that do not have dragons of their own."

The cadets flooded into the mess hall, and Senndra and Rita followed them. They saw that only a fraction of the cadets were present, a testimony of the devastation of the attack. As they entered the hall, they stopped at a table and told their names to an officer who marked them off of a list. Then they moved into the hall and took a seat at one of the tables.

"What do you think is going on?" Rita asked. Her hands were moving nervously, and Senndra did her best to calm her.

"I don't know, but everything is going to be all right," she said. "We have the dragons protecting us and…"

"Sowpa!" Rita interrupted. "I haven't heard from her since just before the attack." She rose quickly to her feet and was about to bound out of the mess hall, but Senndra restrained her and forced her back into her seat.

"Don't worry about her," Senndra said. "I'll have Feddir find her before we leave."

"But what if she got killed in the attack?" Rita was bordering on hysterical, and she tried to rise again.

"I'm sure she's fine," Senndra said as she kept Rita in her seat. "She is a dragon, you know. She can take care of herself. Now stop making a scene so I can tell Feddir to find her."

Rita calmed down considerably, allowing Senndra to focus on the mental link between herself and her dragon. As she impressed the situation upon Feddir, Timothy sat down at the table. Quickly she sent Feddir in search of Sowpa and turned her attention to the young man before her.

"What news is there of the attack?" he asked.

23

"None as of yet," Senndra answered. She glanced at Rita, who was scanning the room, and saw that her panic had apparently started to wear off. Senndra turned back to Timothy. "Your guess is as good as mine as to who staged the attack or where it came from. As to casualties…I shudder to think what they might be."

"Great," Timothy muttered under his breath. "Just great." Out loud he said, "What happened in the battle? I was in my room when it started. Just barely made it out of the building before it was torched. I ran up here as fast as I could, but got sidetracked multiple times by enemy dragons. By the time I got here the battle was over."

"I don't have any details," Senndra said. "The only thing that I know is that apparently we won."

"Yes, we won the first round," Lemin said. Senndra had not seen the instructor approach and was surprised at his interjection. She noticed that he was accompanied by Vladimir as he often was.

"What do you mean 'the first round'?" Timothy asked

"He means that the attack isn't over yet," Vladimir answered. "The dragons that we defeated were only the front guard of the real attack force. Our scouts have brought news that another force, several times larger than the one that we have, is approaching even as we speak."

"Which is why the evacuation is being called," Lemin explained. "There is no way that we can hope to defeat them, so we are leaving."

"Do you know where they came from?" Timothy asked.

"No one knows for sure," Lemin answered, "however, my suspicion is that it is an attempt by Molkekk. I am, however, uncertain as to what he hopes to accomplish by it."

"Eight months have passed since the last attack," Timothy said thoughtfully. "Eight months is enough time for us to grow complacent, but not enough for us to rebuild our forces. What if this is just one part of a much larger plan? Maybe he is coordinating this attack with several others."

"That is possible," Vladimir said, "but where would he attack? There are only two places that an army can enter Magessa, and both of them are protected."

"Protected, yes, but perhaps not by a large enough force," Timothy countered. "From what I have heard, many of the soldiers which were stationed in Saddun have been assigned to different posts. The only way that we managed to hold that city in the first attack was by a considerable amount of luck. Actually the more logical attack for Molkekk would be through the pass that Belmoth protects. Heaven knows that that city is severely undermanned. Molkekk could attack either of those cities or both of them and would be assured of success."

"In either case, Molkekk knows that our force of dragons could cause him grief, so he is removing them before they can do anything," Lemin said. "That much is clear to me now."

"But the academy doesn't house all of the dragons in the country," Vladimir argued.

"A large majority of them do live on or around this mountain," Lemin said. "Added to that is the fact that dragon operations are usually based out of the academy. The destruction of this place will at least temporarily hinder the effectiveness of our dragons."

"A temporary reduction in our dragons' effectiveness is all that Molkekk needs to get a foothold inside the country," Timothy said. "In any case, I think it is clear that this attack isn't our main problem."

"Correct, which means that we need to get messages to Belmoth and Saddun," Lemin decided. "I think the evacuation is heading to Belmoth, so they will be warned. That means that someone still needs to go to Saddun."

"Well that's not me," Timothy said. "I already ran that course once and don't want to do it again."

"What about your dragon?" Rita asked. Everyone turned to look at her, not because of the question, but because she did not normally interject into conversations.

"A dragon?" Timothy said. "No, not me. I don't have one."

"I suppose I could go," Vladimir said to Lemin. It sounded as if he did not really relish the idea.

"No, I think I'll do this myself," Lemin answered. "I am of much higher rank than you, obviously, and as such will probably be received better. Plus I am an elf and so will be shown more respect."

"How are you going to get there?" Senndra asked. "Are you going to borrow a dragon from someone?"

Lemin gave her a look of disbelief. "How about I just use my own?"

"You have a dragon?" Senndra blurted and immediately wished that she hadn't.

"Do I have a dragon?" Lemin retorted. "What kind of question is that? How do you think you get to be a dragon rider without a dragon?"

"Well, Timothy doesn't have one," Senndra said, gesturing to her friend.

"That is another case entirely," Timothy said with a wave of his hand.

"Why don't you have a dragon?" Rita asked suddenly. "How are you going to be a dragon rider without one?"

26

"I'm not," Timothy answered. "I never intended to be one. I didn't come here to train to be a dragon rider, but a dragon slayer."

"Oh," Rita said in a small voice and fell silent.

"Anyway," Lemin changed the subject, "it's settled. I am going to Saddun to give them the news and perhaps bring some back."

"You'd better hurry," Vladimir remarked. "The enemy is beginning to circle to the east."

Lemin left without another word, and Vladimir sat down at the table with his friends. Senndra was about to ask him a question when she felt a whisper at the back of her mind. Immediately she identified it as Feddir and listened to what he had to say.

"Feddir found Sowpa!" she said, interrupting Timothy. She ignored the clueless expressions from the boys and turned to Rita, who grabbed her in a hug. Senndra hugged her friend back, but their exuberance was cut short by an order for the evacuation to begin. Quickly the cadets scrambled to their feet and headed out of the mess hall. The two officers at the door were speaking with each cadet, making sure that all of them without a dragon large enough to ride would have a way off of the mountain.

"I don't need a dragon," Timothy said when it was his turn. "I'll walk." One of the officers was about to argue, but the other pulled him aside and whispered something in his ear. The first officer looked at Timothy with a strange expression and motioned for him to pass. Once outside the cadets quickly found their dragons and mounted them. The air was filled with dragons taking flight, and in ten short minutes, the academy was deserted.

******

Josiah raised the ax and hacked at the limb with all his might. The tool's sharp blade sheered through the wood, and the branch fell to the ground. Josiah leaned on his ax and wiped the rain out of his eyes. Six other cadets were also chopping at the tree, and another half dozen were carrying the wood away. Already all of the branches had been stripped from the tree, and the axmen were starting to work on the trunk. Josiah wiped his face again then raised his ax for another strike. He froze at the top of his swing and let the tool fall to the ground beside him. A horn was sounding from the north wall; a horn that was reserved for one thing: trouble. Josiah sprinted for the nearest staircase. Taking the steps two at a time, he raced up them and onto the wall. The rain made movement along the wall perilous, and with his attention focused on his footing, he almost didn't see spots of light on the plain outside the city. They continued to appear out of the rain, and his mind flew back to an event little more than half a year ago when a dwarf army had approached the city in much the same manner. The only difference was that the dwarf army had been significantly smaller and had not possessed as much siege equipment. The current army was not unprepared in this aspect, and Josiah could count scores of catapults, not to mention ballistae, battering rams, and disassembled trebuchets. The army's infantry and cavalry were also well-prepared; already the leading edges of ten legions could be seen, and as they advanced, more became visible behind them.

Josiah's mind spun as he took in the massive army. For a few fleeting moments he wondered what the purpose of trying to hold the city would be. Surely the army before him would be able to crush the city without much trouble and then move onto the rest of the country. With a shake of his head he dismissed the thought and ran for the stairs. When he reached the ground, he made a beeline for the mess hall and burst through the doors at full speed. The meal was in full swing and most of the cadets were there.

"Enemy army outside the wall to the north!" he bellowed, and the hall became deathly silent. "Everyone, get to the wall!" he shouted; when no one moved he added, "Move, move, move!"

28

The cadets suddenly burst into motion. Food was left uneaten on the tables, and no one stayed behind to clean it up. Shouting and the sound of boots thudding on the stone floor echoed through the room as the soldiers rushed out of the hall and into the night. Or maybe it wasn't night; Josiah couldn't tell. The dark clouds overhead blocked all light from reaching them. Within minutes the hall was empty, so Josiah hurried out and headed to the wall again. Cadets were already taking their places, some stringing their bows while others were preparing rocks and boiling oil to drop on the enemy. Engineers were manning the siege equipment mounted on and behind the wall. If nothing else, they would have more equipment to fight back with, Josiah thought grimly. Quickly he ascended the stairs and strode down the wall to a point a few hundred yards from the gatehouse. The problem with the city was that there were so few soldiers to protect a relatively long wall; nevertheless, he knew that the fiercest attack would come at the gate.

"Commander." The statement came from behind Josiah, so he turned and saw that Cirro had arrived. Behind him two hundred cadets filed onto the wall and took their stations. All of them had bows and quickly readied them for use when they had reached their positions.

"Captain," Josiah said and returned Cirro's salute. "What of the other Captains?"

"They are on their way as we speak, sir," Cirro answered.

"Good," Josiah responded. Turning to the cadets that had arrived, he ordered Cirro, "Tell them to take it easy for right now. The enemy is still a good ways out and this dratted rain will decrease the sighting ability of their engineers. We shouldn't be receiving any fire for some time."

"As you say, sir," Cirro answered and turned to relay the order to his men. When this was done, he turned back to Josiah. "What is the plan, if I may ask?" he said.

29

"I don't know," Josiah answered. "The General is going to want to meet with the commanders in the southeast tower, so I'm off."

"It's kind of different, isn't it sir," Cirro commented. Josiah gave a questioning look to his Captain who continued. "The old General was too much of a coward to have his headquarters on the wall. He tended to hide out behind our lines."

"That man was not fit to lead an army," Josiah stated firmly. "The new General, on the other hand, is a very capable commander, and they tell me that he has also been in several battles before, so we can be sure that he won't run. In fact, I feel almost safe under the man's command, even if we are facing this massive force," Josiah motioned to the army to the north. "Anyway, you know the drill; if the enemy attacks when I'm gone, don't lose your head."

"No sir, I wouldn't dream of it," Cirro assured him. Josiah jogged to the tower that the new General used as a headquarters in case of an attack and entered the bright interior. In actuality, the tower was lit by only a few candles and two lanterns, but the contrast with the darkness outside created the illusion of a brightly lit room. The General was already in the tower, but no other commanders were, so after saluting, Josiah took a seat at the table where the General was seated. A map of the city and surrounding areas was spread on the table, and small figurines indicating enemy and friendly forces littered it. One glance at the number of enemy figurines made Josiah's heart sink dramatically. From the wall it was obvious that the enemy force was large, but he didn't realize the true enormity of it.

"So what do you think, Commander?" the General asked, staring at Josiah.

"It's a lot of men, General," Josiah answered, his gaze fixed on the enemy forces.

"Oh, this isn't a sure number of soldiers," the General explained and waved at the enemy figurines. "Our intelligence estimated that this is how many soldiers they have, but that is only an estimate. The true number could be several thousand more or less than what I have here."

"What of their siege equipment?" Josiah asked. "Is there any estimate on how much of that they have?"

"Our best guess is around five hundred pieces total - about half of them being catapults," the General answered. "That is only the equipment we can see, though. They could have some further back in their formation that we can't see now."

"I wouldn't worry about the catapults," Josiah advised. "When the wall was rebuilt, its thickness was doubled, and its construction is sounder than that of the old one. The catapults' projectiles shouldn't damage it too much, at least initially. The real problem is going to be with the trebuchets and ballistae. They have enough range and power to really wreak havoc on our men and siege equipment."

"So you think that the trebuchets and ballistae are our biggest problem?" the General said thoughtfully as he stared at the map.

"Not necessarily," Josiah said. "The enemy has so many foot soldiers that if they got in their heads to simply charge the wall and use ladders, they would succeed purely due to their massive numbers. And if they gain the wall, we are almost defeated."

"Agreed," the General commented. "If they overrun the city, our only option for survival will be to run away, and running isn't something I like to do."

"Nor I, General. Nor I."

******

Thunder shook the wall, and the rain continued to pour down on the soldiers. Josiah's only consolation was that the enemy was experiencing the same things that he and his men were. A strong wind whipped down the wall, biting through the clothes that the soldiers wore and making them shiver. Josiah looked over his shoulder at the city behind him and saw a long line of servants, cooks, and other workers that the city housed making their way through the south gates. During the meeting with the General, it was decided it would be safer for all of the noncombatants to leave the city until the battle was over. In addition, a messenger was leaving to request help from Feling, but Josiah did not feel hopeful that they would arrive in time. It was also resolved that the only sensible course of action for the soldiers was to hold the city as long as possible and then fall back as slowly as possible in order to buy time for reinforcements to arrive. Everyone agreed that the city should not fall into enemy hands, so people were standing by ready to torch it when a retreat became necessary. Josiah glanced down the wall and saw soldiers ready in every quadrant. During the reconstruction of the wall, meurtrière, or 'murder holes' as the soldiers fondly referred to them, had been added, and men were standing at them ready to dump boiling oil and rocks on any attackers that got too close to the wall. At least the city would not be as easily taken this time.

Josiah looked proudly at his men standing in perfect order and waiting for the attack. About a quarter of them had bows, and these had them strung and ready, waiting only for the order to draw, aim, and fire. Behind them stood soldiers with swords, axes, maces, spears, and pikes. Each had a determined look in his eyes that indicated that the enemy would be hard pressed to take their position. Unfortunately, Josiah knew that the enemy was up to the task. At the edge of the wall, several of Josiah's men stood unarmed. They crouched behind the crenellations and beside the murder holes, waiting for unlucky enemies to venture too close to the wall. Down the wall a hundred feet stood a short, stocky tower, and mounted atop it was a mangonel. This machine was similar to a catapult but had a sling on the end of the arm. It was designed to throw numerous stones at a time, and Josiah knew that the outcome of the battle might lie with this machine and others like it.

The enemy was getting closer, almost to within siege engine range. Josiah gave an order and the infantrymen moved in among the archers and readied their shields. In the event of a catapult or ballistae attack, they would raise them to shield the bowmen. The enemy army seemed to halt its advance. Even from his position Josiah could see that their engineers were mounting the catapults and ballistae and readying them for an attack. The dismantled trebuchets were also being assembled and teams of men were dragging massive stones to them.

"So you think that we're going to survive this?" The question came from Josiah's right, and he turned to see Cirro standing there.

"I wish I knew," Josiah replied. "I'm not worried about the catapults. Their range and power is probably not enough to damage the wall severely. What I *am* worried about is the trebuchets and ballistae. They both have enough range to reach the wall and do some damage. We can deal with the ballistae if we duck when they fire, but if they fire them randomly, we may not fare so well. The trebuchets have a long enough range that they should be able to drop rocks almost straight down on the wall. That may not do too much damage to our soldiers if we're lucky, but they could mess our siege equipment up pretty badly."

"Elohim protect us," Cirro muttered; Josiah silently agreed.

The enemy engineers worked quickly, but even they could not beat the speed of the wall's battle machines. All down the wall, orders were given and the tower-mounted mangonels and ballistae released their missiles. Josiah watched as the machine near him hurled its load of stones toward the enemy ranks. The stones, each about as big as a man, would have been devastating had they reached their target; however, they fell short

33

of the enemy's lines by a good thirty yards. The machine was quickly reloaded by its crew and again it let its load fly, this time with more force. The boulders arched through the air, and as he watched, Josiah knew that they would hit their target this time. They smashed into the enemy lines, bouncing in all directions and crushing men and equipment wherever they went. All along the enemy line, siege equipment was being damaged and destroyed, but for every piece that was hit by a missile, three more were not damaged. To make matters worse, more equipment was being brought up to replace that which was destroyed. The wall was able to make one more barrage before the enemy siege equipment was ready to fire. The catapults fired first, and as Josiah had predicted most of their boulders never even reached the wall but dropped short. Those that reached the wall hit it and bounced off, making no impact for their efforts. Next up to fire were the ballistae, and their effect was much more serious.

"Shields up!" Josiah yelled when he saw the massive javelins hurtling toward the wall. His men obediently raised their shields, but the armor did little good. Wherever the weapons hit, they slammed through the shields and killed the men under them instantaneously.

"Under the wall," Josiah ordered his men, and they all crowded to the crenellations. Josiah followed them and peered through an arrow slit. The enemy ballistae were firing at will now, and their javelins were raining onto the wall. Josiah's men crowed further under the short wall that offered them protection. Josiah glanced over his men again and saw that most were cowering and fear was in many of their eyes, but he was pleased to see determination as well. These soldiers would die fighting; they would die serving their country. A man appeared down the wall. He was running toward Josiah's position, and the commander watched him with interest, waiting to see if he would bring any news or orders. The man sprinted the last few yards to Josiah and crouched down beside him.

"Commander?" he asked.

"That's me," Josiah answered.

"Order from the General," the messenger said. "He has decided that you aren't doing any good up on the wall, so you are to take your men to the base of it and wait out the siege equipment attack."

"Very good," Josiah said. "I understand."

The messenger offered a salute to Josiah and headed off down the wall again. Josiah turned to his men and immediately wondered how he was going to relay the message to them. The normal channels of communication would not be effective in their current position, and he could not think of any other way. Finally he turned to the soldiers next to him.

"Everyone follow me," he told the men and sprinted to the opposite side of the wall. Quickly he bounded down a set of stairs, only looking back when he had reached the bottom. He was pleased to see that his plan had worked, and his men were following him. With curt hand motions he ordered them to spread out along the base of the wall. When everyone had settled in, he sat down on the wet grass to wait.

******

Senndra slid off of Feddir's back and jogged through the rain toward a building that had been cleared for the cadets from the academy. Rain fell in the city of Belmoth just as it had at the top of the mountain, and Senndra wondered if it would ever stop. She ran the last few yards to the building and passed through the door into a large room. Already it was beginning to fill with cadets, so she hurried to what was clearly the girls' side and threw her few provisions on the floor, claiming a spot. She did not see anyone that she knew, and she was already feeling tired from the frenzied activity of the last few hours, so she lay down with her head resting on her pack. She closed her eyes, but despite her tired state found it difficult to fall asleep. The fear and surprise that she had felt in her dragon and the sudden evacuation of the academy all puzzled and worried her, and the constant rain did nothing but exacerbate the fear. She knew that Timothy was on the other side of the hall somewhere, but right now she wished that she could see and touch him. Then again, he was often less than comforting. Their relationship had grown in the past six months, albeit slowly due to the pressures of academy life. At the same time, Timothy seemed to be all over the map emotionally. Sometimes he was frank and open with Senndra, but other times he was cold and emotionally distant. The constant switching in attitude was certainly out of character for him, and Senndra didn't know what to think. Apparently despite how well she thought she knew a guy, boys were still weird. Eventually the swirling of thoughts exhausted her, and she fell asleep.

Senndra woke with a start. The building was still shaking from a particularly loud clap of thunder. The lights were out, and all of the cadets appeared to be asleep. At least the chorus of snores seemed to indicate as much. Senndra rolled over and closed her eyes again, but sleep would not come. She lay there for fifteen minutes before she rose and headed for the door of the building. It was still raining outside, so she wrapped her cloak tightly around herself and stepped out into the downpour. At a fast pace she trotted to the wall at the north of the city and reached it in only a few minutes. She located a staircase to the top and ascended it quickly. Once on the wall she moved to the northern edge and looked out over the plain on the other side. The wind blew the rain into her face, and stung her eyes, so she turned her face away. Out of the corner of her eye she saw a slight movement, so slight in fact that she almost missed it. She jerked her head back to the plain and stared out into the darkness, but nothing was visible. Slowly she swung her gaze across the whole plain, and out of the corner of her eye she again saw a slight movement. This time she didn't jerk to face it but froze and watched it from where she was. She became aware of a figure moving across the open field, and as she watched, more figures became visible. Turning her head toward the figures, she was finally able to see them clearly. The stocky forms of dwarves and gangly forms of goblins were still several hundred yards out, yet they were approaching the gate at a quick pace. It took Senndra a few precious seconds to realize what she was seeing, and the enemies moved closer to the gate. She regained her senses and burst down the wall at a dead sprint, yelling a warning to the guards at the gate. She was too far away for them to hear what she was saying; however, the dwarves and goblins heard her and quickened their pace. Senndra reached the gate and, without checking her pace, leaped down the stairs that led into the gatehouse. The men on duty there were startled by her quick appearance and jumped to their feet, pulling their swords from their sheaths.

"The gate, you have to close the gate!" Senndra cried urgently between gasps of air. "Enemies are approaching; they're about to enter the city."

The soldiers hesitated, so Senndra rushed past them and began to pull at the large wheel that controlled the gate. For a second the soldiers did not know what to do with the female cadet before them. She appeared to believe what she was saying, but then again maybe she was up to some mischief. The men dropped their swords and began to crank at the wheel. There was really only enough room for two at the wheel, so Senndra surrendered her place to the two soldiers.

Gathering her breath, she shoved open the gatehouse door and rushed out to where the gates where slowly closing. The goblins had pulled ahead of the dwarves in their frenzied race toward the closing gates, and Senndra saw that they would reach them long before they were sealed. Swiftly she pulled her bow from the quiver on her back and strung it. Snatching an arrow from her quiver, she placed it on the bow string, and pulled it back. Closing one eye, she sighted down the arrow and drew a bead on the chest of one of the goblins. She released the arrow and watched as it sailed straight and true into the chest of the target, throwing him backwards onto the wet ground. Already her hands were pulling another arrow from the quiver, and in an instant it was flying at another goblin. The darkness masked the true numbers of the enemy, but by the noise, Senndra knew that there was a multitude. Quickly she loosed another arrow into the goblins, but they were already in the gate. Senndra sent a fourth arrow into the goblins and knew that she would never survive their onslaught.

Still, she slung the bow over her shoulder and drew the short sword from its sheath on her quiver. To her left and right she heard the iron-shod boots of the watchmen coming down from the wall, and she was thankful that she would not be facing the goblins alone. Five heavily armed men joined her, but even they looked pathetically small compared to the force that was attacking. Quickly they drew their swords, stepped in front of Senndra, and braced themselves for the attack. Senndra stabbed her sword into the dirt, jerked her bow from its place across her shoulders, and nocked an arrow. The goblins hit the five soldiers in front of her, immediately bearing one to the ground and viciously engaging the other four. A goblin jumped into the gap where the fifth man had stood, but before he could swing his weapon, Senndra dropped him with an arrow through his throat.

They heard the roar of a rushing wind above them, and a massive form slammed into the ground between the soldiers and the gate. The ground shook with the impact, throwing goblins and humans alike to the ground. A thunderous roar came from the huge beast, and goblins shrieked and ran away only to find their escape cut off as the city gates shut with a crash. A dragon's head materialized out of the dark silhouette and swept away the goblins immediately in front of the soldiers. The dragon's eyes met with Senndra's and she immediately recognized Feddir. Rage filled his eyes, and with a massive sweep of his tail he hurled the remainder of the goblins into the closed gate. His neck flew out, and a goblin arced through the air, smashing into the ground less than ten feet from Senndra. Feddir's head flashed forward again, and two dwarves sailed upward into the side of the gatehouse. They bounced off the rough stones and crashed into the ground near

Feddir's front foot. The dragon's massive limb rose into the air and slammed down on the two bodies, smashing them to pieces and shaking the ground.

Senndra stared at her dragon in shock. Before today, she had never witnessed such viciousness from him, but now she had seen it twice in the last few hours. He coiled his legs and leaped into the air, clearing the gate by only a few feet. She scrambled to her feet and raced up the stairs to the wall; as she did so, dragons of all sizes and colors screamed over her head toward the enemy.

As she reached the top of the wall, the shrill sound of a bell broke across the city calling the soldiers and cadets to defend wall. She turned and looked out across the city. For a few seconds everything was dark as if nothing had happened; then people began to spill from buildings, most still pulling on their armor or strapping on their weapons. With incredible speed they raced toward the wall. Senndra jogged to the far edge and peered over into the darkness on the other side. Except now there was no darkness. The enemy, realizing that the time for stealth was past, had lighted thousands of torches, revealing the siege engines that were assembled less than half a mile from the wall. In the sky, dragons circled the goblins and dwarves that fled back toward their lines. Senndra smiled, knowing that the dragons would make short work of the enemy siege machines.

One of the catapults snapped forward and fired its boulder at the city. Senndra could tell that something was wrong when the arm of the machine came forward too far and flung its projectile into the dirt a few yards in front of it. The machine seemed to burst into splinters and large pieces of wood flew in all directions, killing several of the people around it. The other catapults fired without problems and an imposing barrage of boulders hit the wall, shaking it to its foundations. Senndra fell to her knees and stayed there for a few seconds, stunned by the force of the attack. By the time she pulled herself to her feet, the battle had taken a sudden, unexpected turn. The number of dragons in the sky had more than tripled, and Senndra knew that the tide of the battle had changed. The dragons were in a fierce aerial battle, letting loose frightful roars as they hit and unleashed streams of fire at each other. Already the ground was littered with the bodies of the great beasts, and as Senndra watched more of them fell out of the sky and crashed into the ground.

The first soldiers reached the wall and stampeded up the stairs. Wasting no time, they rushed to the city's defensive machines and began to retaliate to what had become the catapults' constant pounding on the wall. Javelins and rocks flew from the various machines on the wall and crashed into the enemy ranks, wreaking havoc on them. The enemy machines struck back with increasing intensity. All along the wall, javelins and boulders hurled men and machines off of the wall. Pieces of the wall were smashed off of the whole and flew into the city, crushing whatever was in their way. The enemy was faring no better except for the fact that they were not being bombarded by as many projectiles. The javelins and rocks smashed siege engines and soldiers alike; however, for every one that was killed, another was ready to step up into his place.

In the sky the dragons were not faring well either. They were outnumbered more than two to one and were struggling just to stay alive. Slowly they fell back toward the city, being closely followed by the enemy dragons until they were within range of the city. The ballistae and archers on the wall turned their fire on the enemy dragons and drove them away under a heavy rain of razor sharp projectiles. Wearily, the dragons landed in the city and rested. Their numbers had been cut in half in the short time that the battle had taken place, and many of those that remained were badly hurt. And still the catapults pummeled the wall, smashing pieces off and making it weaker with every blow. Off to the west a small army of dwarves made a foray at the wall, but the archers drove them back with little difficulty. A group of goblins rushed the gate and threw up several ladders. The fighting was intense for a few short minutes, but eventually the ladders were thrust from the wall and the goblins, those that remained, retreated. The catapults continued to assault the wall, whittling its strength down a little at a time.

The sun was just beginning to rise in the east when disaster struck. The continual pounding of the catapults on the city wall had weakened it to such an extent that it gave way with a mighty crash, and a large section collapsed into nothing more than a pile of rubble. Senndra was sleeping at the base of the wall a hundred yards away when this happened, and she jerked awake with a start. It seemed to her that the world was falling apart, but as she quickly rubbed her eyes and looked around, she realized that it was much worse. She jumped to her feet and joined the other off duty soldiers or cadets who were rushing as fast as they could toward the hole in the wall. Though the wall was destroyed, it still provided a formidable barrier to the enemy. The rough stone that had collapsed into the hole was traversable, but not easily, and it was still being guarded by archers on either side. Many of the invaders were dropped as they tried to enter the city, but the massive flood of soldiers could not be held off indefinitely. Senndra arrived at the breach in time to see the first of the enemies struggling the last few feet into the city. With no time to think she slung her bow from her shoulders and let arrow after arrow fly into the enemy ranks. Several other cadets were doing the same thing, and scores of enemies fell with arrows protruding from their bodies. Even so, many of the dwarves and goblins made it across the mound of stone and threw themselves at the small group of defenders that had accumulated. Senndra still had her bow in her hand when suddenly she found herself facing a sword-wielding goblin. Frantically she reached for an arrow, realizing as she did so that she would be much too late to save herself. As the sword descended, she felt herself being thrust out of the way and watched as Timothy stepped into the scene. In one fist he held his sword and in the other was clenched a one-handed battle ax. Both weapons were raised to catch the blade of the goblin which they did with a loud ringing sound. With a swift twist of the ax, Timothy trapped the goblin's blade, leaving his own sword free to be brought down and thrust upward into the goblin's belly.

Senndra rolled over and pushed herself to her feet. She drew her short sword and stepped toward the line of city defenders, waiting to take the place of the first one to fall. She did not have to wait long; a soldier fell with a sword through the stomach, and the victorious goblin stepped forward to take advantage of the gap. With an almost delicate move, Senndra stepped forward and slammed her sword into the goblin's throat, pushing it until the hilt brought it to a stop. With a sideways slash she freed the blade, and the goblin collapsed to the ground. Senndra stooped down and retrieved the soldier's shield then stepped into the line of defenders. A dwarf swung at her, but she blocked the blow with her shield. A slash at the dwarf's unprotected side dispatched him, and another enemy stepped into his place. The fighting continued for several tense minutes, the attackers refusing to give up, and the defenders knowing that if they fell, the city would fall with them. Slowly the invaders seemed to be gaining the advantage as the defenders gave ground inch by inch. Their line was being stretched, and in a moment, the enemy would be able to swarm around the edges and attack them from behind. Just at that moment, when everything seemed lost, a roar was heard overhead. It startled most of the combatants, and they looked up in surprise, but Senndra knew the sound of a dragon and was able to maintain her presence of mind. A well-aimed thrust dropped the soldier in front of her, and she braced herself for the shock of the dragon hitting the ground. A large reddish gold dragon landed on the mound of rubble that had once been a wall. His massive bulk crushed at least a dozen soldiers immediately, and a flick of his tail sent more flying in all directions. The enemies still outside the city suddenly found themselves face to face with a dragon which seemed to them to be all claws and teeth. With terrified yells they turned back toward their lines; the dragon sent several fireballs chasing after them before turning his attention to the goblins and dwarves still inside the city. One snap of his jaws devoured one of them, and sent the

42

rest scurrying straight into the swords of soldiers who slew those that remained. Senndra wiped her blade on the clothes of one of the fallen dwarves and slid it back into its sheath. She held onto the shield that she had acquired and walked slowly to where Timothy was kneeling on the ground.

"Are you all right?" she asked when he was within earshot. It was then that she noticed the blood dripping from the fingers of his left hand and pooling on the ground beneath them. "What happened?" she cried. She rushed to his side.

Timothy said nothing but raised his left hand so that she could see the wound. A deep cut ran from near his elbow to three inches from his wrist. As she watched, the flesh of the cut began to slowly close, but it only continued for an inch. Timothy, exhausted by the battle and the sudden use of magic, collapsed face first onto the grass, unconscious. Senndra rushed to his side, rolled him onto his back, and grabbed his left arm. Holding the gaping wound shut, she yelled for help to the men around her.

******

The army outside Saddun continued to attack the city wall, but boulder after boulder crashed into the sturdy defense with little or no effect. Finally the barrage stopped and an uneasy silence hung over the battlefield until the sun rose. Slowly the defenders came out of hiding and began to stand on the wall. They could see the enemy army to the north looking like a black plague that covered the land. Their camp was several miles square, and every inch of it was covered with tents, soldiers, or siege engines. People started to gather at the side of the camp closest to the city and the area began to swell with the influx of soldiers. The mass of black continued to swell until it burst like a dam letting out water, and the soldiers set out on a headlong rush at the city wall. The machines on the wall opened fire as soon as they came within range, but this did not deter the massive swarm of enemies. It appeared as though the entire army was coming, and they would not be turned aside for anything. Their war cry became clearer as they grew closer to the wall, and the courage of many defenders failed at the sound. As the swarm came within bow range, the archers opened fire on them, and many fell by the arrows, but many more reached the city wall.

Ladders could be seen in the crowd of attackers, and in no time they had been thrown up against the wall, warriors crawling up them. Pike men scurried up and down the wall, pushing the ladders down, and the other hand to hand soldiers beat back the enemies that ascended the ladders, but there were too many. The enemy swarmed past the soldiers and onto the wall, almost overcoming the small defending force. The soldiers of Magessa were barely able to pull together and retreat off the wall and across the city. The enemy army, composed of a mixture of goblins, dwarves, orcs, and even humans gave chase, killing the stragglers. Frantically the army of Saddun tried to turn and fight several times, but in every instance, Molkekk's army succeeded in driving them south. At the south end of the city, the army made a valiant stand, digging in their heels and trying to hold back the onslaught, but to no avail. With the full force of two hundred thousand soldiers, the enemy drove the cadets out of the city and onto the surrounding open fields. The attacking force quickly placed their archers on the wall and, with a steady rain of arrows, drove the army of Saddun away from the city that they had strived so hard to defend. As the army fled for their lives, Molkekk's soldiers did not follow. Apparently they had accomplished their purpose and were in no hurry to move further into the country.

The bad weather seemed to follow the army as it retreated south toward Feling, the capital of Gatlon. Josiah already missed his horse as he strode at the head of his legion, which had been decimated in the recent battle. Only three hundred of the original thousand remained, and these were mostly wounded, some so grievously that they were being carried by their comrades. The rest of the army had suffered as many casualties as Josiah's soldiers, and altogether there remained little more than two

44

thousand warriors. Clearly defeated, they limped toward their destination at a slow pace, but one that would, nevertheless, get them there before the enemy. The mood of the army was not angry, nor was it defiant. Indeed either of these would have been better than the despair that had settled over the soldiers. It was in these conditions that they entered the city of Feling.

Josiah and his soldiers sat outside in the elements as the high ranking officers of the army went inside to have a conference with the ruling council of Gatlon. He sat with his back against a building and pulled his cloak tighter around his body trying to preserve the heat that his body was struggling to generate. His clothes were thoroughly soaked, and a sharp wind cut through the city, chilling him to the bone. He wished that he could have gone inside with the General to confront the council. At least he would have been out of the rain, if not warm. Unbeknownst to Josiah, the General was wishing he could be outside instead of inside. Even the warmth of the room could not counteract the cool reception he had received. He had expected the council to be cooperative, but when he met with them, he found them to be quite the opposite.

"What the heck do you mean there is no confirmed sighting?" he all but yelled at the spokesman of the council. "We were right there staring at the largest army that I have ever heard of. Don't tell me that isn't a confirmed sighting."

"We are just taking into consideration that you have clearly been in a stressful situation…"

"You're right I was in a stressful situation," the General interrupted. "Facing down more than one hundred thousand enemies with only a few thousand men at your back is definitely stressful!"

"There have been no other reports of such a large army, so we are simply considering the possibility that the stress of the attack made the army appear to you to be bigger than it actually was," one of the councilmen said in an understanding tone. The

General got the definite impression that the councilman was patronizing him, and he exploded.

"What about the rest of my men?" he shouted. "What about the fact that they saw the same army that I did? Are you saying that all of us, being veterans of at least one battle, were so traumatized by an insignificant attack force that we imagined a much larger army and fled before it? Because if you are, you are insinuating that my men are cowards as well as crazy, and that is something that I will *not* stand for!"

"I will ask you once to refrain from shouting in the council chambers," the spokesman said. "If you do so again, you will be forcibly removed."

The General looked at the six council chamber guards scattered around the room. They were clearly ready for action. He glanced back at the five officers that he had brought with him. He knew the guards wouldn't stand a chance against his men if they did try to throw them out, and in a sadistic sort of way he really wanted to pick a fight.

"Who's going to throw me out?" he asked. "Them?" He gestured to the guards. "They would probably have trouble throwing an old blanket out, much less six armed soldiers." At the insult, every guard reached for his weapons, but the council spokesman raised his hand to restrain them.

"I will tell you only once to remove yourself from our presence," he said in a low tone. "If you do not, your good health after your expulsion cannot be guaranteed."

"I'm very frightened," the General said in a tone that said the exact opposite. "I will leave now, but only because I need to take my army and be on my way immediately. Otherwise I would be happy to show your little guards what real soldiers can do. As it is, you're going to need everyone that you can spare when the enemy gets here."

46

"No, we won't need any men when the enemy gets here," the spokesman muttered under his breath. The statement was not intended to be heard by anyone, and was so low that only the particularly sharp ears of the General picked it up. The General had turned to leave the chambers, but at the statement, he deliberately stalked across the room to the council spokesman. When he turned, every guard in the room drew his weapon and headed to detain him. They were too slow to stop the General from reaching the spokesman, grabbing the front of his shirt, and pulling him close to his face.

"I would slit your throat now; however, you haven't officially joined the enemy yet, and as such any act against you is treason," the General growled in such a way that every man in the room heard him. He felt the hands of two guards on his shoulders, pulling him away from the spokesman. For a second he considered fighting them, but thought better of it and allowed them to roughly escort him to the door. Every one of his officers was staring directly at him, begging with their eyes to be allowed to lay into the guards, but he prevented them with a slight shake of his head. Just as he was almost to the door, the spokesman spoke again.

"Threatening a council member is a severe crime," he said. "You do realize that, don't you?"

"Not if the councilman in question is corrupt and a traitor," the General responded, turning to face the spokesman.

"Say what you like," the spokesman replied. "What you have done is a crime, and I can't allow criminals to run rampant over this county." To the guards he said, "Take him to the dungeon. We will try him tomorrow, but with all of the witnesses in the room, the trial should be very brief."

"I would not try to restrain me in this way," the General warned the spokesman. "If you do, it could go very badly for you. Keep in mind that I do have more than two thousand men at my command, and none of them will be very pleased when they hear what you have done."

"I will not allow the pleasure of the masses to affect the way in which justice is served," the spokesman responded.

"I would commend you for that if justice was being served," the General stated clearly. "As it is, all that I can say is, may Elohim be merciful to you; because if my men do not kill you, our enemies will not be gentle even though you are turning to their side."

The spokesman said nothing but merely motioned with his hand for the guards to take their prisoner out. One of them relieved the General of his sword and the two that had his arms led him out of the room. They were closely followed by two more of the guards who had their weapons drawn and were making sure that the following officers kept their distance.

"So are you in on the treachery as well or are you simply following your authority?" the General asked the guards that were leading him. When they were silent, he tried another tactic. "Do you really think that they will treat you well simply because you chose to join them? Ha! The best treatment that you can expect is to be forced to fight against your own brothers as the army sweeps across Magessa."

"Shut up," one of the guards blurted out. "You know nothing of what you speak. Molkekk is merciful to those who realize their mistakes and follow him."

"What do you mean 'Molkekk is merciful?'" the other guard demanded, stopping in mid-step.

"You were not to know of the plan until it was too late," the first guard said. "Yes, the plan is for the council to surrender the city along with the entire county of Gatlon to Molkekk's army."

"Has madness taken root in the council?" the other guard retorted. "Molkekk is the sworn enemy of Magessa. There's no way we can abdicate to him!"

"Don't be a fool," the first guard growled. "Molkekk is more powerful than our entire country put together, even if we could get all three counties to cooperate. You know that politics will prevent that from happening, so we don't stand even the most remote chance of being able to resist him."

"You have taken leave of your senses as well, I see," the other guard stated coldly. He drew his sword and pointed it at the first guard. "I hereby place you under arrest for treason against the country of Magessa. Drop your weapon, or I may be forced to harm you."

"You idiot, you know I am the better swordsman," the first guard said as he drew his sword. "You don't stand a chance."

"And neither do you," the General said and stepped between the guards. "I already insulted your ability to use that weapon, and I stand by that. I could incapacitate you even without a weapon."

The first guard gave a roar of rage and swung his sword in an overhanded strike at the General. The General watched with amusement at the sloppy attack and swiftly sidestepped the blow. The guard's sword dug into the dirt, and in a flash the General stepped forward and smashed his armored fist into the guard's face. The man dropped to the ground, and the General wasted no time in turning to the guard behind him.

"Are you for Magessa or against her?" he asked the stunned man.

"For her, sir," the man stammered.

"Good," the General said. "Send the message throughout the city that an army of the enemy is approaching. Gather the soldiers and order an evacuation of the civilians. I also need you

49

to figure out who is behind this treachery and lock them in the dungeons. We will leave them to the tender mercies of Molkekk's soldiers. As for those loyal to Magessa, tell the civilians to fall back to the Vänern River and follow it all of the way to Sulmon if necessary. Everyone who is capable of wielding a weapon, however, is to join my forces."

"Yes sir," the guard said and disappeared among the buildings of the city.

******

The enemy was attacking again. This time boulders from their siege machines smashed into the wall of the city, but they would soon be quieted by a counterattack from a platoon of dragons. The enemy dragons would attempt to protect the engines, but experience had proven time and time again that it was much easier to attack the clumsy machines than it was to defend them. The dragons of Magessa split into two groups and hit the machines with one while attacking the defending dragons with the other. As had happened many times before, the defending dragons were simply unable to properly protect the equipment, and the attacking dragons quickly laid it to waste. They turned and headed back to the city, followed closely by the enemy dragons; however, these fell away when they came within range of the city's ballistae.

Senndra watched the skirmish without much interest. She had seen the same thing happen twice before, and both times the result had been the same. She only wondered how long it would be until the enemy realized that their strategy was not working, or worse, repeated the action and sprung a trap when the dragons of Magessa attacked them. If the latter happened, the result could be disastrous for the defenders. As it stood, neither side could gain the upper hand in the battle. The defenders were outnumbered too heavily to consider an attack, but the attackers could not breach the city walls. All of their attempts to do this were thwarted by the defending dragons. If they chose to involve their own dragons, the defenders would simply draw them into range of the city's ballistae, and they would be forced to withdraw or be killed. If, however, a trap were to drastically decrease the number of defending dragons, Molkekk's forces would be able to attack with the knowledge that their own dragons could more than take care of those defending the city. Because of this, the dragons of Magessa were very careful every time they ventured from the city walls. They thoroughly checked their surroundings for traps and completed their missions as quickly as possible so as to get back to the protection of the city.

The dragons soared back over the wall in a crowd of many colors and dispersed to various parts of the city. They were all staying in the city rather than the nearby mountains so as to be ready at a moment's notice. This was an essential part of the defense strategy since the dragons composed the backbone of the defending force. Because of this they were catered to so much that Senndra feared Feddir might become spoiled. She spotted Feddir landing some distance into the city, and Senndra considered going to meet him but decided against it. Instead she headed down to a place where the other cadets often chose to congregate. The hangout was an old, abandoned military building which the cadets had appropriated for their own use. Senndra entered the building and was rendered blind momentarily by the sudden decrease in light. As she grew accustomed to the dim light, the features of the room as well as its occupants came into view. Old chairs and couches, several of them occupied by cadets, stood against the walls, and a large table occupied the center of the room. Senndra crossed the room to a row of cupboards situated over a counter and opened one filled with glasses. She filled one of the glasses from a pitcher that stood nearby and carried it to the table in the center of the room. She sat on one end next to Timothy and across from Vladimir. Several other cadets were seated at the table as well, and all of them were involved in an energetic discussion. Timothy looked up as Senndra sat down and nodded to her.

"We're discussing battle plans," he explained. "Lemin decided that now was as good of a time as any to get some real life experience, so we are reviewing the proposed plans concerning the defense of Belmoth as well as plans concerning the extermination of the threatening army. Lemin also instructed us to see if we could come up with any plans of our own. If we do come up with any ideas that he decides have merit, he said that he would suggest it to the Grand Admiral of the city."

"I see," Senndra said. She pulled a stack of maps toward her and glanced over them. Marks and words covered them, obviously indicating the positions and movements of troops in different battle plans. Senndra's training in battle maneuvers immediately kicked in, and quickly she began to eliminate plans that would not work. One plan pitted the defending dragons against the attacking dragons, a skirmish that would almost certainly end badly for the defenders, yet the plan still depended on the victory of the defending dragons. This was only the first of roughly half the plans that Senndra discarded based on obvious flaws. Next she began to look more carefully at the plans and discard more of them because of less obvious flaws, but ones that would, nonetheless, spell defeat for the forces of Magessa. In only a few minutes she had decreased the number of feasible plans to five then to two and finally to none.

"None of these plans are any good," she said out loud, still looking at the last plan. She tossed the map and accompanying papers onto the stack of discarded battle plans and looked up to see that the other cadets had stopped arguing and were looking at her.

"It's true. All of these plans have fatal flaws in them," she reiterated.

"What about this one?" Timothy pulled one of the maps out of the stack and smoothed it out. As he did so, the sleeve of his shirt rose up his arm, revealing the last several inches of his wound. It had been neatly stitched up, and Senndra thought that perhaps the healing process had been helped along by magic.

"I really liked this one," Timothy continued. "It could use some finishing touches, but all of the major parts are here, and there aren't any major flaws."

"This one?" Senndra asked. "This particular idea depends on the supposition that our wall-mounted siege machines will be able to fire on their soldiers. This is simply not going to happen. There is no way they will come into range of our equipment. Nothing we have control of would be enough incentive to convince them to leave the safety of their camp and draw them into a danger zone."

"What about the other plans?" a cadet that Senndra did not know asked. "Are you telling us you went over every one of them and found something wrong with each one?"

"Actually, that is exactly what I am saying," Senndra said matter-of-factly. "I could take the time to go over every single one of them with you, but that would waste a lot of time."

"Well, why don't you show us one that won't work and explain why," the cadet said.

"I already did that, but I'll do it with another one," Senndra said. "Take this one for example." She chose the first plan that she had eliminated and slapped it down on the table. "The success of this one hinges on our dragons being able to defeat those of the enemy in a head-on fight. We have less than half as many dragons as them, so that simply is not going to work. Besides that..." She stopped in midsentence and pulled the map closer for a better look.

"Actually, this idea is pretty good," she commented after several minutes. "Besides a few minor flaws and the major one that I mentioned, this actually has potential to succeed."

Timothy grabbed the map and began to look over it for himself. His critiquing of the plan took longer than Senndra's, and as he was studying it the other cadets looked at him expectantly. Finally he raised his head and looked at the cadets surrounding him.

"She's right," he said. "It does have a few problems with it, but none that we can't fix." He passed the plan to the cadet next to him and pulled an unmarked map from another stack on the table and placed it between himself and Senndra. He grabbed a pencil and began to scribble on the map, quickly drawing the position and movement of several units of the army. Senndra reached for a pencil and began to add shapes and words to the side of the map closest to her. She sketched out the positions of several groups of infantry as well as adding three archer positions. She also sketched several maneuvers for the cavalry, mending the mistakes that she had seen in the original plan and adding several of her own maneuvers. Finally she turned her attention to the problem of the enemy dragons. It was obvious that the number of dragons for Magessa was significantly less than that of Molkekk, so they would not be able to defeat them in an all-out battle; however, if they had the support of heavy ballistae, they would have a good chance of being victorious. After pondering the problem for several minutes, Senndra added a few mobile ballistae to the slopes of Rebel Mountains and scribbled a question mark beside them. In words, she described a maneuver that she thought might succeed in drawing the enemy dragons within their range.

When she had finished, she raised her head and looked at the other cadets around the table. They had all looked at the plan and were scribbling on separate sheets of paper. Every so often one of them would reach for another piece of paper or a pencil, but otherwise there was almost no movement besides the scribbling of pencils on paper.

Senndra reached for her glass and took a draught of the liquid. She decided that it was some sort of fruit juice, though she wondered where the cadets would have gotten juice from. As she was pondering this question, Timothy put down his pencil, sat up, and stretched. He rose from his chair and crossed the room to the cupboards, chose a glass, and poured himself some of the contents of the pitcher. After tasting the liquid, he walked back to the table and sat down beside Senndra.

"Well, that went well, I think," he said. "I was able to rework some of the problems with the original battle plan, and from what I saw of your side, it looks like you did even more than I did. If everyone else does half as much as we did, I think that we should have a decent plan."

Senndra nodded her agreement. She glanced at the plan that Timothy and she had drawn up and scanned it for any obvious mistakes but didn't find any. The other cadets were still working after she finished her critiquing, so she turned her attention to Timothy.

"How's your arm doing?" she asked quietly so as not to disturb the others. He was taking a drink, and her question caught him off guard. Instinctively, he began to reply but started coughing instead.

"I'm so sorry! Are you okay?" Senndra asked, ready to help him. Timothy lifted a finger indicating that she was to stay back and continued coughing. Senndra had a worried expression on her face as her friend hacked and coughed for a few minutes. Finally he managed to clear the liquid out of his lungs and took a deep breath.

"My arm is okay," he gasped in a hoarse voice. "My lungs, on the other hand, aren't feeling so well."

"I'm so sorry. Are you okay?" Senndra asked again. Timothy nodded, and Senndra began to relax when he suddenly went into another fit of coughing. When he had finished, he looked up at her.

"I think I'm actually okay, now," he said in a much clearer voice. He wiped a tear from his eye then pushed up the sleeve of his shirt so that the entire scar was visible. "Apparently it was very bad to begin with, but the military surgeons managed to stop the bleeding and stitch it up. When I came to, I found all of that work already done plus something else. Vladimir had been in to visit me and used magic to speed the healing process along a bit. I should be able to get the stitches out tomorrow."

"That's good," Senndra commented. "We're going to need everyone that can fight if the enemy attacks again, and you're one of the best that we have."

"Actually, we really don't need all that many infantry soldiers," Timothy contradicted her. "The dragons and a few archers are all that are really needed to keep the enemy infantry at bay."

"You know as well as I do that they're doing the exact same thing in their camp that we're doing here," Senndra said. "The chances of them creating a plan to bypass our defenses are just as good as our chances of doing the same to their defenses, maybe better since they have more warriors at their disposal. If they do that, we're really going to need all of the soldiers we have and then some. We'll really need you, since you can work magic."

"Work *with* magic," Timothy corrected her. "I've already explained magic to you about a hundred times. I don't 'work magic,' I simply put it together so that it does what I want. Or rather, what Elohim wants."

"How do you do that?" Senndra asked, interrupting Timothy. "How do you know what Elohim wants?"

"Sometimes He speaks to me like a person would speak to me," Timothy answered. "Sometimes I can hear Him speaking to me in my head, but most often I just know what He wants me to do. I can't really explain it; I just know. There was actually one time that I didn't even know how to do the specific bit of magic that He wanted me to do. I just let Him work through me, and before I knew it, I had already done what I didn't know how to do."

"So He speaks to you frequently, but what about you? Can you speak to Him?" Senndra asked.

"I can, and do so often," Timothy said. "Anyone can talk to Him whenever they want to, but whether He responds or not is a different story. Sometimes He will answer me right away, and sometimes it takes a long time for Him to answer. Sometimes it seems like He doesn't answer, but that is simply because I am not looking at things in the correct light. Very often He will use something that I read or see to answer my question, and if I am not in the correct frame of mind, I can miss those answers very easily."

"Maybe He doesn't answer sometimes because He doesn't hear you," Senndra suggested.

"No, that has never happened and never will happen," Timothy said. "In His Holy Book He wrote, 'Call to Me and I will answer you.' He always hears those who call on Him."

"Then why do bad things happen to people who trust Him?" Senndra asked. "Did they not ask Him to protect them from evil, or did He not hear them?"

"Neither answer is necessarily correct," Timothy answered. "Elohim hears every prayer prayed by men, and He always answers, but He does not necessarily answer the way that we would like Him to answer. Perhaps, in your example, the righteous who trust in Him did ask for His protection. That does not necessarily mean that He will give that protection from all evil. There is no doubt that He answered, but maybe that answer was 'No.'"

"But why would He do that to His people?" Senndra asked. "Why would He allow them to suffer when He would have to do so little to take that suffering away?"

"No one knows the answers to questions like that," Timothy said, "because no one knows the mind of Elohim. One answer is that Elohim has given us free will and, for the most part, will not interfere with our choices. The choices made by some people may be what causes the bad things to happen to others. There are many other answers to your question; for instance, perhaps He allows things to happen so that His people can be strengthened by the experience. Like I said, no one knows the mind of Elohim, but we do know this: there is nothing that happens in this life that He cannot or does not use for His own good and the good of His people."

"If He uses everything for good, then what is the purpose of the recent attacks on the country?" Senndra asked. "Surely they cannot be used for good."

"Oh, yes they can," Timothy responded. "Just one way that they could be profitable is if the uncertainty of them causes the people of this country to turn back to Elohim. There is really nothing better for bringing people back to Him than hard times."

"If that's the purpose for these attacks, I guess we can assume they will not end very soon," Senndra decided. "I know that since the last attack, there has not been a massive revival in the nation. On the other hand, this last attack did bring many of the soldiers back to Elohim. I have noticed that a lot more of them believe in Him and talk about Him now than did when we were not at war."

"First, we do not know if the purpose of these attacks is to bring the nation back to Elohim," Timothy said, "however, if it is, I think that perhaps we will not see the end of it very soon. You were right when you said that many of the soldiers that did not use to believe in Elohim now do. Facing death is a very unique experience, and not many people can do it without having

58

assurance that if they do die, they will be going to a better place. Those who trust in Elohim know that they are going to be with Him when they do die, and this makes fighting much easier. By this same token, the reason that the nation as a whole has not turned back to Elohim is that the fighting has not touched them yet. Which is why I think that perhaps this battle will not be finished very quickly and that it is a distinct possibility we will not be able to hold the city. If the enemy gains entrance to the country, they will essentially take the war to all of its inhabitants. When faced with death, they will find, like the soldiers did, that it's easier to face death with the knowledge that they will be with Elohim when they die."

"It's also easier to face adversity when you know that He has your back, so to speak," Senndra commented.

"That is also true," Timothy said. "But then again, we never know if my theory is true or not. Perhaps the purpose of the attack was to bring the military back to Elohim, and they will, in turn, take their belief in Him back to the rest of the country. And then again, maybe the purpose of the attack has nothing to do with that at all. Often times it is very difficult to determine such things."

"So the only choice that we have is to do our duty and hope that Elohim will fight for us," Senndra said.

"No, when we obey Elohim, we *know* that He will fight for us," Timothy said. "Of course, as we said, His plan may involve the defeat of this city; however, you never know what the plan of Elohim is, so never give up without a fight. Now, let's get back to this plan to save the city."

******

Josiah trudged through the mud at the head of his soldiers and again wished for his horse. The soldiers were marching obediently after him, but he knew that they were feeling weary and depressed just like he was. Their ranks had been complemented by soldiers from Feling, but not as much as had been hoped. They had also been joined by the majority of the civilians from the city, and Josiah knew that they would be a liability in a battle. Even so, he knew that accompanying them was the only decent thing to do, so he kept his mouth shut and marched. Several hours after leaving Feling, a halt was called, and Josiah took the opportunity to sit down. His men followed suit, and soon all of the soldiers were resting in various positions. Josiah looked up to see a messenger approaching, and he stood to his feet. The messenger gave a salute, and Josiah returned it.

"The General has ordered a rest of one hour, sir," the messenger said. "You are to have your men ready to go in forty-five minutes."

Josiah acknowledged the statement with a nod, and the messenger saluted again and left. For forty-five minutes the army rested; there was not much movement since the soldiers were tired and the civilians were frightened. The few animals with the army were also relatively still, as if sensing the mood of the group. Finally the soldiers climbed wearily to their feet and they were off again, marching over the ground that excessive rain had turned into a bog. They marched for hours, the monotony broken only occasionally by the breakdown of equipment or some other problem. They took one more forty-five minute rest that day and after that marched until dusk.

When the sun began to set, they stopped and pitched camp in the mud. The next day they struck camp before the sun rose and were off again. The rain had finally stopped, and the sun peeked out from behind the clouds that had been hiding it. The weather was warmer now, and the mood of the company was much brighter, but the ground was still muddy, making their pace rather slow. Even with this impediment of their progress, the borders of a forest could be seen to the south by the third night. They pitched camp when the sun set and were up again before dawn. Tired out from their long march, they plodded the last miles to the forest.

Two

The trees on the edge of the forest were the shortest, and even these stretched more than forty feet tall. The noises issuing from between them were just as would be expected from any forest, which was somehow not what Josiah had been anticipating. The elves' forest should have a mystical and foreboding feeling about it, he thought, but instead there were the natural sounds of birds and animals. Occasionally these beasts could be seen between the trees; they looked like perfectly normal animals running about their own business, but the men in the army knew better. Rumor had it that the elves were able to communicate with the animals and used them to patrol the borders of their forests.

Josiah wondered why a halt had been called. The Reaumur Mountains rose to the east, so there was really only two options for the army; either they could follow the edge of the forest to the southwest, or they could take the easier path directly south into Dublack. No matter what the decision was, the army needed to keep moving in order to stay ahead of the enemies that were sure to be advancing in their wake. Perhaps the decision had been made to go through the forest, Josiah considered. In that case, the General had probably sent a party of men into the forest to gain permission from the elves. It was a time-consuming, yet necessary formality. Not only was it important for the elves to know about the enemy attack, but entering their woods without permission was a dangerous thing to do. Before the people of Magessa had invaded the land, the elves had been one of the only groups to worship Elohim, and as such they were almost constantly under attack. They had set up many traps and enchantments to protect their borders, and many of these devices were still in working order.

The army stayed outside the forest for an hour or two. Josiah couldn't really tell how long it was, nor did he care. Leave that to someone else, he decided, and promptly fell asleep, leaving orders with one of his soldiers to wake him up when the army was ready to move. His sleep was not filled with dark and stormy nightmares; in fact, he didn't dream at all.

When he woke, he felt perfectly rested, almost as if he had not been marching for the last two days. The camp around him was strangely silent, and he began to investigate it. At first he thought that all of the soldiers and other people were asleep, but he realized this would not account for the silence of the animals. He walked to a nearby corral and saw that the animals were walking about inside, eating and opening and closing their mouths as if they were making noise, but no sound was issuing from them.

"They are making sound, you just can't hear them," a voice behind Josiah said. He turned. There stood a man he had only seen once before, on the plains outside of Magessa. The man's sandy blond hair was still cropped short, and even when Josiah examined him closely, he still could not determine which race he was. Perhaps he was all of them, Josiah thought, and perhaps he was none of them. When he looked into the man's eyes, he still saw the indescribable love he had seen at their last meeting.

"This is a vision," the man said. "You are seeing the camp exactly as it is, but you cannot hear them, and they cannot see you or me." A guard paced past Josiah not two feet away but didn't give him so much as a glance.

"Why are you here?" Josiah asked. He was slightly fearful, but more than that, he was eager, anxious to hear what the man had to say.

"I am not 'here' as you say," the man said. "This is not the earth as you know it. Rather we are in the spiritual dimension and can merely see what is happening on the earth. Therefore, the question that you should be asking is 'Why are *you* here?'"

"Well then, why am I here?" Josiah asked.

"The enemies of Elohim again threaten Magessa, and only you and your army stand in their way," the man said. Anger at the fact he had just stated showed in his eyes and voice. "Their numbers are insurmountable, even more so than the last time you saw them. They have been reinforced by a large army of dwarves; that is why they stayed at Saddun for so long. But now your reprieve is gone, and they are following you with vigor."

"We can't hope to win if we stand against them, can we?" Josiah asked.

"That is not for you to decide," the man answered. "You are called only to obey Elohim and leave the outcome to Him. There is, however, wisdom in strengthening your position so that you have the best chance of defeating them. You should retreat to where the Vänern and Pelé Rivers cross. If you receive help from the elves and the ogres, you may have a chance of survival."

"Why are you telling *me* this?" Josiah asked. "I am not in command of the army. You should be speaking to the General. He has the authority to do what you are suggesting."

"The General is a fair, just, and wise man, and he is a believer in Elohim," the man said, "but his belief is more

64

ceremonial than anything else. He does not believe enough to see me even if I chose to appear to him."

"But couldn't you make him believe? Couldn't you make him see you?"

"That is not the way that I would have it," the man said. "There is nothing that I cannot do, but there are a few things that I will not do. Forcing someone to believe is one of those things."

"Very well," Josiah said. "I see that it falls to me to do this thing. What shall I do if the General does not heed my advice?"

"You are to go to the elves and ask them for their assistance," the man responded. "From there go to the place where the Vänern and Pelé Rivers cross. You must do this under any circumstances; the fate of Magessa rests in your hands."

"This all seems plausible when I'm standing here talking to you," Josiah said with panic rising in his voice, "but what about when you are no longer here? How will I do what I have to do when you are gone?"

"When I am gone?" the man repeated. He began to fade from sight as he said, "I am never gone. I will be with you, even though you cannot see me."

First the man and then the rest of the surroundings faded from sight, and Josiah found himself in complete darkness. He blinked, and light flooded his vision, blinding him momentarily. He blinked again and waited for his eyes to grow accustomed to the light. He found himself looking up at the sky and realized that he was lying down on his back. For a moment he had trouble remembering what had just happened to him. What had he been dreaming about only moments before?

It came back to him in a flash, and he pushed himself to his feet. His body ached, but he forced himself to jog toward where the General's tent had been erected. The insignia on his uniform allowed him passage by all of the guards, until he found himself face to face with a massive man standing at the entrance of the General's tent.

"I have urgent news for the General," Josiah said and made sure that his rank insignia was plainly visible. The guard studied Josiah for a minute, then stepped aside from the entrance of the tent. Josiah pushed the flap aside and entered, waiting for his eyes to adjust to the dim interior. The General sat at a makeshift table with several other men, some of whom Josiah recognized but some of whom he did not. All of the men looked up when he entered. The General looked at him, waiting for him to speak.

Josiah remembered himself and offered a salute. When it was acknowledged, he dropped it and stood where he was, trying to think what he should say.

"If I could have a moment of your time alone, General," he finally said in order to gain time. The General must have seen by Josiah's face that it was important because he nodded to the men in the tent and motioned for them to leave. The men stood and filed out past Josiah, leaving him and the General alone. The General was looking at Josiah again, and Josiah again began to search for words.

"We are to enter Dublack," he finally said. "At the command of Elohim," he added as an afterthought.

"At the command of Elohim?" the General asked. "What do you mean?"

"I mean that a messenger from Elohim has told me that I must leave the camp and go to the elves," Josiah said. "He said that we must send an envoy into Dublack forest to request assistance from the elves. Meanwhile, the army is to fall back to where the Pelé and Vänern Rivers cross. The messenger said that if we have the help of both the elves and the ogres, we might be able to defeat the enemy."

"No, I cannot allow that to happen," the General said after a moment's hesitation. "I must keep every available man between the enemy and the rest of Magessa. We have a responsibility to protect the country."

"We will be protecting the country," Josiah reasoned. "If we move now, the messenger seemed to indicate that we would arrive at the Accri forest before the enemy would."

"That's not a chance I'm willing to take," the General said. "There is a possibility, a good one in my mind, that the enemy will overtake us before we ever reach the ogres. I will need my army to be at full strength when that happens."

"General, Elohim says that we won't get stuck in that situation," Josiah said. "If we follow His commands, He will watch over us."

"Faith like that may be good enough for you, but I cannot stake the fate of the country on it," the General said with a shake of his head. "Even if I dispatched messengers to the elves, the chances that they would come to our aid are minimal."

"Why?" Josiah asked. "They came to help us the last time we were attacked."

"True, but the politics were different back then," the General said. "The elves have withdrawn from dealing with us humans at all, and it does not seem likely that they will see fit to help us."

"Withdrawn from dealing with us? Why?" Josiah asked.

"Apparently you do not follow politics very much," the General said. "Actually, not too many people know what happened. It would seem that the elves believe, and it appears rightly so, that the governing body of Gatlon is corrupt. They have also not been treated fairly of late, and this has driven the wedge further between us."

"So it would seem that we are alone in this battle," Josiah said. "But," he added, "the messenger of Elohim said we need to do this thing."

"That may be," the General said, "but I already told you I don't have enough faith to stake the fate of the country on the goodwill of the elves. So once again, the answer is no. I will not do what you have requested."

"Then you leave me no choice," Josiah sighed. "The messenger also said that I have to do what needs to be done, and I will do it alone if necessary."

"That is deserting in time of war, a crime that is severely punished," the General said, though his voice was not threatening.

"I know that, sir," Josiah answered, "and still I must obey Elohim. No matter what punishments come, I must obey Elohim."

"I wish I had faith like you," the General said. "As it is, you have left me in a tough position. I cannot have my commanders randomly deserting the army, which is what may happen if I allow you to walk away unpunished."

"I am sorry if I cause you any inconvenience," Josiah said, "but I have already told you what I must do, and I will not be moved in my resolve."

"I was afraid of that," the General said. "I cannot afford to have a prisoner in this army, as it would slow us down and consume resources that we cannot spare. Also I cannot see putting a man such as yourself in custody. You have more than proven your bravery and worth, and I do not wish to imprison you for deserting."

"I am sorry for the choice that you are forced to make, but it appears that you must choose between two bad things."

"Ah, but that is where you are wrong, Commander," the General said. "There is a third option that I have not mentioned yet. I do not like it, but it appears to be the best thing considering the circumstances.

"Commander, I hereby order you to take an envoy to the elfin capital and present our request for help to them. After that you are to rejoin the army at the Accri forest no matter what the response to your envoy may be. You are ordered to surrender command of your legion to me, and I will reassign it as I see fit. You may take anyone that you deem necessary with you for the envoy, up to ten persons. Good luck and Godspeed, Commander," the General finished. "Heaven knows that we need you to succeed."

"Understood, General," Josiah said. He saluted and turned to head out of the tent but was stopped by the General's voice.

"Send the other men back in when you go out, Josiah."

Josiah stepped out into the sunlight and motioned for the other men to re-enter the tent. He headed across the camp to where his legion was and ordered a soldier to locate his Captains and have them meet him. Then he began to gather his gear together and stuff it into his pack. He was just finishing when the first of his Captains began to arrive. Within five minutes, the four Captains that had left Saddun alive had gathered.

"I'll make this as brief as possible," Josiah began. "I have received an order from the General to take a delegation into Dublack Forest and request aid from the elves. Meanwhile, he will take the rest of the army around the edge of the forest toward the Accri Forest. After I and my delegation have presented our requests to the elves, we are to rejoin with the army at the Accri Forest. I am to surrender command of my legion at least for the course of the mission, though I don't know if I will resume command when I return to the army."

"I am coming with you, Commander," Cirro said immediately.

"I am allowed to take up to ten people with me, but I don't think that I can allow you to come," Josiah said. "You are a Captain, and as such you have responsibilities to the army that I don't feel comfortable relieving you of."

"Get real, Josiah," Cirro said. "Your legion is not much more than a company as it is. I think it will be just fine without me."

"You're absolutely right," Josiah conceded with a humorless laugh. "There really aren't enough soldiers to justify four Captains."

"With your leave, I would also like to accompany you on your mission," Brandon, one of Josiah's other Captains, said.

"So be it," Josiah said after a moment's hesitation. "Two Captains should be more than enough for the number of men that still remain in the legion. We will be leaving as soon as the envoy is filled. Do you have any suggestions as to whom I should take?"

Suggestions were plentiful, so while Cirro and Brandon left to pack their things, Josiah began to track down the people that they had recommended. As time was short, he found only three of them but determined that they would be enough for an envoy. He allowed them time to gather their gear before returning with them to where he had met with his Captains earlier. Cirro and Brandon were there with packs and weapons strapped to their backs and around their waists.

"You ready to go?" Josiah asked them. They hoisted their packs onto their backs in response. "Then let's roll out."

Just as they were starting to walk toward the border of Dublack forest, they heard a shout coming from behind them. They turned around to see a man hurrying after them. He had a pack on his back and weapons strapped around his waist. Josiah thought that he recognized him but couldn't be sure. As the figure drew closer, he was able to make out the features of his face and immediately recognized Petra Bentinck. Josiah and his companions waited until Petra reached them.

"Permission to accompany you, sir," Petra said, gasping air between words. It was evident by his appearance that he had thrown his gear together very quickly and had run all the way just to catch Josiah's group before they left.

"Permission granted," Josiah said. He knew Petra from the dwarven attack half a year ago and had grown to like the man. He would certainly be an asset to the group, which was still well below the ten person limit that the General had given Josiah.

The group turned back toward Dublack, and advanced toward it with no further delay. When they reached the edge of the wood, they held back, afraid to trespass on the elves' property, but Josiah walked under the trees as if he were simply taking a leisurely stroll. His friends were emboldened by his conduct, and followed him, though they were all on edge. Josiah took the lead and was followed directly by Brandon, who had his hand on the hilt of a battle ax secured to his belt. Petra took the rear, looking in all directions to make sure that they were not surprised. He also had his hand on the handle of his weapon.

Josiah could still not get over the fact that the forest was not as mysterious as he had expected. The ordinary sound of water dripping from the tree leaves was in the air, and every once in a while a drop would splash onto Josiah's head. Further into the forest, the underbrush grew thicker, and the pace of the group slowed considerably. They no longer walked in a single file line but spread out, each making his own way as best he could. They came to a small river and had to follow it a half mile downstream before a crossing presented itself. When they were safely on the other side of the river, they stopped to rest.

"How do we know that we're going south?" Cirro asked as they sat on a fallen log.

"That's a good question," a soldier put in. The three members of Josiah's party previously unknown to him were Devon, Stephen, and Heath. At first Josiah was not able to tell Stephen and Heath apart since they were identical twins; however, he had devised a way to distinguish between them. Stephen, the older of the two by three minutes, wore a ring on his left hand, and the hands of Heath were bare. It was the younger twin that had voiced the question, and Josiah looked at him for a long moment before answering.

"We don't really know, I guess," he finally answered. "Not for sure anyway. But there is something. I don't know about the rest of you, but ever since I entered the forest, an invisible force has been leading me. Maybe it is pushing me, I don't know. That feeling is all that I have to go by, though."

"That feeling has nothing to do with the fact that you're actually going in the right direction," a voice behind Josiah said. The group jumped and spun around just in time to see a tall man step out from the shadows thrown by the trees. He was a little over six feet tall, had black hair and piercing eyes, and was wearing a drab green cloak. A bow and quiver were strapped to his back, and a short sword hung from his waist.

"I am Josii, by the way," the man said and extended his hand toward Josiah. Josiah scrambled to his feet and took the offered hand. As he shook the man's hand, he looked into his eyes and knew immediately that this was an elf, one of the inhabitants of the wood.

"My name is Josiah Pondran, and I have come at the command of Elohim," Josiah said.

"Is that so?" Josii questioned. "And what business do you have in Dublack?"

"I told you, we're here at the command of Elohim," Josiah repeated. "He has sent us here to warn you of the recent attack on Magessa and ask for your assistance."

"That is not a question for me to answer," Josii said. "Only the king can decided whether we go to war or not."

"Where is the king, then?" Josiah asked. "I must speak to him as soon as possible."

"We are still thirty miles north of Lêf, our capital," Josii said. "The path there covers rough terrain, and we do not have many hours left in this day, but if we hurry, we can still reach it before nightfall."

"Then let's get going," Josiah said. He and his friends lifted their packs onto their backs and followed Josii away through the trees.

The forest Josii led them through did not look any different than what they had been traveling through previously with the exception that the underbrush which had been slowing them down was no longer present. It was to their left and right and sometimes behind and in front of them, but it never covered the path that they followed, if you could call it a path. Josiah could see no evidence of a trail except that which he stood on. It seemed to zigzag in and out of the trees, and Josiah tried to discern its winding course, but no matter how hard he tried, he was unable to do so. Time after time it seemed as though they had come to a dead end, but Josii would always make an unexpected turn, and there would be room for them to walk again.

Josii had been telling the truth when he said that the route covered rough terrain. During their first few miles, the group gained several hundred feet in altitude. Josiah knew from his geography lessons that this variation in terrain was the foothills of the Reaumur Mountains. The ground became rockier as the group got higher, but even so they made good time. Finally the ground leveled off, and Josii informed them that they were finished going up. The rest of the journey would be downhill. There was still plenty of light to navigate the forest, but it was slowly fading, and Josiah wondered how their guide expected them to reach Lêf before sundown. The group's pace increased as they traveled downhill, and the walking became easier. Even though Josiah had worn light armor for the mission, he had begun to feel the weight of it as he climbed and had expected that going downhill would be easier for him in this respect. Now, however, he could still feel the weight of his armor albeit in a different way. As he hiked down the hill, he had to take care to keep his balance, for with every step he took, the weight of the armor increased his speed, and he had to be careful to not start running down the hill. The trees were clearing up considerably, and the underbrush between them began to thin out, making the going quite a bit easier than before. Their speed increased, and in less than ten minutes they had reached a new mode of transportation.

Josiah finally understood how they were going to reach Lêf before dark. The Vänern River cut through the forest in front of them, and three canoes were tied to a small pier that jutted out into the water. A shack stood a small distance from the pier, and it was to this building that Josii walked. The door of the shack, or what Josiah assumed was the door, had no handle, but a small hole was visible to one side. Josii pulled a small piece of metal from his pocket, slipped it into the hole, twisted, and withdrew it. Hooking his foot underneath the door, he pulled upwards, and, to the surprise of his companions, the whole wall slid upward, disappearing as it reached the top of the door frame. Josii stepped into the shack and was back almost immediately with several paddles.

"Carry these down to the pier," he ordered. "All of you do know how to use a paddle, correct?" he asked, almost as an afterthought.

Everyone indicated that they did, indeed, know how to use paddles, and Josii brought out one for each person. In no time, they were on their way. Josii was in the lead canoe with Heath and Stephen while Cirro, Brandon, and Devon occupied the second canoe. Josiah and Petra were in the rear canoe. The group set out in this order, paddling very little since the river's current was strong enough to pull them downstream at more than twenty miles per hour. The person in the rear of each boat used their paddle for steering, but this was also not a difficult task since the river was very wide and the current kept the canoes in the middle.

The time spent in the canoes was uneventful, to say the least, leaving Josiah with a chance to study the forest. The trees at the edge of the wood had been large, but the ones in the heart of the forest were colossal. He could not see how tall they stretched, but the trunk of each tree would have required at least three men to reach around it. The underbrush was back in force, filling, it seemed, every available space between the trees. Water still dripped from the trees, but something was different. Josiah had noticed, for the last several miles, the absence of animal activity in the area, and the cause for this was soon obvious. Houses in clearings appeared for the first time beside the river and grew more numerous downstream. These houses had many lanterns hanging from them, and Josiah wondered how long it took to light all of them. Accompanying each house was a large waterwheel. Josiah had seen these before and knew that they were used mainly to grind grain, but these waterwheels did not have adjoining houses big enough to accommodate such equipment. Elfin was becoming more evident, and the buildings along the river's edge were getting closer and closer together until there were no trees at all separating them.

The river took a large bend, and as the canoes rounded it, Josiah was confronted with the most amazing sight he had ever laid eyes on. Lêf, the famed capital city of the elfin nation, lay before them, and it was even grander than Josiah had imagined. Buildings and towers made from strange substances rose from both sides of the river. Glass, a material not unknown to Josiah, but also not common to him, was used in abundance in these buildings. Three large bridges crossed the river, connecting the two sides of the city, and huge systems of docks lined the edges of the river. Buildings covered the ground as far as Josiah could see, and he was more than a little surprised to discover that they were built after a system that was very similar to that of human cities. Lanterns and torches covered the buildings and bridges, and again Josiah wondered how long it took to light all of them. Josii led the canoes to one of the many docks where the travelers got out of the watercraft and tied them securely to rings.

"The king's palace is about a mile from here," Josii told the humans when they had finished tying up the boats. "His court will not be in session, so there are two choices. Either you can stay at my house and wait until tomorrow to talk to him, or we can go straight to the palace and determine whether he will see you or not."

"Let's go to the palace first," Josiah spoke up. "If we can't see him today, we will be more than happy to take you up on your offer; however, our information and request is urgent, so I need to see him as soon as possible."

"As you wish. Follow me," Josii said and led the humans away from the water and into the city of the elves. The streets were wide and clean and did not have sewage running down them as was seen in most of the cities in Magessa. Josiah decided that the elves must have enclosed sewage systems like those of a few of the bigger human cities. Josiah was also struck by the orderly flow of traffic in the city. The way that people waited their turns at intersections and stayed to one side of the road was entirely different than the chaotic activities that were the traffic in most cities. Also, the lanterns were hanging everywhere, keeping the streets lit even though the light was quickly fading.

The buildings of the city were very different than those of the human cities. These structures were taller than Josiah had ever seen, the tallest stretching upward for more than ten stories. The sight made Josiah dizzy and he had to look back down at the road, which was just as different from human cities as any other part of the city. First of all, the road was made of stone and had designated areas for vehicles and animals and for pedestrians.

Also there were no booths lining the streets as was common to human cities.

"No, you won't see any of them here," Josii said when someone commented on their absence. "All of our shops are inside the buildings. This helps to decrease the congestion of the streets and gives the city a neater appearance."

"Imagine that, Josiah," Petra whispered. "No booths outside. I'd like to see this city in the daytime. It must look very strange."

"What about drainage ditches?" Heath spoke up. "I don't see any, nor do I see any sewage."

"And you won't see any in the time that you stay here," Josii informed him. "We have gone to great lengths to make the city clean, and this holds true for water and sewage. Underground pipes carry water from the river to the buildings and carry sewage out of the city."

"How is that possible?" Brandon asked. "Water can't flow up from the river to where we are, and surely it can't flow to the tops of the highest buildings."

"Actually it does both of these things," Josii said. "I can't explain to you how it works since I am not well acquainted with the machines that make it happen; however, I do know that a water wheel gives power to the contraption."

"Amazing," someone in the group muttered. The others were stunned to silence and remained that way as they walked the rest of the distance to the castle of Lêf. They were so engrossed with the amazing sights of the city that had they been by themselves, they would have missed a building relatively unimpressive by comparison to the surrounding structures. It was surrounded by a swath of open ground and looked more like a castle than the seat of elfish power. It was not particularly tall, nor did it have any of the other details characteristic of the other elfish buildings. In fact, its architecture was almost human in appearance. It was not particularly large as it stretched for only two hundred yards along its façade and was only two hundred yards deep. The basic square shape was supplemented by a circular tower at each corner and a smaller turret in the middle of three of the walls. The gatehouse was set in the middle of the front wall, and a large, circular, and seemingly unfinished tower rose from the center of the castle. Tall, thick stone walls formed the perimeter of the castle, but no moat or other defense was visible. The gate was double; a thick pair of iron-bound oak doors were fronted by a massive iron portcullis, making it a difficult entrance to break into. Both the doors and the portcullis were open but guarded by two soldiers who held pikes. Josii led the party through the gate and into a courtyard that separated the castle walls from the tower in the middle. Guards patrolled the walls and courtyard, and a group of them sat in the gatehouse to be called upon if trouble arose. Though the guards were dressed in full body plate armor, they moved as if they were not encumbered by it very much. Their helmets were made of metal and had been shined until they reflected their surroundings. A loose vest with the image of an oak leaf embroidered onto it covered the breastplate of each man and was tucked into his belt. Each man wore a sword at his hip and carried a bow on his back. In addition to these, several of the guards also carried longer weapons, like pikes or spears.

Josii led the staring humans across the courtyard to the door of the tower in the middle of the castle. He knocked firmly on the thick oak door and stepped back to wait. Moments later, it scraped open and an elf dressed in royal attire stepped out.

"What is your business?" he asked.

"I have travelers to see the king," Josii answered. "Before you turn them away for the night, let me say that this is something that cannot wait until tomorrow. The king needs to know about it immediately."

"Well, what is it about?" the elf asked. "I'm not going to believe that it's urgent simply on your word."

"It's about an attack on Magessa," Josii said shortly.

The elf stared at him for a second, then scurried inside the castle with a vague gesture for them to follow. They stepped through the doors and into a massive foyer where the elf told them to stay while he hurried through another door. As they waited for the elf to return, the group shuffled nervously in the hall under the watchful eye of two guards. Josiah noticed immediately that these were not ordinary guards. They were covered from head to foot with a cloak that they wrapped completely around their bodies; the only visible armor was their helmets which were topped by crests in the form of dragons. A sharp bulge in their cloaks indicated the presence of a sword, but they did not carry bows. Instead, a hollow tube extended over the shoulder of each, and Josiah wondered what they were for.

"What are those tubes on their backs?" Devon finally asked their guide. "I've never seen anything like them."

"That is because they are specific to the elves," Josii whispered. "Very few people know they exist, and no one but a few elves know how to make them or operate them. They are called death-tubes by many, though elves call them stringless bows. They fire projectiles through the air at high speeds, have a longer range than bows, and have the ability to pierce armor. In a word, they are more efficient. I don't know exactly how they are operated; like I said, only a few elves know that. I do know that something is placed in it and a trigger like that of a cross bow is pulled. Then, if the operator is skilled, the target falls over dead."

"So they are magic weapons," Brandon said in a tone of awe. "I always heard people say that all elves were magicians, but I never believed them. Now I see that even soldiers can use it. Amazing."

"If you think that's amazing, watch this," Josii said with a mischievous grin. He walked over to the wall and manipulated something there. Suddenly half the lamps in the foyer blew out and a gasp came from the humans. A few seconds later the lamps were instantaneously relit, and the humans gave an audible gasp of awe.

"What the heck was that?" Stephen blurted.

"We call it electricity," Josii said. "I don't know exactly how it works, but when you flip the switch on the wall over there, the lights come on and when you flip it again, they go off."

"Are all of the lights in the city like these ones?" Josiah asked.

"For the most part," Josii answered. "There are a few exceptions, but the vast majority of them are electric."

"That would make things a lot easier," Josiah commented. "I was thinking about how long it would take to light every single light in the whole city. I guess when you can turn them all on with a single switch, it eliminates that problem."

"Yes, it does," Josii said. He was about to say more but was interrupted by the other elf entering the foyer again.

"King Einor will see you," he said. "If I were you, however, I would take as little time as possible."

"Don't worry; what I have to say will only take a few minutes," Josiah said. "Are we all going in or just me?"

"Everyone may enter, though I must warn you now that you will be relieved of your weapons while you are in the presence of the king."

"Very well," Josiah answered and followed the elf through a set of doors and deeper into the castle. They wound through several halls, all of which looked exactly the same, and finally arrived at a set of double doors which were being guarded by six men with stringless bows.

"Please remove your weapons and give them to the guards," the elf who was guiding them said when they had reached the doors. Josiah hesitated for half a second before sliding his sword, sheath and all, from his belt and handing it to one of the guards. All of his men followed suit, and when the last had been relieved of his weapons, they were led through the doors and into the throne room. The hall was not particularly large though the ceiling was vaulted, extending upward for at least two stories. Guards with stringless bows were interspersed through the hall with two standing by each of ten pillars which lined the sides of the room. Four more guards stood near the throne, and though they had their cloaks wrapped completely around themselves, Josiah figured they would be able to move at a moment's notice if the need arose. Ignoring the rest of the room, Josiah marched straight toward the throne and the man that sat atop it. Behind him he could hear his men following him, and this gave him a certain amount of courage. When he reached the steps of the throne, he bowed slightly and stood still, waiting to be addressed. Behind him his men flanked him on either side so that they formed an arrow head with him at the tip.

"Welcome, messengers from Magessa," King Einor said. "What is your business here?"

"We come with news of an attack, your majesty," Josiah answered, taking a step forward to separate himself from the people behind him. "A large army suspected to be under the command of Molkekk attacked us several days ago at the city of Saddun. We held them for as long as we could, but they quickly overcame us with superior numbers and drove us out of the city. We gathered what remained of our army, which is now headed to where the Vänern and Pelé Rivers cross. There we will meet the enemy in battle, though the outcome of such an encounter will likely not be favorable.

"We cannot hope to succeed with the few soldiers that we have left, so the General of the army of Gatlon has sent me as an emissary to ask for your aid in the battle that is to come. I humbly ask for any assistance you may be able to offer us in the fight against our enemies."

"That must have really damaged your pride," King Einor said after a moment.

"I don't know what you mean, your majesty," Josiah said.

"Oh yes, you do," Einor responded. Though he kept his tone even, the anger was evident in his voice. "Your people have treated my people poorly in dealings with us for the last several decades. If you were content to ignore us, that would be one thing, but you aren't. Instead you take advantage of us in any way you can. Yet despite all of this behavior, when the enemy comes knocking, who do you run to for help? Why should we help you after the despicable treatment that we have received at your hands?"

"An unfortunate situation that I am truly ashamed of," Josiah answered, lowering his eyes. "I was unaware of the presence of such a problem until just recently, and I am truly ashamed of the actions of my people. Let me say, though, that not everyone agrees with u. I am very proud of and thankful for your conduct at the last attack on Saddun, and I know that your people are held in high esteem among soldiers.

"As for those who take advantage of you, that was largely the work of the council of Gatlon, if I am not mistaken. It has been discovered that they were in league with Molkekk, and were planning on surrendering the district to Molkekk when he attacked. They have been dealt with, according to as much justice as could be afforded them.

"Finally, I am here not solely at the command of my General. I am here first and foremost on the authority of Elohim. He sent a messenger to me and told me that the only way we could hope to defeat the enemy was to acquire the help of your people and that of the ogres. He told me that I was to come here, with or without the permission of my commander, and ask for your help."

"That is very interesting," Einor said after a few minutes of thought. "I was not aware that only a few people could commit the kind of abuse that has been going on for decades. Of course, the most unforgiveable trespass has only begun to occur recently. Slavers have started to kidnap our people and sell them to people north of Magessa. They had large groups of well-trained soldiers to pull this off, so don't tell me that the military is sympathetic with us." Josiah tried to interject, but Einor cut him off.

"Also, Elohim may have ordered you to come and ask for our assistance, but He did not order me to comply with your request. For all I know, you are simply lying in order to get our help. Well, I'll tell you now that you will not get it no matter what lies you spin. The elves have borne the abuses of humans and fought their battles long enough, and we will not do so any longer. Fight your own battles for we will not help you."

"You may feel no obligation to help us, sir, and that I can understand," Josiah said. "The fact that you have endured these abuses all while helping fight our battles is incredible, and I can understand why you're angry. You may also not care what Elohim has told me to do, and I can also understand that, because I could very easily just be lying in order to obtain your help, though I assure you that I am not. Therefore, I am appealing to your humanity. We do not deserve your help, but what about the people from Belvárd and Rampön? What about all of the women and children who will be killed by the enemy? They are not responsible for your anger toward us, yet they will share in the consequences if you make this decision. I have fought with you before, and my men have died beside yours. My opinion of you could not be higher, and when this war is over I will do everything within my power to put an end to the abuses you have endured. But there will be no chance for me to right the wrongs if we are wiped out, at which point you will have Molkekk as your neighbor. I don't think he'll be better than us, so if nothing else, think of yourselves and help us."

"You are very bold to tell me to think of myself, human," Einor said. "In the forest we can hold out almost indefinitely. Molkekk will not find us as easy to defeat when he is forced to fight us in our homelands. We do not need your help to remain free from Molkekk, nor do we need to even venture out of the safety of our forest. From now on, our policy concerning your race will be isolation."

The last statement was made with such finality that Josiah knew nothing he could say would sway the king's decision. And he couldn't blame him for his choice either. If Josiah had been in the same situation, it was very possible he would have decided the same thing. Slowly he turned his back to the king and passed back between his men. As he walked, he picked up speed until he hit the doors of the throne room at a jog. He slammed them wide open and walked out, followed closely by his companions. Josii, however, remained in the throne room, and after the doors closed with a bang, turned back to the king.

"Einor, are you sure you're making the right decision?" he asked.

"I never know if I am making the right decision anymore, brother," Einor said as he slumped down in his throne and put his head in his hands.

"My gut tells me we should distance ourselves from the humans as much as possible, yet there is a persistent doubt at the back of my mind. What if I am choosing incorrectly?"

"What do you think that Elohim is telling you to do?" Josii asked. "You must always follow His word first of all."

"I don't even know what Elohim wants anymore," Einor said without lifting his head. "I've asked and He is silent. I don't know what to do."

"Do you truly not know what He wants, or do you simply not like what you know He is telling you?" Josii asked.

"I don't know," Einor said. "One second I'm sure that I should help the humans, but the next second I am certain that we should remain isolated from them. After everything that they have done to us, that is the wisest course of action. Then I'm back to thinking that I should give in to my compassionate side and help them."

"Why do you think that isolation is a good option?" Josii asked. "Is it because of the abuses the elves have endured at the hands of the humans, or is it because it's the course of action that will affect us least of all? Sitting back and watching things happen without intervening is a tempting option many times. Almost as often, it is necessary to suppress this tendency and take a hand in what is happening around you."

"Maybe you're right," Einor said as he raised his head and looked at his brother. "But even if I do choose to help the humans, it will be completely my choice. I am not hearing anything from Elohim in this instance."

"I know that we elves typically have a unique relationship with Elohim and can hear Him as an audible voice," Josii said, "but He never promised to speak with us this way. Most humans do not talk with Him in that way, yet in my dealings with them I have found that those who seek Him discover what His will is for them. Continue to pray, but also read His words that He has given us. Perhaps the answer to your question is hidden in them."

"Perhaps, brother," Einor said.

Josii saw that he had said everything he could to his brother, and that the choice to help or deny help to the humans was now out of his hands. He hurried out of the throne room and after the humans, knowing that without a guide they would get lost in the expansive halls of the castle. He found them arguing about which way to go when the hall that they had been following dead-ended. Taking the lead, he showed them the way out of the castle tower and into the courtyard. He slowed his pace when they passed through the gate and stopped only a few dozen yards past it.

"What are you planning on doing now?" he asked as he turned to face them.

"Our job here is done," Josiah said curtly. "We may as well be heading out."

"Right now?" Josii asked with a raised eyebrow. When Josiah nodded he added, "It is too late; the sun has already set. Besides that, how do you plan on finding your way out? I presume that you don't know the way, and even though you may be content to function on no sleep, I have to rest at some point or another."

"You mean elves can't go without sleep for days?" Stephen asked. "All the legends say they can."

"Elfin legends also paint all humans as weak, not only because of their inability to use magic, but also due to their small physical appearance," Josii commented with a sideways glance at Brandon's massive build and two-handed sword. "I would not put too much stock in legends if I were you."

"Enough about legends," Josiah said. "If we aren't leaving tonight, what are we going to do about lodging?" he asked Josii.

"I have a house on the west edge of the city," Josii said. "It's not very fancy, but it should be big enough to house all of you for one night. Plus," he added with a grin in Josiah's direction, "since we will be going west tomorrow, you could say that we're actually getting started on the journey right now."

"We are very grateful for the offer," Cirro said before Josiah could say anything. "I'm sure that Josiah, as our leader, will be more than happy to accept it."

"Yes, thank you for the offer, Master Elf," Josiah said. "We will be delighted to share your roof with you."

"Well, that's settled, so follow me, and we'll get there as quickly as possible," Josii said and started off down a street at a quick pace. As they walked, Josiah found himself at the head of the group alongside Josii. He did not speak to him for several minutes, but finally he could no longer resist the urge to ask a question that had been burning at the back of his mind.

"Why is the castle so different from the rest of the city?" he asked, turning to his elf guide. "The rest of the city has tall buildings and graceful architecture, but the castle looks like it was made by humans. It looks nothing like the rest of the buildings."

"It was made in a different time period," Josii answered. "Actually, it is one of the only original buildings of the forest that is still standing. All of the others have been demolished to make room for more modern structures."

"I don't know anything about the elfin time periods," Josiah said. "What period are you talking about?"

"The story is long, so I will wait until we get to my house to tell it," Josii said in answer.

It took the group another fifteen minutes to reach Josii's house. Josiah was anxious to hear the story, but Josii insisted on preparing a meal despite the protest of his guests. First, he started a fire and hung a kettle of water over it. Next he assembled a simple stew of potatoes, vegetables, and meat which took about a quarter of an hour to prepare. When he had placed it over the fire to cook, he retrieved the kettle of water which was now boiling and poured it into a tea kettle along with some tea leaves. While he was preparing the tea, he pointed out where his dishes were kept, and Josiah and his men set the table. When they were finished, they sat down and waited for the elf. Josii placed the tea on the table, took a seat, and leaned back in his chair. He cleared his throat and finally began the story that everyone was now anxious to hear.

"Long ago, before the recorded history of Magessa, there was only one race on the earth. A people that had the traits of all of the races lived together, and were in fact the whole of the earth's inhabitants. Now there was great sin on the face of the earth. Every man did what was right in his own eyes; if he wanted something that belonged to someone else, he killed that man for the possession. If he wanted land that someone else owned, he killed him for it. If someone insulted him or he simply did not like someone, he killed them. The sin of the people was so great that Elohim actually regretted creating them and sought to purge their uncleanness from the land.

"In all of the earth there was only one man who was righteous in the eyes of Elohim. Elohim told him that He was going to destroy the earth and that the only way to save himself and his family was to build a great boat and place his wife, his sons and their wives, and some of all the animals on it. The man followed the commands of Elohim even though he did not live anywhere near any water. When the boat was finished he gathered animals from all over the earth and placed them and his family on the boat. Once they were all on board, Elohim shut the door.

"Elohim opened up the gates of heaven and poured rain down on the earth for forty days and forty nights. He also opened up the fountains of the earth, and they spewed their water onto the surface of the earth until it was flooded. Not even the tallest mountains showed above the surface of the water and all living things, except those that were on the boat, died in the flood.

"After the rain stopped falling, the boat and its inhabitants floated about on the surface of the water for almost a year. At the end of this time, the man took a bird and let it out of

88

the window of the boat. The bird was gone for almost an entire day, but it eventually returned, for there was nowhere for it to land. The man waited for a week and then sent the bird out again. This time when the bird returned, it had a tree branch in its mouth, for the water had receded enough for the trees to show. Another week passed and the man again sent the bird out. This time it did not return, and the man knew that the waters had receded completely. The door to the boat was opened at this time and the man, his family, and all of the animals left. The man immediately made an altar and offered sacrifices on it to thank Elohim for saving him and his family from the flood. When Elohim saw this, He determined in His heart that He would never destroy the earth with water again and sent a rainbow to seal the promise.

"The family that left the boat began to repopulate the earth, and in only a few generations, a significant number of them were living together in one community. As normally happens when a large number of people live together, one man took the position of king. Now it had only been a few generations since the flood that had wiped out everything on the earth, but the hearts of men forget quickly, and this king decided that he wanted to be as powerful as Elohim. In order to accomplish this feat, he ordered his subjects to build a tower that would reach to heaven. Then he would be able to overthrow Elohim and be more powerful than Him. The people labored day after day, and their tower stretched up into the sky for many stories.

"One day Elohim decided to come down to earth and see what the people were doing. When He discovered what they were doing, His anger was aroused against them, and He struck their tongues so that they spoke different languages and could not understand each other. The brick makers could not understand the builders, and the builders could not understand the overseer. They tried to continue with the tower, but without the ability to communicate they were unable to accomplish anything. They split into groups of people that spoke the same language and moved away from each other. As each group intermarried with itself, a certain set of characteristics came out in it and a race was born. One group of people took on the features of elves; another, dwarves; another, orcs; another, mountain ogres; another, forest ogres; and another, humans. When the group that would become the elves left, they wandered about for several months, looking for a suitable place to live. They wandered into Magessa through the gap in the mountains that Saddun now blocks and eventually decided to settle in this forest. When they first settled, they built a city, and at the center of it sat a tower that was never finished as a reminder of what happens when people try to challenge Elohim. Eventually the elfin nation outgrew the borders of Dublack and moved across the mountains into East Dublack and up into the South Leborum and Leborum forests. Those that remained here gradually displaced the older buildings with newer and better ones, but there is one structure that we have preserved against the ravages of time. The unfinished tower that we built when we arrived as well as the wall surrounding it remains in our city and serves as the king's abode. It still stands in order to remind us that no one can challenge Elohim and hope to win."

The room lapsed into silence as the elf finished his story, and the humans leaned back in their chairs to consider what they had just been told. The elf took a sip of tea that no one had seen him pour for himself and rose from the table. He tested the stew hanging over the fire and stirred it before returning to the table. The humans were passing the tea pot around the table when he returned, so he took another sip of his drink when he sat. He knew that the humans would accost him with questions after they had served themselves, and he prepared himself for the onslaught.

"How long ago did those events take place?" was the first question; it came from Cirro.

"Like I said, this story was before recorded history, and as such there is no reliable date that can be given to it," Josii answered. "There are some who guess that it took place five thousand years ago. Others say it was no more than two thousand. No one knows for sure."

"If it occurred before recorded history, how do you know that it happened at all?" Josiah asked.

"A good question," Josii replied and took a sip of tea. "The account of the tale has been handed down from generation to generation orally since it happened. A few of the details became distorted during this time, and the true account was given to us a relatively short time ago by Elohim."

"What about the castle of the city?" Brandon asked. "Why does it have walls surrounding it while the rest of the city is unprotected?"

"The forest is the only protection that our lands need against any foe," Josii answered. "However, we did not know this when we first arrived, so we built a walled city. The newer city has no such defenses, but walls of the castle have been saved along with the tower."

"I have heard a similar tale to the one that you have just related to us," Stephen commented. "It was, of course, from the humans' perspective, and a few of the details were different, but as a whole it was very similar."

"That really isn't surprising," Josii said. "The flooding of the earth was a very significant event, and everyone knows it happened, just like everyone knows that Molkekk exists and lives to the north of Magessa. The story of the flood was passed down to the children of each race, but as time passed, the details were skewed, making every version slightly different. As I said, the elfin account was also slightly incorrect as we found out when we were given the actual account by Elohim."

"How did you get the story from Elohim?" Josiah asked.

"One of our prophets was chosen by Him to relate to us the events of the history of our nation before we started to record

91

the history. This man wrote down all of these things since the creation of the world until our history began. Many of these events had been lost, and we were very glad to have regained them."

"Lost? What kinds of things were lost?" Josiah asked.

"One of our most treasured pieces of history that we received at this point in time was that of our fickleness concerning Elohim," Josii said. "These stories tell of how our nation followed Elohim but kept falling away from Him. Every time we did so, He would draw us back to himself by invasion, drought, slavery, or some other evil. We look back on this to remind us what happens to those who turn away from Elohim. Only death and misery waits down that path."

The people around the table lapsed into silence again, and Josii rose to check the meal. This time it had finished cooking, and he removed it from its place above the fire. He carried the heavy pot to the table and set it in the middle. He placed a ladle in the food and returned to his seat. After offering a quick prayer for the food, Josiah began to ladle the stew out into the individual bowls, and for the next several minutes there was no conversation as everyone ate.

"Hey Josii, what happened after we left the throne room?" Heath asked as he wiped his mouth. "I noticed that you stayed behind after we left."

"Well, the king seemed set against sending any assistance when you left, is that correct?" the elf asked.

"Yeah, that's what it seemed like," Heath answered.

"He acts like he knows what he is going to do, but he actually isn't as positive as he pretends," Josii said. "On the one hand, his past experience with the humans leads him to believe that the best policy concerning them is isolation. On the other hand, he also knows in the back of his mind that Elohim wants him to send aid, though he tries not to admit this. One minute he wants to send aid and the next he is set against sending help of any kind. The man is struggling, and only Elohim knows what he will decide."

"So everything is not as hopeless as it seems?" Josiah asked. "I was thinking that perhaps someone else should have come to plead our case rather than me."

"No, the fault does not lie with you," Josii assured him. "Your plea was very effective, and I believe, though he did not show it, that it almost persuaded him to promise to help you."

"But will help come?" Petra asked. "If the king doesn't know what to choose, is that really much better than an outright refusal to help?"

"I don't know what the chances are that he will decide to send assistance," Josii said. "The only thing you can do is pray to Elohim that the king will send the help you need."

"That is good advice," Cirro commented. "Perhaps we should do it right now."

Everyone agreed, and together they bowed their heads and asked Elohim for His help. After the prayer, the conversation dwindled as the people started to nod off. Josii showed them where they were to sleep, and one by one his guests went to bed. Eventually only Josii, Josiah, and Petra remained at the table, and the conversation turned to what was going to happen the next day.

"We can't take the river to where we're going to meet up with the army since that is upstream from here," Josiah commented.

"No, we can't do that," Josii agreed. "The only way to get to the Accri Forest is on foot."

"But isn't it almost a hundred miles from here?" Petra asked.

"Yes, it is," Josii answered. "If we were all elves, we could probably make it in a day or two, but as it is…"

"It'll probably take us at least five days," Josiah finished.

"We may not even be in time to be of any help in the battle," Petra said.

"First of all, though every man counts, and only a few can turn the tide of a battle, let us be realistic," Josii responded. "There are only eight of us, and from what you have told me, there are probably more than one hundred thousand soldiers in the attacking army. The only real help Magessa's army will get is from the elves, if they decide to send reinforcements."

"You said there are eight of us," Petra commented. "Does that mean you're planning on accompanying us?"

"King Einor may still be debating what to do, but I already know what Elohim wants from me," Josii said. "I will accompany you and help in whatever way I can."

"But I thought we already established that we won't even get to the forest in time to be of any help," Josiah said.

"That is not established at all," Josii said. He rose from the table and retrieved a map from another room. When he returned, he shoved the chairs away from the table and spread the map out on it.

"You said that you left the army when it was on the edge of Dublack Forest somewhere around where it meets the mountains," Josii said as he stabbed a finger onto the map. "If we assume that was right here, they had a little more than a hundred miles to go. Right now we have a little *less* than a hundred miles to go. Granted, you have spent an entire day in the forest, and the terrain until we get out of the forest will be rough, but armies move at a much slower pace than a small group does. We may not reach Accri Forest before they do, but we should be in time to help them fight."

94

"Well, if we have that far to go, then we had better get some sleep," Josiah said as he stood and yawned. Petra and Josii followed his advice, and in minutes the house was silent except for the steady breathing of its inhabitants.

******

Josiah awoke to sunlight streaming through the windows of the house. He rubbed his eyes in surprise and sat up. He had figured that the foliage of the forest was too thick to allow sunbeams through it. He climbed to his feet and found out he had actually been right. The foliage *was* too thick; however, a hole in the canopy allowed a single sunbeam through, and that beam had found his face. Josiah stretched and stepped through a doorway into the dining room of the house. All his companions and their host were sitting around the table, eating breakfast in a leisurely manner.

"What's going on?" Josiah asked as he took a seat. "If we're planning on making twenty miles today, we should have already started."

"Have some tea," Josii said and handed Josiah a cup. "We aren't moving out today."

"Why not?" Josiah asked as he took the cup and sipped the hot drink. "We should get moving as quickly as possible. I thought we agreed on that last night."

"Yes, we agreed on it last night, but there is new information today that has changed our plans."

"Are you going to tell me what the new information is, or are you just going to sit there and make me wonder?" Josiah asked after waiting for a moment.

"King Einor has decided to send troops to accompany us to Accri Forest," Josii said in an offhanded manner. "As such, we have to wait until they are ready to move. That will probably take two days."

Josiah jumped to his feet and gave a deafening whoop. When he landed, he looked at his friends, who were grinning at him. He gave another, smaller whoop and then sat down.

"What are the details?" he asked Josii. "How many elves is he sending? When exactly are we leaving? How long is it going to take to get there now?"

"Slow down!" Josii laughed. "You sure are different than you have been since I met you. I would never have guessed you would get this excited about anything."

"Cut the chatter and tell me the details," Josiah said. It was obvious that he was still excited, but he was doing his best to contain himself.

"The king is sending half of the city's standing army and has sent messengers to the rest of Dublack, ordering our reserve army to assemble. He has also sent messengers over the mountains to the other elfin forests, but we really cannot count on them getting here in time to help in this particular battle. All told, you should have between five and ten thousand elves at your back when you join back up with your army. And did I tell you that some of our Megaeras will be in the army?"

"Megaeras? What are Megaeras?" Josiah asked.

"Megaeras are what we call our soldiers with the stringless bows," Josii explained.

"They will certainly be a welcome addition to the army," Josiah commented. He thought for a moment, then asked, "How long is it going take to get to the Accri Forest now that we have more people traveling with us?"

"Don't worry about the elves slowing you down," Josii said. "Remember that they made the trip from here to Saddun in much less time than we are allotting for the trip to Accri Forest. Of course, we do have to wait a couple days for them to gather, which will put us considerably behind schedule. Even so, if my estimations are correct, we should arrive in time."

"Couldn't we start now and have the elves catch up to us when they're ready?" Josiah asked. "From what you said, they're more than fast enough to do that."

"They are fast enough to do that," Josii replied, "and we can start whenever you wish; however, I would council you against leaving until they do. The assistance of the king is shaky at best at this point in time, and you taking off would only make it easier for him to withdraw his support. Then you would be counting on the arrival of elves that would never come."

"I don't like to delay our return, but if you think that's best, I will do it," Josiah said. "As you said, we should still arrive in time."

"Then have some breakfast," Josii said and slid a plate across the table to Josiah.

Josiah and his men spent the rest of the day getting a tour of the city from Josii. Everywhere they went, the elf had something to say about that particular area or building. One of the largest buildings had a fence around it along with other security measures. This, Josii pointed out, was the manufacturing plant for the stringless bows. The facility employed less than one hundred elves, but all of them were the most intelligent of the race to such an extent that they were all considered to have magical powers. This notion was only fostered by the fact that they made stringless bows, one of the most effective of the magical weapons that were available. The factory only produced two of the weapons a week; however, this was better than when it was first founded. At that time it had only produced one of the weapons every month.

Another interesting building was the elves' temple to Elohim. It was not particularly flashy, but what it lacked in décor it made up for with its design and architecture. The building took up the most ground space of any building in the city and was only two stories tall, making it an unusual sight in the city of skyscrapers. The central part of the building was a large dome. On either side of the dome rose a relatively thin tower, each of which bore a banner attached at the top of the structure and which fell almost to the ground. These flags bore depictions of many stories that the humans recognized and several that were foreign to them. All of the stories involved Elohim. Near the ground, the pictures stopped and writing covered the last several yards of the banners. Some of the lines Josiah recognized as coming from the holy books of Elohim, and he assumed that those that he did not recognize also came from those books.

The group passed into the temple, and the humans discovered how simple it really was. The whole dome covered one large room filled mainly with benches. A balcony circled the edge of the building and was also filled with benches, all of which faced the center of the building where a large altar made of a single stone stood. The ordinary benches and stone altar seemed out of place compared to the décor of the rest of the building. Gold covered everything from the doors to the walls. Large pillars of gold with artistic designs carved into them ran around the edge of the building, and even the plain-looking altar sat atop a stage that was overlaid with gold. Chandeliers of electric lights hung from the ceiling, but were unlit at the moment. Instead, the inside of the building was illuminated by sunlight drifting in through the many windows of the structure.

Josii took the humans to one of the two towers that stood on either side of the dome. Compared to the main building, the tower was dull and boring. It was of typical construction, with a large spiral staircase filling it entirely. It had two floors, but both were small and obviously not used for any real purpose. The roof of the tower was just as Josiah had imagined; crenellations ran around the edge, preventing any careless soul from falling off, and the actual roof was no more than a flat surface that could be walked on. The structure itself was nothing special, but the view from it was amazing. One of the elves' streets stretched away from them in a straight line, and they could see for nearly half a mile until a building interrupted their view. From their vantage point, they were also able to see what had been blocked from their sight at ground level. The path to the doors of the temple was bordered on each side by a tall hedge, which was all they had been able to see when they approached the building. On the other side of the hedges stretched huge gardens of flowers, bushes, and trees. Paths crisscrossed through the gardens, and gazeboes were stationed at strategic points so that people could rest in them. Fountains were seen periodically throughout the garden, often at the intersection of two paths. Figurines and statues could also be seen along the paths.

The rest of the city tour went by quickly, and sooner than he had expected, Josiah found himself back at Josii's house. The sun was setting, and the first day of gathering the elfin forces was ending. Josii reported that around twenty-five hundred elves had been gathered from Dublack and that messengers had been dispatched to the other elfin territories. Josiah went to bed glad of the knowledge that elves were going to be on his side, but praying fervently that they reached the battlefield in time.

The next day was a flurry of activity in Lêf. Warriors poured into the city, and by noon the number of soldiers had swelled to fifty-five hundred. The humans spent the day meeting with the upper officers of the elfin army and explaining the situation to them. Troops continued to arrive throughout the afternoon, and finally, just as the sunlight was fading from the forest and the electric lights were coming on across the city, a large force arrived from the east. They bore a different design on their armor than the rest of the soldiers, and Josiah learned that they were from East Dublack. It was necessary for him to meet with the leaders of this army and explain the situation again, but he didn't mind. Their soldiers brought the number of elves to just over eleven thousand. The meeting with these officers continued late into the night, and Josiah was exhausted when he finally made it to his bed. He fell asleep immediately, his last thought being that he needed to rest for the march the following day.

Three

Senndra sat astride Feddir high in the sky above Belmoth. The sun had set almost an hour before, and the darkness provided perfect cover for the movements of troops. During the day, siege engines had been disassembled and moved into the mountains. This gave them better range as well as better protection, and was in and of itself nothing to attract the attention of the enemy. The movement of these engines was completed just as the sun was setting, and the activity in the city turned to moving troops. The moon was just beginning to rise, and the confusing shadows it cast provided the cover needed for the plan to succeed. As the infantry, archers, and cavalry moved into position, they were only able to see just well enough to stay in rank. Five hundred horsemen, two hundred foot soldiers, and three hundred archers were gathered just inside the gate of the city, and as many archers as could be spared were stationed on the wall on either side of the gate. Senndra couldn't see any of this from her position high in the sky. In fact she couldn't see anything except the dragons immediately on either side of her, but Timothy had explained the finalized battle plan to her, and it was engraved in her memory. Everyone should be in position and simply waiting for the enemy to make their move which would signal the beginning of the attack.

Several minutes passed without incident. Senndra began to worry that the enemy would mess the plan up by not acting as they had in the past, but just as she was thinking this, she saw something far below her. A pinprick of light started in the enemy lines and flashed across no-man's-land toward the city wall. This light was followed by a dozen others. More continued to appear until in only a few seconds hundreds of them were present in a blinding barrage of flaming projectiles.

Senndra smiled to herself. The enemy had congregated its siege engines in front of the city gate, hoping to open a hole there. That was the signal for the troops of Magessa to spring into action. The soldiers behind the city gate would burst through and split, with half of the archers and infantry going along the wall one way and the other half going the other way. The cavalry would continue forward until they were just out of range of the enemy and finally split into two companies. Each company would circle around to hit the concentration of enemy siege equipment from the side, riding toward each other. When they met in the middle, they would rejoin forces and ride back toward the city, hopefully drawing out some of the enemy soldiers.

Five minutes passed and still the siege equipment pounded the city wall. From her height, Senndra could not hear anything, but she had stood on the wall of a city as it was pounded by catapults and could well imagine what the archers on the wall were feeling. She looked down and thought she could see movement. She squinted, and the movement began to shift all over the place. It was just her imagination playing tricks on her. She shifted her eyes back to the enemy siege equipment just as a pinprick of light, a flaming projectile, flew backward into the enemy ranks. Suddenly shapes could be seen flooding down the line of siege engines. No noise could be heard from below, but dark masses could be seen flowing down the line of siege engines from either end. As they came to each piece of equipment, it was apparently rendered useless and did not fire again. In less than a minute the cavalry had joined up and turned back toward the city.

******

Timothy stood at the base of the wall of Belmoth, an enormous recurve bow in his hands. He had received the weapon from Lemin earlier that day. The weapon was massive, five and a half feet long, even though it was a recurve bow. A quiver of arrows with thick shafts accompanied the bow; some of the arrows were bodkins, and some of them were equipped with broad heads. Timothy selected one of the bodkin arrows and nocked it on his string. He glanced to his left and saw Vladimir standing there. Vladimir also had a bow, but it was significantly smaller than Timothy's. His quiver contained arrows that were standard for an archer and, like Timothy's arrows, half were bodkins and the other half were broad heads. He too selected an arrow, nocked it on his bow string, and waited.

The siege equipment had ceased firing which meant the cavalry had done its job and disabled the engines. It also meant that soon the horsemen would arrive back at the city gate, and, if all went according to plan, they would have a crowd of enemies close behind them. Timothy cocked his head to allow his ears the best vantage point for listening and focused on the vibrations of the ground. A faint thrumming in the earth slowly grew in intensity, and was accompanied by the sounds of yelling and jangling tack. He kept his eyes pointed into the darkness, searching for any sign of activity. Fifty feet in front of him he saw horses appear, seemingly out of thin air, and he tensed for combat. Suddenly the darkness was broken as a hail of flaming arrows arched over the battlefield, showering sparks onto the earth. The rain of sparks was surprisingly bright and showed the archers of Magessa exactly how far away the enemy soldiers were.

Timothy drew his bow back and held the string next to his cheek. At the command of fire, he released the string,

103

smoothly drew another arrow, and nocked it on the string. The cavalry had reached the wall by this time and had split again, each half following the wall in opposite directions. The command to aim was given again, then the command to fire. Cries of pain could be heard above the sound of horses' hooves, but Timothy ignored them and nocked another arrow. The enemy appeared out of the darkness, and the commands to draw and fire were given very quickly.

The front row of enemies was cut down, but more enemies flooded out of the darkness. The command of fire at will was shouted down the line, and Timothy shot three arrows in quick succession. The enemy was getting dangerously close; the infantry protecting the archers took a step forward and slid closer to each other, pressing shoulder to shoulder. Arrows whizzed from both the top and the base of the wall until the archers were no longer able to safely fire. Seconds later, the enemy hit the shields of the infantry with a tremendous crash. The fight was bloody, and soldiers fell everywhere, opening holes in the defenders' line. The archers drew short swords and fell back toward the gate. Their weapons were no match for the swords and shields of the enemy foot soldiers.

Timothy whipped his sword from his back scabbard and stepped toward the first enemy to approach him. This was the first time Timothy had ever seen a goblin, and he shuddered at the sight of it. Taught, green-tinted skin stretched across bones that appeared too large for the creature. The creature's muscles, though not incredibly large, were well toned. It wore a torn and tattered uniform, and its only armor was a shield.

In the instant Timothy took in its appearance, the goblin swung its sword in a short, powerful arc aimed at his head, but Timothy caught the blade of the weapon on his own sword, letting it slide off to the side. The blow had been glancing, but the force of it staggered Timothy. He recovered and slashed at the goblin's side, but his blow was stopped by the creature's shield. The goblin slashed at Timothy again, but the cadet ducked underneath the blade and spun, slashing at the creature's left leg. The force of the blow was so powerful that the blade sliced cleanly through the goblin's ankle. The goblin pitched sideways and as he extended his shield hand to catch himself, Timothy slashed upward, catching it under the chin. One more slash separated the shield from the goblin.

Timothy snatched up the shield, fastening it to his left arm as best he could. Almost instantly, he was under attack from three more enemies, and he danced sideways to escape their jabs and slashes. He raised his shield and used it to catch the blades of two of his adversaries. He didn't see the sword of the third goblin until it was under his shield. As he leapt backwards, the tip of the third sword sliced through his uniform, barely drawing blood from his stomach. The goblin had overextended himself on his blow, and Timothy brought his sword up, cutting through the creature's wrist. The goblin stumbled backward, giving a scream of pain that made Timothy want to cover his ears. Instead, he spun to face the other two enemies, blocking their blades again. He stepped back and was able to get his first good look at them. Both of them were orcs, and were not of large build. One was left-handed, and Timothy immediately started watching him closely. The right-handed orc jumped forward and attacked with an over-handed hack at Timothy's left side. Timothy lifted his shield and caught the blade on it, but realized too late that had left himself open to an attack from the left-handed orc. Already the creature was aiming a swipe at Timothy's side, and Timothy was barely able to raise his sword and intercept the blade.

The goblin's sword slammed into his own with such force that he was not able to keep his wrist straight. His hand snapped backward and the blade of his sword dug into his leg. The orc tried to press his advantage by swinging at Timothy's now exposed side. Timothy punched his shield forward into the right-handed orc and threw him backwards, then yanked his sword out of his leg and swung it upward, batting the blade of the left-handed orc aside. He brought his blade around in a tight arc, slashing at the orc's chest. The orc was not prepared for the swift attack and was unable to get his shield up in time to defend himself.

Timothy stepped back as the orc fell in half and turned his attention to his other adversary. The orc hesitated in approaching him, but a dwarf jumped past him and swung his battle axe in a heavy over-handed attack at Timothy. Timothy knew that the axe had the edge and force to cut through armor, so he swung his shield to meet it, smashing it sideways. The dwarf staggered forward and impaled himself on Timothy's waiting blade.

Timothy stepped backwards to allow the dwarf to slip off of his blade and continued backward as the enemy started to close in around him. The first several enemies he was able to dispatch due to his superior swordsmanship, but for every one he killed, several stepped into his place. These soldiers did not have swords, which he could easily defend against; clubs and battle axes were more common and a much greater threat. These new, heavier weapons began to hammer away at him, and he was forced to rely on his shield even more than he had before. His sword was rendered almost useless except for the few odd stabs he was able to deal out with it. The new brand of warrior quickly drove him back until he had joined up with the remaining archers and infantry, frantically trying to hold their own against the press of enemies.

For a few more desperate minutes, the defenders stubbornly held their ground until the sound of their salvation met their ears. The ground shook with the pounding of horses' hooves, and a cry came from five hundred mouths. The cavalry had returned from their circular route and came in behind the enemy soldiers. The enemy faltered momentarily, giving the defenders enough time to form a line; then the horses hit. The enemy soldiers were cut down and trampled under the horses hooves; suddenly what had been a threat only moments before was now a scared horde running away. The archers and infantry pulled back to the gate in order to stay out of the way as the horsemen did their work. The riders crisscrossed the battle field, killing the soldiers that had survived the initial attack.

Just as it seemed that the soldiers of Magessa were victorious, a roar sounded from the north. Out of the darkness burst a dragon followed by two more, then a dozen more. In the blink of an eye, dragons were everywhere, torching the ground and killing the soldiers of Magessa in every way possible. The ballistae mounted on the wall immediately began firing at the dragons, but many of them were too slow to get off any shots at all and were crushed by dragons. The gates of the city groaned and began to swing open, as the seemingly endless force began to rush through them.

Timothy stood on the field outside the gates. The horses and soldiers were panicking as they rushed in vain to get away from the dragons. Once again Timothy found Vladimir at his back, and he was thankful for it as he drew his bow. He selected a broad headed arrow and nocked it on the bow string. He located a dragon and, keeping his eyes on it, drew the string of his bow back to full draw. The dragon was closing in on him rapidly, so he quickly released the arrow. It sped toward the dragon, hitting just in front of where the beast's leg joined his body. The sharp tip of the arrow smashed through the relatively weak scales and sank up to its black feathers. The dragon began to zigzag as it tried to stay aloft, and Timothy knew instantly that his arrow had penetrated the creature's heart. The dragon continued to drop as it flapped its wings twice more before it slammed into the ground, sliding through the soldiers that remained outside the city. A handful of horsemen and infantry were crushed before the gigantic carcass slid to a stop.

Timothy nocked another arrow and looked at the fallen dragon. It gave one more feeble beat of its wings and fell still. Timothy looked again to the sky and saw a dragon flying straight toward him. Already its mouth was open as it prepared to rain a torrent of fire on the human that had just brought down one of its brothers.

"Vladimir, do something fast!" Timothy shouted as he released his arrow.

Vladimir spun around and a sparkling bubble flared up around the two friends as well as several nearby soldiers. The dragon fire hit the bubble and spattered across its surface before extinguishing. Timothy's arrow flew through the bubble with no trouble and slammed into the dragon's still-open mouth. The dragon gave a gurgled scream as it dropped like a rock and hit the earth just a few yards in front of the bubble. The bubble had vanished as suddenly as it had come. The dragon plowed a deep furrow through the dirt and spun to a stop mere feet from Timothy. The beast's tail swung around, and Timothy grabbed Vladimir and jerked him down to avoid contact.

Timothy wasted no time getting back to his feet, nocking another arrow, and targeting another dragon. He drew his bow back, but as he released the string he was startled as a group of ten dragons burst over the city wall. His arrow veered right and bounced off the targeted dragon's chest scales, but the dragon was saved only momentarily. The dragons from the city were reinforced by forty more, and in the blink of an eye the battle changed again. Now dragons battled dragons above the city wall, allowing the remaining soldiers to rush through the gates. Timothy reluctantly turned as well and fled with the other men through the gates and into the city. Ignoring the pain that flared in his wounded leg, he raced to the top of the wall and took his place among the rest of the archers. Vladimir was only a few steps behind him, and he took a place beside him.

"That was amazing, what you did out there," Timothy said to Vladimir. "How did you pull it off? I didn't think you were powerful enough to create a shield that large that was still able to stand up to dragon fire."

"I didn't do it," Vladimir said simply.

108

"But if you didn't, then who?" Timothy asked with a puzzled look.

Vladimir shrugged his shoulders, but his eyes pointed up toward the sky.

******

Senndra hung tight to Feddir's saddle as he shot through the air, an enemy dragon hot on his tail. The plan for baiting the enemy dragons had worked perfectly. The dragons of Magessa had attacked and appeared to momentarily gain the upper hand. Then they allowed the enemy dragons to break their formation and drive them toward the east. Already they were over the mountains and quickly covering the distance to the ballistae that were hidden among the rocks. In the dark it was impossible to see anything, and Senndra only knew that they had passed over the siege weapons when she heard the hiss of them discharging their missiles directly into the dragons overhead. Silhouetted against the moonlit sky, the dragons were easy targets for the siege equipment, and many were hit with the projectiles. Several dropped immediately while scores more sustained injuries and fell back as Feddir and his compatriots turned to head back toward the city. The enemy dragons stubbornly continued to follow, though it was with considerably less vigor than before.

The dragons pulled within range of the siege equipment mounted on the city wall, and Senndra felt Feddir laugh across their mental link. Moments later, hundreds of arrows of all sizes launched from the wall and arched through the air on an intercept course with the enemy dragons. Too late the dragons saw them, and the arrows cut into their ranks, injuring at least half their number. In a flash the dragons of Magessa banked in sharp turns and flew into the enemy, slashing with their talons and teeth.

The archers on the wall could no longer fire for fear of hitting their own dragons, but that was of no consequence. The weakened enemy was no match for the fresh dragons of Magessa that burst from the city and joined the others in an all-out attack.

Fire flashed across the sky, and dragons screamed as they were torn apart and forced into the ground. Beasts from both sides rained from the sky into the city and onto the field outside of it. The fighting was bitter, and Senndra was forced to hold on with all her strength as Feddir rolled and banked through the mindless melee, striking at every enemy within his reach. The enemy ranks seemed to have swelled, and Senndra figured they must have been reinforced; even so the battle seemed to be in favor of the army of Belmoth. And still the enemy dragons attacked.

At a signal, all of Belmoth's dragons burst upward, leaving the enemies behind and within easy range of the archers and ballistae on the wall. A flock of arrows flew up and slammed into the enemy dragons, killing several and wounding many more. They were struggling to recover when the defending dragons dropped back down on top of them.

The enemy dragons finally seemed to realize what a dire situation they were in and tried to flee, but there was no escape for them now. They were systematically hunted down one by one and overwhelmed. Still they held on and even rallied themselves together for one more attack, but this attempt was easily repelled. Then they fled in earnest, heading for their lines, but there was no sanctuary there. As they approached the lines of Molkekk's army, no missiles came from the enemy siege equipment. Perhaps the soldiers thought that all of the dragons were their own, returning victorious from the fight. Perhaps they did not want to risk hitting their own dragons with the missiles. Whatever its cause, one thing was certain: the hesitation was deadly. The dragons of Magessa dropped down on the enemy siege engines and tore through them with their claws and tails. With the siege engines gone, they were able to return their attention to the enemy dragons.

Dawn was just breaking as the defending dragons returned from hunting down their counterparts. Death and carnage met their eyes and the eyes of the soldiers on the wall as the sun flooded the earth with its brilliant rays. The enemy army had disbanded and fled in the night, leaving the entire camp and all of its contents. Several trails of discarded equipment showed that they had escaped in all directions with only a very few of them heading back to Vollexa Temp. This army of Vollexa Temp had effectively been broken.

The leaders of Belmoth's army sensed a trap and sent out squads of eight horsemen to investigate each direction the enemy appeared to have gone. All the soldiers returned with the same message: Molkekk's army had fled and was not going to return. They also brought back a small portion of the contents of the enemy camp. Next, a squad of dragons was sent out to scour the countryside for the enemy, and they returned with the same message.

The gates of the city finally opened up and the people spewed out, prepared to pillage the enemy camp. From the wall, Timothy could see all that happened. He saw the commanders of the army trying to maintain command of their soldiers but to no avail. The rush for the enemy tents was turning into an all-out race, and Timothy knew what would happen when the people reached them. The fighting and quarreling would begin as the soldiers each tried to carry off the best of the loot for themselves.

Quickly, Timothy scanned the sky for dragons and located a few of them still circling over the enemy camp as well as two which were approaching the city. Frantically he waved his hands at these two and motioned for them to land on the wall. As they drew closer, one of them dropped toward the wall while the other one pulled upward and blasted overhead. Timothy hunched over as the dragon passed and waited for the small whirlwind that accompanied its presence to subside. When he looked up, he saw that the other dragon had landed on the wall and was perched on it less than a hundred yards from where he was. Its tail was curled around a tower and pieces of rock had been knocked loose where its feet had set down. Timothy began to run toward the dragon and its rider, and as he approached he realized that luck was with him. The dragon was a muddy brown color which meant his rider was Senndra. Senndra had slid off of her dragon by the time Timothy reached her.

"The army is going berserk," Timothy shouted when he was close enough for his voice to reach her. "They're going on a looting rampage, and if they are allowed to reach the enemy camp, we'll cause more casualties to our own army than the enemy ever did."

Senndra didn't say anything, but the look in her eye indicated that she understood perfectly. Without hesitation, she scrambled up onto her dragon and spoke to it. Before she was even properly seated in the saddle, Feddir had burst from the wall and was banking sharply around. He gave a series of roars to the dragon with which he had approached the wall, and the two of them flew toward the enemy camp.

The dragons that had been circling the enemy camp were now returning to the city, but another series of roars turned them around. Altogether, nine dragons slammed down onto the ground well in front of the unruly army and roared as loud as they could, sending jets of fire into the sky. Their impact with the ground was so violent that Timothy saw the soldiers in front get thrown to the ground. Even the wall underneath him shook slightly. He saw the tongues of fire first and then the roar reached him. The force of it made his knees involuntarily tremble, and he saw that the army which had only moments ago been eagerly rushing forward, come to a sudden stop. Already many of the soldiers were rushing back toward the city. Even though the beasts bore the insignia of Magessa, they were not about to rush into them, frenzied as they were. Another set of roars from the dragons sent the remainder of the army after their compatriots.

Timothy let out a breath he hadn't known he was holding and gave a sigh of relief. He turned and almost ran into Vladimir. After a quick apology, the two friends walked down the wall.

"That was quick thinking on your part," Vladimir commented as they walked. "I would never have thought of using dragons to stop that."

"I don't know what the soldiers thought they were doing," Timothy said more to himself than to Vladimir. "Or maybe they weren't thinking at all. That seems more likely."

"No, they were thinking," Vladimir said. "They were thinking about themselves and that is all. They weren't thinking about the consequences of their actions, only about what they thought they would gain from them. The only question now is, how are they going to be punished for their disobedience?"

"How much of the army broke ranks?" Timothy asked.

"Well, Lemin had the soldiers from the academy in strict order, and none of them would dare to disobey him, so they stayed. Other than that, there was one, maybe two platoons and a few odd squads that didn't break."

"What drives the thinking of men when they will forsake everything to loot an enemy camp?" Timothy muttered. "Surely that is not what Elohim would have them to do."

"I hate to break this to you, but I don't think very many of the soldiers here care what Elohim wants. From hearing the way they talk, only about one in five actually believe that Elohim exists, and of those, who knows how many care about following His commands."

"You're right, unfortunately," Timothy said with a sigh. "It seems no one is interested in following Elohim anymore. Maybe the reason for this attack *is* to punish us."

"We won the battle. How is that a punishment?"

"It may be more of one than you realize," Timothy answered as he started down the stairs. "Victory seems to be almost too much for these soldiers. This time it drove them into an insane frenzy. There is also the fact that the more victories we

113

have, the cockier the soldiers will get. If the enemy gets wise to that fact, they could fake a retreat and then reform and fall on our men when they rush out of rank after them. The result of something like that would be devastating."

"What it really comes down to is this," Vladimir said as he stopped at the bottom of the stairs and faced Timothy. "The condition our country is in now is deplorable. People who worship false gods or no one at all far outnumber those who worship Elohim. If He chooses to uphold us, that is His prerogative, but if He chooses to hand us over to our enemies, He has ample reason to do so."

"True," Timothy agreed and ended the discussion with that one word.

******

The whip whistled through the air and cracked as it hit the man's bare back. The man grunted and jerked slightly against the bonds that held him to the whipping post but showed no other signs of the pain the strike had caused him. This man was a true soldier and had volunteered to be the first to receive his punishment. The man with the whip struck again, and this time the one being punished showed no outward signs of the anguish he must have been in. Instead he clenched his eyes and laid his head forward on the post. The whip struck again with such a loud cracking sound that Senndra cringed inwardly. Still the punished man made no move.

The area surrounding the whipping post was completely silent except for the sound of the whip striking flesh again and again. The post, along with nine others, had been erected in the field outside of Belmoth. The others were still empty and their operators were dragging the men that they would have to punish toward them.

In that way the soldier who was already being whipped was different. He had not struggled against the punishment.

Instead, when the army had arrived to begin the whipping, this soldier had been standing by the post, waiting. A ring of people had surrounded the posts as he was being fastened to it. The soldiers that had obeyed their orders stood on one side and the vast majority of the army stood on the other side. It would take all day for all of the malefactors to be punished.

When the soldier was securely fastened, the punisher raised his whip and brought it down with amazing force and a tremendous crack. The soldiers who were waiting to be punished gave a collective gasp and pulled back, but dragons surrounded them, so there was no hope of escape. The whip struck again, and the man tied to the post jerked. Some of the condemned soldiers tried to break away, but a roar from the dragons stopped them dead in their tracks.

The other nine men who had been assigned to whipping duty grabbed the closest soldiers and began to drag them to their posts. One final crack of the whip, louder than any of the rest, stopped all action for a second. The man doing the whipping unfastened the other's hands, and the young soldier collapsed on the ground. All eyes watched as two men ran out, hoisted the unconscious man onto their shoulders, and took him toward the city. Once they had broken through the circle surrounding the whipping posts, everyone came back to life. The punishers dragged their protesting victims to the posts and tied them to them. Now the place came alive with the cracking of whips on bare skin and the screams of men in pain.

When Senndra could no longer stand the sound of anguish, she quietly slipped out of the circle and walked away. The sounds followed her into the city, and in an attempt to escape from it, she slipped into the nearest building. She shut the door and let her head fall against it. She stood that way for several moments before straightening and turning to see what building she had entered. The interior of the building which the cadets had converted for their own use was before her, and she immediately felt more comfortable in the familiar setting. She fell onto a couch and laid face down on it, trying to force the screams of the punished men from her memory. She lay that way until she lost track of time. She tried her best to push the horrifying images from her mind, but found that they simply would not leave. Finally she rose from the couch and started to pace in front of it.

Back and forth she walked, trying to get her brain to think about something, anything. Yet every time she started thinking about something else, the men getting whipped jumped back to the forefront of her thoughts. Finally she could pace no more. Pulling a chair from beneath the table, she sank into it. She let her head fall onto the table top and felt paper there. Raising her head, she pulled a sheet from the pile that stood there and looked at it.

A blinding light flashed and a series of scenes flew before her eyes. Saddun's gates stood open, barely hanging on their broken hinges. Smoke curled from the burned remains of buildings, and the streets were deserted. Another city flashed before her eyes. This one was not burned down, but smoke curled from it, and several of the buildings were aflame. People ran through the streets as they were chased by soldiers clad in dark armor.

Next was an army marching through heavy rain, sloughing down a muddy road. It was followed by another army, this one hoisting flags which bore the insignia of Molkekk.

Senndra hadn't even thought about the man in her vision for the past six months. It took her several moments to recognize him; he seemed much older than she remembered and the light shading of his jaw indicated the beginnings of a beard. Nevertheless, she was able to identify Josiah as he led a group of men through a forest. She wondered how he had fared since the dwarves had attacked, but didn't have much time to ponder this as the scenes changed quickly.

Josiah and his friends were in a city, though not one that Senndra recognized. The buildings were taller than any she had ever seen, and the sky was filled with lights even though it was night. They stood before someone who appeared to be a king, and then another army was marching, this one through a forest. The scene changed one last time, and Senndra found herself staring at nothing. There was light everywhere, but there was nothing there, just the light and despite the carnage she had witnessed, she felt strangely calm.

Then in a flash she found herself back in the building in Belmoth. The paper she held slid from her fingers and fell to the table. She slumped back in her chair, unsure of what to make of her vision. The last time she had had a vision, it had come true which was enough to convince her to take this one seriously.

What she wasn't as sure of was if what she had seen had already happened or was still to occur. Was there anything that she could do to stop it from happening? The more she thought about the questions, the more confused she became, and her thoughts swirled around with no real pattern to them. She also found that her eyelids were becoming heavy and slowly closing. She fought the urge to go to sleep for some time but lost in the end. That was how Vladimir found her later, slumped down in her chair with her head resting on the table.

******

The General sat atop his horse and assessed the situation around him. His army stretched from the Orc Range on his left to the Accri Forest on his right. At their backs was the Péle River with no good way to get over it. All in all, the situation was not as good as Josiah had made it out to be, but, then again, it was better than any the army would have found elsewhere.

At the thought of Josiah, the General's mind went to his soldier and the mission he had started out on. Would he be able to convince the elves that they should aid the humans? Would he even be able to find his way to Lêf? And if he did convince the elf king, what were the chances the elf reinforcements would be enough to turn the tide of battle? The enemy army was not in sight yet, but the General's scouts had informed him that it was not far away and would arrive by nightfall. They also brought reports of the strength of their numbers and all of these reports were disheartening. It appeared that their numbers could have even grown slightly since their attack on Saddun.

A commotion started at the Accri Forest and steadily grew. The General turned to see what it was about and saw the massive forms of ogres lumbering out of the trees. Finally there was some good news. With the ogres added to his men, there was a slightly better chance of holding off the enemy, but their chances were still not good.

The General kicked his horse and rode toward the forest to greet his reinforcements. As he approached, he began to realize just how huge the ogres really were. Every one of them was at least ten feet tall, and their limbs were as large as trees. Some carried massive clubs, others battle axes, and others humongous crossbows. The bows were so large that they shot bolts as long as the General's arm. The General swallowed and was very glad that the ogres were there to fight on his side.

The General approached the ogre leading the army and saluted him. Sliding from his horse, he approached the ogre commander and again saluted. The ogre returned the gesture.

"So, you are the General of this army, little one." The ogre's voice boomed out, and the General had to make a conscious effort not to flinch.

"That is correct," he replied. "I am the General."

"We are here to aid you in the coming battle," the ogre said. "You are the one who is wise in military strategy, so we are at your disposal. Where would you have us go?"

"I have a plan that might do some significant damage to the enemy," the General said. "It is a bit risky, but I think that it could work. Since your men will have a large part in it, I would like to discuss it with you before we implement it."

"Very well," the ogre said. "Explain this plan to me."

The General and the ogre walked off together, the General doing most of the talking and the ogre only interjecting every once in a while. An hour later, the ogre commander had agreed to the plan, and the army started to prepare.

Night had fallen by the time the enemies arrived, and the General fully expected them not to attack until the following day. However, they immediately prepared their battle lines and started advancing on the thin line of Magessa's soldiers stretched from the mountains to the forest. They also set up their siege engines and began to hurl rocks at the soldiers, but these did very little damage and served only to cause a small amount of worry.

As Molkekk's soldiers approached they were able to get a clearer view of the small, Magessian army that stood against them. Only men composed the line, and they were spread rather thinly. Perhaps too thinly, the commander of the attacking army thought, and he ordered his men to approach with caution. He also ordered several squads of horsemen to advance on the line and test its strength. These horsemen received light fire from bowmen, but that was all. No one bothered to follow them when they retreated back to their own lines. Molkekk's commander was still not convinced of the forces of his adversary, so he ordered his line to spread out until it stretched from the mountains to a point opposite the Accri Forest. He ordered the advance of his men and stopped the incessant firing of rocks from his siege engines.

The enemy line slowly advanced on the forces of Magessa, uncertain of what might be hiding, but certain that their numbers would be more than sufficient to deal with it. When they came within range of the other army's bowmen, they quickened their pace. The army of Magessa fired on them again and again, but the damage the arrows caused them was insignificant compared to their numbers, and Molkekk's soldiers continued to advance without hesitation.

The distance between the armies diminished until only a hundred yards lay between them, then fifty, then twenty five, then a dozen. The line of Molkekk's army bowed as the soldiers in the middle rushed forward to begin the fight. The first ring of a sword on armor that broke the silence seemed particularly shrill and was followed by many more. Then the whole of the armies collided, and the sound of steel on steel filled the plain for miles around.

The army of Magessa held their line, but slowly they were pushed back toward the river at their backs. A horn rang out from the lines of Magessa, but nothing appeared to change. Those nearest the forest saw shadows coming from the trees, but they were unable to cry out before the ogres swept them away. Clubs and battle axes swung as the ogres punched their way through the enemy ranks. Their movements were obscured by the darkness as they used a specialized rushing technique. The ogres at the front of the army were the only ones doing the killing, but these were constantly changing, rolling down the outside of the army and falling in again at the rear. Then they would charge forward again and gain momentum until they again hit the enemy soldiers. This movement allowed the ogres to charge out of the forest and down the front line of the enemy. And in all of these maneuvers, they were completely silent. Never did even one of their soldiers give a roar to indicate that they were present. In this way they swept through the enemy ranks, a deadly tide that took many lives.

The ogres finished their charge and fell in with the rest of the defenders, dispersing among them so that they covered the entire line. As they did this, they removed massive crossbows from their backs and loaded them. As soon as they were set in the line, they fired a deadly volley of darts at the enemy ranks. The darts smashed into the enemy soldiers, many of them dropping more than one man. The ogres reloaded and fired two more times before the enemy soldiers retreated out of their range.

The commander of Molkekk's army sat atop his black horse, watching his soldiers flee back towards him. In the darkness he was unable to see what had frightened them, and he was furious with them. Nothing that the humans could throw against them should have incited such a retreat. A chorus of triumphant roars came from the army of Magessa, and the commander finally understood. Somehow the humans had convinced the ogres to fight for them, and these brutes had put fear into the hearts of his men.

Well, he could deal with ogres just as efficiently as he could deal with humans.

******

Josiah's legs were tired, but he was holding up much better than he had expected. He had been relieved of his armor and weapons, which had been given to elves to carry for him. Despite this fact, he was still considerably slower than the elves. He looked to his left and spotted Cirro who had also relinquished his weapons. Cirro was walking beside Brandon who had elected to keep his armor and weapons and yet was still able to easily maintain the pace. Josiah was unable to locate the rest of his men in the crowd of elves, and he suddenly wished that Josii had accompanied them on this march. The elf could have served as a useful liaison between the humans and elves, making the allies feel more connected; however, he was a dragon rider and had stayed in Lêf. He would arrive at the battle among the ranks of his platoon.

The elves indicated they would run again and Josiah broke into a jog as the soldiers in front of him did. The army would run for an hour or so before stopping, and Josiah was thankful for the physical conditioning he had received at the academy. Even without his equipment, he was hard pressed to keep up.

The plain rolled by as the army followed the Vänern River toward the Accri Forest. There was not much to see, making the run very boring. Josiah had found that the only way to drive away the boredom was to think about something else, so he turned to sword-fighting maneuvers. Mentally he reviewed every cut, parry, and thrust that he knew multiple times. Then he turned his thoughts toward strategy. He invented an army and set it up in a specific formation. Next, he created another army and arranged it in a formation that was able to counteract the formation of the first army. Finally, he rearranged the first army to counteract the other, and continued to do this until he tired of it.

The army slowed to a walk, and Josiah slowed with it. His thoughts about strategy having been disturbed, he started to recite the names and uses of every medicinal plant that he knew of. Following this, he recited geography and did his best to envision where each physical feature was.

The ground beneath Josiah's feet grew rockier, so he returned his attention to his surroundings. The army had left the river, though it could still be seen off to the left, as they continued due west. They were now approaching the hills on the southern end of the Orc Range, and boulders spotted the ground ahead of them. Soon they would be traveling uphill. Josiah dreaded this, but he knew this also signified that they were nearing the end of their journey. The sun was beginning to set and a crowd of lights to the left indicated that there was an army gathered there. Slowly the army of the elves came to a halt, and scouts were sent out to reconnoiter the discovered army. They returned, and the army moved again, though this time they headed south. No torches were used to light the way of the soldiers when the sun had fallen completely behind the horizon. Instead, they used the light of moon to navigate the rough terrain.

It took them half an hour to leave the mountains at which point the army stopped again. The elves who had been carrying the humans' armor returned it, and Josiah finally understood what was happening. The battle had already started, and they were going to enter by attacking the rear of Molkekk's army. When the humans were armed, the army set off again.

******

The General pulled his men into a tighter line, and though this strengthened the formation, it also shortened the line. Still, there was nothing else to do if the army was to have any chance of survival. The enemy army had retaliated with fury once they recovered from the ogre attack, and now they stood on the brink of destroying the army of Magessa. Many of Magessa's soldiers had already fallen as had a good number of the ogres. There seemed to be no way to stop the frenzied attack of Molkekk's army. The shriek of metal on metal screamed across the battlefield, drowning out the screams of the wounded and dying. The ogres were currently holding the line together, but that could only last for so long.

The General spurred his horse forward and began shouting orders to rally his men. If they were to die here, they would go down fighting, and he would lead that final charge. He reined his horse to a halt and slid from it. As he strode toward the fighting, he drew his sword and held it in front of him. As he continued, his pace quickened to a run and he gave a battle cry. The soldiers who had fallen back to rest saw him and gathered to him, running behind him and screaming. By the time they hit the enemy, their numbers had swelled to a score.

They hit like an anvil, showing the fury and bravery of men who know that they are about to die, and slammed through the enemy's front line. They quickly penetrated deep into the enemy line, killing as many as came within the range of their weapons which flashed like lightning through the darkness. One of the soldiers dropped, then another. Still the others pressed on, dying one by one as they continued. Eventually the momentum from their charge faltered and disappeared entirely, and they found themselves trapped deep behind the enemy lines. They quickly formed a tight circle and fought with everything they had, but they could not prevail.

Slowly they were killed one at a time, and the General knew that it would only be a matter of time before he passed from this life as well. He tucked himself behind his shield to better protect himself, but as he did so, an enemy soldier hacked at him and slashed his right calf. He recovered in time to use his shield to protect himself and then to dispatch the enemy. Another soldier pressed him and then another, but they were both killed by crushing blows from his sword. He dispatched a third enemy but not before receiving a wound to his right hand. He glanced down at the scratch and as he did, he caught sight of a dead soldier. Quickly his eyes moved from soldier to soldier, all of them lying dead on the ground, and for the first time he wondered what the purpose of resisting Molkekk was.

A sharp pain stabbed him between the shoulder blades and shot down his spine. He looked down and saw a sword blade sprouting from his chest. He felt the vibrations on his broken ribs as the weapon was withdrawn, and he crumpled to the ground in a heap. In that moment of pain, he knew that resisting Molkekk by following Elohim was worth all that it cost. He knew that Elohim would not let his men die on this battlefield. And then his sight went black.

******

"No!" Josiah screamed as he cut his way through the enemy army.

He and a group of elves had been making their way toward a dozen men who had somehow become trapped deep behind the lines of Molkekk's army. As they approached, the defenders had been killed one by one until only one man was left standing. The figure looked familiar, but in the chaos of battle Josiah couldn't ascertain who it was. He realized it was the General only seconds before an orc stepped up behind him and stabbed a sword through his back. Josiah's arms swung even more powerfully as he fought to reach his fallen commander. He broke through several enemies and fell to his knees beside the General.

He was aware that the elves he was with were now around him, but the General's broken body filled his vision.

Dropping his sword and shield, he sank to his knees beside the fallen man. He knew the General was dead even before he felt for a pulse. Tears ran down his face and mingled with his sweat, but he didn't even notice. Instead he lifted the General's body and embraced it for a long time.

His tears slowed and stopped, and he gently laid the body on the ground. Reaching for his sword and shield, he lifted them again and rose to his feet. His face was hard as he turned to face the army that had killed his respected commander. In that moment, he felt nothing but an incredible anger. It bubbled up within him until it reached his mouth and burst out in the form of a roar. He lifted his head to the sky and let out another roar of pain and anger so savage that the enemies within earshot stepped backward slightly. Lowering his head and raising his sword, Josiah advanced slowly on the nearest enemy. The soldier moved to defend himself but could not stop the blinding stroke from Josiah's sword.

The elves with Josiah moved in around him, and together they pushed toward the line of defenders still desperately holding their ground. The elves' blows were strong, but not even they could compare with Josiah's strokes. They slashed their way through the enemy lines until they forced a path to the army of Magessa. There was a brief scuffle there before the soldiers realized the elves were their reinforcements and accepted them into their lines.

The elves strung their bows and unleashed a deadly rain of arrows on the enemy army, driving them back temporarily. The Megaeras were particularly deadly in this capacity. They fired their weapons just as quickly as the other archers and could shoot farther and with more force. Everywhere enemies fell as the stringless bows penetrated their armor. Even so, the massive numbers of the enemy could not be compensated for, and after a slight retreat they were again pressing the defenders. Slowly, the line was pushed backward toward the river, and eventually the

Magessans would be forced into it. There was nothing, it seemed, that could stand up to the massive numbers of Molkekk.

Josiah looked up and down the line and saw his comrades falling like leaves in autumn. The only hope of survival would be to escape across the river, but there was not a ford for miles and the river had too swift a current to swim. Nevertheless, several of the soldiers had come to the same conclusion as Josiah and were throwing aside their armor. They dove into the river and were quickly swept downstream.

Josiah's thoughts turned to Elohim. Surely He could rescue them from their plight, but would He? Josiah let his sword and shield drop to his sides and bowed his head, knowing that he was making himself extremely vulnerable, but not caring. Fervently he petitioned Elohim for His help, begging for deliverance from the enemy.

As he prayed, he became aware that the sounds of battle were growing dimmer and eventually came to a complete stop. They had been replaced with the sound of hundreds of stones hitting the ground. Puzzled, Josiah raised his head and stared at what had only moments before been a raging battlefield. Hail stones the size of boulders rained down on the enemy army which was now in full retreat as they tried to escape. The hail stopped, however, before it reached the army of Magessa, leaving the elves, ogres, and humans there unharmed. The soldiers of Magessa stood with their weapons hanging limply at their sides as they stared at the phenomena. Not only was the hail massive, but it was also only falling in a very narrow strip, effectively creating a wall between the two armies as it piled up.

Josiah watched the miracle for a while but eventually forced himself to move. Regardless of how long it took, the army of Molkekk would find a way through or around the wall, and the army of Magessa needed to be gone by that time. As Josiah ran up and down the lines, gathering as many of the soldiers as would come with him, a plan was forming in his mind. A forest stood nearby, and the trees from it could be lashed together to form a sort of floating bridge. He was certain that with the ogres' strength and the elves' intelligence, they could get it to work. He put the men he had gathered to work cutting down trees before leaving to find the commanders of the assembled armies. No matter which way he looked at it, the project was going to be a big one, and he would need the cooperation of all of the soldiers to complete it in time.

Four

The death of the General left the human army without a commander, and though it was not a problem so far, the lesser officers knew they would have to choose someone to command them before long. They immediately began to look for someone suited to the task, and several men stepped forward. They each coveted the high position of authority, but wisdom prevailed over the plans of man. The army's officers determined that none of these men would make a good General, and so they turned their attention to another man.

They decided that Josiah was the best choice for the position they needed to fill. Not only had he been able to mobilize the army extremely quickly and direct them in building a bridge across the river, he also had no current responsibilities since he had relinquished command of his men when he had left for Lêf. Naturally there was dissent from the people who wished the position for themselves, but eventually they acquiesced and decided to appoint Josiah as their General.

Josiah was hard at work chopping down a tree when the news arrived. He had already met with several elves and decided how many trees would be necessary to span the river and was working with the other soldiers in an attempt to reach that number. Already, massive stacks of logs lay near the bank, and more logs were added to their number regularly. A group of elves and ogres worked at the river bank, lashing logs together and pushing them out into the current. A long rope had been attached to the front log so that the front of the line of logs would not drift downstream. The logs currently reached to the center of the river, and in another half an hour they would span its entire width.

Josiah wiped the sweat off of his forehead with the back of his hand and the messenger told him the news. He leaned on his axe as the words were spoken, then turned back to his work when the man had finished.

"Do you not have any commands for your army, General?" the man asked. Josiah stopped swinging his axe and turned back to the messenger.

"Tell them to rest and be ready to move out this afternoon," he said and turned back to the tree.

The ogres and elves worked quickly, and by noon a floating bridge spanned the length of the river. Though it was wide enough for four men to walk shoulder to shoulder, the men went across in a single file line. Even so, the bridge rocked on the water and more than one soldier fell off of it and had to be helped back on. Despite several delays, the soldiers moved quickly, and all the humans had crossed the river well before sunset. The elves crossed next, as night began to fall, and the ogres followed them. At last, just as the sun was beginning to rise, the final soldiers crossed and the bridge was cut loose to be swept downstream.

Josiah watched the logs as they were swept out of sight before turning back to his army. They stood in orderly rank and file, but it was obvious that they wanted to move. Josiah sighed, and with one last look at the river, ordered his army to march. The ogres followed him, and the elves took the rear. They moved quickly into the distance as, behind them, the army of Molkekk awoke and charged in to finish them off, only to find themselves blocked by the river that had prevented their quarry from escaping on the previous day. The cries of rage coming from the enemy soldiers faded into the distance as the newly combined forces of Magessa and her allies put more distance between themselves and their enemy.

As the army moved away from the river, Josiah sent one of his officers to find all of the soldiers in the army who still had horses. Within fifteen minutes seven soldiers stood before him, holding the bridles of their mounts.

"Don't worry, I'm not going to take your horses away," Josiah said with a grin. The soldiers stared at him, not sure what to say, and Josiah rolled his eyes. "I need you to ride through Belvárd and tell them about the invasion. Each of you must go in different directions and cover as much territory as possible. Go to all of the major cities and tell them that there is simply no way that we can hold them off; they will have to flee to Rampön."

"Yes sir," the riders answered and saluted before hoisting themselves into their saddles. They turned their horses to the north and dug their heels in, sending their mounts into a trot.

"May Elohim go with you," Josiah called after them. He watched for a few seconds before turning back to his army. On his orders, his trusty Captains had already started the soldiers marching, putting them well ahead of him by now. He started after them and, since their pace was relatively slow, was able to catch them in less than thirty minutes. He was met by Cirro, who was chagrined at having been separated from his friend.

"Cirro, you are officially my second-in-command," Josiah said before Cirro could say anything. "If you want a title, I can think up one for you."

"I don't really care about a title," Cirro said. "What I do care about is keeping you safe, which I can't do if you keep disappearing like that."

"Here we go again," Josiah muttered under his breath and began to mouth the words that Cirro was already speaking.

"You're an important asset to the army now, and you are jeopardizing a lot when I don't know where you are."

"Come off it, Cirro," Josiah said, rather irritably. "Nothing's going to happen to me just because I'm not in your sight every second of the day. I'm just as safe at the back of the army giving orders to my soldiers as I am at the front leading them on this frightfully interesting march. Besides, this army just lost one General, and it seems to be getting along fine, so why should my death affect it all that much?"

"There are precious few people in this world that make good Generals, and we were lucky to have two in this one army. If something happens to you, it's unlikely we could find someone who could effectively replace you."

"It's nice to hear that," Josiah said sarcastically. "No one in the entire army can do this job, a fact which I seriously doubt, so I can't do anything without you babysitting me. It's nice to know that you care so much. Besides, I already said I'm not in any more danger at the back of the army than I am at the front with you."

"Come on, Josiah, don't be like that," Cirro said. "You're my friend, and I don't want anything to happen to you. But the army also needs you, and in my opinion that is far more important than any personal relationship. And concerning your safety, you might be just as safe from Molkekk's soldiers no matter where you are in the army, but they are not your only enemies. Why do you think the late General didn't associate more with his men? Why do you think he was always surrounded by his guards? He was too much like you to allow himself into that situation unless it was necessary. No, if he wasn't afraid that others would harm him because of his position of authority, he would not have had the guards; however, he *did* have that to consider, and so do you."

"I know all that, Cirro, but I simply won't believe any of my men would harm me until I have evidence to the contrary. Until that point, you can still offer me your protection, but please, don't do any more than that."

"I will do as you command, General," Cirro said in a tone that shouted his displeasure. "I will say one last time, however, that you take too many chances for a person of your intelligence."

"Logged and noted," Josiah said and started off, leaving Cirro to catch up with him.

The army marched west across the bottom of Belvárd, following the Vänern River toward the gap between the Rebel and Vankor Mountains. The plains allowed them to see a great distance on every side. On the right hand was the county of Belvárd with its many farms starting at the Pelé River and spreading away from it as they followed branching creeks and canals. The county was sparsely populated compared to the other two in Magessa, though three large cities around the river made this fact less than obvious. In the interior of the county, however, there could be up to several miles of distance between houses. Besides allowing for larger farms, the large distances between the dwellings also allowed for an incredibly diverse population of the races rarely seen in Magessa. Orcs, elves, both mountain and forest ogres, and even a few dwarves all could be found with relatively little trouble. Many of them had settled in the county to lead a life of farming and only associated with other people when they sold their produce or bought supplies. There were also a small minority that had chosen to settle in the cities.

The intermingling of races had even given way to intermarrying between them, a practice that the humans of Gatlon and Rampön found detestable. Still, the practice continued despite the opposition from the rest of the country, and now half-breeds formed a sizable portion of the county's citizens. These mongrels, as humans tended to call them, were often indistinguishable from the other races, but they were looked down on and often discriminated against. As a result, many of them had retreated to farms where they did not have much interaction with anyone.

Josiah had entertained ideas of help from the army of Belvärd; however, Cirro had crushed these hopes with his superior knowledge of the social and military trends of the region. Several dragon outposts had been established in the county, and as a result many of the dragon riders settled there. The fact that the county could only be entered from the two adjacent counties gave the people of Belvärd a measure of security; therefore, they did not keep a standing army, but instead relied on the dragon riders to deal with any military problems that might arise. Only a few generations ago, many of the people knew how to handle a blade and were able to form an army if necessary; however, the current generation had seen this practice as unnecessary and discontinued it.

With these thoughts in mind, Josiah decided how he was going to best fortify his chosen position, the gap between the two mountain ranges at the bottom of Rampön. The dragons that the messengers would come across would help greatly, but they would not be able to hold off the entire might of Molkekk's army. He would have to send messengers throughout Rampön and request all available soldiers, hoping they would arrive in time. The county of Rampön probably had a standing army of thirty or forty thousand, but they would be scattered over a large area. And even after they were contacted, they would still have to travel to the bottom of the county. All told, they would probably only have a few hundred additional soldiers in two days, maybe ten thousand in five days, and twenty thousand in a week, if they survived that long. Molkekk's army would be stalled at the Péle River, but that could only last so long. If they also took time to pillage Belvárd, it might give Josiah's army enough time to build up a sizable force, but that was just a guess. The army might stick to the bottom of the country and move straight across to attack.

"We have to offer them something that they can't refuse," Cirro said from beside Josiah, jerking him from his thoughts.

"What do you mean?" Josiah asked as he shook his head. He didn't understand how Cirro could have read his thoughts.

"I was just thinking that we really won't have any better of a chance of holding off the enemy at the mountains than we did at the river," Cirro explained. "We can send for help, but who knows how long it will take to arrive. What we need to do is flaunt something in front of the enemy army, something they can't help but chase after. If we can keep them following it for long enough, it should give us time to fortify our position and receive reinforcements."

"What do you have in mind?" Josiah asked. "Molkekk's troops seem to be hell bent on the fall of Magessa and nothing else."

"Molkekk may be bent on our nation's fall," Cirro said as he stepped over a rut in the ground, "but his troops are still mortal. They'll have their best interests in mind over the interests of their master. If we collect enough articles of value and put them in the army's path, the soldiers' first thoughts will be to collect them. If we're lucky, they may even fight over them and decrease the army we have to face."

"So we use the oldest trick in the book and play to their greed," Josiah said skeptically. "But what do we have that could possibly lure them away from their task? We're poorly equipped as it is and have nothing we can spare."

The dilemma seemed to stump Cirro, and he was silent for some time as he thought. Josiah was thankful for the silence and turned his mind back to figuring out how to fortify his position, but for some reason his thoughts kept drifting back to Cirro's idea. After all, why wouldn't it work? All they needed was something that the enemy soldiers would want, and then their selfish nature would take over.

It's interesting, Josiah thought, *how often people are deflected from their paths by something they think they want. All too often, though, it is only after they waste many years to catch that thing that they realize they were only chasing shadows. It is such a depressing commentary on our nature.*

Josiah again forced his thoughts to how he was going to position his men between the mountains at the bottom of Rampön. The Vänern River would protect their right side, but it would also be a disadvantage to them. If the enemy crossed to the other side, Josiah would have to split his already slim force to cover both sides. If only he could get more men, but there again was the original problem, he needed more time. And the only feasible way to make more time would be to harry the enemy with strike attacks, but for that he would need more men, men he didn't have.

"Why are you chasing shadows in your mind, Josiah?"

Josiah looked up and saw the same man that he had seen on the plains outside of Magessa when he had been chasing the dwarves and more recently when he and the army were resting near Dublack. This time the man wore a full set of silver plate-armor though it didn't seem to hamper his movement at all. A shield was slung across his back, and a large two handed sword hung in a sheath behind it, the handle sticking up over his right shoulder. A heavy bow was also under his shield and stuck out over his left shoulder. He carried a helmet under his arm, leaving his face uncovered. Again Josiah was struck by the love that he saw in the stranger's face.

The sound of a sword sliding from its sheath drew Josiah's attention to Cirro who had drawn his weapon with the intention of pointing it at the stranger. His sword never made it fully out of the scabbard, however, for when he looked at the stranger, what he saw stopped him cold.

"Put your sword away, Cirro," the man said and put a hand on Cirro's shoulder. "There is a time for that, but it is not here when you are among friends." After a moment's hesitation, Cirro slid his sword back into its sheath and let go of the hilt. The man left his hand on Cirro's shoulder for a moment before removing it and turning his attention back to Josiah.

"I see that you have convinced both the elves and the ogres to help you," the man said as he scanned the army.

"Yes, I did exactly what you said, and still we failed to defeat the enemy," Josiah said hotly. "Why? Did I somehow fail to do something that I was supposed to do? What went wrong?"

"Nothing went wrong," the man said, unfazed by Josiah's outburst. "You did exactly as I told you to do, and you accomplished what I said you would. I never said you would defeat the enemy, I simply said you would survive, and you did, didn't you? I tell you the truth, you would be dead at this moment if you had failed to follow my instructions."

"And what good is being alive when I am powerless to stop the army currently overrunning my country?" Josiah asked. "Answer me that."

"Where there is life, there is hope," the man answered. "If you are alive, you have a chance of stopping the enemy; you have no chance of that if you are dead."

"And will I be able to defeat them? I thought that you said they have even more men than they did the last time they attacked Magessa."

"I did say that, and you have fewer men than you did last time, but these facts do not diminish the power of Elohim. He is still able to deliver you."

"Well then, what shall I do?" Josiah asked in a somewhat more respectful voice. "Should I make a stand at the pass between the Vankor and Rebel mountains?"

"Yes, you need to do that, but you will be driven from your position there," the man answered.

"What's the point of fighting there then?"

"There are many battles in a war, yet only the last one matters," the man said. "Win the last battle, defeat the enemy, and you win the war. You may not win the next time you encounter the enemy nor the time after that, but if you trust in Elohim, He will not fail you."

"Listen to the man," Cirro interjected. "You have told me many times before that the reason we fight is not because we know we will win, but because we know our cause is right. You cannot back down just because you fear that you may lose."

"What's up with him?" Josiah asked and jabbed his thumb over his shoulder at Cirro. "I thought when I was having a vision they couldn't see me."

"You are not having a vision," the man said with a smile. "You are not there, I am here."

"Right. Does that mean you aren't leaving this time?" Josiah asked.

"I am afraid not," the man said. "I will leave shortly, but remember, I am with you even if you don't see me. I will lead you, so don't stray, chasing after shadows; leave that to your enemy." The man smiled and began to fade. Within seconds he was completely gone.

Josiah and Cirro stood staring at the space where the man had been standing only moments ago as the army continued to march past them. Neither found what they had just witnessed to be unbelievable, but still they were a bit stunned. They stood in that way for several moments, half expecting the man to reappear, but he didn't.

"Chasing after shadows!" Josiah exclaimed suddenly. "That's what he meant. All that we need to do is find several pack animals and form them into a caravan. A few men can drive it toward the enemy army, and when they come within sight scatter a few articles of gold on the ground and drive the caravan away.

By the time the enemy catches the caravan and finds out there's nothing in it, they will hopefully be some distance from here."

"I thought you didn't like my plan," Cirro said with a small laugh. "That would work though. As long as we can find enough to entice them with, we should be able to stall them."

"And your job is to find those types of items," Josiah said. "Once you have them, assemble the caravan and set it out so that the enemy will see it." Cirro didn't move immediately, and Josiah added, "You may start now."

"Josiah, I thought we already had this discussion," Cirro reprimanded.

"Don't worry about me, Cirro," Josiah reassured his friend. "I need to talk to the General of the elves' army, and I'll stay with him until you finish your task. Surely he has enough guards to satisfy even you."

"I don't know." Cirro's expression changed to a smile and he chuckled. "He only has thirty men in his personal bodyguard. Maybe you should get him to take on a few more." Josiah glared at Cirro who just laughed and said, "Make sure you stay with him."

"What, you're going to trust me to walk myself all the way to where he is?" Josiah asked in mock surprise.

"Perhaps it isn't the best idea, but time is of the essence," Cirro said.

Feeling just a bit juvenile, Josiah stuck his tongue out at Cirro. Cirro just laughed and jogged away toward the front of the army where the supply wagons were. Josiah turned and started toward the rear of the army where the elves were positioned. As he approached, he was struck by the odd look of the elfin ranks. Many different uniforms were present, each indicating a separate region of the elves' forest. Two insignia were the most common among the soldiers, one of them being from the king's army of

Dublack and the other that of the army from across the mountains. They were not in two large groups but were instead dispersed among the other elves. The stories that Josiah had heard about the elves had made him believe that they were stern beings who were always in order; however, they were anything but this description. The elfin army was not in any ranks but moved as a group of mingling soldiers who laughed and joked among themselves. Near the back of their ranks were three or four lines of soldiers and among these Josiah spotted their General and headed toward him. He was stopped by three guards and asked his business. Quickly he gave his position in the human army, and he was let past with no further delay. The General heard him coming and turned to face him. He was tall even for an elf, and his build was massive. His hair was bound in a tight ponytail which hung down his back. He appeared to be about twenty, but Josiah knew that elves showed their age less than humans and placed this one's age at about forty-five. He wore a full suit of leather armor as most of the elves did and carried a bow and sword. His helmet was not on his head, allowing Josiah to see his eyes, and he immediately liked what was before him.

"Good morning, General," the elf said before Josiah had time to speak. "That is, if you can find anything good about it."

"By the grace of Elohim, we are alive," Josiah said. "Surely that's cause for rejoicing."

"Well spoken," the General said and offered his hand to Josiah. "I saw you in Lêf but was not able to introduce myself. My name is Nathan Valosh."

"I am Josiah Pondran," Josiah said as he shook the elf's hand.

"I do remember the name, though I do not recall you being a General when you were in Dublack," Nathan commented.

"That's because I wasn't at the time," Josiah explained. "I was a simple Commander then. The General of our army was killed in the battle at the Accri Forest, and I was promoted to fill his spot."

"Well in that case, congratulations on the promotion, though I am sorry to hear about your leader," Nathan said. "Now, what is it that you came to see me about?"

"My men are working to create a diversion to slow the enemy down, but they may need help," Josiah explained. "I was wondering if you had any magicians among your men who could create an illusion."

"I have a few," Nathan answered. "Exactly what kind of illusion do you have in mind?"

"I know very little about magic, so I don't know how hard this will be, but I need, if possible, for them to make our army appear larger than it is so that the enemy will be less likely to follow us."

"That would be very difficult," Nathan answered slowly. "Creating such an illusion would take a lot of power, and I don't believe I have enough men to do it." Josiah's countenance dropped, and the elf hurried on. "There is one thing I *can* do, however. I believe I have enough magicians to implant images into the minds of the foremost soldiers in their army. That would start the wave of fear which would ideally flow back through the ranks. It might accomplish the same things as an illusion would."

"Well, if you think it will work, I would appreciate it if you would have your men do that."

"Think nothing of it," Nathan said amiably. "After all, it's helping me just as much as it's helping you."

"Oh, and one other thing. My body guard is very picky about my safety, and since I sent him to do a task for me, he told me I would have to stay with you until he finished."

"You're always welcome to join me," Nathan said. "It'll be nice for a change to have someone around who isn't so respectful that they won't even carry on a conversation with me."

"It's lonely at the top," Josiah quipped.

"Actually, it is," Nathan answered. "As soon as you can, you should renounce your Generalship and go back to being a commander. Commanders have all the good times."

Five

Senndra opened her eyes and stared at the ceiling from where she lay on the couch. She had a crick in her neck from where her head had been propped up on the armrest all night, but otherwise she felt refreshed. Slowly she sat up and rubbed her eyes, looking around the room at the same time. The place was deserted, and Senndra didn't feel like getting up yet, so she lay back down and closed her eyes.

Suddenly the door slammed open, letting in a burst of cool air, and Senndra snapped her eyes open. Timothy and Lemin were the first two people to enter, followed by the Grand Admiral of the academy in Belvárd and several other officers that Senndra did not recognize. Vladimir brought up the tail of the procession and closed the door behind him as he entered. The officers took seats around the large table in the middle of the room as Vladimir crossed the room to where Senndra lay on the couch. His eyes met hers, and he motioned for her to get up. She did so, stretching as she rose, and followed him out of the building. The air outside was much cooler than it had been the previous day, and Senndra looked up at the sky to see if the sun was hidden by the clouds. There was not a cloud in the sky, and the sun was shining in full brilliance. A sharp wind was blowing across the city, and she hugged herself and looked at Vladimir.

"Why is it so cold?" she asked. "Just yesterday it was too hot."

"No one knows what's up with the weather," Vladimir said. "Some time last night the wind started to blow, and we figure that the temperature started to drop then, but we don't know for sure. Ever since, it has been getting steadily colder, and it's anyone's guess as to when it will bottom out."

"It's a north wind," Senndra commented as she looked toward the north. "Maybe Molkekk sent it."

"That's the rumor being spread around, but I don't believe it," Vladimir said. "Molkekk is just a man, and a defeated one at that. Last time I checked, even though he has allied himself with Oglemophin he doesn't have the power to control the weather."

"The most recent reliable information that we have on him is over ten years old," Senndra shot back. "It could very well be that he has gained more power over those years."

"I think some people are too quick to assume that everything they cannot explain is an evil power," Vladimir said. "Perhaps it is simply that winter is coming on early this year."

"And I think you aren't open enough to the idea that perhaps this did come about by Molkekk's power," Senndra responded.

"I've never known you to be so eager to believe magic is the reason for something," Vladimir said. "What is wrong with you?"

"I've been having these dreams," Senndra started. She looked at Vladimir to see if he would roll his eyes at her, but he appeared to be paying attention to her. "The last time that I had one, it turned out to be true, so as you can imagine, I'm ready to believe the same about these ones."

"What kind of dreams?" Vladimir asked.

"Dreams of death and carnage," Senndra answered. "In them, Saddun is defeated and burning and so is another city. A Magessan army marches away from the cities with a massive army bearing the sign of Molkekk following them. I can't help but wonder if they are true."

The door banged open, and Timothy stepped out into the open air. The smile on his face disappeared as he saw the solemn looks on Senndra's and Vladimir's faces. He looked from one to the other and back again for several moments.

"What's up?" he finally asked.

"Senndra's been having dreams," Vladimir answered without taking his eyes off Senndra.

"What kind of dreams?" Timothy asked, a worried look starting to form on his face.

"Bad ones," Vladimir said. "In them, Saddun has fallen and Molkekk's army is marching across Magessa. Senndra said the last time she had a dream like this one, it came to pass; so, do you think these things will happen?"

"I don't know exactly," Timothy answered. To Senndra he said, "What happened at the end of the dream?"

"There was a bright light and then I woke up," Senndra answered. "I mean, there was the bright light, but at the same time there was nothing to be seen."

"We'd better let them know," Timothy jerked his head toward the door he had just come out of. "Come on," he said and motioned for Senndra to follow him.

Senndra followed him into the building where the officers were discussing plans in an animated fashion. When the cadets

144

entered, all the officers hushed up except for one man who had his back to the door. He continued to talk and motion for several seconds before he realized everyone else had fallen silent. He turned to face Senndra then, his face beginning to turn red around the edges.

"What is it, Timothy?" Lemin asked in an irritated tone of voice. "I thought you were supposed to be keeping people out, not letting them in."

"Yes, sir," Timothy answered. "But something has come up. I think you need to hear about Senndra's dreams."

"Dreams?" one of the other officers said incredulously. "What in heaven's name do dreams have to do with anything?"

"It is not common, but Elohim sometimes uses dreams to communicate with His people," Lemin answered, his face suddenly serious. "What were your dreams about?" he asked Senndra.

Senndra recounted again everything that she had seen in her dreams, leaving out nothing. When she finished, there was silence in the room for several heartbeats as the officers looked at each other and at her. Lemin's face, especially, showed worry.

"You can't seriously be considering believing what she says," the man who had spoken previously finally exclaimed. "It's a blasted dream. It doesn't mean anything."

"And what if it does mean something, Tiberius?" Lemin countered. "What if it is a warning? If it is, and we ignore it, our destruction will be upon our own heads."

"I say it's just a dream," Tiberius growled as he stood and leaned across the table, staring Lemin down.

Lemin calmly stared back.

"And I say that it might be more than that," the elf finally said. "I'm not saying it is a warning or prophecy, but it might be, and I don't see how we can ignore that."

"Because I say that it is nothing," Tiberius said harshly. "Don't forget who the magician is, old man. Who do *you* think that you should listen to?" he asked of all the officers seated.

"Sit down, Tiberius," a person Senndra recognized as the Grand Admiral of Belmoth said. "I think Lemin has a valid point. It would cost us but little to send a scout to confirm whether the dreams are true, but if they are and we do not act, the consequences could be dire."

"I had a dream last night that informed me that we should take all of our men and assault Vollexa Temp," Tiberius sneered. "Maybe we should do that. No, wait! My dream was that there is a fertile land across the Sea. Maybe we should send explorers over there. If we decide to check out the validity of every dream anyone ever has, we would be doing nothing else."

"I wholeheartedly agree with you," Lemin answered the outburst. "However, this dream appears to have the marks of Elohim's message in it. I think it could be a warning from him."

"A warning from Elohim?" Tiberius laughed harshly. "Didn't anyone ever let you in on the secret that those stories are only for children?"

"And hasn't anyone ever told you to have more respect for your superiors?" Lemin asked in an even tone. "Last time I checked, I held the rank of Admiral; whereas you are only a Commander. You should at least address me as 'sir,' not 'old man,' and if you are going to call me an idiot, you should at least preface it by saying 'with all due respect.'"

"The Admiral is correct," the Grand Admiral of Belmoth said over the snickering from the other officers. "You will have more respect when addressing him, or I will be forced to punish you."

"Feel free to insult anyone of your own rank," Lemin interjected with a ghost of a smile on his face. "I don't imagine, however, you will find the term 'old man' very pertinent." There was more snickering and a few choked laughs which the Grand Admiral silenced with a glare.

"Admiral, please refrain from encouraging the juvenile behavior that has so far ruled this meeting."

"Gladly," Lemin conceded. "Back to the matter at hand, I believe, though I am not positive, that Senndra's dream could very possibly be a premonition of things that are to come, if not a vision of things that are happening at this very moment. If we ignore it, we could fall prey to the enemy, and we will have no excuse except that we ignored the warning of Elohim."

"With all due respect, sir," Tiberius interrupted, "I don't believe in Elohim, and frankly I don't think anyone else here does except for you. Secondly, I am very well acquainted with magic, which is the only way the dream could possibly mean anything, and I don't think it was sent by magical means."

"Concerning your first claim, Commander, I know for a fact that you are wrong," Lemin argued. "And concerning the dream, you know this because of your extensive experience in magic? I was under the impression that magical ability came from Elohim."

"You have been sorely misled, Admiral," Tiberius said in a strained voice as he tried to keep his emotions in check. "Magic has nothing to do with religion of any type, and yes, I don't believe that the dream was anything more than a dream because of my magical experience with such things. And considering that I am the only magician in here, I think I am the authority on such things."

"Are you sure you are the only magician in here?" one of the officers Senndra recognized from the academy said, and winked at Lemin. "It seems at least two of them have slipped in without your noticing."

Tiberius glanced at the door and turned back with a frown.

"I don't see anyone..." he said and stopped midsentence when his gaze rested on Lemin. The elf was still sitting in his chair with his hands folded in his lap, but in front of him a display of sparks flashed and sparkled. The sight was mesmerizing, and Senndra found herself being drawn to it until Lemin waved it away with a flick of his wrist.

"Ah yes, Admiral, some of us here are aware of your magical abilities, though it would appear not all of us were," the Grand Admiral of the academy of Belvárd said.

"Knowing how to do a few tricks does not make you an expert," Tiberius argued.

Timothy snorted and rolled his eyes. "You apparently are not aware of exactly who is sitting before you. If you or I are lucky, we will be half as skilled as he is by the time we die. You know the elf who slew Molkekk and confined him to his tower?"

"His name was Jothnial," Tiberius retorted. "Besides, this couldn't be him; he died in that battle."

"I never said he was Jothnial," Timothy said. "That would be unrealistic. No, this is the leader of the squad of magicians that Jothnial was part of."

"It's too bad Jothnial wasn't a better magician," Lemin commented offhandedly with a wink at Timothy. "If he had been more focused, I bet he could have been as good as me."

Everyone at the table turned to Tiberius, expecting him to respond, but he remained silent.

"Oh, one more thing," Lemin added. "Religion has everything to do with magic. Now, back to the matter at hand. I think we should investigate Senndra's dreams before it is too late for them to do any good."

"I agree," the Grand Admiral from the academy of Belvárd said. "Timothy, have Vladimir take a message to my General and tell him he is to have three dragon riders leave the city and scout the county of Belvárd. If they see anything out of the ordinary, they are to report it immediately. Then watch the door and make sure no one else comes in."

"Yes sir," Timothy answered and exited the building.

"You may go as well," the Grand Admiral said to Senndra, but Lemin held up his hand for her to stop.

"If you don't mind, Grand Admiral, I would like to question her a bit more."

"As you wish," the Grand Admiral responded.

"Besides this one, have you had any other dreams lately that could be prophesies?" Lemin asked.

"When we were still in Belvárd, right before the attack, I dreamed I was in Vollexa Temp," Senndra answered.

"Here we go again," Tiberius muttered, but everyone ignored him. Senndra glanced at Lemin who nodded for her to continue.

"I was in a tower; I assume that it was Molkekk's tower, though I don't know that for a fact. Anyway, there was a man there, and a voice which I knew belonged to Molkekk was speaking to him, questioning him about the attack which was about to happen. When I woke up, the enemy dragons were upon us, a part of the plan that I heard outlined in the dream. I also heard that half of Molkekk's army was supposed to attack Belmoth and the other half was to attack Saddun. I don't see why, if two parts of the dream came true, that the third part shouldn't, which is why I was concerned about the dream I just had."

"And well you should be," Lemin told her. To the other men in the room he said, "If her first dream came to pass, then the events of her second dream would logically follow. The question is: is there anything else in the dreams we might be able to use to our advantage?"

"There were a few things in the first dream that I can think of," Senndra offered. "Molkekk's man mentioned they would constantly be sending reinforcements to their army in Magessa, so our troubles are far from over. The enemy may still attack Belmoth again, and they will be adding to the numbers of their army to the east. The man also mentioned that the sea would be on their side. I have no idea what that means, but it sounded bad."

"Most likely it means that they will try to use boats in their invasion of the country," one of the officers said. "That means we will have to keep an eye on the ocean too."

"Yes, but that isn't a new consideration," Lemin countered. "We always knew that someone could do it. Besides, if we can keep his men from landing or destroy the ships before they are able to reach shore, we may come out on the upper hand because of it."

"Did they make any indication as to how many soldiers were supposed to be in each attack?" the Grand Admiral of Belmoth asked.

"Oh, yes, sir, he did say that each attack force was supposed to have a half a million men in it."

"Half a million!" the Grand Admiral exclaimed, following it with a curse. "There's no way we can stand up against a force like that."

"If what Senndra saw is correct, we already have done it, sir," Lemin said. "Both of the attack forces were supposed to have half a million men, and we defeated one of those forces not long ago.

"What about striking at the head of the beast? Did they say anything about Vollexa Temp that we could use against them?" Lemin asked Senndra.

"I got the distinct impression from the way that they were talking that most of their troops were being deployed, sir," Senndra answered. "From what they said, I think the city of Vollexa Temp should be all but deserted."

"That will help if we decide to attack Vollexa Temp," one of the officers commented.

"Of course, we don't know for a fact that the city has no defenders," someone else countered. "We didn't destroy all of the soldiers that attacked this city, and they had to go someplace. Besides, we all know about Molkekk's ability to raise armies in only days."

"I don't know if the soldiers we defeated will go back to their master," Lemin commented. "If I were in the service of Molkekk, I don't know that I would want to go back to him after a failure. He doesn't take failures very lightly. Besides that, they said they would be sending all additional forces to reinforce the troops in Magessa."

"Then you think we should attack the city?" the Grand Admiral of Belmoth asked.

"I never said we should, but I think we should always keep the possibility in mind," Lemin returned.

"Well, let's pretend we did decide to assault Vollexa Temp," the Grand Admiral postulated. "How would you go about doing it?"

"The city is landlocked, so there is no way we could use ships to approach it. It is also surrounded by a marsh, with only one main road leading to it, which effectively eliminates a land attack. That is, if you wanted to lead a surprise attack, which is what I was assuming."

"Surprise would not hurt our chances," the Grand Admiral admitted, "however, if our information is correct, it sounds like a frontal attack would also work."

"Why not both?" a commander asked. "We could stage a frontal attack on their gates and at the same time coordinate a sneak attack with dragons."

"That might work," the Grand Admiral said thoughtfully.

"Actually, I just thought of a better idea," the commander interrupted. "We have a whole lot of armor we captured from the enemy soldiers. If we dress ourselves in it, we could approach the gate without arousing suspicion. Before we are close enough for anyone to ask us for a password, the dragons can attack, thereby taking the attention off of us. We can then have the dragons drop men onto the gate and open it for us."

"A much better idea," the Grand Admiral admitted. "Get me a map so we can start planning this campaign."

"Surely you can't be actually contemplating this madness," burst out Tiberius, who had been holding his peace for some time. "The mission would be suicide!"

"So be it," the Grand Admiral said. "If you do not want to be part of this suicide, leave now. If you stay, I will expect you to say nothing else concerning the intelligence of the mission."

Senndra looked around the table, and her gaze locked on Lemin. The elf was inconspicuously giving her a sign to leave, so she edged away from the table toward the door. In the flurry of activity which was turning the room into an army's headquarters, no one noticed her open the door and slip out.

******

As the army neared the Rebel Mountains, Josiah and Nathan got their first look at the position they would have to defend. On the opposite side of the Vänern River, the Vankor Mountains rose right next to the shore, making it difficult for anyone to proceed on that side. What remained was a stretch of land, perhaps a mile in length, between the Vänern and the Rebel Mountains. There was a small outpost by the road running through the pass; however, since it was so deep in Magessa's territory, there were basically no defensive structures. An abandoned stone quarry was located nearby in the mountains and would provide stone if the army had enough time to erect any defenses. Nevertheless, the enemy army was close behind, and if they continued at their current pace, there would hardly be enough time to dig in, much less build structures for defense. There was some hope, though, for Cirro had not yet implemented his strategy for distracting the enemy.

Levvy, the ogre General, had also joined them, and together the three were scoping out the territory before the rest of the army arrived. The terrain was good in that the mountains would prevent the enemy from sneaking around behind them, but the pass was really too wide to effectively defend unless they could erect some defensive structures. All three Generals were not optimistic about their chances of winning, but they also knew there would be no better place to make their stand. They were now approaching the outpost in the gap to assess its capabilities, and as they drew nearer, they had their first glimmer of hope.

The outpost had been erected during the time when the people of Magessa were eradicating their enemies from the southern lands of the country and so it was built to withstand significant attacks. Its front wall was perhaps two hundred yards long and tall enough to prevent anyone from scaling it without ladders. It also had wall defenses and murder holes in order to give the defenders the advantage in the event of a siege. The walls themselves were a strategic wonder; there were actually several walls spaced five or six feet apart and each taller than the one in front of it. This prevented enemies who had scaled the outer wall from easily reaching the defenders who were on the other walls. All in all, the outpost was almost a fort; nevertheless, it was rather small compared to the area that the army would have to defend.

"As soon as we receive word that your plan has worked and that we will have more time, we can start mining stone and create a wall across the length of the pass," Nathan said to Josiah.

"But will we have enough men to protect the entire length, even if we do have a wall?" Levvy asked.

"I've been doing some quick math, and I think we should have more than enough," Josiah assured him. "If each of our soldiers only protected four feet, we would need less than fifteen hundred men to cover the entire length. I know your men can cover more area than that, so we should have plenty of soldiers. The real question is if we will be able to hold them here."

"If they bring their whole might against us, we will never stand," Nathan predicted. "They have too many men, and even if they lose a few thousand, they'll still have hundreds of thousands left."

"That's where the dragons will come into play," Josiah countered. "I have news that several dozen of the riders have already been contacted and will be joining us as soon as they are able. Granted, the enemy may be reinforced with griffins and dragons, but we will still have an advantage."

"So what we need now is an advantage on the ground," Levvy said. "We have enough men to dig a reasonable trench as well as erect a palisade in enough time, even if we can't build something more substantial. That would hold them for some time at least."

"If only we could make the mountains fall," Josiah commented grimly. "Then we could cut off their pursuit altogether."

"Well, that's not likely to happen anytime soon, so don't hold your breath," Nathan said. The three Generals continued to strategize as they approached the outpost, but without more information on the approach of the enemy, they couldn't do much else. They reached the fort and entered, informing the inhabitants that they were under attack. Since the outpost was deep in the heart of Magessa, the garrison was very small, only twenty-four strong plus the blacksmith, cook, and other attendants.

The senior officer of the outpost, Captain Merick, saluted Josiah and invited him for refreshments.

"We don't have time for that," Josiah answered. "The enemy is on our doorstep, and we need to get ready for their attack as soon as possible."

"An enemy army this far south?" Merick asked. "I don't think that's very likely, sir."

"You also probably didn't expect to see an elf and an ogre walk into your outpost an hour ago, but here they are," Josiah said, pointing at Nathan and Levvy.

"The matter of enemies aside, if you are a Commander, where are your troops?" Merick asked. "For that matter, where are any of your men?"

"First of all, the rank insignia may deceive you, but I actually hold the rank of General at the moment," Josiah responded. "I just haven't had time to replace it, being pursued by half a million enemies as we have been."

"Half a million!" Merick exclaimed, but Josiah cut him off.

"Second of all, if you want to see our men, come up to the top of your watch tower with us. You'll see them up there; however, I would hurry. The ogre is sometimes very impatient."

Levvy pulled his lips back from his teeth, and a low growl rumbled deep in his throat. Merick looked in his direction and nodded quickly.

155

"I believe you, but how in heaven's name are we supposed to stand up to half a million men? I only have twenty-four soldiers, and most of them should have retired long ago; we'll be swept aside like dry leaves."

"We have a sizable army following us," Nathan assured him. "There are less than twenty thousand all told, so we'll still probably be swept aside like dry leaves, but we'll give them one heck of a fight. The only question I have for you is: will you stand and fight with us? If you don't wish to, I will understand perfectly and allow you to go on your way."

Merick was silent for a full minute, clearly contemplating what he had just been told. Half a million soldiers, and these Generals wanted him to stand with them against the enemy! There was no way they could survive. On the other hand, the three men before him seemed calm and collected, almost as if they thought they would win the ensuing battle. He had never been exposed to a real combat situation, but if he ever was, these were the type of men he would want leading him.

"I will stay and fight," he finally answered. "I would like, however, to give my men the same choice you gave me, if that is alright with you, sir. As I said before, many of them are well advanced in years, so I don't know how they will respond to this."

"Very well, but be quick about it," Josiah told him. "We have preparations to make."

The Captain nodded and hurried off to find his men, and Josiah, Nathan, and Levvy headed back outside to take another look at the outpost and its surroundings. The army didn't arrive at the pass for another three hours, and when it did, the soldiers were exhausted. The Generals ordered their men to pitch camp and get some rest while they waited for news. An hour later, Cirro came galloping back toward the outpost with three men behind him. Josiah saw them a long way out and went out to meet them. They pulled their horses to a stop in front of him and dismounted.

It was obvious that they were exhausted from their ride, so Josiah dismissed them to go get some rest. Cirro, however, he pulled aside as they walked to the camp.

"I trust from the expression on your face that it went well?" Josiah asked.

"It went better than well!" Cirro burst out. "We didn't even have to drop anything for them to find. All that we did was parade the caravan in front of their army, and they started chasing after it like a pack of dogs after a rabbit. They were pillaging the houses and farms that they encountered, so if we're lucky, they'll do the same further up into Belvárd and give us even more time."

"How quickly are they moving?" Josiah asked.

"With all the ransacking they're doing, they barely make ten miles a day if that," Cirro answered. "Even if they take a straight course from where we think they'll overtake the caravan to this pass, we'll have at least a week to prepare."

"Good work," Josiah told his friend. "You have given us the best chance to defeat the army that we have had in a long time. Now go get some rest. Tomorrow we have some serious work to do."

******

As Senndra walked south, she found her dragon and urged him, through their mental link, to meet her outside the south gates of the city. She did not expect any trouble getting out of the city and encountered none. The guards at the gate nodded to her as she passed them, but besides that, no one saw fit to notice her. Once outside the walls, she bore slightly east toward the mountains and continued walking until a shadow covered her. She stopped moving and looked up, shielding her eyes from the sun. Feddir was circling above her, his scales glittering dully in the bright light.

157

Feddir circled one more time before landing on the ground a short distance in front of Senndra. Senndra jogged to her dragon and climbed his leg to get to his back. She had forgotten to bring a saddle, and immediately regretted it. Even though she didn't expect to have to fight while on Feddir, the trip would still be long and uncomfortable with her riding on Feddir's rough scales. Feddir must have picked up on her thoughts because he showed her an image of them flying back to get a saddle.

"I guess we could," Senndra answered out loud. "There are already going to be several dragons leaving the city, so we should blend right in with them." Feddir projected another image into Senndra's mind, and she chuckled. "No, I don't suppose too many people are going to stand in the way of a dragon, are they?"

Senndra felt Feddir's muscles bunch underneath him, and she grabbed a spine directly in front of her. They shot upward in a blast of air, and in a few moments were on their way back to the city, soaring high in the sky. Feddir kept his wings extended for the most part, gliding from one updraft to the next and only giving his wings one long, lazy flap every once in a while. Almost before they were up in the air, they were at the city, circling over the parade field where the dragons took off and landed. Feddir spiraled three times around the field before coming in for a perfect landing and hardly scratching the turf as he hit the ground.

Senndra jumped down from his back and hurried across the field toward the bunk house where she was quartered. She reached the dwelling in only a few minutes and didn't slow her pace as she burst through the door, swinging it closed behind her with a resounding bang. She took the stairs two at a time, almost crashing into another cadet but reaching her room without any mishaps. She grabbed her weapons from the closet and strapped them on quickly. Next she grabbed her saddle from its place in the bottom of her closet and hurriedly scanned it to make sure it was in good working condition. With it tucked under her arm, she jerked open the door of her room and almost rushed out, straight into another person.

"Oh, Senndra, it's you," the person said. Senndra finally realized she knew the young man who stood in front of her. They had been in several of the same classes at the academy and were in the same training squadron.

"Hi," Senndra said breathlessly. She hoped that her clipped answer would discourage any conversation. It didn't.

"Where are you off to in such a hurry?" the cadet asked. "You look like you've been running."

"That's because I *have* been running," Senndra answered. "Now I am going to go ride my dragon."

"For any reason in particular?" the cadet asked. "Because I could come with you if you wanted."

"Actually, there is a specific reason, and no, you can't come," Senndra answered. The cadet stood there waiting for an explanation, but Senndra didn't feel like giving one, so she simply stood opposite him.

"You want to tell me what that reason is?" the cadet asked finally.

"I'm going on a scouting mission," Senndra answered. "I need to leave as soon as possible, hence my running, so if you could move out of the way, I would be grateful."

"Of course," the cadet said, sounding just a little hurt. "Anything you want."

Senndra hurried out of her room and past him, but as she reached the top of the stairs, she stopped. She had been abrupt and even a little rude with the other cadet, and she was immediately sorry for it.

"I'm not trying to blow you off or anything," Senndra said as she turned to face the other cadet. "It's just that I'm in a bit of a hurry and need to leave now."

"I understand, Senndra," the cadet said. "You have something to do, so go do it."

Senndra stared at the young man and tried to figure out what he was thinking. The words that he had chosen seemed to indicate that he was being sarcastic, but his tone seemed to indicate otherwise. It was almost as if he understood the situation and had no problem with Senndra being so curt with him. Senndra stared at him for one long moment and was about to spin around to head back down the stairs when she realized why he was there.

"Oh, by the way, Rita was at the practice fields last time I checked," she told him. "I think she's still down there, though I don't know that for a fact."

"Thanks," the cadet said and Senndra hurried down the stairs and back to the parade field. Feddir was lying down now, letting the sun warm his scales as he scratched absent mindedly at a spot just behind his front leg. He opened one eye when he sensed Senndra nearing him and blinked at her.

"Come on, Feddir, I don't have time for this," Senndra said as she held the saddle out in front of her. Feddir looked at her with what could only be described as a grin and rolled slowly onto his stomach. Senndra grunted and reached up to place the saddle on Feddir's back, but he continued rolling until he was on his other side with his back to her. He twisted his head around so that he could look at her and gave another grin.

"Feddir, stop playing around," she growled at the dragon. "You know this is important. Besides, if you don't behave, I'm going to tell Lemin to turn you into a frog. He's a magician, you know, so he could do it."

Feddir jerked his head around to stare at Senndra again, this time with his eyes wide. A question floated across their mental link, and Senndra had to force herself not to smile.

"Yes, I'm quite sure that he would have no trouble at all turning you into a toad, even with how big you are. And even if it is difficult for him, he'll be very angry with you for not cooperating. After all, this mission was his idea."

Senndra felt chagrin and anxiety from Feddir, and the dragon rolled over onto his stomach, allowing Senndra to place the saddle on his back. Quickly she threaded the straps underneath his stomach and buckled them securely. When she was finished and had checked everything to make sure it was in working order, she climbed into the saddle. She slipped her feet through the leg loops and tightened them so that she could ride without her hands. Feddir waited until she was finished before jumping into the air and riding an updraft. As soon as he had reached a sufficient height, he tilted his wings and allowed a breeze to push him southeast.

The wind which had been cold on the ground was freezing at the higher altitude, and Senndra wished that she had remembered to bring a flying jacket. As it was, she was not willing to go back for the extra clothing. Instead, she hunched over the back of her steed, letting his head break the wind and his body heat warm up her hands and face as she laid them against his bare scales.

Despite this arrangement, the trip threatened to be miserable. To escape the uncomfortable situation, she slipped into a light sleep. Her dreams were sporadic and made no sense whatsoever, vanishing from her memory as soon as she awoke. She straightened from her position on her dragon's back and stretched to get the kinks out of her back and neck. She felt a burst of surprise come from Feddir, which jerked her to complete consciousness. Leaning over and out from her mount, she saw the capital city of Belvárd but spotted nothing that would have

161

surprised Feddir. The city appeared to be in perfect condition, and as far as she could tell, nothing was amiss. Then she noticed the large cloud of black smoke coming from the south. She looked in that direction and thought that she might be seeing something, but the smoke obscured her view of everything.

An image from Feddir flashed through her mind, one of the area that she had just been staring at. His eyesight was much better than hers and pierced the smoke to detect what she had missed. A large army spread out across the land, covering several miles with its first line. As they came, they burned and pillaged whatever they encountered, killing whoever they could lay their hands on. Their device was not visible, but Senndra knew who they were. She encouraged Feddir to get closer, and he slowly dropped until they were only a hundred yards above the ground. The symbol on their flag was now visible: a gigantic bat, black as night. The symbol itself struck dread into Senndra's heart for she now knew for certain that they were fighting Molkekk, bane of Magessa.

As she watched, the soldiers came to another house. They didn't even bother seeing if the door was open, but instead rammed it with their shoulders until it smashed inward. They entered with drawn swords and emerged moments later with a man, woman, and three children. Senndra watched, horrified as the soldiers killed each of them, laughing as they did so. They entered the house again, smashing the windows and anything else that would break. A table became firewood and dishes were smashed on the doorstep. They stripped the house of everything of value before finally leaving. Shortly thereafter, smoke began to seep out of the doorway and through the smashed windows of the structure, and within minutes the whole building was aflame.

Senndra watched in horror as the dark soldiers were demolishing the house. She felt the anger rising in Feddir and had to prevent him from diving down and tearing the soldiers apart. It wasn't that she wouldn't have been happy to see justice served so soon; rather, she knew that they had been concealed in the smoke so far, and revealing themselves might endanger their mission. She had to get news of this back to Belmoth, but first she would circle down to the bottom of the county and see how far these evil forces spread. She also needed to find out if the army that was sure to have resisted them had by some miracle survived, or if it had been destroyed.

Feddir's anger made him hard to control, and at first he resisted Senndra's orders to fly south, preferring instead to drop down and eradicate as many of the enemy soldiers as he could. Senndra was persistent, however, and in the end, the dragon complied with her command.

Soon they had left the enemy army far behind, though the evidence of their destruction was obvious for as far as the eye could see. Buildings smolder, animals and people lay dead on the ground, and trees had been slashed down. Everywhere the earth screamed of the massacre that had just occurred, but there was no help, no one to serve justice. It took all of Senndra's power to keep flying south and not return to attack the enemy.

Further south, the wreckage was just as bad, if not worse, than it had been before. Burned-out houses, towns, and cities were marked by columns of smoke rising from the land. All of the trees had been slashed and hacked down, and the humans and animals who had not escaped lay dead in the dust. Even the grass had been turned to dirt by the hundreds of thousands of feet which had marched across it. And just when Senndra thought things couldn't get any worse, they did.

The next city she flew over appeared to be one of the first to be hit by the army. It had been burned clear to the ground, and a good portion of its wall had been knocked down, but what caught Senndra's eye were the rows of sticks that stood in front of the city. At first she could not tell what they were, but as she drew closer, she just about vomited with the realization. Scores of people had been mutilated and impaled on spikes in front of the city, sending a message to the world: this is what happens to those who oppose Molkekk. When Senndra could no longer bear the sight, she pressed her face against Feddir's neck and kept it there until they were well past the city.

As the dragon and rider approached the Vänern River, there was still no sign of life, and hope of finding any slipped away altogether. Then, just as they were about to turn back toward Belmoth, they spotted activity in the gap between the Vankor and Rebel Mountains. They dropped in for a closer look, fully expecting to find another army of Molkekk's men. Senndra was shocked to see two elfin flags, an ogre flag, the flag of Gatlon, and the flag of Belvárd hanging from the walls of the main tower of the outpost which stood in the pass, while the flag of Magessa flew from the pole at the structure's center. A mixture of feelings welled up inside of her- surprise, relief, thankfulness. She hadn't realized until now how bleak the whole situation had seemed, but now there was hope. No matter how small the force might be, there were still soldiers in Magessa who were resisting the advances of Molkekk's hordes. Excited at this unexpected good luck, Senndra ordered Feddir to drop, and the dragon immediately began to spiral downward. As they came nearer to the ground, they were able to see thousands of figures working to fortify the pass, bringing stones in from one of the mountain ranges and building a wall with them. When they noticed the dragon, they scattered in fright but came out of hiding when Feddir didn't breathe fire at them or attack them in any way. Feddir landed, and the men approached with their weapons drawn, obviously ready in case he suddenly decided to attack. Feddir let out a soft purring which Senndra recognized as a chuckle. He sent her a scene of him blowing fire on all of the soldiers, and their armor doing them no good.

"Of course their armor wouldn't be of any help if you actually decided to attack them," Senndra told him in a low voice. Then she had a sudden thought. "Can you actually produce flames now?"

Feddir let out another low purr and twisted his head around to look back at Senndra, pulling his lips up from his teeth in a smile. Other than this action, there was no answer, but Senndra understood. Her dragon could breathe fire with the best of them. She smiled at the unexpected good news, slid off of Feddir's back without another comment, and approached the leader of the soldiers, making sure the symbol on her uniform was in plain view. She stopped at the leader's order and identified herself upon request. Finally the soldiers allowed her to approach, though they still eyed her and Feddir with suspicion.

"Can I please speak with your General?" she asked. "I have been sent from Belmoth and have information that may be of help to him."

"Sent from Belmoth, huh?" the leader said suspiciously. "And why would a dragon rider come from Belmoth? Last time I checked, there were no dragons there."

"Well, your information is at least a week old," Senndra retorted. "The academy for dragon riders was attacked, so we evacuated down the mountains to Belmoth. Now please take me to your General, or admiral, or whoever is in charge."

"I'll need more proof than a uniform before I take you to him," the leader said. "You could easily have taken it off one of our dead soldiers."

The statement silenced Senndra. What could she do to prove she was who she said she was? Really, there was nothing other than her uniform that distinguished her as a warrior of Magessa. She noticed one of the soldiers talking to the leader and strained to hear what they were saying, though she gave no outward indication of her effort.

"It's the brown dragon, sir," the soldier said. "They say its rider was one of the ones who came to Saddun when the dwarves attacked. I remember it like it was yesterday."

165

"So now just because the rider of a brown dragon was supposedly at Saddun six months ago, we should believe this person?" the leader asked.

"He's not *a* brown dragon, sir," Senndra called out. "He's *the* brown dragon. There's only one of them known to exist at the moment. From what I hear, he's actually only the second one in recorded history. Send a message to your leader and tell him that the brown dragon and his rider are here. Hopefully they will know who I am."

The leader of the soldiers was silent for a moment, but he could see nothing better to do. After a moment of indecision, he called one of his men and whispered in his ear for a few seconds. The soldier nodded and hurried away toward the fort. Senndra walked back to Feddir who had spread himself out on his side, exposing his underbelly to the sun's rays. Senndra sat on the ground just behind his front leg, leaning back against him and closing her eyes. It was an old dragon rider's trick; it put the soldiers around her at ease, but at the same time she was able to see what was going on through the images that Feddir sent to her. As it was, the soldiers didn't do anything except keep a good distance from the dragon.

With nothing else to do, Senndra decided to question Feddir about his previous ambiguous statement. She sent him an image of him breathing fire along with a quizzical expression. He responded with surprise and puzzlement.

"Who was the dragon in that image?" he seemed to be asking.

Senndra responded with a feeling of sternness and presented the image again. Feddir sighed, and Senndra could feel his embarrassment. He erased the image of himself breathing great streams of fire and replaced it with one in which a small tongue of fire was coming out of his mouth.

166

Senndra now understood why he had avoided her question and even had not told her to begin with when he first found that he had any flame abilities whatsoever. Even if it was irrational, he was embarrassed that the other dragons were able to sustain large fire jets for minutes at a time while he could hardly create any flame at all. Senndra promised not to tell anyone else, but was herself ecstatic. Once dragons were able to create fire, the ability expanded quickly. If he followed normal development cycles, Feddir would be able to fight with his flames in a matter of weeks if not days.

Feddir was still embarrassed but less so than before. Senndra smiled to herself and made herself more comfortable against Feddir's side. She hadn't been there for more than half a minute when Feddir sent her another image; three people were coming toward them from the castle. One of them was obviously an ogre, she could tell even from this distance, but the other two could have easily been humans, elves, or orcs. Not that it mattered much to Senndra, but she liked to know what she was going into so that she didn't get surprised.

She waited until the men were only a hundred yards away before rising from her spot beside Feddir and brushing off her clothes. Feddir lifted his head to look at her, then glanced at the three men approaching. They didn't impress him much, and he didn't even bother getting up.

Senndra rolled her eyes at the dragon and took a deep breath, finally turning to face the three men who were now only a stone's throw away. The one on the left was an ogre as Senndra had decided before, and she was now able to identify the one in the middle as an elf and the one on the right as a human. The human appeared familiar to her, though she couldn't quite decide who he was or where she had met him before. Perhaps at Saddun. His appearance was so different even from what she had seen in her vision that it wasn't until he was less than twenty feet away that she finally recognized him.

******

Josiah had heard about the brown dragon before, and as he approached, he scanned the beast from head to tail. Rumor was that the dragon didn't have scales and couldn't breathe fire, but the sun glinted off the beast's side, disproving one of those rumors. All in all, the dragon appeared to be a healthy specimen, and Josiah tried to guess its age. He was not very familiar with dragons and as far as he knew, it could be twenty years or six months. He turned his attention from the dragon to the rider and had a strange feeling they had met before. In fact, it was probable they had met, he decided. There were dragon riders at Saddun during the whole fiasco with the dwarves half a year ago. Recognition stunned him for a moment as he realized who the rider was. This was Senndra Felling, daughter of the famous elfin warrior, Jothnial. Josiah had fought beside her in the dwarf attack and, as he recalled, she was a force to be reckoned with.

"Yes, I am already acquainted with General Pondran," she said with a glance at the emblems of rank affixed to his uniform. "Though last time I saw him, he was not a General."

"Yes, that makes sense," Nathan answered. "He was just recently promoted, though I must say that the governing authorities probably won't recognize his promotion as valid."

"They'll probably just demote him like they did last time," Senndra said with a smile on her face. "But it looks like he's doing better than he did last time, though," she added with a glance at his shoulder. "Last time he didn't even get to wear the rank patches."

"What do you mean 'last time'?" Nathan asked. "You mean this isn't the first time he's been a General?"

"There was that one time though technically I was an Admiral, not a General," Josiah answered quickly. "I guess I never mentioned it, but when the dwarves attacked Saddun, and we set out after them…well, let's just say that the General wasn't ready for battle, much like the rest of us. The only difference was that he split at the first sign of danger. The commanders needed someone to combine all the armies and decided I was the best man given the situation, and the ogre General agreed. It didn't last long, but I didn't really care. I brought as many of my men out of the battle alive as I could; that's all that really matters."

"I would tend to agree," Nathan concurred. "Anyone who wants the rank just for the power that it brings is not a good person for the job. That being said, perhaps we should make sure Josiah remains a General," he added with a wink at Senndra.

"No dice, General," Josiah shot back. "I'll happily go back to being a commander as soon as I can. Like you said, they're the ones who have all of the fun."

"Do you have time for refreshments?" Levvy asked Senndra, before his companions could get into a long discussion. "While we're doing that, perhaps you could give us the information that you said you had."

"Yes, I guess I have time for that," Senndra said.

"Could I have the honor of escorting you?" Josiah asked with a small bow.

"Why certainly, General," Senndra answered and placed her arm through his. Then the three Generals and Senndra turned and headed toward the castle.

Six

The trio stepped onto the newly constructed drawbridge of the outpost which spanned a freshly dug ditch. Senndra looked down as they crossed and saw that the ditch was about ten feet deep with pointed stakes in the bottom and steeply slanted sides which butted up against the walls of the outpost. Altogether it would make a reasonable defense against the invaders.

"Welcome to Castle Far Point," Josiah said as they stepped off the bridge and under an arched gateway.

Heavy wooden gates on either side were reinforced with metal strips and studs, and in front of them an iron portcullis hung open. Immediately inside the gatehouse was a courtyard of moderate size. The number of soldiers patrolling the area and the walls had been decreased to a minimum, freeing as many of them as possible to work on the fortification of the pass.

Across the courtyard, a solidly built door led to the keep. The foyer they stepped into was very small and immediately emptied into a larger room with few furnishings. A ladder was bolted to the far wall and led to a trapdoor in the ceiling. The group passed through a doorway on the left, entering a dining room where they sat down at a table. Josiah and Levvy disappeared but returned moments later with two pitchers of water and some glasses. Josiah also held a plate of food which he placed in front of Senndra.

"We've already eaten our midday meal, but you look like you could use something after your trip," Josiah commented. Senndra hadn't remembered until that moment that she hadn't even had breakfast, nor had she noticed how hungry she was. She was acutely aware of her hunger now, however, and after briefly thanking Elohim for her food, began to eat. As she was eating, the others made small talk, occasionally asking her questions but mostly leaving her alone; however, when she had finished eating, their attention immediately shifted.

"Tell us about this information you brought," Nathan said and took a drink of water.

"After listening to you talk, you may already know a lot of it," Senndra said as she pushed her plate away. "You already know about the enemy army and that they're moving north, pillaging the land as they go."

"Yes, but how far are they going?" Levvy asked. "We still don't know how much time we have before they come back to attack us."

"You'll have plenty of time," Senndra answered. "When I saw them they had almost reached Angárd and didn't seem to be in any kind of hurry. My guess is that they'll loot as much of Belvárd as they can before they come back, unless something changes."

"I would almost rather have them back here attacking us, instead of preying on innocent people," Josiah commented. "There's not much we can do about it though, and according to what Senndra said, we may have several weeks to prepare. That is, unless there are any more of Molkekk's soldiers around that we don't know about; though I would find that hard to believe, given the number of troops already here."

"Even Molkekk has a limit to how many soldiers he can sustain at one time," Nathan agreed. "I don't think that he could have many more than half a million."

"You don't know, do you?" Senndra asked in unbelief, looking from one General to the other. "Of course, I guess that's understandable, since you've been cut off from new information for the last several weeks."

"We don't know what?" Nathan asked.

"Saddun wasn't the only city attacked by Molkekk," Senndra answered.

"What?!" the Generals exclaimed all at once. "What other cities did he get?"

"If you mean how many did he capture, the answer is none," Senndra said. "Well, unless you count the dragon academy."

"What happened up there?" Josiah asked, a worried expression on his face. "I thought you came from there."

"No, the academy was attacked by dragons and griffins, probably at the same time as the assault on Saddun," Senndra informed him. "We drove off the enemies and then evacuated to Belmoth before they came back. Unknown to us, we had just stepped from the pot into the fire; hundreds of thousands of Molkekk's soldiers were knocking on the gates of Belmoth. With our dragons added to the force already at the city, we held our ground and even, with Elohim's help, were able to drive them off. That's why they sent the dragon scouts down here, to see if the same thing had happened to the east."

"You mean Molkekk could have fielded as many as a million soldiers?" Josiah asked in astonishment.

"We were never sure how many were attacking Belmoth, but that's possible," Senndra answered. "We also have some

172

inside information that he has more troops to reinforce the ones already here."

"Elohim save us!" Nathan exclaimed. "Where in heaven's name did he get so many soldiers?"

"Who knows where people like him get their followers," Levvy answered in his gravelly voice. "He probably offered them riches and glory. There are many that would take that bait."

"How are we going to defend against them?" Nathan asked. "They have just as many men as we thought they did, and they could be getting reinforcements of who knows how many soldiers."

"The situation really hasn't changed that much, if you think about it," Josiah responded after a moment. "We already suspected the number of their army, and the addition of a few extra soldiers won't really tilt the battle too much in their favor. After all, what are a few thousand among half a million?"

"Plus, we now have time for our own reinforcements to arrive," Levvy added.

"That's right," Senndra agreed. "When I take this information back to Belmoth, they'll almost certainly send a squadron of dragons to assist you. I'll also spread the word on the way back that you need assistance."

"We have already sent out our own messengers, but any help you can provide would be appreciated, particularly any dragons you can bring," Nathan assured her. "If we had a functioning air force here, it would go a long way toward being able to hold them off or even defeat them."

"Yes sir," Senndra said, then added, "By the way, how many men do you have here? If I had the exact number, it would probably help convince people that you need help."

"Let's just say we're easily outnumbered twenty to one," Nathan answered. "Actually it's probably worse. That should be enough to convince anyone. Oh, and be sure to mention the fact that we're holing up right on the border of Rampön. That should speed up the bureaucrats in their decision making."

"I'll be sure to mention it," Senndra said. "Is there anything else I should know?"

"Not that I can think of," Nathan answered. He looked at the other two, but they just shook their heads.

"Very well," Senndra said. "Then I will carry news back that a massive army has indeed attacked Saddun and gained entrance to Magessa. I will tell them that there is an army of defenders at the border of Belvárd and Rampön who are trying their best to hold the enemy off, but who need help immediately."

"We're outnumbered twenty to one as well," Nathan reminded her.

"Of course," Senndra agreed. "You're outnumbered badly; you need reinforcements immediately."

"One other thing," Levvy mentioned. "We need as many supplies as we can get. We have enough for now, but our army is burning through them at a fast rate."

"Very well," Senndra said and waited for a few moments. "If that is all, I should probably be on my way. Thank you for the food, and I will do my best to bring you reinforcements."

"We know you will," Josiah said and rose when Senndra did. "I'll see her to the door, gentlemen," he informed the other Generals.

Josiah and Senndra left the keep and stood in the courtyard for a moment. Though they had not noticed it while there, the castle had been rather dark, and their eyes needed time to adjust to the sunlight. Josiah headed for the castle gate, but Senndra held him back.

"I'll just have Feddir come here to pick me up," she said, sensing Josiah's intent. She added with a small chuckle, "After all, he can cover the distance a lot faster than we can."

"I guess that's true," Josiah conceded. He stood for several seconds, letting an awkward silence grow. "So, how have your studies at the academy been going?" he finally asked in an attempt to break it.

"They're going well," Senndra answered. "I've been making good grades, and I'm almost ready to graduate."

"How close is almost?" Josiah asked.

"I have another year. Of course it's going to be a lot more than that if we keep getting attacked and whatnot."

"I know what you mean," Josiah commented. "It seems like most of my training in battlefield tactics and hand-to-hand combat has been on the job. I imagine it'll be that way until we defeat Molkekk once and for all, which I don't see happening in the incredibly near future."

"It could be closer than you think," Senndra said. "There's no set plans as of yet, but there may be an attack on Vollexa Temp soon."

"There's no way it could succeed," Josiah argued. "Molkekk has an incredibly vast host at his disposal..."

"All of which are either here or being directed here as reinforcements," Senndra interrupted. "All together, it leaves Vollexa Temp nearly empty."

"I don't believe Molkekk would make such an important mistake," Josiah disagreed. "Surely he knows we'll attack him if given the chance.

"It wasn't really his mistake," Senndra said. "If he had succeeded in taking both Saddun and Belmoth, he wouldn't have to worry about such an attack because we would all be occupied.

However, we defeated his army at Belmoth, an event for which he was clearly not prepared."

Josiah suddenly smiled, and Senndra looked at him quizzically.

"I was just thinking," Josiah explained with a shake of his head. "Not so long ago, the name Molkekk struck an insurmountable fear into my heart. I mean, at Saddun we wouldn't even say his name, mostly from fear, I guess. I never would have thought I'd be fighting his army before I graduated from the academy, much less considering that we might actually be able to defeat him."

"I guess when I think about it, I'm a little surprised too," Senndra agreed. "I never would have even considered the idea that we might be able to stand up to him."

"And now, his name is just another word," Josiah said. "I use it all the time in battle meetings and regular conversations. It holds very little fear now."

A roar of wind rushed down into the castle as Feddir dropped out of the sky and landed with a thud. The guards on the wall staggered backwards from the force of the wind, but Senndra figured they would have done so even if there had been no physical reason. She did note, however, that they held their ground.

"I guess it's true: fear of the unknown and untested is much stronger than any other fear in the world. See you in a while, General," she called over her shoulder as she jogged up the stairs to the wall and climbed onto Feddir's back. She waved down at him just before Feddir sprang from the wall. His wings flapped downwards in powerful strokes that pushed him and his rider up into the sky. Within minutes he was soaring north back toward Belmoth.

******

176

"It's not that I don't trust him, it's just that…"

"You don't trust him," Lemin finished Timothy's sentence for him.

"Well, yes," Timothy conceded. "I don't trust him and with good reason. Only a fool would put his trust in someone who doesn't trust in Elohim. That trust will be broken eventually."

"I would tend to agree with you," Lemin said. "Putting faith in someone who doesn't believe in Elohim is often dangerous, but not this time, I think. Tiberius may not believe, but he is not an enemy of Magessa. He hates Molkekk as much as anyone else here and, in my opinion, will do whatever is necessary to be rid of him."

"I am required to be respectful to you and abide by whatever you decide; however, I am in no way required to agree with you, so let me say right now that I don't," Timothy said bluntly. "Agree with you, that is. I normally don't have this feeling about people, but with him, I can't help but be suspicious. I have a bad feeling about what he might be up to."

"And I don't think he's up to anything," Lemin said. "Your feelings are founded entirely on the fact that he disagreed with us in front of our superiors and made fun of Elohim. Nothing he has done indicates in the least that his allegiance is to be doubted."

"I'm not saying he's working with Molkekk," Timothy argued. "There are other ways a person can be a menace besides working with the enemy. We know nothing about him, and it's not exactly like my feelings tell me what's wrong with a person. Maybe he talks too much. Maybe his view of the world will hurt our cause; I don't know. All I can say is that I have a bad feeling about him."

"Logged and noted, Timothy," Lemin said. "I'll take what you have said into consideration."

"Which is another way of saying you'll just ignore it," Timothy muttered as he left the room. It wasn't that he disliked Lemin, but the elf could be extremely hard to get along with sometimes. Maybe it was the fact that he was usually right, and Timothy didn't find it any easier than the next person to admit that he was wrong.

"Maybe he *is* right," he told himself. "Tiberius probably just makes me edgy because of some completely unrelated issue. I'm sure he's a fine officer and is an asset to anything that he is included in. Perdition! Not even *I* can convince myself of that!"

Timothy was so lost in thought that he almost ran over another cadet. He began stammering his apology until he realized the cadet was Senndra. Instantly the discussion with Lemin was forgotten as he looked his friend over from head to toe.

"Well, it looks like you got back in one piece," he commented. "Please tell me the trip was a complete waste of time, and that you failed to turn up anything of importance."

"I wish I could," Senndra sighed.

"So your dreams were real?" Timothy asked.

"As far as I can tell," Senndra answered. "The army of Molkekk is currently marching all over Belvárd, killing and pillaging. They're more than five hundred thousand strong now, not to mention that they'll probably be getting reinforcements."

"Please tell me you have good news in all of that," Timothy begged. "A massive elf army is coming to wipe them out or something along those lines."

"An army is digging in at an outpost, named Castle Far Point, on the south border of Rampön and Belvárd. They have a large army, but against the numbers that Molkekk has…They're outnumbered at least twenty to one, probably worse."

"I shouldn't have asked," Timothy muttered. Louder, he said, "Lemin's in his office. He probably wants to see you. I guess that's why you're heading there right now."

"If I can make it without running someone over," Senndra answered with a smile. "Most people make that a whole lot easier than you do."

"Well, have fun with that," Timothy said as he moved past Senndra. "I was just in there and, well, I guess you could say I softened him up for you."

"What do you mean?" Senndra called after him.

"I think he'll just be relieved to have someone that doesn't disagree with him, is all," Timothy called back before disappearing from sight around a corner.

Timothy was in a bad mood for the rest of the day. Not even Vladimir with his suggestion of playing Lex Tanna could make him feel better. He realized the effect that he was having on everyone and chose to hide away in the library. Forsaking the fiction genre, the type of book he normally read, he wandered aimlessly. He scanned the shelves as he passed, meandering through the geography, medicinal, and historical sections.

As he was passing through the science section, a book that did not belong caught his eye. It was a large grey book tucked in the middle of a series of small blue books, and Timothy turned to take a closer look at it. Its title, *Molkekk*, did not seem to fit in the science section, so Timothy took it from its spot on the shelf. Dust coated it in a thick layer, almost as if the tome had not been touched in years. When Timothy opened it, dust fell from the cover and puffed up from the pages. Timothy flipped to the title page and scanned those surrounding it until he found the date the book had been written: only a year before Molkekk had been imprisoned in his tower. He flipped back to the title page and froze in shock as his gaze drifted down to name of the author.

Jothnial Felling, the very elf who had defeated Molkekk, had written the book that Timothy now held in his hands.

Several hours later, Vladimir found Timothy sitting in a library chair. The light had already faded outside, and dinner was long past. In fact, most of the inhabitants of the city had already gone to sleep. Timothy sat with one leg slung over the arm of the chair and his back against the other; a large grey book lay open in his lap, and he was reading it intently. Vladimir walked softly up behind his friend and peered at the pages of the book, frowning at the strange characters he could not decipher.

"I didn't know that you could read the Old Tongue," Vladimir commented. The sudden break in silence didn't startle Timothy as he had expected it to.

"I don't," the cadet said without even looking up. He flipped a page and continued reading.

"That's weird," Vladimir said. "It's doesn't seem like that's much of a picture book."

"What do you mean?" Timothy asked and finally looked up at Vladimir. "Why would it be a picture book?"

"Well, if you can't read the Old Tongue, I don't see any other way you could get anything out of it," Vladimir said.

"You're crazy, it's not in the Old Tongue," Timothy said and turned back to the book. He froze, then turned back to Vladimir, a strange look in his eyes. "What happened to this book?"

"What do you mean?" Vladimir asked. "Nothing happened to it. It's still right there in your hands."

"That's not what I mean," Timothy said. "It used to be in plain language that I could read. Now it seems like it's written in the Old Tongue."

"It's good to see you're coming around," Vladimir said. "You had me worried there for a bit."

"What do you mean?" Timothy asked. "How could this book change like this?"

"It didn't change," Vladimir said. "When I came up, it was written in the Old Tongue. You must have fallen asleep and dreamt that you read it because there's no way you could have read this." Vladimir took the book and hung it in front of Timothy's face. Timothy took the book back and stared at it with a puzzled expression. Slowly he flipped through the pages, trying to decipher the strange characters.

"You fell asleep, Timothy," Vladimir said. "You dreamed you were reading the book, that's all."

"But I was actually reading it," Timothy argued. "It was written by Jothnial; I can even tell you what the title is. It's one word: *Molkekk*."

"And how can I tell if you're right?" Vladimir asked reasonably. "I surely can't read the title. It's in Old Tongue characters. Look, Timothy," Vladimir said, when Timothy continued to flip through the book's pages. "I know how realistic dreams can be sometimes, but all of the facts are against you this time."

"But why would I have taken it from the shelves in the first place if I couldn't read it?" Timothy wondered. "That doesn't make any sense at all."

"Maybe you picked it out because of its pictures, I don't know," Vladimir started.

"There aren't any pictures," Timothy interrupted, flipping the pages of the book in front of Vladimir's face. "You already brought my attention to that fact."

"Look, I don't know why you chose it, but the fact is, you did," Vladimir said. "And the fact remains that you can't read the book. The only logical explanation is that you fell asleep in the chair."

It took a few more minutes, but Vladimir finally convinced Timothy. He took the book from his friend and guided him out of the reading cove. With a glare at the book, Vladimir tossed it onto the small table beside the chair and followed Timothy out of the library.

The next morning was a jumble of rumors and gossip. The common thread in all the stories Timothy heard was that the army was expected to move out that morning. But when noon rolled around, and there had been no orders to do so, Timothy went to see Lemin. He could hear several voices coming through the door, so he knocked and waited for a muffled voice to tell him to come in. Senndra, Vladimir, and another cadet Timothy didn't personally know already occupied the space in front of Lemin's desk, and the elf behind the battered wood looked harried.

"Timothy," Lemin said as he entered the room. "I wonder how many others are going to join us before we're through with this. I suppose you're here about the rumors as well."

"I am," Timothy said. "So are they true? Are we going to mobilize soon?"

"I've already been to the Grand Admiral of the city to talk to him about the situation," Lemin said by way of an answer. "It seems that no matter which way you look at it, the meager forces currently occupying this city will have to be split in some way. We have to send reinforcements to the army fighting at the bottom of the county, but it has also been decided that we can't give up this opportunity to stage an assault on Vollexa Temp."

"And interestingly, while Tiberius used to be against the attack, now he is an adamant supporter of it," Senndra put in.

"Is that a reason to be against it, or what do you think that means?" Timothy asked.

"I supported the attack in the beginning, and I have not withdrawn my support yet," Lemin said. "Just because someone you may not particularly like decides to support a cause is no reason to abandon it."

"I suppose you're right," Timothy said. "So we have to somehow split the army into two and send them in different directions. Is the decision of how the split will occur causing the delay?"

"There still have to be some men at this city to protect it, so the army has to be split three ways," Lemin said. "But in answer to your question, no, that's not really the prroblem While the Grand Admiral of Belmoth thinks we need to attack Vollexa Temp, *our* Grand Admiral is of the opinion that we should send all our available men south to help defend the country. He thinks that we should secure our own land before worrying about going on the offensive."

"I would tend to agree with him," Vladimir said. "We can't really go gallivanting off on an attack mission when we have enemies occupying our territory. It's just not a strategically wise thing to do."

"But at the same time, the best defense is a good offense," said the cadet Timothy didn't know. "If we can destroy Vollexa Temp, the threat of Molkekk would be gone, once and for all. Also, there's the chance that when his army learns that we're attacking his city, they'll go back, thereby relieving the pressure on our country."

"That's only if they hear about the attack," Vladimir pointed out. "Ideally they'll never get news of the attack, and if they do, we will be long done with it. Besides, the chance of them abandoning their conquest to travel all of the way back to Vollexa Temp on a rumor is very slim."

"So after all the facts are on the table, what's your opinion on the situation?" Timothy asked Lemin. "I know you said that you still support the attack, but isn't it more important to keep the country safe? It seems, from what I've heard, that we'll need all the troops in the south that we can spare."

"That is what it seems like, but looks can be deceiving," Lemin countered. "This may just be a ploy of the enemy to get us to let down our guard in Belmoth so that they can come back from the north and take it. Maybe we should stay here; I just don't know."

"What about the elves?" Timothy asked suddenly. "A force of their soldiers is already with our army and the ogres at Far Point, but they have to have more soldiers than that. Maybe we can count on them to send more assistance."

"We might be able to," Lemin said, "but that's a small hope, given the past record of what humans have done to the elves. Granted, they've already assisted us, but that doesn't mean they'll consent to a full-fledged war."

"Well, there's only one way to find out, isn't there?" Vladimir commented. "We have to make a trip to their forest and see where they stand."

"That might actually be one of the best uses of our time," Lemin said. "If we can secure the help of the elves, we would have an advantage over the enemy because we would be able to flank them. Of course, enlisting their help will be harder than you think. We'll have to convince not one but four kings to help us."

"It may be harder than I think, but it's still worth a try," Vladimir persisted. "Their help may be our only hope for survival."

"I think you're right," Lemin said. "The only question is, given the disarray of the country, who has the power to form a treaty with them?"

"The ruling councils of Gatlon and Belvárd are missing; nobody has heard from them since the attack," Senndra said.

"Since the only ruling body left is that of Rampön, it seems logical to get their permission."

"That will take too long," Lemin objected. "I've had a small amount of experience with the council, and it seems they take forever to decide the smallest things, much less something as important as this. No, we need to have a single person who can agree to a treaty."

"A single person or several of them?" asked the cadet Timothy didn't know. "What if we got several of the highest ranking officers to sign the agreement? That'll probably be the best we can do, given the circumstances."

"You're right; I don't know why I didn't think of that," Lemin said, rising from his chair. "William," he said, addressing the cadet, "I am hereby appointing you as a messenger to go and see if the elfin kings will agree to a treaty. You are to escort those sympathetic to us back here so that we can meet and determine the details. While you're gone, I'll get approval from the highest ranking officers. Hopefully they'll see the importance of this, but even if all of them don't, I'll find some way to push it through."

"Yes sir," William said and saluted. He dashed out of the room, and the door closed with a bang.

"You realize the council won't be happy, right?" Timothy said.

"Oh yes, I realize that," Lemin said. "But right now, I'm just trying to save the country, and I don't really care who doesn't like it."

Seven

"General!"

Josiah jerked awake at the shout and sat up on the couch he had been napping on. He rubbed his eyes and turned to face the man who had woken him. The messenger was a soldier, now standing ramrod straight in front of his superior.

"At ease, soldier," Josiah said. "What news do you have?"

"The enemy is approaching, sir," the soldier said. "Scouts have reported the main body of their army to still be a day or two out, but smaller scouting forces have been seen only a few hours away."

Josiah stretched and stood as he thought through this new information. A week had passed since they had reached Castle Far Point, and already reinforcements were pouring in. Their numbers had already increased from twenty thousand to twenty-five thousand, and they were expected to increase to thirty thousand before the end of the day. Even so, many of these men were not soldiers but simply citizens who had answered the call of their countrymen. It was obvious that most of them had never held a sword before; in fact, many of them had arrived armed only with pitchforks and other improvised weaponry. They still had no news concerning any reinforcements by dragons, and their forces were looking rather thin compared to that of the enemy.

Josiah thanked the soldier and dismissed him. He stretched again to get all the kinks out of his body and then headed for Nathan's quarters. When he arrived, the elf had already been informed of the news and had a sand table set up with a rough likeness of the surrounding area and small markers to indicate soldiers. As Josiah entered, the elf looked up and greeted him.

"So, what about the wall?" Josiah asked as he leaned on the sand table and looked at the scene depicted there.

"The wall is obviously not finished, but it's in reasonably good shape," Nathan answered. "It has finally been extended along the full mile we're protecting and has been built fifteen feet high in most spots. It should be wide enough to withstand ram or catapult attacks, but we won't know until it's tested."

"Now that's something I hope never happens," Josiah muttered as he studied the table. "We should revisit the question of force size. Given our numbers, how long can we hold this position?"

"That all depends," Nathan said. "We have roughly twenty thousand men now, but even so, they're going to be spread pretty thinly if we are to cover the whole wall. The real trick is to figure out where they are most likely to attack, so that we can post the ogres there."

"There havn't been any reports of dragons or griffins accompanying the army, have there?" Josiah asked.

"Not as of yet," Nathan answered. "As far as we know, we're just going to have to deal with their massive ground force."

"And that'll be enough trouble in and of itself," a low gravelly voice said. Nathan and Josiah looked up to see that Levvy had joined them. "Even with all our preparation, we will still be badly disadvantaged. Only by the grace of Elohim will we be able to hold them off."

"If only the dragons would arrive," Josiah commented. "Then we would have an advantage they would find very difficult to counter."

"But we have no dragons, and there is no point in wishing for them," Levvy said. "If they come, that is all well and good, but until that happens we need to decide what to do with the men we have."

"Right," Nathan agreed. "Now, here's what I think. If we spread my soldiers down the wall so that there are archers along the whole length and set a concentration of ogres at the castle, where I think that they will most likely attack, our firepower will be properly dispersed. Then the humans can form squads and reinforce the other soldiers at various points along the wall, but also be ready to move at a moment's notice. That way they can move to give assistance wherever it is needed."

"We have some horses, so we could put together a cavalry unit," Josiah said. "They would be very useful in quickly giving help to various points along the wall, and if the enemy breaks through, they'll be invaluable."

"It looks about as good as anything we can do with the soldiers we have," Levvy rumbled. "We'll just have to fight like fury to make up for our deficiency of numbers."

"How are we doing on supplies?" Josiah asked. "How long can we last on the food we have?"

"We have a supply that should last us about month or so if we are careful," Nathan said. "I wouldn't worry about food, though. We can easily get more if we need to."

"What about arrows?" Josiah asked. "What about arms and armor?"

"We have enough arrows for now, and we're producing more even as we speak," Nathan answered. "We'll run out before this battle is over, but that's to be expected. As for arms and armor, we have exhausted our supply, so every new person who comes has to fight with what they bring."

"Well, that can't be helped," Josiah said. "I guess we've done just about everything that we can to prepare for this. Now it is in the hands of Elohim."

"What would you say our chances of survival are?" Levvy asked.

"Not good," Nathan said after a moment of silence. "But we'll fight like hellfire and make them remember us no matter the outcome."

"Today is a good day to die," Levvy said.

"Um, they actually won't be arriving until tomorrow or the day after," Josiah commented.

"Oh shut up, you know what I mean," Levvy said. "Now let's go make sure that our men are in good order. I may be prepared to die, but that doesn't mean I want to do so."

******

The enemy army stretched out across the plain, darkening the land for miles around, and all Josiah could think about was how the scouts had been wrong. It was only hours after his meeting with Nathan and Levvy, and the full army was already here. Oh well, today might not be such a bad day to die. In the sky the shapes of griffins could be seen circling the area, but thankfully no dragons had been spotted...yet.

The mere sight of the army facing them was enough to frighten some of the defenders into abandoning the line. The holes left were quickly filled, and the soldiers of Magessa stood resolute, daring Molkekk's army to attack. A flight of boulders hurtled overhead, and Josiah looked back to where a set of newly made trebuchets hid behind the castle. The engineers were already resetting them for another salvo, adjusting the weights in order to get more distance on their shots. Another swarm of rocks flew over the wall, most of them falling short, but the ones with the most distance smashed into the front lines of the enemy army.

The enemy was quick to assemble their own siege equipment, and soon they were pounding the recently constructed wall with boulders of all different sizes. The defenders hunkered down and took cover, seeking to wait the attack out. They knew projectiles for the catapults were not very abundant on the plain, and that the enemy would run out eventually. Boulders smashed into the wall, knocking pieces off and killing soldiers; nevertheless, the defenders refused to move, and eventually the rain of rocks lessened and ceased entirely.

A few of the braver men peered over the wall to see what the enemy was doing. Their siege equipment was quiet now, and their soldiers were forming up into a line. News traveled quickly down the defenders' line, and the soldiers resumed their watch from the wall. It took a full hour for the enemy army to line up, and when they did, they looked even more impressive than they had before. Instead of advancing, however, they stood in perfect order as a man on horseback detached himself from the ranks and rode toward the defenders' wall. He held a white flag in his left hand and continued riding until he was within shouting distance of the castle. Josiah looked down from the castle wall as the rider reined his steed to a halt and dismounted.

"The great Lord Molkekk sends you greetings," the man bellowed his message. "The great Lord Molkekk does not wish for anyone to be harmed without reason and so gives you the opportunity to surrender before we attack. If you surrender, you will be taken prisoner and treated well. If, however, you refuse this offer, you will be swept aside by his mighty army."

"Molkekk does not wish people to be needlessly killed?" Josiah asked. "Then what exactly happened to that entire area?" he said and gestured northward. "You pillaged, plundered, and killed with no restraint. That fact aside, we will never surrender to the enemy of Elohim! He has already delivered the army to the north into our hands, and He will do the same for you. So either you surrender to us or be gone so that the battle can start."

"You scorn the generous offer that the great Lord Molkekk has made to you?" the man said in surprise.

"You bet I do," Josiah shouted back. "In fact, he can take his offer and eat it for all I care! Now I suggest you go back to your own army before one of my men shoots you. I can only keep them in check for so long, you know."

"It is in your best interests to accept this offer," the man argued. "If you don't, you will be killed and swept aside as if you were nothing."

"Elohim will be our commander," Josiah retorted. "With Him as our leader, we cannot lose. Now this is your last warning: get back to your army, or you will be killed."

"Elohim?" the man snorted. "He does not exist."

"Drop him," Josiah told the man beside him. The archer placed an arrow on his bow string and drew it back to full draw. The messenger was still shouting, and the archer took little time to aim before letting fly. The arrow flashed through the air and buried itself in the messenger's throat. He fell like a sack of potatoes.

Silence settled over the field for some seconds as the impact of what had just happened sank in. The enemy army started to mobilize, and slowly it began to advance. The front was a mile long and several hundred lines deep. It was so intimidating that Josiah had a fleeting thought about running away. He shoved the thought out of his mind and diverted his attention from the enemy to his own men.

The trebuchets were firing again, dropping as many boulders into the enemy ranks as they could, but for every person that they killed, several hundred more remained. The enemy army started to march double-time, and soon they were within range of the archers. The defenders let fly, but the large shields and effective armor of the enemy prevented many of them from being hurt. They stopped for a moment, and their own bowmen returned a devastating rain of arrows, which slammed into the defenders and killed scores of them. Archers pitched off of the wall all along its length, and Josiah had to force himself not to think about the casualties. Instead he gave the order to fire again, and his men rained another storm of arrows down on the enemy - again with little effect.

"Conserve the arrows," Josiah ordered. "Wait until the soldiers get close enough that we can effectively shoot into the gaps of their armor."

So the defenders waited on the wall as the enemy army advanced. The details of the enemy soldiers came into focus as they drew nearer. The armor they wore was extremely well made metal, with hardly any vulnerable spots in it at all. The helmets they wore had disfigured designs on them in an attempt to frighten their enemies.

Josiah heard a growl to his left and turned to see the ogres setting their crossbows. He smiled grimly and peered over the wall at the advancing force which had, as of yet, been virtually unharmed by arrows. The ogres raised their bows to their shoulders. A resounding roar echoed across the castle, and the twanging of hundreds of ogre bows made Josiah's heartbeat quicken. Before his very eyes, the army that had seemed to be invulnerable to ranged attack was cut down by the deadly ogre arrows. Several hundred of the soldiers dropped to the ground, but the rest of them continued marching, undeterred by the trebuchet rocks and now the ogre arrows that whistled around them. The ogres reloaded and fired again and again as the enemy army approached. Everywhere their arrows struck, the dwarves sustained massive damage, but the effect was negligible compared to the whole army.

Josiah continued to wait, saving the arrows of his men. Using a spy glass, he was now able to see weak spots in the neck, armpits, and waist of the enemies' armor, but only a very experienced archer would be able to make a successful shot at this distance. The army inched closer until finally they were well within the range of the archers. Josiah sent the command to have his soldiers load and draw their bows. The soldiers did so, and Josiah inhaled to give the order to fire. Suddenly a blast of wind knocked Josiah off his feet, and half a dozen soldiers near him were flung off of the wall. Josiah recognized the victory scream of the griffin before he saw it climbing sharply into the air. He jumped into a crouching position and looked to see what the damage was. Upwards of thirty griffins climbed into the sky, each having cleared the wall of several men.

"Bows up!" Josiah shouted. He watched as his soldiers climbed to their feet and readied their weapons. They were obviously shaken, but more than that, they wanted to repay whoever had done this to them. The griffins circled overhead and swooped back in for another attack. This time, however, they did not come in on a horizontal path, which would have provided an easy target for the bowmen. Instead, the griffins dove vertically at archers, pulling up only at the last instant and throwing men in all directions.

Josiah rose to his feet again and glanced out at the approaching army who had cut the distance from them to the wall more than in half. The urgency of getting rid of the griffins hit Josiah, and he dove under the claws of one of them to reach the bow of a fallen archer. He grabbed the weapon and several arrows and rolled over onto his back, nocking one of the arrows and dropping the rest. He rolled up onto his knees and pulled the bow to full draw. Spotting a griffin making a long looping pattern in the sky, he started to follow it. A movement from the corner of his eye drew his attention, and he swung around. Only a few dozen feet away, a griffin was flying straight at him, claws extended. Acting purely on instinct, Josiah released the arrow and dove to the side, landing facedown on the wall and covering his head with his hands. Warm liquid splashed across the back of his hands and neck, and he raised his head. The griffin was splayed out on the ground, the fletching of Josiah's arrow visible from beneath the creature.

His eyes lingered on the scene for only a second. Grabbing an arrow and spinning to the left, he drew sights on another griffin. Smoothly, he pulled the string back and released, watching with satisfaction as the arrow sunk home into the griffin's chest. He stooped, grabbed another arrow, and brought it up to the string of his bow.

Without warning, pain tore into his shoulders, and he jerked forward, losing his bow and arrow in the process. His feet rose off of the wall, and he looked down to see it rapidly falling away. A glance up confirmed that it was a griffin that had grabbed him and was now carrying him up into the air. Josiah reached for his sword, but when he tried to move his arm, pain shot through it. He strained, pain coursing from both shoulders to the rest of his body, but he was still unable to reach the sword. He tried again, but his efforts were yet again rewarded only with agony. The pressure on his shoulders suddenly disappeared, and he found himself weightless. Instinct caused him to throw his hands up over his head and grab the first thing that he felt: the claw of the griffin that had just released him to plummet to his death.

The griffin was surprised and a little frightened at Josiah's reaction. Never before had a human grabbed onto its claw. It closed its claw, crushing the human's hand, and opened it again, but miraculously the man would not let go. The griffin tried again, but the human stubbornly kept his hold. Trying a new maneuver, the griffin pulled its wings in and dropped into a dive.

Pain flared from Josiah's left hand as the griffin crushed it in its claw again. His agony was replaced with horror as he felt himself become weightless again as the griffin dropped toward the earth. For several long seconds, the weightlessness persisted, and Josiah watched as the earth flew upward to meet him. Just when he thought there was no hope, he heard the snapping of wings opening above him and felt a jerk as they caught air. His grip on the griffin's claw held by the smallest margin, but his arm jerked upward, straining at the shoulder joint and jerking it out of its socket.

Josiah didn't feel the pain of his new injury over the agony of his others. With a grunt, he reached with his right hand and pulled his sword from its scabbard. He swung the weapon upward with an angry shout. The tip cut into the belly of the griffin but caused little real damage. Josiah shouted in frustration and was about to try again when he saw the wall rushing to meet him. He hit the stone with a sickening crunch, and his grip on the griffin was finally broken. He bounced backward off of the stone and fell the fifteen feet to the ground. The jolt of his contact with the earth snapped his head backwards into the packed soil. Stars flashed across his vision; then all was black.

******

Cirro saw Josiah get carried off by the griffin, but there was nothing he could do about it. He gripped a javelin in his hand and let it fly at one of the beasts approaching him. The heavy spear didn't hit the beast fully but only managed to cut through one of its wings. Cirro ducked as the griffin blasted over him and came to a crashing landing on the wall, knocking a mass of soldiers over the sides. It floundered to its feet and faced Cirro, strangling out a most annoying cawing sound as it did.

Cirro pulled his sword from his belt and slowly approached the beast. The most dangerous part of the creature, he knew, was the beak. Rumor was that a griffin could bite through an inch of steel, and though Cirro doubted the claim, he didn't want to test it. He spotted a bow and arrows, but they were too far away, and he very much doubted that the griffin would allow him to get off a shot.

The griffin's head shot toward Cirro who jumped backwards, tripping over a loose stone. He scrambled to his feet, swinging the sword in front of him to dissuade the griffin from making any more attacks. The beast lunged at him again, and this time Cirro was able to spin to the side and slash at its head. The wound was superficial and only served to enrage the griffin. It jumped forward, simultaneously lunging with its head, throwing Cirro onto his back directly under the beast. His sword arm slammed into the stone with enough force to jar his sword loose and send it tumbling off of the wall. Cirro and the griffin stared at each other. Malevolence shone from the beast's eyes as it drew its head back for one final thrust.

A thrust which never came; the griffin gave a scream of pain and twisted around. Cirro saw an ogre clinging to the back of the animal. When it stopped moving, the ogre planted his feet and jerked its wings, flipping it backward onto the wall. The huge foot descended on the animal's neck with a snapping sound. With a mighty heave, the ogre flung the body of the dead beast off the wall before turning to help Cirro to his feet.

Cirro nodded to the ogre in thanks. Then they turned to go in different directions, the ogre to fight the other griffins and Cirro to go find Josiah. He dashed down the wall as quickly as he could, jumping over dead bodies and other obstacles. He stooped down to grab a fallen sword as he ran and gripped it tightly in his right fist. He reached a rough set of stairs that had been built up to the wall and dashed down them two at a time, all the time searching for Josiah.

He spotted the griffin first. It was closing in on its prey, the human that was so much more difficult than any of the other ones. Cirro gritted his teeth and started to sprint toward the beast.

He began to yell as he approached, and the griffin looked up just in time to see him hurtling through the air toward its head.

Cirro hit the animal with all the force that he could muster. The blow knocked it backward though it did not actually harm it. The griffin swung its head to the side, flinging Cirro off onto the ground. Cirro's breath was driven out of him when he hit the dirt, and he lay on his back for several moments trying to draw air into his lungs.

Just as he was drawing in his first, ragged breath, he felt a beak clamp around his leg and lift him up into the air. Cirro had lost his sword and so reached into his boot for another weapon. The dagger he withdrew was no more than six inches in length and didn't even reach the griffin's body. Cirro slashed frantically, but it did nothing. The blood began to drain to his head, making him feel as though it might explode. Soon he would pass out.

******

A yell pulled Josiah from his sleep, though it did not get him to open his eyes. Something warm and sticky splashed onto him, and his mind struggled to figure out what it was. He forced his eyes open, seeing only fuzzy shapes at first, but slowly those shapes came into focus. He had a massive headache, and when he tried to sit up, his head pounded in pain. He spread his arms, and his hand came in contact with something round and hard. It felt like a staff, so Josiah pulled it toward himself and tried to use it to push himself up off of the ground. Pain stabbed through both shoulders and he was unable to use his left hand. Gathering all his willpower, Josiah used the staff and his right hand to lift himself from the earth and onto his feet.

He leaned heavily on the staff as he forced his eyes to make sense of the image that had again blurred. The first thing he saw clearly was a mass of feathers, and the memories of being carried by the griffin crashed back into his mind. The sense of danger jerked his mind to complete consciousness, and he saw the griffin holding Cirro in its beak at almost the same instant he

197

realized that the staff on which he was leaning was actually a spear.

Josiah tried to grip the spear with both hands, but pain flared from his left in protest. The fingers, he noticed, were twisted oddly, and he wondered how badly it had been damaged. Shoving the thought away, he grabbed the spear tightly in his right hand and stabbed it forward into the griffin's chest. His shoulder screamed in protest, and he was only able to make the spear penetrate six inches into the beast.

The griffin screamed in anger, dropping Cirro onto the ground and batted the spear away with a claw. The wound on its chest was deep though not serious enough to slow its attack. It shrieked again and lunged at Josiah who ducked out of the way and stabbed the spear through the griffin's wing. The griffin shrieked in pain and jerked its wing back, ripping the spear from Josiah's grip and flipping it over next to the wall. It screamed again, staggered back two steps, and turned to face its other attacker. Cirro clutched a bloody sword in his hand, and the griffin sported another cut. Distracted as it was, the griffin did not see Josiah dash around it to where his spear lay. He retrieved it and turned to face his adversary, but was cut down by the flying body of Cirro. The two men fell into a heap, and the griffin advanced on them with sounds of delight. The humans who had caused it so much pain were finally about to be dispatched.

Josiah groaned and rolled over, extracting the spear from underneath him. His grip was near the head, and he pushed the weapon back until its butt hit the wall. The griffin was on top of Cirro by now so Josiah yelled at it. The griffin looked up but did not move. Josiah let go of the spear to grab a rock and fling it at the animal. The rock bounced off of the griffin's head, and the creature went ballistic. It reached Josiah in one bound and reared its head back for a thrust. Josiah frantically reached for the spear and wrapped his fingers around it. With a jerk of his arm, he yanked the spearhead upward just as the griffin jabbed downward. The spearhead caught the griffin in the open mouth

198

and, braced against the wall as it was, smashed through the back of the creature's head.

Josiah didn't even notice the pain in his shoulders as he rolled sideways, away from the giant body as it crumpled to the ground. He lay there for several minutes, catching his breath and finally taking inventory of his body. Both of his shoulders, he noticed, had large puncture wounds in front and back from the claws of the griffin. His left shoulder was also out of joint, and his left hand was crushed. The rest of his body was covered with bruises and cuts from hitting the wall, but he would survive.

Slowly Josiah rose to his feet and staggered over to where Cirro was still lying on the ground. He was unconscious and required some extra encouragement to awaken, but Josiah was able to provide it. Josiah steadied Cirro as he got up, and together the two friends climbed the stairs to the top of the wall. The first thing that met Josiah's eyes was the mass of black soldiers marching toward the wall. The front line was a handful of yards away, and for the first time, Josiah realized what a pathetic barrier it was. The enemy army would sweep straight over it and carry the defenders along with them. Anyone who stood in their way would be crushed. There was no hope of fighting against them.

The second thing Josiah noticed was that the griffins were no longer attacking. They circled high above the city and watched the scene unfold beneath them, waiting for the battle to end so that they could feed on the dead. Determination filled Josiah, and he turned to Cirro.

"I think my left shoulder is out of joint," he told his friend. "Get it back in, will you?"

Cirro looked at the shoulder and placed his hands on it. He felt the bones underneath the skin and positioned his hands. In one deft motion, he pulled the bones back into alignment, causing a stab of pain to flare through Josiah's shoulder. Josiah could tell immediately by the lessening of his pain that his shoulder was back to normal. He looked around and saw a shield on the ground before him.

"Take that shield and strap it to my left arm," he told Cirro. "I can't grip with my hand, so you'll have to fasten it extra tight."

Cirro retrieved the shield and slid Josiah's left arm through the straps. He tightened them as much as possible, wiggling the shield to test his work. The piece held, and he stepped back.

"Thanks," Josiah said. "Now, let's give this dratted army what for."

"Yes sir," Cirro said and grinned for the first time in a long time. "I've been wanting to fight someone my own size. Those griffins are interesting to fight, but they're so large. Now these soldiers," he gestured to the army on the other side of the wall. "They shouldn't be so hard, I think."

"Now you're thinking optimistically," Josiah commented. "There's a million and one of them, but they're your own size. I think you could even find the good side of having to eat the food at the academy!"

The front line of the army reached the wall, and ladders they had previously held sideways were stood up and laid against the wall. One of them slammed down between Josiah and Cirro, and in seconds a climbing soldier's head popped into view. Cirro made a lazy sweep with his sword, sheering off the top of the ladder along with the soldier's head. The decapitated body toppled off of the ladder, but in seconds another soldier rose in its place. Cirro swung his sword again. The soldier leaned backward to escape the movement. It almost looked as if he might hang on, but then he lost his balance and toppled backwards.

A second ladder slammed up against the wall in front of Josiah, and he drew his sword arm back for a strike. A soldier came into view, holding his sword above his head in order to stop any downward strokes, and Josiah almost laughed to himself at the attempt at protection. He dispatched the soldier with a stab and turned to another ladder that had just crashed up against the wall. He swung the shield on his left arm into the face of the soldier there, throwing him down. A slash of his sword killed another soldier coming up the ladder on the right, and Josiah immediately turned back to the one on the left to kill a soldier there.

Sweat was already pouring off of him, and his wounds ached terribly, but he refused to quit. For several minutes he continued to switch back and forth between the ladders, knocking soldiers off in turns. By this time, reinforcements who had previously been scattered by the griffins were returning to their places on the wall, along with soldiers who had been stationed in other areas. The increase of defenders made the task of keeping the attackers off the wall much lighter, and the soldiers who had valiantly held them off were now able to have a rest.

Josiah stepped back and allowed two men to step in and take care of the ladders he had been in front of. He slid his sword into the scabbard and bent over to catch his breath, resting his palms on his knees. Cirro was similarly fatigued and stood next to Josiah, catching his breath as well.

"Come on, General," Cirro said after a minute. "Let's get you back to safety."

Josiah consented, and Cirro led him back to a position on the higher castle wall which was not currently being scaled. Nathan and Levvy were there along with a contingent of ogres and elves, including a squad of Megaeras. The two Generals were in an animated conversation, talking loudly and gesturing at the soldiers below them but stopped when they noticed Josiah approaching.

"Good night!" Nathan exclaimed. "You look terrible, man. What happened to you?"

"I got into a fight with a griffin," Josiah answered. He smiled slightly and added, "Not to be cliché, but you should see the other guy."

"You faced a griffin and came out of the encounter alive?" Levvy asked in surprise. "Fire and brimstone, you're tougher than most ogres!"

"Cirro helped," Josiah said and gestured to his body guard. "And really, it's only by the grace of Elohim that we came out of it alive."

"And severely hurt. Sir," Cirro addressed Nathan, "General Pondran has serious wounds in both shoulders as well as a crushed hand and several other, less serious wounds. I know he would never ask, but perhaps you could spare a healer?"

"Of course," Nathan said. He motioned to one of his guard, who approached. "I need you to see to General Pondran. Do whatever is necessary to heal him; I want him in good order as soon as possible."

"Yes sir," the elf answered with a salute. He took Josiah to the side and began to move his hands over the various parts of his body, mixing physical and magical means to ascertain the damage.

Satisfied that his commander was being cared for properly, Cirro turned his attention back to the battle. The soldiers on the wall clearly had the advantage and were easily holding their ground as they cut down the attackers who continued their attempts to scale the ladders. Men with pikes were also moving up and down the walls, shoving ladders off wherever they could. This was only a setback for the attackers, who would immediately raise the ladders again. Altogether, though, it looked as if the defenders might be able to hold off the attack.

Then the archers entered the fray.

Up to this point there had been no action from the enemy archers. Cirro presumed this was so that they wouldn't hit their own soldiers; however, in their inability to capture the wall by sheer numbers, they had thrown caution to the wind. Swarms of crossbow bolts and arrows rained down on the wall, striking and killing attackers and defenders indiscriminately. Bodies piled up on the wall and spilled off both sides, falling on the men who had managed to get under cover. Then as quickly as it had started, the assault was over, and the enemy swordsmen were making another rush on the wall. This time there was nobody on the wall to impede their advance, and they swept over the barrier in a mighty wave.

The defenders were taken completely by surprise at the sudden attack. They crouched under the protection of the wall, waiting out the archers' attack, and suddenly they were being engaged in hand-to-hand combat again. Despite their surprise, they fought well and were able to hold the line, though they were driven backward by the onslaught. The Generals were forced to abandon the castle to avoid being surrounded and directed the retreat of their men. Josiah, gripping his sword in his right hand and, still having a shield strapped to his left arm, was directing a staggered retreat pattern. As one group of soldiers retreated a few yards, another group would hold the line. After the first group had turned and was set, the second group would turn and retreat past the line, and the process would repeat itself. The army switched back and forth for almost a mile, and the enemy was still hot on their heels.

Molkekk's army had given very orderly chase up to this point, but frustrated as they were with their inability to catch their prey, they finally broke ranks and rushed forward with reckless abandon. Josiah immediately gave the signal, and his men stopped retreating and advanced as a line. All along the line, the other soldiers did the same thing, and the soldiers of Molkekk broke upon them as they hit. For several minutes all was chaos as the enemy army tried to reform while at the same time attacking.

The defenders kept up a slow advance the whole time and swept over thousands of the enemy.

And then the dragons arrived.

At first no one could tell whose side they were on, but they made their loyalty clear very quickly. The first thing they did was begin to harry Molkekk's soldiers and force them backward, giving the soldiers of Magessa a much-needed rest.

One of the dragons broke away from the flock and circled the defenders three times. Then he straightened his flight out and sailed in for a landing behind their lines. The dragon was massive even by dragon standards. It was fully one hundred and fifty feet long and had a wingspan to match. Its claws were larger than those of most dragons, and its teeth looked deadly even from a distance. Its scales were black with traces of white, a combination that Josiah was not aware existed. But the biggest surprise was the rider himself, for as Josiah watched, none other than Einor, king of Dublack, dismounted. Another dragon, this one of regular size, landed to the side of and slightly behind the first. Another elf jumped off this beast, jogged up to stand beside the king, and together they approached Josiah, Nathan, and Levvy.

"Josii!" Josiah called when he recognized the king's companion. "King Einor. I can't tell you how good it is to see you."

"Good to see you again, Josiah," Josii said. He grabbed Josiah's outstretched hand and pulled him into an embrace. He slapped the other man on the back before letting him go. Josiah staggered backward and coughed.

"Well, I *used* to think it was good to see you, but now I'm not so sure," he gasped.

"Enough of the pleasantries," Einor said. "General Nathan, what is the situation on the ground here? We saw some of it on the way in, but not enough to be able to adequately grasp the situation."

"It's not good, sir," Nathan answered. "Well, at least it wasn't before you got here. We used to be at the castle about a mile east of here, but they drove us from that position, and we have been retreating ever since. I don't know the extent of the casualties that we have sustained, but I do know they have been heavy."

"With the ogres and humans, how many soldiers do we have in all?"

"We had twenty thousand when the enemy first attacked, but I have no idea how many there are now," Nathan answered.

"Whatever the numbers are, we don't have anywhere near enough men to face Molkekk's army, even with your dragons," Josiah put in.

"Our army is tired, and we are barely holding on as it is now," Levvy added. "Given the condition this army is in, there's no way we could defend anything but a heavily fortified city."

"We need to continue to fall back," Nathan said. "Any contact with the enemy at this point could be fatal."

"Very well," Einor said after a moment of thought. "Our dragons will keep their army at bay while you put distance between yourselves and them. We will harry them if they try to follow you."

"Good plan, sir," Josiah said. "We'll commence a faster retreat immediately."

"Do it quickly," Einor said as he and Josii turned to go back to their dragons. "We won't be able to hold them off forever."

"Yes sir," Nathan said. The three Generals waited for the king to climb back onto his dragon and take off before they started to move. As the massive beast swept over them, they sprang into action, sending orders for their men to form marching ranks and begin the trek north.

As Josiah watched his men form up and move out, he couldn't put aside the feeling that their retreat was useless. Wouldn't they have had just as good of a chance of holding the enemy off at Far Point as they would anywhere else? With a shrug he put his misgivings aside and led the army up the Vänern River.

Eight

Senndra pulled her coat tighter and hugged herself for warmth. Even the warmth of Feddir's body was not enough to chase away the chill at this altitude. The dragons were so high that the features of the ground far below them looked like small children's toys. Trees were the size of toothpicks, rivers appeared as tiny rivulets, and mountains didn't seem high or impressive. The wispy clouds floated below the dragons as they winged their way north toward Vollexa Temp.

Senndra was glad that she had remembered her heavy riding apparel this time; it consisted of a bulky coat and pair of trousers worn over her armor which did a good job of locking in her body heat. However, even with these clothes, her face and hands were still cold, and she spent a great deal of time riding with her face down and her hands in her pockets. Luckily, the majority of the trip was behind them. They had been flying for an hour and a half and were expected to arrive in little more than another half hour.

The several hours after Senndra returned were fraught with the usual rumors accompanying news in an army. Nobody knew what was happening, but everyone had their own opinion.

The most common story was of a disagreement among the higher ranked officers as to what was to be done, a story which Senndra knew to be correct. Whatever the reason for the delay of the action, it was broken early that night when the infantry was informed they would be moving out immediately. The dragons would leave the next morning.

Senndra had met up with William later that night and had discovered that he had encountered an army of dragons with elfin riders over Belvárd. After the first few minutes of distrust, he learned that the elves were headed to relieve the army in the south of Rampön. His mission now moot, William had turned around and headed back to Belmoth. The news of the elf army ended all argument as to what was to be done, and the order to march was given.

And so, Senndra found herself astride her dragon only miles from the city that she had been brought up to fear, preparing to attack it. Already, if she looked hard enough, she could see the walls and defenses of Vollexa Temp far below her. An unnatural mist originated from the tower in the middle of the city and flowed out past the city walls before dissipating. The mist hid the whole city from view, preventing the dragon riders from ascertaining what they would be facing when they attacked.

A group of scouts had recently returned and reported that the infantry was only a few miles from the city gate. When the dragons arrived at the city, it would be time for the attack to commence. The plan was for the dragons to deposit their riders near the east wall of Vollexa Temp. This would relieve the beasts of their burdens as well as putting a force on the ground in the city. The hope was that such a threat would prompt the defenders to allow the attacking infantry, dressed as they were in enemy armor and uniforms, immediate access into the city to help deal with the attackers. They would only learn of their mistake after the infantry had gained a foothold in the city.

The thirty minutes it took to reach Vollexa Temp felt like hours. The dragon riders prepared for the drop by readying their weapons and rehearsing the plan in their minds to make sure everything would go correctly. They would be dropped right into a hotspot and would have to come out swinging in order to survive. Immediately after being set down, they would have to fight their way to a defendable position, and chances were that many of them would never make it.

Senndra tested her sword to ensure it had not been frozen into its sheath by the low temperatures. The blade stuck momentarily but was easily pulled free. Next, Senndra loosened the fasteners on her riding clothes so that she would be able to easily slip out of them when she hit the ground. Her preparations were barely complete when Feddir began to drop through the clouds. For a moment the dampness of the clouds soaked into her clothes, and then they were through. The city, now clearly visible, was still a mile away, but that distance would be covered in only a minute or two.

Senndra crouched low over Feddir's back as his speed increased. The air screamed past her ears and stung her eyes, but she forced herself to look ahead. The wall approached quickly, and in a moment they were over it. Feddir dropped to six feet above the ground and fanned his wings to slow his speed, just as they had practiced. Without giving herself time to think, she threw herself sideways off of Feddir and hit the ground, the landing jarring her whole body and knocking the breath out of her. She scrambled to her feet, shoved her bulky riding clothes off, and drew her sword. With adrenaline pumping through her body and giving her an energy boost, she sprinted to the city wall where the other dragon riders were already gathering.

When Senndra reached the wall, she had a chance to look around and take stock of the situation. The mist covering the city had disappeared when she had crossed over the city walls. It was just an illusion, as she had suspected, and now the city was clear. The sentries on the walls had finally spotted the invading force and were scurrying off to sound the alarm. In less than a minute a bell was pealing across the city, drawing soldiers from their beds.

By now all the dragon riders had dismounted and gathered, and they began to skirt the courtyard, looking for a way up onto the wall. They found what they were looking for in the form of a tower with a spiral staircase winding up it. They entered and ascended the steps, encountering some enemies about half way up. The brief battle which ensued left the opposing soldiers and one of the dragon riders dead. The invaders met another group of enemies at the top of the stairs, but these were again dispatched easily. Using the wall, the dragon riders reached another section of the city and descended into it. Houses covered this part of the city, and the dragon riders separated into squads of ten, moving through the buildings and clearing them of all inhabitants.

By this time bells were sending their alarms across the whole city, and the enemy troops were assembling. Molkekk's men began to search the entire city, looking for the invading force and were quickly attracted to the commotion in the residential district of the city. They formed ranks and began to move through the houses, searching for the invaders. The dragon riders were expecting such an attack and scrambled to get into their ranks. By the time the city defenders reached them, they were ready.

Molkekk's soldiers hit the invaders and immediately began to drive them backward. They pushed them back through the houses toward the wall. The skirmish was brutal and many soldiers from both sides fell. The dragon riders fought with the ferocity of tigers, but they could not compete with the numbers of the enemy. Thousands of troops continued to pour out of the enemy barracks, swelling the ranks of Molkekk's army. The attackers could no longer stand up to the defending force and began a full-fledged retreat, practically running back to the city wall.

When they reached the wall, they found their way blocked by more enemy soldiers. They smashed into these with all their strength. Not even the superior numbers of Molkekk's forces could keep the dragon riders off the wall; they hacked and stabbed their way up the stairs to their desired destination. This, however, opened them up to the fire of enemy archers. The first swarm of arrows killed three of their number and wounded a half dozen more. The next barrage did even more damage. The invasion was turning into an all-out slaughter.

Then the dragons intervened. A mass of flying, fire-breathing beasts dropped out of the clouds and dove toward the city. They slammed onto the ground and wall wherever the enemy soldiers were gathered, smashing men underfoot and killing others with their flames. The battle was turning in favor of the attackers.

******

Timothy was in one of the first ranks of soldiers, and so was afforded an unobstructed view of the gates of Vollexa Temp. They were every bit as impressive as he had imagined, and he shuddered at the very idea of trying to storm them. If such a tactic were tried, many soldiers would die, of this he was sure, so he found himself fervently willing their plan to work. The army came to a halt about a hundred yards from the massive gates and waited. No one came to challenge them; in fact, nothing happened at all. Timothy's hopes died, and he realized their scam had failed. They would have to assault the gate if they were to ever get into the city.

Suddenly the gates gave a groan as they began to swing slowly open, and the army gave a collective sigh of relief. Timothy let out a breath that he had been holding and motioned for his men to begin moving. He had been put in charge of a group of soldiers with magical abilities of varying skill levels; one of them was his friend Vladimir. He would lead them in an assault on Molkekk's tower; hopefully their combined power would be able to destroy it.

The army quickly mobilized and marched in through the gates of the city. A squad peeled off from the army and disappeared into the gatehouse. Moments later, they reappeared with blood on their swords. The army marched into the city and spread out. A commotion was coming from the east end, so they quickly made their way there.

Timothy separated his group from the rest of the army and led them toward the tower which occupied the center of the city. Only the tallest spires of the structure showed, but even they looked ominous. As the magicians drew nearer to the building, the walls hid it from sight. Timothy did not have trouble locating it, however; it was rank with the evil magic spreading from it like a blanket over the city. It was so blatant that even the weakest of magicians would have been able to sense it.

The group finally came to a gate separating the tower from the rest of the city. This entrance was nowhere as large as the main gate of the city and was barred with a score of locking spells. Many of these had deteriorated with time, but two had been created recently and were a force to be reckoned with. Timothy tried to break them by himself but was unable. The whole group of magicians prepared to apply their energy to the task, but Timothy felt uneasy. He couldn't decide what he was feeling, but one thing was sure, it wasn't good. Pushing the feeling aside, he gave the order to begin, and the whole group of magicians began to batter the gate. As they worked, Timothy's unease returned, this time stronger. He tried to push it away again, but it would not be denied. As the magicians continued, the feeling grew until Timothy was beginning to feel that he couldn't take it anymore. Then, in a moment of utter clarity, Timothy understood.

"Stop!" he shouted to his magicians. They froze and looked at him, but it was too late. Timothy cursed and threw his arms up in front of his face protectively. An explosion from one of the gate's spells ripped across the distance and flung the magicians backward. They landed on the ground several yards away while bits of stone and wood from the gate rained down around them. Timothy rolled sideways to avoid a boulder-sized piece of rock; off to his right Vladimir was spinning a protective web over himself and the surrounding magicians. The stones from the wall bounced off of the shield and fell harmlessly around its perimeter. When the dust finally began to clear, Timothy tried to survey the damage. He was quickly able to locate all the squad members. Everyone had been injured to some degree, but no one had been killed.

"Is everyone alright?" Timothy called out, more to reassure his companions than for his own edification. "Everyone regroup on me."

Slowly the magicians got up from where they had been thrown and staggered toward Timothy. They all looked awful, cuts and bruises covering their faces and any flesh unprotected by armor. Timothy guessed that he must look just as bad. Nevertheless, there appeared to be no broken bones or other serious injuries as Timothy had previously deduced, and the magicians cautiously stepped through the destroyed gate.

Molkekk's headquarters, which had been barely visible above the arch of the now-shattered gate, could now be seen in all its maleficent glory. It towered so high above the ground that it produced an odd sense of suffocation in Timothy. Or perhaps the feeling was caused by the sense of dark magic that seemed to boil out of the structure in a dark mist. The nearer he came to the tower, the darker the sky grew, and the more poignant his sense of foreboding became. Absently the magician wondered if the regular soldiers saw the same thing or if it was simply a bright, sunny day to them.

Though level at first, the path to the tower almost immediately began to rise, climbing the mound of earth and rock

213

the structure was set atop. The foundation was so high that even the first story windows of the building soared above the tallest buildings below, affording an unobstructed view of the entire city. As Timothy studied them, he had the distinct feeling that eyes watched him from every pane of glass. What it must be like to live in this city every day! The tallest spires of the tower loomed five or six stories above the base, and flashes of magic jumped and crackled between them. The lightning would sometimes descend to the dozens of lower turrets covering the structure's faces, but only for a few seconds before returning to its apex. A small door at the bottom of the tower granted access to the building, and it was to this entrance that the broad road led the magicians.

It took ten minutes to reach the tower, much longer than Timothy had expected. And then there was the problem of the door. The entrance was only two feet high and obviously not intended for any one of the seven races to use. Timothy chuckled to himself over the attempt to keep intruders out of the tower and cast a shrinking spell. In no time at all, the magicians were the appropriate size and entered the tower easily. A long stone hallway greeted them. They moved down it to a door at the far end. The door was massive, towering above them by at least four times their current height, so Timothy released his shrinking spell and they returned to their normal sizes.

"Wait a moment," Timothy said, stopping one of the group from opening the door. "This may be a bit overdue, but I think it's time to prepare for what we're about to encounter. If anyone has anything to say that might help us with what we are about face, I would like to hear it."

"I have some experience with the wizard Molkekk," Lemin spoke up and every eye turned to him. "There isn't a lot I can say that will prepare you for the specific spells or traps we might run into; indeed, I don't know if there is anyone who could give you such information. I will give a caution and an encouragement, though. First, remember that Molkekk is not some demi-god that we cannot stand up to. He is sufficiently powerful to change his shape at will, but he is still as mortal as we are. In fact, he is an elf by birth. He *can* be defeated, and we have more than enough skill and power to do it.

"To temper this, let me say that Molkekk is one of the most powerful magicians of this age. Not only is he powerful, he is clever. He is one of the most subtle magic users, magician or wizard, I have ever met. Don't be surprised if you stumble into his spells unawares. He also favors spells that attack the mental and emotional aspects of the targets. We will have to specifically guard our emotions and mental abilities."

"How do you know so much of Molkekk?" Timothy asked. "Have you fought him before?"

"That's a long story for a different time," Lemin answered. "Ask me when we get out of this infernal place, and I'll tell you."

"Very well," Timothy said. "Does anyone else have anything to say?"

"This squad was put together because of our respective strengths," an elf said. "Stick to what you do best and trust everyone else to do their job."

There were a few more suggestions, but none that Timothy hadn't heard before. When there was nothing left to say, the magicians assumed a tactical formation. Due to his affinity with wards, Vladimir was the first through the door. He moved quickly, scanning for traps while the others followed cautiously behind him. They entered a large foyer with a staircase climbing each wall. In addition, there were three doorways: one to the left, one to the right, and one straight ahead. Timothy drew his sword and moved to the middle of the room; his men followed suit, gathering around him. He carefully scanned each hallway and staircase before moving toward the stairs on the left. Slowly he approached and stepped onto the first step. His foot sank right through the plank, disappearing half way up his shin. Quickly he stepped back from the stairs and drilled them with a hard stare.

A noise in the hall they had just come from grabbed the attention of the group, and the magicians spun around to face the doorway. The sound of steps echoed through the door, and several of the magicians began to mutter under their breath. The footsteps stopped, and Timothy sensed a flow of magic. A figure stepped through the door, and half of the magicians released their spells.

Timothy recognized Lemin just in time and reigned in his own. Lemin raised a hand, and a thousand fireworks exploded in front of him. When the flashes had cleared, he glared at the magicians.

"Next time, would you please look before you attack?" he asked. "It's possible that your rearguard might move a bit more slowly than the vanguard." Without waiting for a response, he strode across the room to join the group. "What's your feeling?" he asked Timothy.

"Well, I thought these stairs were the best option, but I guess I was wrong," Timothy said. "They're just an illusion. When I stepped on them, my foot just went straight through."

"And the doors?" Lemin asked.

"Obvious fakes," an elf answered. "I can feel that from here."

"Well, let's go open the doors and make sure," Lemin said. His eyes never left the steps as he was talking. Carefully he placed a foot on the bottom step of the staircase. His leg went through the planks just as Timothy's had, and he looked down for a moment, studying it.

"It would appear as though it is an illusion," Lemin commented offhandedly. "On the other hand..." The magician closed his eyes and knelt down by the stairs, feeling along their surface. His arms and legs disappeared into the illusion followed by his whole body as he continued to move forward. He reappeared under the stairs, crawling across the floor on hands and knees, feeling every step he took. Finally he reached the far wall and simply disappeared through it. The magicians waited for several moments, but nothing happened. A few of them went over to the wall where Lemin had disappeared to examine it. They found nothing and returned as puzzled as ever.

"If you're looking for me, I'm up here."

The magicians looked up to see Lemin standing at the top of the stairs. The group was shocked, and no one spoke for a moment.

"How did you get up there?" Timothy finally shouted. "We saw you disappear through the wall down here, but how did you get up there?"

"I climbed the stairs," Lemin shouted. "Or rather, I crawled up them."

"But there are no stairs," one of the magicians interrupted. "They're just an illusion."

"The real illusion is that the stairs are an illusion," Lemin countered.

"What do you mean?" Timothy shouted. "We all saw you go straight through the stairs and disappear through the wall."

"That may be what you saw, but that isn't what happened," Lemin responded. "The illusion which seeks to make you think that the stairs are an illusion created the image of me crawling across the floor. I even felt like I was on the floor the whole time, but all the while, I was actually going up the stairs."

"How is that possible?" Timothy called as he stepped through the bottom step. "I sense no magic."

"Which doesn't make sense," Lemin said. "You should have at least felt the magic of the illusion if the stairs were truly fake. This is Molkekk's headquarters and his magic. Be prepared to encounter things that you have never encountered before. Keep walking forward. I can see you walking up the stairs."

Timothy stepped forward again, this time the illusion reached up to his knee. A few more steps and he was completely engulfed. Then he was through and walking straight toward the wall that Lemin had disappeared into. He closed his eyes and continued to walk, encouraged by Lemin. Three more steps and he knew that he was close to the wall, but he refused to open his eyes. Another two steps and his strides began to falter. Then he felt a hand grab his arm and pull him forward. He opened his eyes and found himself in another hall. He turned around and looked at the staircase that he had just ascended. Both sets of stairs, on the right and left walls of the foyer, followed the wall up to the same location. From here, there appeared to be nothing unusual about them.

"Now that wasn't so hard, was it?" Lemin commented. Timothy shrugged and glanced back at the hall behind them.

"I'll scout down the hall while you make sure the rest of them get up the stairs," Timothy said.

"Sounds like a good plan to me," Lemin said. He began talking to the magicians still at the bottom of the stairs while Timothy started down the hall. The walls glowed faintly, and Timothy was cautious as he advanced. It was a foregone conclusion that something unnatural was going on here, and he didn't want to be caught off guard again. There were niches in the wall, and he went to examine one of them. The only thing in it was an ordinary-looking piece of rock which Timothy picked up and studied. Using all his concentration he looked for spells of any sort: illusions, wards, booby traps. He found nothing and placed the rock back on the pedestal. Still something nagged him

218

about it and after only another two steps he turned around to examine it again.

He stopped dead in his tracks at the anomaly that presented itself. If he were to guess, he would have estimated that he had covered about half of the distance of the hall, but now Lemin and the top of the stairs looked to be more than twice that distance away. Something felt different, like he was less enclosed, and as he looked up, an oath escaped his lips. The ceiling had been high before, perhaps ten feet, but now it was twice that. He knew before he turned back to the niche with the rock that it would be larger than before. Sure enough, he had to stretch as high as he could to reach the rock he had examined earlier. He pulled it off of its shelf; it was larger than before though no heavier.

An inexperienced magician might have assumed everything had grown in size, but Timothy knew better. As soon as he had seen the increased height of the ceiling, he knew that he had shrunk. It was magic, a booby trap he hadn't anticipated, and he chided himself silently. He had been so focused on finding the spells that he had walked headlong into one of them. But that mistake was in the past; what he needed to do right now was apply his brains to the situation. He was smart enough to get out of this. All he had to do was think of the solution.

Lemin had mentioned that Molkekk specialized in spells that attacked emotionally and mentally, and Timothy could feel those effects right now. Fear and anger were inexplicably bubbling up in him, and if he allowed them to do so they would incapacitate him. This threat was relatively simple to combat since he had been warned of its coming.

On the other hand, the attack on his mental abilities had taken him by surprise. Twice he had not recognized a spell for what it was. This place was clouding his thinking. Now he had to come up with a way to beat this hall, but his mind kept jumping to other subjects. Maybe he was overthinking this. For all he knew, he could escape the way he had come. It seemed unlikely, but even if it failed, he would know more about the enchantment. Taking the rock from the pedestal, he jogged toward Lemin and the growing crowd of magicians at the top of the stairs. He covered the distance quickly, but just as he was half way there, the world seemed to explode around him. Now that he was paying attention, it was easy to see the hall growing, or rather him shrinking.

The sudden change in size caused him to stumble and drop the rock he had been carrying. He rolled onto his back and lay there motionless for a while, trying to focus his thoughts. He'd shrunk twice, meaning he was probably a quarter of his original size. He had a rock, but was unsure of why he'd held onto it. It's only unusual quality was its utter lack of any interesting characteristics. If only Senndra were here, she could solve the mystery. He shook his head. Why, out of everyone that he knew, had he thought of Senndra? It was because this rock reminded him of her. Now he was just being crazy; how could a rock remind him of a person? He was getting nowhere and knew it.

Slowly he sat up and rubbed his head. The other magicians were starting to enter the corridor from the end of the hall and he briefly thought about trying to warn them, but knew they wouldn't see him at this distance, especially with his decrease in size. Instead he took up a post in the middle of the hall and waited.

******

Senndra was so happy to see the infantry arrive that she could have kissed them all. Even with the aid of the dragons, they had been very hard-pressed to hold off the enemy soldiers. The appearance of the infantry changed all that. They attacked the rear of the enemy ranks, using the element of surprise to kill many of them before they realized what was happening.

Joining the ranks of the dragon riders, the combined forces mounted an assault on the enemy, pushing them back in a deadly onslaught. Steadily they had forced them to retreat toward the gate of the city, exacting such a heavy toll on their numbers that only two or three hundred escaped from Vollexa Temp. The dragons continued to chase the hapless soldiers, and the invaders of the city had lost sight of them some time ago. By now the soldiers of Magessa were putting into effect the plans which they had prepared for after the city had fallen. Guards and sentries were placed along the walls and at the gates. Half of the total number of dragons took two or three riders each and headed back to Belmoth to defend the city in case an attack was made against it. The soldiers that remained in Vollexa Temp cleared out the entire city, killing those who resisted and rounding up the others. They placed their prisoners in a section of the city separated from the rest in such a way that it would function effectively as a prison.

The soldiers finished rounding up their captives and placing guards on them, but even as they worked, they cast uneasy glances at the tower in the middle of the city: Molkekk's abode. A squad of magicians was supposed to have infiltrated it at the commencement of the attack, and though more than two hours had passed since that time, there was still no sign of them. The soldiers who were off duty began to gather on the walls around it, watching expectantly for something, anything to happen that would indicate that their men had been successful. The day marched on, the sun rose into the sky, sending scorching rays down, and still the tower stood tall like a black, skeletal talon in the middle of the city. The heat forced the soldiers to strip off their armor to keep from overheating, and though the temperatures dropped slightly as the sun sank again toward the horizon, they remained unusually high.

Senndra had retired to a shady spot under the wall in an effort to escape the heat. There was some relief in the wall's shadow, but even so she was very uncomfortable. She lay back, closed her eyes, and dozed fitfully for a while. When she awoke, the sun had already disappeared behind the tower occupying everyone's attention and was continuing its steady, downward march. It would be completely gone in less than an hour, she estimated.

The shadow that Senndra was in had attracted several dozen people, and more were still making their way toward it. Senndra recognized William and called to him, indicating the open ground around her. William, along with two other soldiers, one female and the other male, came toward Senndra. They still wore their armor, and the perspiration on their bodies was evidence of their discomfort.

"Hey, Senndra," William said. "Anything happened with the tower yet?"

"Nothing at all," Senndra replied with a sigh. "Two of the magicians that went in are my friends, and I'm beginning to worry about them."

"You know that Lemin went in with them, right?"

"He went in with them?" Senndra repeated. A worried look lingered on her face. "I didn't know that."

"Don't worry about him," William said with a chuckle. "If I had to place a bet on someone coming out completely unscathed, I'd put my money on him. He's the best magician I've ever seen."

"Just how many magicians have you seen, Will?" his male friend asked in a mocking voice.

"Oh, sorry for my rudeness," William said, ignoring the question. "Senndra, these are my friends Richard and Alyss. Richard and Alyss, this is Senndra."

"Nice to meet you," Senndra said as she climbed to her feet and extended her hand to Richard and then to Alyss. "So what have you guys been up to lately?"

"We were doing an independent exploration of the city," William explained. "We figured we might as well know our way around the place if we're going to be here for a while."

"And we stumbled across a library of sorts," Alyss interjected. "Actually it's just a large storage building that contains scrolls and books. Nothing's organized, but it's vastly interesting."

"I might want to see that sometime," Senndra said. "It sounds like an adventure all by itself. Albeit one that happens safely in the confines of a respectable building," she added in response to William's raised eyebrow. "I mean, come on. Not everything that's interesting has to involve running around and fighting."

William and Richard looked at each other for a moment. Then they turned back to Senndra.

"Yeah, they pretty much do," Richard said.

"Don't listen to them," Alyss told Senndra. "They're like that all the time. Everything has to be gung-ho and macho with them."

"Typical boys, I suppose," Senndra said with a wink at Alyss. "They're all immature to the core. Can't take anything seriously unless they're bashing away at it with a sword, at which point, it's very hard to take *them* seriously."

"Well, she's got us completely figured out, doesn't she, Richard?" William said to his friend. "Hey, Senndra, you must know a lot of guys to understand us so well."

"Yeah, almost no one realizes that we're actually very immature at heart," Richard stated with mock seriousness. "And that part about the sword…pure brilliance."

"Actually everyone knows young men are like that," William said in a low voice.

"They do?" Richard said, feigning surprise. "No, they don't. Are you serious?" William nodded his head with a sense of extreme gravity. "And here I was, thinking we had everyone fooled."

Senndra looked at Alyss, who rolled her eyes. Apparently these antics were not new to her. The boys exchanged a few more playful remarks as the girls waited for them to come around to a more pertinent topic. When it appeared that this wouldn't happen soon, Alyss intervened.

"Doesn't anyone here think it's odd that this entire operation," she waved her hand at the city around her, "was launched and carried out by kids? I mean, I know we're supposed to be 'young adults' and all, but isn't this sort of thing supposed to be done by older people? You know, people with actual experience?"

"Hey, if the real adults aren't willing to step up to the challenge, I guess us imitation ones will have to fill in for them," Richard joked. "Seriously though, I hear a lot of them are down south, holding off the might of Molkekk's army. They can't be everywhere at once, you know, so everyone has to play their part; that means us, too."

"I know all that," Alyss said. "I just was wondering what happened to the entire army of Rampön. Belmoth was being attacked long before the enemy was at the bottom of Rampön, yet we got almost no help. It seems to me that the numbers of our army should be much greater than what they are now."

"I know what you mean, but I don't have an answer for your question," William responded. "Fully mustered, the country should be able to field an army of at least half a million. I know that includes everyone who can fight, but at the moment we only have a fraction of that number. It's almost as if some people are living in a different world and don't even realize we're in danger. Let's pray they haven't gone over to Molkekk's side. After all, his arm can reach very far."

224

"That's a nice thought," Senndra commented. The group lapsed into silence for a few moments.

"I just had an interesting thought," Richard finally said. "You know how we have been brought up as children to hate and fear Molkekk? Well, who would've guessed we'd be sitting here in the evil city waiting for our own men to destroy Molkekk? I mean, it used to be taboo to even use his name, but now…" he trailed off.

"This is kind of weird, but you know what I find the most odd about this whole thing?" Senndra asked. "I always associated this place with evil and everything bad. I even thought it would be a disgusting, messy place, but it's neither of those. It's clean and well kept."

"I thought the same thing," Alyss admitted, "but I didn't say anything because I thought you guys might think I was strange."

"You *are* strange," Richard said. "Just because you found someone else who agrees with you doesn't mean that your ideas aren't weird."

******

"Timothy checked out this hall already," Lemin said, scanning for the younger magician. He was nowhere to be found. "I guess it must be safe if he didn't come back to warn us."

"Or he got eaten by a particularly nasty booby trap," another magician spoke up.

"That's a possibility, but I don't really want it to be true," Lemin said. "Let's pretend he made it through safely and just keep our defenses up."

"Sounds like a good plan to me," Vladimir spoke up. He wasn't convinced the hall was safe to traverse but didn't want to think about the possibility of Timothy being dead.

The magicians made their way warily down the hall. It was rather boring; the walls were painted a flat grey and only broken periodically by niches with pedestals in them. Lemin relinquished the point position to another magician and stopped to examine one of the stones. He scanned it every way he knew how and didn't find anything. Still, something tickled the back of his mind, like a star at night that you can only see out of the corner of your eye but which disappears when you look straight at it. Digging into all of his skill, Lemin scanned the rock again. There was the glimmer, and this time he knew what it was.

"Stop!" he shouted without ever taking his eyes off of the rock. The command was useless; they had already stopped and were staring at something in front of them.

"Lemin, I think you're going to want to see this," one of the magicians called.

Lemin pocketed the rock and looked up. The magicians had gathered around something that was holding their unwavering attention. He pushed through the crowd until he could see what they were looking at. A one and a half foot tall Timothy stood in the ring. A rock like the one Lemin had was beside him.

"You're small," Vladimir said.

"Nothing gets by you, does it?" Timothy said disgustedly.

"So you picked up one of the rocks," Lemin noted.

"Yes," Timothy agreed. "It reminded me of someone."

"Senndra?" Lemin asked. Timothy nodded "Well, it would, wouldn't it?" the elf muttered to himself.

"What was that?" Timothy asked.

"It doesn't matter," Lemin said with a wave of his hand.

"So you see that Timothy has been shrunk and the only thing you notice is a rock?" Vladimir interjected. "I don't get it."

"It's because I already know what happened to him," Lemin said. To Timothy, "Based on your size I'm assuming it's happened twice."

"That's right," Timothy said.

"What's happened twice?" someone asked.

"He shrunk," another magician answered. "Obviously, this is a half-way hall."

"And what, exactly, is a 'half-way hall'?" Timothy asked.

"It originated with a man who was renowned for his logical approach to everything," Lemin began. "This man was so convinced that logic was the supreme medium that if anything could be proven logically, he considered it to be true, even if experience discredited it. One day this man announced that it was useless to try and move around since it was impossible to get anywhere. His reasoning was this: to get from one point to another, it is first necessary to pass through the point halfway between the start and the destination; however, once this halfway point is reached, there is another between the person's current position and the endpoint and so on and so forth. Of course, experience discredits this argument because people get places they're traveling to all the time. However, a magician decided to use the idea as inspiration for a spell. The notion was to create a hall, enchanted in such a way that anyone who walks down it would never reach the end. Basically, the spell makes it so that once a person enters the hall, he will be shrunk to half size once he reaches the halfway point of the hall. It doesn't matter if he only takes ten steps into the hall and then turns around, once he is only five steps from the door that he just entered, he will shrink to half size. In this way, it is impossible to get anywhere in a hall such as this, and it is therefore impossible to escape."

"But wherever there's a spell, there is a way to counteract it," Timothy reasoned. "The only thing left for us to do is figure out how to do that with this particular one."

"And the only way to figure out how to counteract the spell is with logical thinking," Vladimir added. "Ironically, that's the exact thing that got us in this mess in the first place."

"If we're going to reason logically, then we need to know the facts," one of the magicians put in. "What do we know about the spell?"

"If you move halfway from your current position to either of the ends of the hall, you will shrink to half your size," Lemin said immediately.

"So what shrinks you and therefore prevents you from leaving the hall in essence is the simple action of moving," Timothy concluded. "But if you shrink by moving, doesn't it seem logical that by doing the opposite you could reverse the spell?"

"The opposite of moving is to not move, to be at rest," a magician said. "That, however, doesn't do anything for us except prevent the spell from shrinking us."

"What if being at rest isn't the opposite of moving?" Timothy asked suddenly. "It seems to me that moving would be an action, being at rest would be neutral, and the opposite of moving would still have yet to be mentioned."

"But then what would be the opposite of moving?" someone asked. "Perhaps by walking backwards you could reverse the spell?"

"The spell wouldn't care which direction you walk," Timothy said. "The hall simply gauges your progress and shrinks you at the appropriate time. No, the opposite of moving would have to be something else entirely."

"I think I might have something," one of the magicians, who was an orc, said. "If you walk forward, you have a speed, that is, you go a certain number of feet in a given minute. If you are not moving, you go zero feet per minute; therefore, the question is, is it possible to go negative feet per minute?"

"You might actually have something there," Lemin commented. "The question is, then, what is speed?" Timothy's eyes widened in understanding.

"Speed is relative, isn't it?" he asked. Lemin nodded.

"What do mean, it's relative?" a magician asked.

"I mean this," Timothy explained. "Let's say you're riding in a carriage at a speed of five miles in one hour. A man is standing by the side of the road, and a fly is in the carriage with you, flying forward at a speed of one mile per hour. To the man on the side of the road, you are traveling at five miles per hour and the fly is traveling at six; however, what is the speed of the man and the fly according to you who are in the carriage?"

"I see," Vladimir exclaimed. "The fly is traveling at only one mile per hour and the man outside the carriage is moving slower than you are. Since your frame of reference is the carriage, then it appears to you that you have a speed of zero feet per second and that the man outside actually has a speed of less than zero. In essence, he has negative speed, which is exactly what we need to attain to get out of this hall."

"Following that example, the only way to attain negative speed is if we remain stationary and the hall moves," Timothy said. "I don't know how the spell currently on the hall will react with any new magic, but if we can use magic of our own to make the hall move underneath us, we can safely move toward the end of the hall and actually reach it."

"I have a question," an elf said. "If moving makes us shrink, and not moving makes us stay the same, then having negative motion would presumably make us get larger?"

"It's possible," Timothy agreed.

"Then we still have a serious problem," the magician pointed out. "On the way to the end of the hall, or rather of the end of the hall to us, an infinite number of halfway points will reach us, each time doubling our size. That means we will continue to grow indefinitely."

"Then the only other thing for us to do would be to stay still," Vladimir said, "and there isn't a way out where we are."

"And there you may be incorrect," the magician said with a grin. "Sometimes the most complex problems have the simplest answers. All that we have to do is create an exit right where we are." He pointed at the floor beneath his feet.

"It can't hurt to try," Lemin agreed with a smile. He knelt down and rapped on the floor. The sound was not solid as would be expected of stone. It gave a hollow thud like that of a wooden floor.

"And it looks like our host has made the task easy on us," Lemin said as he stood. He motioned to the orc, who removed a battle axe from his back. Everyone cleared a circle around him as he raised the weapon above his head and swung it at the floor. The wood gave way, and the axe head sank deep before coming to a halt. The work was difficult, but the orc was clearly used to wielding his weapon for extended periods of time. In less than ten minutes, there was a good sized hole in the floor.

"So, this may not be a big deal for you, but what about me?" Timothy asked as he stared through the hole. Though the next floor was only approximately ten feet below, his size made it equivalent to a forty foot drop. "You'll be able to make it with no problem, but I'll be smashed at the bottom."

"That isn't necessarily true," Lemin contradicted. "If the spell only covers this hall, once you're through the floor you should return to your normal height and be able to land without injury."

"*Should* be able to?" Timothy asked incredulously. "That's doesn't sound too reassuring."

"I didn't say it wasn't a gamble," Lemin said, and with a grin he jumped into the hole.

Nine

Rita was safe back in Belmoth. Due to injuries she had sustained during the fighting, she had been ordered to remain behind when the majority of the soldiers left to assault Vollexa Temp. She had followed the orders, reluctantly by all outward appearances, but in reality she was quite happy with the arrangement. Some people, she told herself, were suited to battle and wars and all the fighting that accompanied it. Others, on the other hand, were not created to live such a life, and though Rita was willing to do her part, she conceded that she fit into the second category.

Therefore, it was with feelings of joy and relief that she watched the soldiers leave Belmoth and set out for the evil city. She retired to the library to read and relax, but found that the commotion of having an army in the city, commotion she dreadfully hated, had distracted her mind to areas she was loath for it to wander. And so it was that in the silence of the library, her thoughts began to stray from the words of the book in front of her eyes.

"Why?" was the first question to assault her. Of course, the most logical reason was that Molkekk was a power-hungry magician who sought to further his authority by conquest of arms. But then, what was she to make of what Senndra, Lemin, and many of the other soldiers said, that Elohim was in control of everything? If He was indeed so powerful, why had He allowed His grave enemy to invade the country of His people? Perhaps He was not as powerful as everyone seemed to think. Maybe He was just another magician with limited power and was therefore unable to protect His people. Then again, maybe He didn't even exist; maybe He was just a myth. That would explain everything, Rita decided. Or would it? The army in Belmoth had just driven off an invasion of half a million, a number of soldiers much larger than their own. By all rights, they should have been crushed without any delay. Instead they had miraculously done the impossible. Of course, the followers of Elohim were quick to claim this as His intercession in their daily lives. To them He had just saved the entire country from invasion.

But if Elohim was real, why did He not show himself more readily? Lemin claimed that His desire was to have a personal relationship with everyone, but if that were true, why had Rita never experienced Him? Her parents were devout followers, so she had attended the gatherings of His followers for as long as she could remember. Until four or five years ago she had even believed everything her parents had taught her. She had believed Elohim was the supreme ruler of the whole world. That He was all powerful and could do anything that He wanted. That He rewarded people for serving Him and punished them when they disobeyed Him. But if that were true, why did evil men so often prevail over good people? Did Elohim lack the power to do anything about it, or did He simply not care?

The most oppressive question, however, was "Where do I fit into all of this?" Rita tried to dismiss it with the simple answer that Elohim didn't exist, so she could not possibly fit into His plans. Every time she tried this approach, the teachings of her parents would return in force, dashing her argument to pieces. No matter how hard she tried, she simply could not deny the fact that

He did indeed exist, so she moved on to a different argument. If He was so powerful and important, what interest could He possibly have in her? He was so big, and she was so small, and He couldn't actually care enough about her to want a relationship with her. That was unimaginable at the very least. This argument silenced most of the questions tumbling through Rita's mind, and the ones that remained, she pushed away.

Realizing she was not going to find the relaxation she desired in the library, Rita left and headed for the city's practice field, making a slight detour to retrieve her bow and arrows. Once at the field, she headed for the archery range and placed her weapons down at the first station. The target before her was only twenty five yards away, and she was able to sink her entire quiver of arrows into the bull's eye. When she had exhausted her arrows, she walked to the target and retrieved them, carefully pulling each from its place in the cloth of the target. She returned to the shooting station, recovered her bow, and headed to a station further down. The target at this station was only fifty yards out and still not much of a challenge for Rita, who easily succeeded in placing all her arrows within the bull's eye again. The target of the next station was one hundred yards away, a distance more challenging to Rita's skill. All of her arrows still hit well within the target's edge, but this time only about half of them hit the bull's eye.

Rita retrieved her arrows and fired them twice more before gathering her equipment and heading back to her quarters. She returned her weapons to their place with her armor and settled onto her bed to rest after the exercise. Her tired muscles were grateful for the reprieve, but her brain had no wish to rest. Instead, it set off on a train of thought that Rita had never considered until the present moment. What if Elohim did care about her and actually wanted to have a relationship with her?

She was becoming more and more certain of this, but even if that were true it could never be, she realized with dismay. She had once believed in Him and served Him, but then she had turned away. No matter the love He might have for all people, He could never love someone who had turned her back on Him, could He? He wanted His people to live righteous lives, but she had sinned so much. Was it possible that He could forgive her and give her another chance?

No, she decided with despair. There was no way someone as righteous and perfect as Elohim could draw near to someone as sinful as she was.

The feelings that accompanied this revelation surprised her. Not long ago she had been arguing that Elohim did not exist, and now she felt despair and utter hopelessness at the realization that she could never be close to Him, could never follow Him again. Sadly her eyes closed, and a tear tumbled slowly down her cheek. What was the point of even living if she could not live to serve Elohim? She knew now that all of her arguments before had been an attempt to run from Elohim, a God whom she could never approach again, and by making them she had ensured she would never be able to go back to Him, the only one that made life worth living.

These dismal thoughts filled Rita's brain, causing tears to spill out of her closed eyes. She began to weep silently and then audibly. Soon her entire body was shaking as she poured out the sorrow she had not allowed anyone to see. Eventually her sobbing subsided, and she fell into a light sleep.

As she slept, a dream began to dance before her closed eyes. In the dream, Rita saw her friends locked in combat with Molkekk's troops. She was shocked to find herself among the ranks of the evil wizard's army, but her body followed these soldiers as if it had no will of its own. Fiercely the two armies fought, and many fell at the blades of Molkekk's hoard. The forces of Magessa dwindled until all that remained were a dozen soldiers. Suddenly a legion of dark storm clouds rose up in the east and swept down on the battle. As the clouds drew closer, Rita realized they were actually a host of angels clothed in armor and wielding swords. The armor shimmered, almost as if it was generating light of its own, and the army's swords were like shafts of pure light. At the head of the army was a man dressed entirely in golden armor of incredible workmanship. On his head was a helmet of gold, and a shield of gold was on his left arm. The device on the shield, a solitary dove, was a mystery to Rita. Doves were most often associated with peace, and yet the leader of this army had one painted on his shield.

Rita did not have time to puzzle over this anomaly because the legions of angels were suddenly upon the two armies. The soldiers of Magessa they passed over without harming, but they hit the army of Molkekk with a ferocity not often seen. Screams of pain and shouts of anger filled the field as their swords flashed time and again, dropping enemies with every swipe.

The angelic advance continued, unhindered by the numbers of Molkekk's army. Every second they came closer to Rita, and then they were upon her. She screamed and dropped to the ground, throwing her hands over her head in a vain attempt to protect herself. The inevitable stabs and slashes never came, and after a minute or two of lying prostrate on the ground, she raised her head to see what was happening. The first thing that she saw was two golden shoes and golden greaves above them. Her gaze continued upward to the belt with a massive two-handed sword hanging from it, then to the golden breastplate, and finally to the man's head. The man had removed his helmet to reveal a face that wrenched Rita's heart, for she instantly knew who it was, though she had never seen him before. His features could not be classified as any particular race, but appeared to be a combination of all of them. His hair was close cropped and sandy colored, and sweat dripped freely from it. But what captured Rita the most were the man's eyes. Love poured out of them and washed over Rita like cool water.

Rita climbed to her feet and reached for her sword. Everything within her screamed for her to stop, and she paused even as her hand was on the hilt of her weapon. She looked again at the man, then at the scene surrounding them. Molkekk's army had collapsed before the might of the angelic warriors, but even as she watched, a pit opened in the middle of the defeated army. The soldiers screamed as they fell into the hole, and moments later a swarm of beings, as black as night and as dense as a swarm of locusts, rose out of the hole.

These beings appeared at first sight to be more angels, but their appearance was actually quite different. The armor they wore bore not the device of the dove but instead the likeness of a hideous dragon. Their armor was so black that it even appeared to suck light into itself, and their weapons were of every kind. The angels quickly regrouped and prepared for the assault from this new threat. The two armies of beings hit each other with a mighty crash, and a fight like nothing Rita had ever seen commenced. Angels and demons, for that is what the second army was, rained from the sky like hail, and still the battle continued.

One member of the evil host detached himself from the rest and flew toward where Rita stood. As he approached, the being removed his helmet to reveal the most beautiful face Rita had ever seen. Light shone from his face, making his features look all the more beautiful, and Rita was shocked to stillness by the sight. The being landed beside her and dropped his helmet on the ground. He glared at the man in golden armor across from him and looked as if he would like to kill him.

The man in golden armor ignored this new person and kept his eyes focused on Rita. Ever so slowly his arms rose until they extended toward her, inviting her to come into his embrace.

"Rita," he said when he finally spoke. His voice was warm and inviting, and Rita found herself wanting to run straight into his arms, but something held her back. "I have been searching for you for a long time now," the man said.

"This man is your enemy," the shining being behind Rita said. His voice was powerful and full of concern. "Do not let him deceive you."

"Come to me, Rita," the man in golden armor said. "I love you and have been searching the whole earth to bring you back."

"Lies, all lies," the man behind Rita spoke. "He is trying to deceive you, so that you will follow him. He does not love you, or he would not ask you to come to him. Ask him; he knows that pain and suffering are what you will find there."

"Come to me, Rita. You are heavily burdened, but I will give you rest," the man in golden armor said.

"Rest? Ha! That is a lie, and you know as much," the man behind Rita accused the man in golden armor. He stepped past Rita and confronted the man directly. "All that awaits her on the path you have chosen for her is suffering. Tell her the truth. Oh yes, I remember now. You don't want to tell her the truth, or she would not follow you."

"So, you wish to sway the girl with your lying tongue and sweet-sounding words," the man in golden armor accused as he shifted his gaze to the shining man. His eyes flashed with an anger that startled Rita. "Your meddlesome ways are very trying, and I will deal with you soon. Mark my words, snake, your defeat is at hand." He turned his eyes back to Rita, and again she saw the love in them. "I am the Way; I am Truth; I am Life. There is only one way to eternal life, and it is through me. I love you, Rita, and if you will but accept, you can have that life."

"There are many ways to eternal life, and none of them are through you, you power-hungry liar!" the shining man shouted. For the first time since his arrival, Rita saw a trace of anger and darkness on his face, but it was quickly replaced again with a look of goodness. He shuffled to his position behind Rita and began to whisper in her ear. "This man is a fake and a fraud.

He has nothing to offer but misery, but I can offer you something greater. I can give you eternal life like he promised before. I can give you unlimited power; anything you want, I can give you."

"Rita, trust me," the man in front of her said. "You know deep in your heart that it is I who speaks the truth, not the man behind you. Come to me, and you will indeed find rest, for my yoke is easy and my burden is light."

"Listen to what he is saying," the man behind Rita said and uttered a curse. "He wants to lay a yoke upon your neck and force you to carry his burden. I want to do no such thing to you. He wants to enslave you, but I will set you free."

"Do not think that lying lips can give you true freedom," the man in front of Rita said. "Only the truth can set you free, and I am that truth."

"Listen to that babbler, spinning his lies like webs to draw unsuspecting people into them," the man behind Rita said. "You know you have already rejected him, now end this thing. Draw your sword and kill this bothersome nuisance."

Rita looked at the man in front of her, but he said nothing at all. He simply stood in front of her with his arms outstretched toward her, begging her to come to him.

"End this thing now!" the man behind Rita hissed. "Draw your sword and run him through. It is the only way you will be rid of him."

Slowly, almost against her own will, Rita began to draw her sword. Inch by inch it slid out of the sheath until she had pulled the full length of its blade free. Carefully she gripped the hilt in both hands and held the weapon in front of her. The man behind her continued to whisper in her ear, urging her to drive the blade into the man in front of her, but when she looked into his eyes, she found she could not. Tears sprang to her eyes and began to run down her face, blurring her vision.

239

"KILL HIM!" the man behind Rita shouted in her ear. The vehemence in his voice was obvious now.

Rita shook her head in despair and dropped the tip of the sword to the ground.

"There is only one way that you can be free of this liar," the man behind her went on in a more reasonable voice. "The holy scripture says that we must put evil far from us. We must kill it so that it cannot harm us. Do it, and be free of this evil."

Rita screamed in anguish and drove the sword forward with all her might, and in that moment everything became clear. The man in front of her sank to his knees, Rita's sword buried to the hilt in his waist between the edges of his breastplate and belt. His arms were still stretched out toward Rita, and his eyes still had the love that had always shone from them though now it was tainted with sadness. There was no surprise on the man's face, nor was there anger. He simply shook his head slowly once and then fell headlong in front of Rita.

A cackle of victory burst from behind Rita, and she turned to see the man who had once shone with light, changing. His face lost all its beauty and contorted into a hideous, leering mask. He gave one last howl of delight before jumping into the air and flying to where his army had finally gained the victory over the angelic host.

Tears flooded Rita's eyes again, and she sank to her knees in front of the man she had just killed. She bowed her head in shame and wept openly over the choice she had just made. She now saw that the man lying before her *was* everything he had said he was. The man behind her had been the liar and had tricked her into killing the only hope she could ever have. As the hopelessness settled over her, she crumpled to the ground and continued to cry.

Rita awoke to find herself crumpled on the floor, crying. She knew of the choice she had made; even if it was subconsciously, she had still chosen, and she would have to live with her decision. The flow of her tears increased as she thought about the man in golden armor, the only hope she used to have. She had turned her back on that man, and knew now that she could never go back.

Ten

Timothy watched Lemin prepare to drop through the hole in the floor. The ten foot plunge would be easy for *him* but more of a problem for Timothy. Well, Lemin had yet to lead the wrong way, Timothy thought as the elf gave a reassuring grin before disappearing. With a shrug, Timothy dropped through the hole; as he fell, he experienced the most unusual sensation. A stone floor smashed the air out of his lungs, and he rolled onto his back and gasped for air.

"You alright?" Vladimir asked. Timothy could see him through the hole in the ceiling above him.

"That depends," Timothy said. "Am I still small?"

"You look normal to me," Vladimir said and swung his legs through the hole. He dropped through and landed beside Timothy.

"Do you need a hand up?" Vladimir asked, extending his hand.

"Please," Timothy rasped.

Vladimir hauled Timothy to his feet and helped him to where Lemin was standing. Soon all the magicians had escaped from the half-way hall and congregated in the passage directly below it. This hall was not enchanted. It led into a small antechamber. The room contained only a few chairs and a small table, and they passed through quickly. The room beyond appeared more promising; it was large, at least thirty feet by thirty feet, and had a number of furnishings. Bookshelves covered the walls while desks littered the floor. Couches and chairs provided places to sit, and there were three chests at the far end of the room.

"We should spread out and see if there's anything useful in here," Timothy said.

"It seems unlikely, but it's worth a shot," Lemin said.

"Be watchful of booby traps," the orc said. "I don't like having to use my axe to cut us out of them."

A faint chuckle went up from the magicians as they spread out and began to examine the contents of the room.

Vladimir migrated immediately to the bookshelves and searched through the titles. He loved books more than almost anything in the world, but right now what he wanted to find was a secret passage that would get them out of here. The classic trigger was a false book that, when pulled, would reveal the passage. At random, he pulled several volumes from the shelves, but to no avail. He was about to begin searching the desks when he noticed the book in his hands. Though the size and shape of the book was not familiar, he recognized the title. The word *Molkekk* was scrawled across the cover in elaborate gold script. Vladimir thought unexpectedly of the book Timothy claimed to have discovered in Belmoth. If the older magician was to be believed, the two volumes bore the same name, but even so, they had more differences than similarities. While the volume from Belmoth had been large and grey, this one was rather thin, with a black leather binding. This book also gave no indication as to who had written it. Was it possible that two people had written two different books with the same name? Timothy was the only other person he knew of who had seen the other book, and Vladimir hoped he would have some insight. He spotted his friend a few shelves over and carried the book to him.

"Do you remember that book you dug up in the library at Belmoth?" Vladimir asked, extending the book in his hands.

"It was named after Molkekk," Timothy answered, taking the black book. "What's this have to do with...What is this?"

"I don't know," Vladimir admitted. "I found it on one of the shelves. Do you think it could be the same book you were reading in Belmoth?"

"It's too thin," Timothy said. He flipped through the pages. "Nothing is the same."

"Do you think it's just a coincidence?" Vladimir asked. "Maybe we should hold onto it. We could examine it more closely when we get out of here."

"An artifact from the dark tower itself?" Timothy asked. "It seems kind of risky. We should ask Lemin what he thinks."

"What I think about what?"

Timothy and Vladimir turned to find the older magician standing behind them.

"This book," Timothy said, extending the volume to Lemin. "Vladimir wants to take it with us, but I'm worried it may have some enchantments on it."

"As far as I can tell, the book is clean," Lemin said after a cursory scan. "This room, on the other hand, is not."

"What do you mean?" Timothy asked as he tucked the book into a pocket. "I don't feel anything."

"And neither did I, initially," Lemin said. "Even now it's hard for me to determine exactly what it is. I told you what
244

Molkekk's favorite spells are. At the moment, one of them is making it extremely difficult for me to focus. I can tell there is an enchantment of some sort, though what it is I don't know."

Timothy looked around the room and saw the rest of the magicians were intent on their search. Vaguely, he realized it made no sense for them to stay in here. Who had suggested that they search one stupid room in this infernal tower? The magic here was strong indeed. Not only was it making it difficult to focus, but it was distracting them from their main purpose.

"We're getting out of here right now," Timothy told Lemin. In a louder voice he called to the rest of the magicians, "Everyone gather up. It's time to move on."

A resounding crash echoed through the room. Both doors had slammed shut of their own accord. Timothy was about fed up with this place. He formed a spell and flung it at the nearest door. He expected the door to explode outward or, at the very least, for sparks to fly when the spell hit a ward. Instead, nothing happened. The thick oak door simply absorbed the magic.

"Trying to leave so soon?" a booming voice asked. It appeared to come from everywhere at once.

"That was the notion," Timothy snapped before he realized what was going on.

"That is so impolite," the voice said. Slowly, almost imperceptibly, the magicians' feet came off the ground, and they began to float upwards. "You just arrived. Welcome to my world. Come in; float around; stay awhile."

"Who are you?" someone asked.

"Molkekk, of course," the voice answered. "Who else would you expect to be speaking to you from the walls of this tower?"

"Well, for a second there I thought you were just a voice in my head," Timothy said. He felt Lemin grab his shoulders and rotate him until they were looking at each other. The half-elf pointed to his head then to his eyes. Timothy understood immediately; this was yet another illusion.

"Do the voices in your head often make your float?" the voice taunted.

"Only after I've had a significant amount of alcohol," Lemin said. He was distracting Molkekk, and Timothy took the cue. It took some snapping of his fingers and waving of his hands, but he finally got Vladimir's attention.

"Keep him busy," he mouthed. It took a few tries, but eventually Vladimir understood.

"I saw the way you escaped from my half-way hall," the voice was saying. "Very clever, I will admit, but you'll have to be much more clever than that to escape this room."

"And exactly what are we escaping from?" Vladimir blurted out.

"Normally I would let you figure that out by yourself, but I'll tell you to make the game more interesting," the voice said. "I call this my utter logic room. In here, logic is supreme; if you can prove something logically, then it is true. I have already proven that gravity does not exist, which is why you are all floating."

Vladimir continued to distract the voice with conversation, and Timothy hoped it would allow him to work unnoticed. To dismantle a spell required either a lot of brute force or an understanding of it, and Timothy was not confident that the group could compile enough raw power for the task. He would have to try to move outside of the illusion, to force himself to see through it, before he could destroy it.

It took all his energy and will power, but slowly his surroundings became translucent. He could see the magicians as they currently were, standing in a circle on the tower floor. There were no bookshelves, desks, or other furnishings; the room was completely empty. The spell itself was of a typical design, but Timothy would have to remain outside of its influence to dismantle it. One wrong thought or move...Suddenly, Timothy was floating again. He had slipped up and been taken in again by the illusion. The voice was still talking, so Timothy pumped his arms, trying to swim through the air. The going was slow, but eventually he reached Vladimir.

"Can you beat him?" Timothy asked.

"What do you mean?" Vladimir asked in confusion.

"Beat him logically," Timothy explained. "Can you beat him at his own game?"

"I might be able to," Vladimir said. "It'll be difficult since he's made all of the rules, but I can try."

"Beat him," Timothy said.

Vladimir rubbed his chin as he thought, trying to compile an argument. A smile crossed his lips, and he interrupted the voice.

"You said you proved that gravity doesn't exist. What about the bookshelves and desks? What about the chairs?"

"They are all bolted to the floor," the voice said.

"I don't buy it," one of the magicians said. "What about everything on the desks? Why isn't that stuff floating?"

"It is all fastened to the desks," the voice explained. "There were several among your number who attempted to move these items. Ask them, if you do not believe me."

"And what about the books?" the orc magician asked. "I took several of them off their shelves, so they clearly aren't attached. Why aren't they floating?"

"They are," the voice said. "Take a look for yourself."

Sure enough, on closer examination, the books were seen to be floating several inches off of the shelves they had been resting on.

"What about the ink in the inkwells?" the orc magician asked. "Why hasn't it floated out of them?"

It occurred so quickly that Vladimir was unsure of whether it actually happened, but for a split second, everything flickered.

"And here's a good question," Vladimir said. "Why did we float to the middle of the room? What stopped us here if there really is no gravity? Why are we not walking around on the roof?"

"You ask a lot of pesky questions," the voice said.

"And you're avoiding the issue," Vladimir responded. "If the ink doesn't float free of the inkwells, clearly gravity hasn't been disproved."

"But if gravity hasn't been disproved, we shouldn't be floating in the air," a magician pointed out.

"And yet, we are floating," Vladimir said. "So if by all rights we shouldn't be floating, but we are, that means this isn't real."

"But if it's not real, what could it possibly be?" Lemin asked. He was openly taunting Molkekk now.

"I believe we call that an illusion, in the magician's world," the orc magician said. "Though I think wizards might call it a failure."

In an instant, everyone was standing on the floor again.

"It's *all* an illusion," Timothy said. The room's furnishings disappeared, and the door at which Timothy had flung his spell earlier was nothing more than a smoldering hole.

"And that, ladies and gentlemen, is how you do that!" Vladimir said with a sarcastic bow.

The magicians didn't linger in the room. They left through the hole Timothy had created and began to wander the long, confusing halls of the tower. For hours they walked, never encountering enchantments or spells or anything, for that matter. Hall led to hall, all of which looked exactly the same.

"We've been here before," a magician said finally.

"What was your first clue?" another shot back irritably. "Was it the fact that we've been walking in circles for the past several hours?"

"No, I just have a head for directions," the first one said. "We were here about half an hour ago."

"And no doubt you wouldn't have brought it up unless you thought it would be helpful," Lemin said. "What exactly are you getting at?"

"There used to be a four-way intersection right here, but now it only turns right," the magician said.

"So what, another illusion?" Timothy asked.

"I don't think so," Lemin answered. "I haven't felt anything, and it's been hours. Molkekk may be able to hide spells, but not for this long."

"So, moving walls maybe?" the orc magician asked.

"It's possible," Lemin agreed. "Let's try this one right here."

Bringing his palms together and thrusting them outward, he cast a spell at the wall directly in front of the group. In a shower of stone fragments, it burst inward to reveal a hidden passage.

"Which way do we want to go?" Lemin asked the first magician who had spoken.

"Straight, I think," the magician answered.

Lemin stepped through the destroyed barrier and walked straight ahead. It was another twenty feet before he blasted through another wall. The hall here led straight to a door which Lemin approached cautiously.

Vladimir moved to the front of the group and raised a large ward. With one swift motion he threw open the door and moved in. Timothy was immediately behind, close enough to be protected by the ward, and scanned the room as they moved quickly to the other side. The rest of the magicians fanned out behind them, searching for traps. After several tense moments, the room was determined to be safe, and they gathered near a door on the far side. Vladimir was set to lead the charge again with Timothy on his heels when suddenly there was a hiss, and the air began to stir.

"He's piping air in!" one of the magician exclaimed. "It's sleeping..." He slumped sideways to the floor, followed quickly by the rest of the squad. Vladimir cast a ward over his mouth and nose while Timothy yanked him bodily through the door and slammed it with a resounding thud.

"Are you alright?" Vladimir asked, but Timothy could barely make out the words. He was feeling woozy and extremely tired. The spores were already in his lungs and beginning to work on him. If he didn't purge now, he would pass out. Gritting his teeth against the pain, Timothy cast a ward on himself, followed quickly by a fire spell. The magic started in his lungs, burning the spores there before sweeping up his throat and out his mouth and nose. Even with the ward, the cleansing was excruciatingly painful.

"Protect yourself," he rasped through parched lips. Vladimir expanded his ward to surround his whole body, and Timothy shot fire through the space around them, burning the spores that lingered there. In a matter of seconds, the air was clean.

"You can drop your shield now," Timothy said. "Are you alright?"

Vladimir nodded and slid down the wall to a sitting position. He regarded Timothy with a look of defeat.

"What are we doing?" he said. "We're just two kids. There's no way we can defeat Molkekk."

"That's just the spells talking," Timothy said. Already he could feel the hopelessness of the situation settling on him.

"I can tell the difference between spell-induced fear and the real thing," Vladimir argued. "Think about it. We've been stymied at every turn by this tower."

"Not so," Timothy interrupted, speaking to convince himself as well as his friend. "We've come this far, and we will continue forward."

"*We* made it this far, but our friends have all fallen prey to a trap," Vladimir said. "If it were Lemin and someone else more experienced than us, they might have a chance, but we're more apprentices than magicians."

"You're selling yourself short, Vladimir," Timothy said. "We may be young, but we're more than apprentices, or they wouldn't have allowed us on this mission. And I certainly wouldn't have been put in charge of it."

"Why were you put in charge?" Vladimir asked, his panic suddenly pushed to the background. His naturally curious nature couldn't ignore the obvious breach in logic. "Why take one of the two most inexperienced magicians and put him in charge of any operation, much less this one?"

"I don't know," Timothy answered. "Lemin was the one who recruited us for this mission and put me in charge. Either he trusts me a lot more than I trust myself, or he knows something I don't. He believes in us much more than I would, but he's the one with all the experience. Maybe we should trust him on this."

251

"But we're just…us," Vladimir said. "Lemin may think we're strong, but I don't see it."

"Maybe that's the point," Timothy said. "Elohim said that in our weakness He is made strong, that He uses the weak to confound the strong. We'll find a way to do this; I'm confident of it."

"If you say so," Vladimir said.

"Not just because I say so," Timothy said. "You need to believe that it's true."

"I'll try," Vladimir said. "Elohim hasn't let us down yet."

"You're right," Timothy agreed. "Now take my hand, and let's finish this thing."

Vladimir grabbed his friend's outstretched hand and allowed himself to be hoisted up.

"Well, there's a closed door behind us, so I guess the only direction is forward," Timothy said.

"Let's do it," Vladimir agreed, and together the two friends journeyed further into the bowels of Molkekk's tower.

******

Timothy and Vladimir stood just outside the doorway before them, staring into the room beyond. Time was deceptively slow in the tower, and it seemed as if they had been here for ages. The fatigue showed on their faces and in the way they held themselves. They clearly dreaded entering the next room which almost certainly contained another trap like the others they had already defeated.

"We're not going to make it through this next one," Vladimir said matter-of-factly. It wasn't a depressing statement or one devoid of hope, but simply a statement of fact.

"All we have to do is outlast him," Timothy said. "We can't go on forever, but neither can he. We just have to have more stamina."

"He'll kill us before he tires out," Vladimir countered. "We'll never get the chance to escape."

"He might kill me, but not you," Timothy said.

"What makes you say that?" Vladimir asked.

"Just call it a hunch," Timothy answered. He turned to his friend and saw the look of confusion on his face. "You seriously haven't noticed?"

Vladimir shook his head, so Timothy gestured to his chest and arms. Scratches and gashes covered his armor, some of which had even penetrated deep enough to injure him. Vladimir, on the other hand, had no injuries to speak of.

"What are you getting at?" Vladimir asked. He knew there was probably an important message behind Timothy's observation, but he was too mentally drained to determine what it was.

"Molkekk apparently has no qualms about injuring or killing me," Timothy said. "Personally, I think I deserve more consideration than that, but apparently not. On the other hand, he hasn't raised a finger against *you*. He wants you alive for some reason, though what it might be I have no idea."

"If you're implying what I think you are," Vladimir began, but Timothy cut him off.

"I'm not implying anything. I know you're not with him, I'm simply pointing out the facts. It appears as though he doesn't want to kill you, which will give you the upper hand."

"Why are you telling me this now?" Vladimir asked.

"Because I sense that one way or the other, this is going to end very soon," Timothy answered.

"You think this will be the last trap?" Vladimir asked.

"I didn't say that, but I think we're nearing the end," Timothy said.

"Well, then, let's not keep Molkekk waiting," Vladimir said, appearing to get his second wind. "What do you think it's going to be like, meeting such a legendary wizard face to face?"

"We'll find out when we get there," Timothy said. "Let's take this one step at a time."

"Fair enough," Vladimir said. He raised a ward and stepped through the door, ready for anything.

Timothy followed immediately on Vladimir's heels, but as soon as he broke the plane of the room, the magician vanished from sight. In fact, everything seemed to disappear, and Timothy found himself staring into nothing. Then again, he would have expected "nothing" to be pitch black, so perhaps he was staring at everything.

White light so vibrant it almost blinded him surrounded every side. There were no floor, no walls, no ceiling, no texture, just white. He tried to walk, then to swim in every direction, but had the distinct feeling that nothing was happening. Then again, with nothing but the white to get his bearings by, he could have been moving at a hundred miles an hour, and he wouldn't know.

"So, magician, you're here at last, caught in my trap."

The voice was disembodied and seemed to come from everywhere. Timothy knew it belonged to Molkekk and said nothing, hoping the wizard would leave him alone.

"You're a traitor, you know that?" Molkekk asked

"I'm just doing my job," Timothy shot back.

"Are you now?" Molkekk taunted.

"I go where they go," Timothy answered. "I didn't choose this place. If it were up to me, I wouldn't have come within a million miles of here."

"And yet, you don't regret being here," Molkekk said. "You relish the idea of what you might do."

"Any chance I might possibly have to wipe you off the face of the earth is a pleasure," Timothy said.

"Now, now, Timothy," Molkekk chided. "Why would you say that to me? I may lose my patience and destroy you."

"Why would you do that?" Timothy asked. "You already own me. I obey you; what more could you possibly want?"

"Your allegiance," Molkekk answered. "Give up these dreams of Elohim rescuing you, helping you out of this. He's a joke. He couldn't even rescue a boy's soul from being sold to the devil. How is he going to rescue you?"

"A boy?" Timothy said, perplexed.

"My little brother," Molkekk all but bellowed.

"Your brother was sold to the devil?" Timothy said. "That sounds like something you would do. You sold him out, didn't you?"

"Of course I did," Molkekk answered. "My brother trusted in Elohim, but he, the supposed all-mighty god, abandoned him just like he has abandoned you to me. There will be no help for you."

"You already own me," Timothy said. "Don't ask me to swear fealty when you know it'll be a lie."

"Very well, then," Molkekk said in a much more subdued voice. "But remember, we had a deal. You protect them, and I deliver on my promise. There is no more to the deal. Simply obeying in this will do nothing for you when Elohim is defeated. And know this: he will be defeated."

"And you remember that it's *your* city that's occupied and it's *your* tower which is infiltrated by the agents of Magessa," Timothy said. "Your time is almost up whether you want to admit it or not."

"You are welcome to your own delusions, of course," Molkekk said. "All you need to do is protect them. That's your end of the deal."

"Protect Lemin and Vladimir, I got it," Timothy said. "You don't have to worry about me. I managed to keep them alive when your whole stupid dwarf army tried to annihilate us. I think I can handle whatever you've got in store this time."

He turned his back, though it was a futile gesture since Molkekk's voice came from all directions.

"One more thing, Timothy," the voice said. "If I die, the deal is off."

Timothy felt a sudden flood of anger boil up inside of him. The deal was already off, he had discovered as much, though Molkekk didn't know that he knew. And if the deal was off, what was still tying him to the wizard? There was no reason to obey him, and Timothy had the sudden urge to disobey no matter the cost. What the wizard's plans were, Timothy had no idea, but they involved Lemin and Vladimir. It was too bad since both were good magicians, loyal to Magessa and Elohim. But Molkekk wanted them alive, so they would have to die. He would do it himself, Timothy decided, and he'd do it in front of the wizard as one last act of defiance.

The white began to fade, and Timothy was suddenly aware of hard ground pressing into his back, shoulder, and the side of his face. Someone was shaking him awake, and he could just barely make out the voice.

"Timothy, wake up," Vladimir was saying.

Timothy cracked his eyelids enough to see the younger magician. The moment he saw Vladimir's face, a sudden urge to be rid of him and break the pact with Molkekk permeated his being, but he pulled it back in check. Molkekk would have to see him die for this to work.

"I'm awake already," Timothy growled. "You can stop thrashing me." He slowly got to his feet, groaning at how stiff he was. "How long was I out?"

"A few minutes," Vladimir answered. "I was worried for a bit, but now you're back and we've got bigger problems."

"Such as?" Timothy sat up and rubbed the back of his neck. As he looked around, he finally understood what Vladimir was talking about. They were back in the room they had left hours ago, the one they had left the rest of the magicians in. Though the air appeared to be safe to breath once more, there was no movement from the others.

"Dead?" he asked.

"No," Vladimir answered. "They're alive but unconscious. I can't get them to come around, no matter what I do."

"Right," Timothy said after a long moment. He rose to his feet and stretched. "Let's see what we can do about this."

It took him less than thirty seconds to come to a conclusion.

"There's a basic stasis spell covering all of them," he told Vladimir.

"I know that," Vladimir said. "I just haven't been able to pull them out of it, which is weird. Stasis spells are usually easy to break."

"That's true, they usually are," Timothy agreed; which meant something else was going on here. He cast a look around the room, trying to pierce the veil of magic surrounding them.

"What is it?" Vladimir asked.

"I don't know," Timothy answered. "You work on taking down the spell, and I'll protect you in case anything goes wrong."

"Wrong?" Vladimir asked. "Like how?"

"We're in Molkekk's tower," Timothy answered. "You name it and it could go wrong."

"Good point," Vladimir said. After a moment of preparation, he began attacking the stasis spell while Timothy scanned the room again, searching for any signs of danger, either physical or magical. As he did so, he began to form a ward around his left arm, carefully taking his time with it. He didn't have the affinity for shields that Vladimir had and it certainly showed in the time it took for him to create them. For almost a minute, nothing changed. The presence of the stasis spell was as overbearing as ever, and Timothy's ward grew stronger, but aside from this there was no indication of any magic. Almost imperceptibly, the situation changed. There was a variation, a flutter, in the stasis spell; Vladimir was defeating it.

It happened so quickly that Timothy almost didn't see where they had originated from, but in an instant two spells shot across the room straight toward Vladimir. Timothy barely had enough time to step forward, deflecting the first spell to the left and catching the second full on his ward. The shield was overwhelmed and blinked out of existence as the spell detonated, spinning Timothy around and slamming him into the ground.

"You need to break the spell, Vladimir!" Timothy shouted over the ringing in his ears from the spell's explosion.

"I'm working on it," Vladimir shouted back.

"Work on it faster!" Timothy said as he rose to his feet. He sent two fireballs, a concussion spell, and a lightning burst toward the spot where the spells had come from.

"This isn't exactly an easy process," Vladimir said. His eyes were closed now as he concentrated on the invisible magic.

"And getting blasted by magic *is* easy?" Timothy shot back. "Just hurry up before I get turned into a pile of ash!"

Timothy intercepted the next spell with one of his own, creating a shower of sparks that burned him as they landed. Dancing sideways around the room, he drew the magic attacks away from Vladimir, giving the younger magician some breathing space as he worked on the stasis spell. Why was it taking so long? How could the thing take so long to break?

"Got it!" Vladimir shouted, almost as soon as Timothy had the thoughts. A ward erected instantaneously in front of him, and he looked right to see Vladimir standing at his side, repelling the now constant attacks coming from the other side of the room.

"Let him have it," Vladimir said in a strained voice as he maintained the shield.

With a nod, Timothy gathered himself and let loose the most stunning barrage of magical power he had ever produced. Non-stop spells of every destructive type flew from his fingers, pelting the other side of the room. Sometimes they disappeared into thin air, evidence that they had contacted the wizard concealed by the illusion spell. Other times they smashed into the stone walls, sending chips of masonry flying in all directions.

Timothy's attack was aided by the other magicians as they shook off the clinging remnants of the stasis spell. The trickle of magic added to the already existent deluge was so small that it was some time before Timothy noticed the effect. While his own attacks had simply held the wizard at bay and prevented him from retaliating, the full might of the magician squad swung the tide of the battle noticeably. A large number of attacks were hitting the target, the largest of which caused noticeable disruptions in the illusion spell hiding the wizard. Through the cracks and breaks, the figure of the wizard could be seen, the shimmering of a ward sometimes around him, sometimes absent.

A particularly large conglomeration of spells hit the wizard in a deafening explosion which shook the tower and rained dust and debris from the ceiling into the room. As the dust gradually cleared, the figure of the wizard appeared from the haze. Clearly his invisibility spell had been broken. Slowly his features came into view, and though many in the room recognized him, none dared to speak his name.

"Molkekk."

The solitary word came from behind Timothy. He turned to see Lemin rising to his feet; the elf had eyes only for the wizard.

"Lemin," Molkekk responded. Though he was across the room, his words could be heard clearly. "It's been a long time, old friend."

"Yes, it has," Lemin said. "Last time I met you, you could still move outside of your tower."

"Things have changed," Molkekk agreed. "Speaking of which, how is your friend Jothnial doing? I still have a score to settle with him."

"He's dead," Lemin answered. "You can settle your score with me."

"Well, I would have preferred to kill him, but a stand-in *is* the next best thing," Molkekk said. "Come then, let's fight this out."

"Now you don't think I'm that stupid, do you?" Lemin asked. "I've brought an army with me, and you think I'm going to fight you one on one?"

"I had hoped," Molkekk answered. "I think you owe me at least that much."

"I owe you nothing," Lemin said simply. "Magicians, on me."

"You may owe me nothing, but I owe you," Molkekk said with a laugh. He raised his hands, extending two tendrils of magic. One wrapped around Lemin while the other latched onto Vladimir. Before anyone could react, the two magicians were sliding across the floor toward Molkekk.

Timothy was the first to react. He sprinted after his friends, eying the large opaque shield Molkekk was creating around himself. In a moment, his prey would cross the boundary and the shield would shut, effectively cutting them off from the rest of the magicians' assistance as well as their line of sight. Timothy gathered magic into a spell and flung it behind him at the ground near his feet. The explosion launched him forward through the shield just before it closed. He landed on his back, sliding a short distance. He drew his sword and jumped to his feet, blade outstretched and another spell crackling at the fingers of his left hand.

"You rat," Molkekk said. "What do I have to do to get rid of you?"

"I'm just protecting them," Timothy said.

"Timothy, stand down," Lemin said.

"But Lemin...," Vladimir began.

"You are to stand down as well," Lemin cut him off. "Molkekk wants a one-on-one battle, and he will get one."

"What about that army you were talking about?" Timothy argued.

"Three hardly constitutes an army," Lemin answered.

"I won't let you fight alone," Vladimir said resolutely.

"Vladimir, I said to stand down!" Lemin shouted.

In response, Vladimir raised his sword and rushed toward Molkekk. The movement was so unexpected of the young magician that Lemin was fully two steps behind him in his mad charge toward the wizard. With a laugh, Molkekk blasted two spells toward Vladimir, one head-on and one which approached him from the side. Vladimir's ward took the head-on spell, but the second hit him full force. There was no explosion, no fireworks of magic, no dramatic flinging of his body across the tower. He simply fell like a sack of potatoes, tripping Lemin who was a half-step behind him. The elf flew forward, belly-flopping onto the floor as his head slapped down against it with a crack. He was out cold before his body ever came to a halt.

"So it's just you and me, magician," Molkekk said. "What's your plan, boy?"

"I thought it was about time I defied you," Timothy said in an offhanded manner. "It's time to break ties, if you know what I mean."

"So you're going to try and kill me?" Molkekk asked calmly. "That nullifies our deal. You know that."

"Our deal is broken already," Timothy retorted. "I checked after we invaded the city. There's nothing here except for your armies and pits full of their victims. You never planned on delivering on your end of the bargain. I can't believe I ever trusted you."

"Think about it, Timothy," Molkekk said. "Would I keep anything of worth here, so close to Magessa? What you're looking for isn't here for its own safe keeping."

"You're lying," Timothy said. "You would keep it here because you play your cards close to the chest. Only this time, I've seen what you hold and it's nothing. Nothing to keep me from doing what I'm about to do."

With a conscious effort, Timothy began to scratch magic together into a spell he was not predisposed to create. Though he had studied its shape, size, positioning, and every other specification concerning it, the task was still difficult. Molkekk didn't stop him but watched with some amusement as he struggled to gradually bring a portal into existence. Once the portal was finished, the last touch was a bit of theatrics. Portals did not transmit smell or images, so Timothy added fire and the smell of sulfur burning so the wizard would know exactly where this one led.

"Hell?" Molkekk asked in a bemused fashion. "You're going to send me to hell? You can't force me into that portal! You aren't strong enough."

"I'll certainly try to kill you," Timothy said, "but that venture isn't a sure thing. On the other hand, there's something you care about almost as much as your own life, something I can affect."

Molkekk's eyes shifted to Lemin and Vladimir lying in a heap only feet from the portal.

"Noooo!" the wizard shouted, but there was nothing he could do to stop it. Timothy's concussion spell had already detonated, unceremoniously flinging the bodies of Lemin and Vladimir through the portal, which snapped tightly shut behind them.

"What have you done?" the wizard bellowed in anger and pain. "How could you do that to your own friends?"

"It wasn't easy, but it was necessary, wasn't it?" Timothy asked, hoping Molkekk would overlook some glaring weaknesses in his strategy, holes in his plan, faults in his reasoning. "You wanted them alive, so I knew no matter how much I like them, they had to go. It was a bit drastic what I did, but I wanted to make it abundantly clear that I'm not your lackey anymore. I had to destroy them, and I had to make sure you saw me do it."

"Stupid magician," Molkekk growled. "What's your plan now that you've killed the only magician who could stop me?"

"It doesn't matter," Timothy answered. "Whatever plans you had for Lemin and Vladimir won't work anymore thanks to me. Your secret weapon will never work now, and though you may kill me, there will be others who will take you down."

"You have no fear of death," Molkekk noted with surprise.

"Why should I?" Timothy asked coldly. "You took from me what I loved most. What else is there but to exact revenge and die?"

"That's not the attitude of a follower of Elohim," Molkekk noted with a slight smile.

"True," Timothy agreed. "Maybe I'm bluffing. Or maybe I just don't care anymore."

"Well then, let's get this over with," Molkekk said. "A good ol' one-on-one wizard fight. May the best wizard win. And I will."

"Who said anything about one-on-one?" Timothy asked. "I brought an army of magicians with me, and I intend to use them."

"How?" Molkekk asked. "Have you forgotten my shield?"

"No, but with a little smoke and mirrors and a dash of distraction, you have," Timothy answered, motioning to the rapidly receding opaque shield surrounding them. Turning his head he shouted over his shoulder, "Magicians, attack!"

He unleashed the fury of his spell on Molkekk, and from behind him a barrage of magic slammed into the wizard. Molkekk gave a bellow of pain as he tried fruitlessly to raise wards against the attack. For several long moments, the attack persisted.

Molkekk continued to scream until without warning an explosion rocked the place he had been standing. The shockwave blasted through the room, knocking everyone to the floor and demolishing entire sections of the walls. Timothy rose shakily to his feet and began to make his way to where the rest of the magicians were.

"Is everyone alright?" he asked, helping people to their feet.

There was some complaining and muttering about pain here or there, but it was quickly replaced with excited congratulations and slaps on the back. They had just defeated Molkekk, bane of Magessa! The celebration was cut short by an ominous creaking from the tower.

"Everyone on me," Timothy called. As he formed a spell, the magicians gathered around him.

"Brace yourselves!" Timothy yelled and threw the spell into the floor. The wood smashed downward under the group and they fell into the next level. This floor splintered as well, allowing them to continue their fall. The next floor disintegrated too, and the group of magicians slammed into the stone floor of the first level of the tower.

"Get out!" Timothy yelled over the din in the tower and made straight for a large hole in the wall. The other magicians were right behind him, and they burst out with no trouble. Timothy ran as hard as he could away from the falling structure and flung himself down the hill supporting the building. His companions followed his example, and none too soon; with an ear shattering explosion, the building blew into a million pieces. The incredible force of the blast concussed across the city, toppling buildings and crumbling walls. Timothy covered his head as the debris fell around him. He stayed like that for some time until the commotion died down. Only then did he dare to raise his head and look around. The tower was nothing more than a pile of rubble. So it was that Molkekk's center of power had become his unmarked grave.

Timothy realized that something was digging into his leg, and he rolled to his side. Apparently, something had gotten into his pocket during the ruckus. With some effort, he dug a small black book from his pocket. This was the volume Vladimir had given him inside the tower. It had come from the room where all the furnishings were illusions, and yet it had not disappeared.

Something was very odd about this book. He would have to read it before long.

Eleven

After the destruction of the tower in Vollexa Temp, there was nothing to incite the army to stay. Most of the city had been demolished by the explosion, and even the thickest walls had breaches in them. Miraculously, very few people had been injured or killed, and the survivors were anxious to leave the place behind. Consequently, the army moved out in the morning. The dragons matched pace with the infantry, providing an escort, even though it was obviously not necessary. The old enemy had been defeated, and there would finally be peace in the region.

The soldiers who had lost their lives in the attack were mourned, and none so much as Lemin and Vladimir. As the only two magicians who had given their lives in the battle against Molkekk, they were already regarded as heroes. Many people felt the loss, but none as keenly as Timothy.

As he led the remains of his squad of magicians into formation with the rest of the army, he could hardly hear the cheers of praise that were shouted at them. When the order to march came, he mechanically walked along, putting one foot in front of the other and not noticing how long they marched nor how much distance they covered. After the order to halt was given he sat alone and stared north to the ruins of the evil city. He hadn't realized how much a part of his life Lemin and Vladimir were until now. With them had gone his sense of direction. He was sitting this way when Senndra found him.

"Timothy," she said gently. He didn't even turn to look at her, so she sat down beside him and was silent.

"They should still be here," Timothy finally said. The emotion was thick in his voice, and it sounded as if he might lose control any minute. "What happened couldn't have been done any other way, I fully believe that, but they deserved better. If only I could have found a better way; if only…"

"You're being too hard on yourself," Senndra said. "You did the best you could and you brought most of the team through it. This is war, and in war there are…" she could barely say it, and when it did come out she was just repeating a lesson from school, "…casualties."

"But what if I could have done something differently?" Timothy asked.

"Molkekk was a powerful wizard," Senndra said. "Defeating him at all is an accomplishment and a great victory. Lemin and Vladimir were glad to give their lives for the cause."

"I know," Timothy agreed. "It worked. I just wish they were still here. For their leadership, their advice, and their friendship. I miss them so much already."

"Oh, Timothy I know it has been hard; I miss them too," Senndra said as she looked up at him. "But Lemin and Vladimir did what they had to do. They died for a good cause, and they did so nobly. They wouldn't want you to mourn them in this way. They're in Elohim's hands now."

"You're right, I'm certain you'll see them again one day," Timothy said. Elohim had proved Himself faithful to his followers time and again, just not to double-crossing backsliders like himself. He rose to his feet and offered his hand to Senndra. She took it, and he pulled her up.

"You're right; death isn't permanent for those who believe in Elohim." Senndra sniffed and wiped a tear from her own eye. Soon the tears were running down her face in small rivers. "Look here," she said with a small laugh. "I was the one who was trying to comfort you, and now I'm the one who's blubbering like a baby."

"It's okay to mourn," Timothy said softly. "Don't hold your feelings in or you'll just feel terrible."

At his words, Senndra dissolved into tears. She pressed her face against his shoulder, crying her heart out. Timothy placed his arms around Senndra and did his best to comfort her, though he had no idea what to say. He couldn't very well tell her that he was the reason Lemin and Vladimir were gone. He couldn't tell her the truth; he would someday, but not right now.

******

Josiah and Nathan entered the walled city side by side. Their scouts had reported that it was a position where they might be able to make a stand, and their assessment appeared to be well founded. The city was deserted due to the advancing enemy army, and the inhabitants had left behind enough provisions to resupply the army. The city was rather large and had a well-built wall surrounding it, making it a good, though not ideal, spot for a confrontation.

Josiah looked up and saw dragons circling overhead. The elves and their dragons had been in constant escort since their arrival, always watching the progress of both armies and leaving only when necessary to slow down the enemy. With this support from the air, the armies of Magessa, the elves, and the ogres might be able to hold their own against Molkekk's host. The recent fighting was taking its toll on the enemy, and their ranks were beginning to thin, though not enough to give the defenders a decisive advantage if they chose to attack head-on. Nevertheless, the progress was heartening and very good for the morale of the troops.

"We can't hold them here, even with the help of the dragons," Nathan said. "The city is too small, and the enemy will just be able to bypass us."

"That's probably true, but we need to do something," Josiah said. "They're marching unhindered across the country, sacking and killing everything they come across, and we aren't doing anything to stop them. If we're to have any chance of defeating them, we need to give our people more time to organize themselves."

"What would you suggest?" Nathan asked. "We're too small to hit them head-on. If we make a stand in a single location, they'll ignore us, as I said before or worse, surround us and wipe us out."

"You of all people know how much I detest cowards and prefer a fair fight, but perhaps it is time to consider other options," Josiah said. "We've been acquiring horses for the last few days, and we have enough now to put together a significant mounted contingent."

"And what would riders do that we have failed to do so far?" Nathan asked.

"They would be swift and able to strike the enemy where we have not been able to," Josiah answered. "A mounted unit could successfully pull off hit-and-runs on the main army as well as on the supply wagons. It could also perform night raids with few casualties, I think."

"I don't believe you are actually suggesting this," Nathan said. "Although you're right, I never thought of you as the type to use tactics like this."

"I don't like the thought, but I can see the definite advantage," Josiah persisted. "If we harry them while they're marching, they'll be forced to march in their armor with scouts going before and behind them. This will slow them considerably; perhaps it will even give us enough time to raise a reasonable army."

"Not to mention the fact that it will annoy the heck out of them," Nathan added. "It will demoralize them and deprive them of needed sleep and rest."

"So you agree to go with this plan?" Josiah asked.

"Absolutely," Nathan said.

"Would it also be possible for you to organize the raids?" Josiah asked. "I have no experience in such tactics."

"We'll plan them together," Nathan said. "That way you'll figure out how to plan them as well. We might even be able to organize two independent operations."

"I wouldn't count on that for a while, but I'd be happy to learn," Josiah agreed.

"Actually, the essential points are pretty easy to learn," Nathan said. "First of all, you need to make sure your men know the basic principles of these attacks. We don't want to actually engage the enemy, as tempting as it may be at times. Our troops will have to be lightly armed so that they can maneuver quickly. Any places that could serve as ambush sights, we can use during the day. If we hide a few men in a small stand of trees, for instance, they can ride out, kill a few dozen men or ruin a few wagons, and then be gone before they are ever confronted. We need to make sure to avoid confrontation. The light arms our men will be using will be no match for someone in full battle array.

"Of course, it'll be easier to attack at night. We won't have to find ambush sights or anything like that. If we're clever enough, we can just ride into their camp, slash a few tent wires, burn some supplies, and be on our way. Again, it won't harm the army very much, but it will kill their morale. I mean, just think what would happen to our morale if we knew that there were enemy soldiers sneaking into our camp at will."

"Not to mention that if we target the right supplies, we could be taking away something necessary," Josiah added. "But what about when they catch on?" he said as an afterthought.

"We have to keep our attacks random," Nathan said. "Attack the front of the column one time and then the back the next. Vary the attacks between their soldiers and their supplies. Don't attack every day, but then some days we can attack more than once. Basically we need to keep them off balance enough that they don't know when we're going to attack, so they have to be prepared all of the time.

"Another thing we could do is get some of the dragon riders to be in these groups. They have experience firing bows from moving beasts and so should be able to use them astride horses. That would give us another advantage in these attacks."

"Why not just use dragons?" Josiah asked. "Couldn't they do more damage with less injury? They could attack just as stealthily as we can on horses."

"No, they can't," Nathan responded. "The enemy has magicians who have likely set up a spell to detect dragons as they approach. That means our dragons won't be able to launch any surprise attacks; if they did, they would get beat up pretty good."

"I don't get it," Josiah said. "Wouldn't the enemy also have spells to detect our soldiers and horses?"

"They can't do that," Nathan answered. "Think about it; they have no dragons, so a spell to detect dragons will work for them. But they have men and horses just like we do. It wouldn't be realistic to set up a spell and expect it to only detect our soldiers."

"I see."

"So, how many horses do we have anyway? How many soldiers can we outfit for these attacks?"

Josiah and Nathan discussed the strategy of using hit and run attacks for a long while. It was getting dark, and the order to halt for the night had already been given by the time they had decided how many soldiers they would arm for the first hit and run raid. The men were assembled, and the unit was given explicit instructions: attack the camp, burn what they could, kill anyone they could, and get out before a direct confrontation occurred. The soldiers liked the idea even less than Josiah had when he first thought of it, but they were loyal to their commanders and set off to complete the mission. Josiah and Nathan rode out with the group until they were half a mile from their camp. They stayed with their bodyguards and watched as their soldiers seemed to fade into the moonless night.

"It shouldn't take more than a minute or two for them to cover the distance," Josiah commented. "If we don't see any commotion soon, we can start to worry." He looked through the darkness and saw hundreds of the enemy's fires burning. He thought he could see tiny figures around them but knew that he was only imagining things. No one's eyes were that good, not even an elf's.

Five minutes passed then ten. They couldn't see anything in the camp, but the lack of activity indicated that the raiders had not been spotted yet. Then, very suddenly, a shout rolled across the plain, and fires flared up all over the camp. Instantly, the camp was a hotbed of activity as people rushed all over it. No single person could be distinguished, but a general clamor replaced the silence that had reigned previously.

A minute and a half later, hoof beats could be felt through the ground. The Generals and their entourage mounted their horses and waited for the raiding party to reach them. A single torch was lit to guide the horsemen to them, and soon the whole party was congregated. When a full accounting had been done, they turned and headed back to camp, pleased with the night's work.

******

Rita stood in the gate of Belmoth and watched as the army approached. Reports had already come in that it was the infantry returning from Vollexa Temp, and the whole city had turned out to greet them. The army was in neat ranks, marching at an unvarying pace toward the city. People had trooped out of the city in droves, lining the road and cheering the army as they marched. The majority of the soldiers were still in the city, and when the returning army came within range of voice from the city, a great roar rose from the walls to greet them.

The show on the ground was nothing compared to that in the air. The dragons that were returning with the army were flying in formation with less than a foot of space between wingtips. A crowd of dragons rose out of the city and flew to meet them, flying in small squads and performing acrobatics. When they reached the returning dragons, they formed an honor guard around them and slowed their pace to match that of the army underneath.

The road to the city gate was straight as an arrow, and the army reached the city in relatively little time. As the first ranks passed under the gate of the city, a resounding roar arose to replace the cheers that had been dying out. Observers moved into the ranks, welcoming soldiers back and giving them food and liquid refreshments. The infantry did not break ranks but stayed in tight formation until they had reached the square of the city. The army marched around the square and took up positions on all sides of it facing the center. The dragons deposited their riders, who took up rank in the formation, and the magnificent beasts flew off to celebrate the return in their own way.

Rita followed the army to the square and took a position in the back of the army. From her vantage point she had a relatively good view of what was happening. A group of high-ranking officers was moving through the ranks of soldiers, shaking hands as they went. When they broke away from the soldiers, they headed to the center of the square and stood in front of a makeshift platform. The cheers died away as the Grand Admiral of Belmoth mounted the platform and raised his hands for silence.

"Soldiers of Magessa," he began. "Welcome back home." His voice was not amplified in any way, but it was still clearly heard in the farthest reaches of the square. "Today is a day of rejoicing for our victory over Molkekk." At these words, the square was filled with a deep resounding roar as all present raised their voices together. The Grand Admiral allowed the cheering to go on for some time before raising his hands again for silence.

"There is nothing I can say that will properly describe the admiration we all feel for you. Any words I try to put to it could use cannot do you justice, so I will not ruin this occasion with many words. Instead I would like to congratulate and thank each of you for going above and beyond the service expected of you. Only in a free country such as the one in which we live can patriotism be cultivated. I also want to make sure that we do not forget the brave soldiers who remained behind to defend this city, a thankless but necessary task.

"This day we have shown that we will not fall quietly to the schemes of anyone. We have withstood the might of one of the most formidable foes in the world, and yet we still stand. Let this be a message to anyone else who would seek to conquer us. We will not flag or fall in the defense of our country. No, as long as we draw breath, Magessa will remain a land of freedom!"

Uproarious cheering and applause followed the Grand Admiral's speech, and continued for several minutes. Eventually the cheers began to die down, and as they did, the Grand Admiral of the academy of Belvárd mounted the stage. He and the Grand

Admiral of Belmoth shook hands, and then the Grand Admiral of Belmoth fell back.

"Today marks a great advent in the history of Magessa," the Grand Admiral from Belvárd announced as the last of the applause was dying away. "We have stood side by side with soldiers not from our own county. Side by side we have beaten back the might of the enemy. Side by side dragon riders and foot soldiers have fought to preserve our freedom, and preserve it we have." At this point the Admiral's voice rose to a shout and the soldiers responded with cheers which lasted for a short time before they were silenced. "Side by side we will fight for the freedom of this country, and as long as we remain united as one, none will be able to overcome us!"

Again cheering drowned out the speaker, and this time he allowed it to go on unhindered as he and the other Grand Admiral stepped down off the platform and, along with their entourage, walked to where the soldiers were standing in formation. They began to shake hands up and down the lines, and the soldiers responded with enthusiasm. For a quarter of an hour they made rounds through the soldiers, greeting everyone they came to and shaking their hand.

Eventually, however, the Grand Admirals started across the square to where they had entered, obviously leaving. Suddenly an officer broke from the ranks and jogged to the platform in the middle of the square. As the Grand Admirals were about to leave the square, the officer on the platform gave the command to come to attention. Instantly every warrior in the place straightened. The Grand Admirals turned to look at the officer on the stage, but he remained silent, his hand raised to his brow in salute. The Grand Admirals saluted the officer, who then dropped his hand but remained at attention. As the Grand Admirals turned to go, silence reigned as the soldiers continued to salute their commanders.

After the departure of the Grand Admirals, the soldiers were allowed to disperse. They quickly spread throughout the city, celebrating as they went. The raucous sounds of parties erupted almost immediately, but Rita passed them all by as she headed to the cadets' haunt. As she approached the building, she could see activity going on inside, and when she stepped through the door, she was swept up in the excitement of the celebration.

Not all the cadets were celebrating, however. In a back room of the cadets' building, a grim meeting was in progress. Timothy sat at the head of the table in the room and presided over a good-sized crowd. Senndra, William, Richard, Alyss, and several high officers were seated around the table.

"Let the people celebrate, but we need to consider what the next step is going to be," Timothy was saying. He had quickly risen to a position of respect among all in the army due to the fact that he had led the group of magicians which had defeated Molkekk.

"Quite so," an Admiral said from the other end of the table. "We have chopped off the head of the snake, but the body will keep on moving, at least until they hear the news."

"Which means we still have to deal with the army traipsing across our country," Timothy agreed. "The last report we have is from William. Would you mind giving that report now?"

"This news is from before our attack on Vollexa Temp," William said, "but as Timothy said, it is the latest report we have. I was under orders to fly to the elf forests and try to obtain their help, but on the way I encountered the elf dragon riders turned out in force. I turned around at this point since my mission was not necessary anymore, so I have no information on the size of Molkekk's army, nor the army that stands against his."

"Thank you, William," Timothy said. "I believe the latest information we have concerning the armies comes from you, Senndra, so if you don't mind please tell us what you saw."

"It wasn't good," Senndra said. "I saw the enemy army marching across Belvárd, killing and pillaging everything they came in contact with. I would estimate their numbers to be at least a half million. They had no dragon support at the time I saw them, but that might have changed.

"Now, concerning the defenders, they were in bad shape. They had been reinforced by elves and ogres, but their numbers were still well below those of the enemy. When I met with their commanders, they were preparing to make a stand at an outpost in the gap between the Rebel and Vankor Mountains, but they didn't seem too optimistic that they would be able to hold that position."

"How many soldiers does our army down there have?" one of the officers at the table asked.

"I don't know exactly, but I would say that they have more than we have here," Senndra answered. "Perhaps twenty or thirty thousand."

"They'll never be able to hold an outpost with such a small force," a General said. "Even with the dragon support, it's debatable."

"Which is why we have to assume they have either been driven from that position or overrun," Timothy stated.

"Then we need to go and give them any assistance we can as quickly as possible!" an Admiral exclaimed.

"Which is why I arranged this meeting," Timothy said. "I do not have any say in that decision, but many of you do. You need to voice your opinions to the Grand Admirals."

"I will do so immediately," the Admiral said and stood up, but Timothy motioned for him to sit back down.

"We may need to give assistance in the fight, but at the same time we also need to fortify this city."

"We do not have enough men to do both tasks," someone commented. "If we do not send all of the help we have to reinforce our army, we won't have a country to defend at all."

"Perhaps you're right," Timothy conceded, "but as I have said, I do not have access to the Grand Admirals. You need to take these concerns before them and see what they believe to be the best course of action."

The meeting adjourned in short order, and the officers left with one mission in mind: convince their Grand Admirals to send aid to the army standing against Molkekk's forces.

******

Senndra awoke the next morning to find the city in turmoil. She couldn't figure out what had happened from anyone since everyone seemed to have their own story. Eventually she made her way to the mess hall for breakfast and met Timothy there.

"What's happening?" she asked as she set her plate down across from him.

"The Grand Admiral of Belmoth is dead," he answered before shoving a forkful of food into his mouth.

"What?!" Senndra exclaimed. "Was he murdered? Who would do such a thing?"

"No, he wasn't murdered; at least, foul play isn't suspected," Timothy answered, wiping his mouth. "It appears he was celebrating the victory by eating a meal of clams."

"Isn't it a little late for clams?" Senndra asked, puzzled by how this information had anything to do with the Grand Admiral's death.

"Yes, it is too late in the year for clams," Timothy answered. "That's the problem. It appears they had gone bad and poisoned the Grand Admiral. The doctor was called at once, but there was nothing he could do. The Grand Admiral was dead before sunrise."

"How will that affect what we discussed last night?" Senndra asked suddenly. "It won't disturb that, will it?"

"I don't know for certain, but I don't think it will," Timothy answered. "Our Grand Admiral seemed more likely to send aid, and since *he* is still alive, he'll have more sway than before. My guess is that we'll be moving before the day is out."

Timothy's guess was correct, and soon after noon, the army was again mobilized. This time they were headed south to intercept the army that was ravaging Magessa. The excellent roads in Magessa allowed them to cover the distance quickly, and by the time they pitched camp, they had marched twenty miles. The next day was filled entirely with marching. As the army moved, they sent messengers ahead, proclaiming the danger and calling for volunteers. All day long people flooded to the army and swelled its ranks. Though some of these men were local militia and well-armed, the bulk of them were normal people and poorly equipped. Very few of them had any armor at all, and they were armed with whatever they were able to lay their hands on. Nevertheless, the sight of all the volunteers raised the hopes of the army. Surely where equipment failed, sheer numbers would succeed.

The army, now several times larger than when it had set out from Belmoth, camped in the open again. They had covered only thirty miles due to the coming of reinforcements, and many people were worried they would not reach the battle with Molkekk's army in time to be of any assistance.

Late that night, dragon riders reported that Molkekk's army was moving up the Vänern River, driving a smaller army of humans, elves, and ogres in front of them. The next morning the soldiers were roused particularly early and after a quick breakfast set to marching again. Their course had been changed, and this time they were headed generally in the direction of Sulmon, the capital of Rampön. Reinforcements continued to join the army all day, and again they were only able to cover thirty miles. By now, however, they were only twenty miles out from Sulmon, and scouts reported that Molkekk's army was less than half a day's march away.

Camp was pitched as usual, and hundreds of fires were built, covering the countryside. Senndra, Timothy, Rita, William, Richard, Alyss, and several others gathered around one of the fires, cooking dinner as best as they could. Their rations were meager since the army had mobilized in a hurry; nevertheless, everyone had enough to satiate their hungry bellies. After they had finished dinner, they sat around the fire, leaning back against logs and piles of equipment.

"I don't know if anyone else has heard this yet, but our scouts are reporting that we could very well engage the enemy tomorrow," Timothy said from his spot against a particularly long log upon which three cadets were leaning.

"Tomorrow?" Alyss asked from her spot beside Richard. "I hadn't heard that." There was a note of worry in her voice.

"I had," William commented. "I wonder why they haven't spread the news through camp yet?"

"Probably because they don't want to alarm the soldiers," Timothy said. "You know how people get nervous and can't sleep when they find out they're going into battle. The last thing we need when we attack the enemy is an army full of soldiers who haven't had a good night's sleep."

"So you don't mind that the news might keep *us* awake?" Senndra asked from across the fire; there was a note of sarcasm in her voice. "Some friend you are."

"We're all seasoned warriors here," Timothy said. "We've been through several battles already, and I don't see that knowing we might be going into another one tomorrow will keep any of us from sleeping."

"Well, I don't know about the rest of you, but I'm a little…apprehensive about tomorrow," Richard admitted. "Sure, I've been in my fair share of battles, probably more than that considering my age, but that doesn't mean I'm thrilled to be going into another one. Maybe this will be the one where I die."

"That kind of talk is bad for morale," Alyss said and shoved Richard playfully. "You'll make the rest of us scared if you keep it up."

"Oh, I think being scared is a good thing, actually," Timothy said. "At least we know he isn't a cocky kid who thinks he's invincible. I'd rather trust someone who I know won't take unnecessary risks."

"But what if we do die tomorrow?" Rita spoke up. "That's a thought I'm literally terrified of."

"You shouldn't be," Senndra said. "If we die, we will go to be with Elohim in heaven. There is nothing to be afraid of, only something to look forward to."

"Maybe for you, but not for me," Rita said. "I turned my back on Elohim, and now He will never take me back. Death may hold nothing but good things for you, but for me there is nothing."

"You can never go so far from Elohim that He will not take you back," Senndra argued. "He is always willing to forgive you, if you will turn to Him."

"I would agree with you for the most part," Rita said sadly, "but you don't know what I've done. He could never take me back; I've sinned too greatly."

"That's simply not true," Senndra protested. "Nothing can separate us from the love of Elohim."

"You don't know what I've done," Rita said simply.

"Maybe not, but I know my own past and there are parts of it I'm ashamed of," Timothy said. "Some of my sins are more recent and larger than others, but I guess it's all the same to Elohim. At least I have to believe it, or I would have given up a long time ago as I'm sure you feel like doing now."

"I don't expect you to understand," Rita said and rose to her feet.

"Listen, Rita," Senndra said, directing the comment to Timothy as much as to the girl. "You may feel like that, but remember this: Elohim loves you and will always take you back. All you have to do is ask."

The cadets watched as Rita walked off into the darkness alone. Senndra looked about ready to get up and go after her, but Timothy laid a hand on her arm. When she looked at him, he shook his head.

"This is something she'll have to work out on her own. As much as you might want to, there's nothing you can do to force the right decision on her. Leave her to herself for a while."

Senndra nodded and sat back. There was silence around the fire as the people there considered the conversation that had just taken place. Yawns sprang to life on many faces, and several cadets got up and went to bed. Those that remained simply stared into the dying fire.

"What could you have possibly done in the past that would cause you to be ashamed?" William finally said, breaking the silence.

"It's not a story I share with everyone," Timothy said. "I try to forget it, as I know Elohim has, but it's impossible for me."

283

"If you'd prefer not to tell it, then don't," William said. "I was just asking."

"Oh, I don't mind telling it," Timothy said. "Perhaps if I do, someone else won't make the same mistake I did. This was five years ago now, back when I was fifteen. I was not attending the academy yet, nor did I have any training in magic, though I had discovered my gift only a few months earlier. As you can imagine, a fifteen-year-old boy with no training will use magic in the most irresponsible ways. I used magic to get what I wanted. If I wanted something from a market vendor, I used magic to help me steal it. If I wanted to eavesdrop on someone, I used magic to help me do it.

"Now it appears that the devils had their eyes on me from the beginning since they recognized me to be a particularly powerful magician. Because of this they put me on the fast track, so to speak, for demon possession. Quickly they nudged me toward wanting more and more power until possession was the only option left open for me. I didn't give it much thought at all and let the demon in.

"That arrangement worked out for a week. I had more power than ever before and was thrilled with it; the demon, however, had other plans for me. Normally demons kill people before they take control of their bodies, but this time he was in too much of a hurry to bother with specifics. The last thing I remember was going to bed one night; apparently the demon took control of my body at that point and had me go up to the city of Sengal where the prophet Gilad was preaching. I'm told I went straight up to him and killed him with a single stroke of a knife I was carrying, but I don't remember any of it.

"As luck would have it, there were several magicians there, and they quickly incapacitated me. Their attacks actually killed the demon, and only a very wise and very strong magician realized what had happened; the others were ready to kill me. Anyway, that magician took me and restored me to my previous health. He tutored me in the use of magic and taught me about Elohim. Two years later he enrolled me at the academy and has been periodically checking on me ever since.

"You see, I didn't do anything really bad by worldly standards. Sure, I killed a man, but that was under the influence of a demon. I also stole and committed many sins, but who is there is this world who hasn't done things like that? No, the truly horrible sin I committed was literally turning my back on Elohim. I allowed a demon into my body and in doing so aligned myself with His enemies. I spat in His face, and yet He says in His word that He is faithful to restore me when I turn to Him. I choose to believe He has forgiven me, and though I sometimes fall back into my old ways and commit sins, He promises to forgive me, and by His grace I am able to live in a way that pleases Him."

"But what you did doesn't seem too bad," Richard commented.

"Perhaps not if you look at it in a worldly light," Timothy said. "However, if you consider all that Elohim has done for us, how He has allowed us to have fellowship with Him even though we grieve Him so much, then you will see that turning your back on Him is the greatest insult you can ever offer Him. Of course, Elohim doesn't rank sins according to their relative severity. To Him, every sin is just as bad as every other sin."

"Well, I would be really thrilled to stay up all night and continue this conversation with you, but I think we should be getting to bed," Richard commented with a glance at the moon.

"Not yet," William said slowly, a pensive look on his face. "I've got more questions, Timothy."

"Not tonight," Timothy said. "You need rest, if you don't want to fall asleep in the middle of the battle. That's about the fastest way to get a ticket straight to heaven."

The cadets yawned, stretched, and dispersed to go to their sleeping rolls. Senndra, however, remained behind and waited for them to leave. She had a question for Timothy.

"Who was the magician who rescued you?" she asked.

"No one you know," Timothy answered in an offhand manner.

"No, really, who was it?" Senndra asked.

"Gillian," Timothy answered.

"Who the heck is he?" Senndra asked in puzzlement.

"Exactly," Timothy muttered. He shook his head in exasperation and headed for his bed roll.

Twelve

"We must consider plans for a battle out here on the plain," Josiah said to Nathan. The two Generals were astride horses at the head of the combined armies; General Levvy was running along beside them. The amazing size of the ogres prevented them from riding horses; however, they were more than able to match pace with the animals.

"He's right," Levvy growled. "You heard what the scouts said; somehow the enemy army has picked up their pace. If we delay any longer, we will not have any time for our armies to prepare before they attack."

"Sulmon is less than ten miles ahead of us," Nathan countered. "We'll be butchered if we engage the enemy out here, but from the city we have a chance. We should be able to reach the city before the enemy catches us."

"You heard what the scouts said," Josiah argued. "They'll have overtaken us before we even cover five miles. And even if we did make it to the city, there's no way they would open up their gates and let us in with the enemy army so close on our tail."

"You know we don't have a chance out here in the open," Nathan said.

"But there is also no chance we can reach the city in time," Levvy countered. "We will simply be attacked in the rear and brought down without a fight if we do not prepare ourselves. At least if we ready our men, we will be able to inflict some damage on that cursed army."

"I will not allow my men to be attacked from behind when I can prevent it," Josiah said. "If you must, continue your march to Sulmon, but my army and I will get ready to face the enemy. Perhaps we will create enough time for you to reach the city."

"This is madness," Nathan said weakly. Though he did not like what was being proposed by the other two Generals, he saw the wisdom of it.

"No, what is madness is to ignore the certain doom behind us until it overtakes us," Levvy growled. "Even if you take your men to the city, my army will stay with Josiah's. It is here that we must take a stand and fight, for if we do not, we will most definitely fall."

"Very well," Nathan conceded. To one of his messengers he said, "Give the order for the soldiers to arm themselves and form battle lines." Josiah and Levvy sent men to their commanders with the same message.

"If we must, we will engage them here, though I do not like the looks of the battlefield," Nathan said. "The flat terrain is not in our favor; it will allow the enemy army a chance to surround us."

"We can't let that happen, no matter the cost," Levvy rumbled. "If they succeed in this, we'll be done for."

288

"Which means we'll need an incredibly long line," Josiah said. "But the length we need will spread our soldiers out too thin. We'll never hold the line with such a strategy."

"Which is exactly why I originally wanted to march straight for the city," Nathan countered. "We may inflict damage by making a stand out here, but there's no way we can survive a head-on attack."

"And there's no way we can reach the city alive," Levvy retorted.

"We've been considering using one strategy or the other, but what if we combine them?" Josiah suggested. "If we have our men begin an orderly retreat as soon as they have assembled into ranks, we may be able to hold off the enemy long enough to reach the city. In addition, the backward motion of our troops should prevent the enemy from surrounding us."

"And what of the city gates?" Levvy asked. "We will still be trapped out on this plain facing the whole of Molkekk's army."

"Even if they don't open the gates for us, we'll still have a solid wall at our backs," Josiah countered. "That's better than being surrounded by enemies on all sides."

"It's a long shot, but it just might work if it is executed properly," Nathan conceded. The conversation was interrupted by a soldier galloping up to the three Generals. He gave a hasty salute before speaking.

"Sir, the soldiers are preparing for battle as you have ordered," he reported to Josiah. "They're forming ranks as we speak and should be prepared to fight soon."

"Thank you," Josiah said. "What condition is the rest of the army in?"

"The elves are also forming ranks as we speak, though I do not know about the ogre soldiers."

"Do not worry about the ogres, General Pondran," Levvy said. "They'll be ready with plenty of time to spare."

"Even fully prepared, our soldiers won't stand a chance against Molkekk's horde," Nathan said. "Don't think I'm trying to back out of this, gentlemen; I am with you to the end. I just want to confirm one last time that we are all in this to the death, for with the numbers they will throw against us, that will likely be the outcome."

"It's actually worse than you think," Josiah commented. "My scouts reported that their numbers have actually grown since we last engaged them. They don't have a definite number, but their estimate is close to a million, all told.

"No, there's no way we can stand against them in our own strength, but the good thing is, we never have to. Elohim will fight with us, and if He sees fit for us to be victorious, we will win. If, however, He ordains that we shall die on this battlefield, so be it. There is no place I would rather die than in the center of His will, and I am certain that this is it."

"As I said last time we encountered this foe: Today is a good day to die," Levvy growled. "Let them come and try their hardest to overcome us. You do not need to be concerned about my men, for they will not be overcome except by death."

"Well, if we are to die here, let us give a good showing of ourselves," Nathan agreed. "They might take this field, but they will pay a high price for it, of that we can be sure."

"The ranks are forming," Josiah noted. "Perhaps we should go and address our men before this battle."

The three Generals turned and galloped to the front of the army, their entourage of guards behind them. Levvy's amazing stride pounded the ground with the horses of the other two Generals. Nathan and Josiah pulled their horses to a halt in front of the army, and Levvy thundered to a stop just in front of them.

"Would you care to do the honors?" Josiah asked Nathan. "Legend says that elves have the golden tongue and know what to say for all occasions. I myself am not a very good speaker."

"Well, the legends are wrong," Nathan said flatly. "I'm no speaker at all, especially not in this capacity. I never know what to say before a battle."

Josiah turned and looked at Levvy.

"I'm afraid I will not be of any help to you," the ogre said apologetically. "We ogres usually just bellow before a battle."

"Then the task falls to me. Help me, Elohim," Josiah said. He glanced at the enemy army which was fast approaching. "I don't think we'll have time to retreat before they hit us," he commented. "We need to fight them to a halt before we start to fall back."

Without another word to his friends, he spurred his horse forward and cantered to the front line. As he looked at the line of swordsmen which seemed to stretch on forever and saw the wall of shields and swords, his throat tightened up, and he could think of nothing to say. As he looked closer, however, he caught glimpses of the soldiers' eyes. Fear was in many of those eyes despite the previous battles they had seen. Immediately Josiah knew what to say. He might not know how to speak to an army, but he knew how to address frightened men.

"Soldiers of Magessa, hear me!" he yelled, so that all could hear him. "As I look at you I see a fear in your eyes, a fear that steals the hearts of even the bravest men. And that fear is well founded. Indeed, the largest army ever assembled is marching against us, and in a few moments we will meet them in battle. They outnumber us heavily, but numbers are not what win battles. No, it is the spirit of the army that counts.

"Yes, they outnumber us, and yes, many of us will die today. I do not seek to conceal this from you. However, I ask only this question: What accounting will you give of yourself? Will we give them this field? Will we give them Sulmon? Will we give them Magessa? No! We will not stand idly by and watch them ravage our country before our very eyes, killing our families. We will make them fight for every inch that they gain from us. Their blood will be the price of their victory, should they gain it.

"Yes, we may die today, but we will give them such a fight as has never been recorded. Their numbers may be great, but that just means they will have more slain when the day is out. For we can gain the victory this day; yes, if Elohim is willing, we can rout this army before us. Yet, even if we do not, fight the good fight and make this a battle they will not soon forget!"

A bellow rang out behind Josiah, and the whole army answered with a resounding shout of its own. The higher voices of men and elves mingled with the low roars of the ogres, and the ground shook with the sound. Josiah drew his sword and gave his own long shout. He turned to find Nathan, Levvy, and the guards at his side.

"Nathan, take the right side of the army; Levvy, take the left. I'll lead the middle, and by Elohim's grace, perhaps we can come out of this together. Do the dragon riders know about our decision?"

"Yes, they do," Nathan answered. "Right now, they're coordinating an attack of their own. They're going to try and time it so that as we hit the front of the army, they will hit the rear."

"Very well," Josiah said. "Now let us get to our positions and lead this attack."

Levvy loped off at a quick pace, followed by his guard of ogres. Nathan and his guards wheeled their horses and trotted off to their position. Josiah pivoted his horse in a circle and scanned the battlefield. The enemy army was approaching quickly but were perhaps two or three minutes out. Many of the soldiers in ranks behind him continued to show signs of fear, but there was also grim determination in their eyes now. Their impatience to attack was evident as they seemed to strain against an invisible wall holding them back. Levvy and Nathan were still trotting to their positions as Josiah slid off of his horse. He pointed the animal toward the army and slapped it on the rump. The lines opened up to allow the animal through and closed behind it. Moments later, there was a commotion behind the front line, and a group of six men stepped out and jogged forward to where Josiah was standing. Cirro was leading the group which also included Brandon, Petra, Devon, Stephen, and Heath.

"What are you doing?" Josiah asked when the men were close enough to hear him.

"The elfin commander has a personal bodyguard; so does the ogre commander," Cirro answered. "You, however, seem to have forgotten about yourself again."

"You needed an entourage to go before King Einor," Petra added. "We figured that you needed one to go into battle, seeing as though you are of an even higher rank than when we went to Dublack."

"Actually, we really just wanted a chance to get at some enemies before anyone else does," Brandon commented with a grin.

"We were a team before, and it seemed to work then," Devon said. "You need a guard, and seeing as though no one else was going to step up and take the job, we gave it to ourselves."

"Once a team always a team," Stephen said.

"Thank you," Josiah said, nodding slightly. He glanced over his shoulder at the enemy army. "Get ready; it's time to attack."

Josiah turned and faced the enemy forces. His sword was already in his hand, but he heard the sound of steel on steel as his friends drew their weapons as well.

For a moment everything seemed to slow down. The sounds faded away, and the enemy rushed forward in slow motion. Out of the corner of his eye, Josiah could see Petra drawing his sword out of the last few inches of the sheath; the action seemed to take forever. Josiah thought that he spotted the wing of a dragon far above the armies, though it could have been his mind playing tricks on him.

With a snap, time returned to normal, and Josiah stabbed his sword into the air as a cry tore from his throat. An answering roar came from the army behind him as they raised their weapons. He slashed his blade downward to point at the enemy and broke into a run. The army surged forward behind him, almost overtaking him and his guards as it rushed forward. The distance to the enemy army disappeared rapidly and Josiah was able to see the soldiers clearly. The sun gleamed off their weapons and armor making them look quite impressive; however, there was a single weakness that Josiah was able to detect. Though the army of Magessa had managed to keep their ranks tight as they charged, the lines of Molkekk's army had fallen apart; there was no pattern to the enemy soldiers.

Josiah barely had time to notice this before the armies smashed into each other. He found himself in the front line of his own army and, as he had hoped, the line held as the other army smashed against it like waves on rocks. The disjointed ranks of the enemy were no match for the orderly form of their opponent. No matter how many of their number rushed the wall of men, they could not open a hole in it, for whenever they overcame a soldier, another stepped into his place.

For several minutes the armies battled like this, Molkekk's soldiers throwing themselves heedlessly against the impenetrable wall. Finally they fell back and began to regroup, and Josiah gave the order to follow them. He knew that there was no way his army could overcome theirs, but he also knew that if he gave them a chance to pick up momentum with another charge, they would have a chance of smashing his line to pieces.

294

The enemy saw the advance and turned to defend themselves. As the fighting began, Josiah gave up his position in the line to another soldier and fell back to evaluate his army. It was holding together well, but it could not hold forever. Already the enemy soldiers were spilling toward the edges of the line, seeking to fall in on the unprotected flanks.

"Fall back!" Josiah roared as loud as he could. All along the line, the call was taken up, and slowly the soldiers began to give way. The enemy soldiers saw the retreat and followed closely. Their toll on Josiah's soldiers was increasing as they continued to beat against the soldiers who were falling back.

"Stand your ground!" Josiah commanded, and his men stood their ground again. For a moment they were forced to fight for their footing, but after a few more backwards steps were again able to form a solid wall. As before the enemy soldiers crashed ineffectively against their lines, but even as Josiah watched, their forces were swarming around the edges of his line. The flanks were bending inward to prevent such a catastrophe, but it was already apparent that the enemy planned to surround the army.

"Retreat running," Josiah ordered. Immediately his troops began a new retreat pattern that he and Nathan had devised. The back half of the army fell back twenty feet and formed ranks with gaps between every man. At a signal, the soldiers who had stayed to hold off the enemy turned around and ran pell-mell toward their comrades. The enemy was so taken by surprise that they hardly had time to give chase before the soldiers had reached their line and slipped behind it. As they passed, a soldier stepped from behind every man on the front line and filled the gaps, making the line ready for another attack. The soldiers who were retreating did not stop but continued to run until they were twenty feet behind the soldiers who now held off the enemy. At a signal, the defending soldiers turned and ran for their own lines which again filled in behind them, bringing the enemy to a halt.

Bit by bit the army leapfrogged back toward the city of Sulmon. The enemy seemed unable to cope with the new tactic and was having difficulty keeping up, much less mounting a serious attack. Then, just when it seemed that the army would make it to Sulmon, disaster struck. A large part of the enemy army detached itself from the whole and began to run toward the city as fast as it could go. They ran faster than Josiah had ever seen anyone run, and in no time they had reached and passed Josiah's own lines. In a flash they wheeled and struck the left flank of the army, sending the soldiers reeling and forcing the leading edge of the army to bend inward to prevent another attack. The soldiers abandoned the left flank and quickly covered the distance to the right. Already the line was bending to prevent a catastrophe, but the damage was done.

From his position Josiah could see the army contort into a gigantic circle and come quickly to a halt. This was exactly what he and Nathan had hoped to prevent by retreating. Now that they had been surrounded, there was nowhere for them to run to, and they would either win the battle or be defeated to fight no more. Even as he looked, the loose circle was being forced inward, pushed by the crushing force of the enemy troops. In the confusion that ruled the center of the ring of soldiers, Josiah found himself face to face with Nathan.

"What happened?" Josiah asked. "How did they get past our lines?"

"I don't know," Nathan answered. "They ran so quickly it was almost as if they had whips at their backs. I've never seen anyone run that fast."

"We have to make a run for the city," Josiah said. "The wagons and such that we sent on ahead should be there already. All we have is soldiers now. I think that if we attack the army in one spot, we just might be able to create a hole for us to escape through. Sure it's risky, and many of us may not make it to the city alive, but it's the best chance we have."

"I agree," Nathan said. His ears picked up a different sound, and he turned to take a look. "There's some sort of commotion on the north side of the army. Now's our best chance to do this."

"Well, then," Josiah said and lifted his sword. "Charge!"

The two Generals and their body guards burst forward in a surge of energy, pushing through the soldiers to the front ranks. Cheers followed them as they continued forward until they found themselves face to face with the enemy. With another shout, Josiah slashed with his sword and pushed ahead into the enemy soldiers.

******

Senndra and Rita helped each other into their armor and strapped on their weapons. Since they were going to be riding on dragons, their armor was light, consisting of leather with very little metal. Their weapons were standard for dragon riders; each carried a one-handed sword and a bow along with a quiver of twenty-five arrows. The quivers strapped on over their leather vests were built to hold a strung bow. The swords were in leather scabbards slung across the girls' backs opposite their quivers. This put the swords' handles over the girls' left shoulders, making it slightly awkward to draw the weapons; however, it was more important for them to have easy access to their arrows. Besides that fact, they had trained for years with swords over their left shoulders.

Feddir stood behind the girls and watched as they prepared for battle. Senndra had already buckled his saddle on, so he was ready to go as soon as they were. His tail twitched in anticipation and smacked into a nearby tree, shaking the leaves off of it. He was excited to be flying into battle again. He scraped his razor-sharp claws across a rock, leaving three deep furrows in it. Then he stamped his legs, shaking the ground with the impact.

"Are you ready to go, Feddir?" Senndra asked over her shoulder, as she adjusted the quiver and scabbard on Rita's back. Feddir gave a roar in answer, and Senndra smiled. She finished with Rita's equipment and turned to her dragon. He had stopped his haphazard and dangerous movements, but even as he sat still, he quivered with anticipation. Using his knee for a step, Senndra vaulted up into his saddle and fastened her legs to it. Rita followed more cautiously and took a seat behind Senndra. She also fastened her legs to the saddle with a second set of thongs.

"We're ready, Feddir," Senndra said to her dragon. "Ready to go and put an end to this madness. We're going to destroy Molkekk's army and return the blessed peace to this country."

Feddir's muscles bunched as he waited for the word that would indicate he could take flight. Every part of his body was coiled like a spring, awaiting the command that would release it. One toe moved slightly as the dragon struggled to stay under control. Senndra sensed the dragon's impatience and only waited for a few more seconds.

"Let's go," she said in a voice barely over a whisper. All of Feddir's muscles uncoiled instantaneously, flinging him and his riders into the air like a rocket. His wings snapped out to catch the air, and with mighty flaps, he rose higher and higher. He gave a roar and released a fireball as he continued to rise. Finally, he leveled out and began to circle the area from which he had just taken off. Some dragons were already in the air and more were leaving the ground and joining them. Soon the whole contingent would be airborne, and they would be able to move out.

From her perch on Feddir's back, Senndra could see the infantry as they continued to march toward the enemy army. She could also see the enemy army only a few miles away, facing an army that was pathetically small by comparison. They didn't stand a chance unless the reinforcements reached them in time.

It took mere minutes for the rest of the dragons to leave the ground. The order was given to move out, and Feddir fell into the middle of the flock of dragons flying to the aid of the beleaguered army of Magessa. It took two minutes to cover the distance to the army, and the dragons were already diving by the time they reached it. They might not be able to destroy the whole army, but they could at least give their allies time to retreat to the city behind them. Just as they were nearing the ground, a wall of fire balls rushed toward them. Instantly the dragons rolled onto their sides to absorb the fire on the scales of their bellies and then turned to face the foe that had just attacked. A sparkle of lights flashed in the air, signifying the death of a cloaking spell, and a flock of dragons and griffins, more than Senndra could count, appeared through the flashes. The dragons turned to face their enemies, and were able to form a line before they were attacked again. Even so, the force of the charging creatures brought them to a halt, and many fell toward the earth before regaining their wings.

In an instant the enemy was in among them, and the dragons were fighting for their very lives. Claw to claw and fire to fire, they challenged these attackers with a ferocity born of patriotism. These defilers were here to pillage and burn their homes and the homes of their riders, and they would not stand for it. Bodies of dragons and griffins rained out of the sky to smash into the ground below, and though the defenders fought tooth and nail, the sheer numbers of their enemy began to overpower them. They took down three or four dragons for every one they lost, yet there seemed to be no end to the enemy's ranks.

Suddenly a swarm of dragons bearing elfin riders dropped out of the clouds and fell on the flank of the enemy dragons and griffins. For a moment they wreaked havoc, killing many of the unsuspecting beasts, but they too were faced with the fact that there appeared to be no end to the enemy, and slowly the armies of Magessa were pushed backward.

Senndra chanced a glance down at the ground to see how the troops below were faring. The elfin dragon riders finally reached the rest of the soldiers of Magessa, and together the combined armies were pushing their way through Molkekk's forces, which had managed to surround them. They were only a quarter of a mile from the city now, and the soldiers on the walls were helping them in any way they could. Missiles of all types were being fired from the wall into the enemy army, though they could not touch the closest soldiers for fear of harming Magessa's men.

A sharp bank from Feddir jerked Senndra back to the aerial battle. A griffin was on his tail, and he was doing his best to shake it. Though griffins were not a serious threat to dragons if they met head to head, they were considerably faster and more maneuverable than the larger, heavier dragons. Using this speed and agility, they were able to maim or kill dragons if given the opportunity.

The griffin behind Feddir had targeted the weaker membrane of his wings, and was closing on that target steadily. No matter how much Feddir banked and twisted, the griffin remained behind him as if he were attached by a line. Acting purely on instinct, Senndra pulled her bow and an arrow from her quiver. Feddir sensed what she was doing and ceased his twisting and banking in order to give her a clearer shot. The griffin took advantage of this by shooting forward and closing in on the dragon's wings. With a gaping beak and outstretched claws, it reached for the wing, but before it could grasp it, Senndra released her arrow. The feathered shaft slammed into the griffin's chest, penetrating the tough hide and killing the creature instantly.

Senndra didn't have to time to gloat over the kill; Feddir banked hard right to avoid a head-on collision and dove twenty feet before leveling back out. Senndra already had another arrow on her string by the time his flight evened, and out of the corner of her eye she noticed that Rita had done the same thing. Both bows sang, and another griffin dropped out of the sky with two arrows protruding from its chest. A blast of heat brought Senndra's head around to see a dragon rushing straight at them. She fumbled for an arrow and got off one shot at the beast's head, but it bounced harmlessly off the scales of its closed mouth. In triumph it opened its maw to douse its opponents in flames. But Feddir was quicker. He fired a stream of fire into the dragon's mouth and rolled sideways. The dragon shot past with a roar of pain, and Feddir started to climb through the sky. He slammed into the belly of an enemy and sent it spinning away before dropping back into a dive, another enemy on his tail.

******

The army had finally reached the gates of the city, and found them thrown wide to receive them. Quickly they began to file into the city, always making sure to keep constant pressure on the enemy in front of them. As they continued to enter the city, the archers on the walls were able to get better shots at the enemy soldiers, and in no time they had them retreating from the walls. The soldiers began to file into the city in an orderly fashion, always keeping a contingent to guard the gate against attacks. Even with the orderly retreat, the movement of the army was painfully slow.

As the retreat was underway, the enemy army pulled back out of range of the archers on the wall and quickly reformed into a more organized formation. Seeing that the larger part of their adversary was still outside of the city, they realized they had plenty of time. They began their advance immediately and marched at an even pace until they came within range of the city's archers again. This time, instead of turning and running, they simply raised their shields and continued their march though at a faster pace.

Suddenly they came to a stop, their shields lowering for a heartbeat to reveal a crossbowman behind each one. In a moment, thousands of bolts were flying at the wall, and the archers threw themselves behind any cover they could find. Many of the bolts found their marks, dropping archers all along the wall, but an instant later the archers who had not been hit rose up again and fired a return barrage. Mixed in with these arrows were javelins from ballistae, and their combined impact devastated the enemy troops. Scores fell at a time, but still they pressed toward the wall, desperate to kill the defenders before they could enter the city.

The sheer impact of the attack from the wall weakened the enemy army to such an extent that when they reached the soldiers congregated outside the gate of the city, they were unable to break through the line. Nevertheless, the fighting was bitter, and many men fell from both sides. The attackers knew that this was their best chance at destroying the army of Magessa once and for all, so they continued to press forward, heedless of the soldiers that had fallen before them. The defenders held on with grim determination and refused to give the attackers any ground whatsoever; they knew they were fighting for more than their lives.

From the battlements of the city, Josiah watched the furious battle raging below him. He had been one of the first people through the gates at the urging of his body guard and had directed the passage of his men into the city for some time, though he eventually left this task in the hands of others and ascended the wall to gain a better view of the battle. The black forms of Molkekk's soldiers spread across the plain like a blight on the face of the earth. There were hundreds of thousands of them, probably close to a million, all pressing against his men, trying to force them to break. The archers from the wall poured arrows into the enemy ranks, and wall-mounted ballistae and mangonels rained their projectiles down with devastating effect. But no matter how many of the soldiers were killed, more advanced to take their places.

Just when it seemed that the black army would surely overcome the city defenders, a glimpse of hope appeared. At first Josiah was not sure whether he had seen it or not, but off to the north he thought he detected some commotion. He stared at the spot, but nothing more happened. Then, just as he was about to turn away, he saw a rip form in the enemy ranks as another army tore through them and headed for the gates of the city. Thousands upon thousands of men appeared as the army continued its all-out break for the city, and Josiah's hope began to rise. Such numbers would definitely be welcome in the battles ahead.

As the army drew closer to the city and Josiah was able to make out more details, he saw that the soldiers were not what he had expected. Some of them were properly equipped with armor and decent weapons, but many of them were not. They had obviously been recruited from their farms and shops to fight against the national threat and were armed with machetes, pitchforks, clubs, and whatever they had been able to lay their hands on. The effect of their attack on the enemy, however, was overwhelmingly successful. They had hit Molkekk's forces on their flank and were able to tear through the unsuspecting soldiers. Even now after they had battled their way to within several hundred yards of the city, they had few casualties of their own.

Josiah switched his attention to his soldiers who were desperately trying to hold the gate. Despite their determination, the sheer numbers of the enemy army were beginning to take its toll, and as Josiah stared, a hole opened up in their lines. The enemy soldiers pushed into the hole, and for a moment it appeared as if they had finally opened a serious breach, but in a concerted effort the defenders pushed them back out and reformed the line. Less than a minute later another breach opened, but it was at that moment that the other army reached the gate.

Suddenly the enemy soldiers found themselves beleaguered from both sides, and breaking into the defenders' ranks was the farthest thing from their minds. The soldiers caught between the two armies were quickly eliminated, and the newly arrived army rushed to reinforce the ranks of the exhausted defenders.

With the number of soldiers facing it leaping by several thousand, the attacking army fell back to regroup. This gave the soldiers of Magessa the opportunity to rush thousands more soldiers into the city. Twice they reformed their ranks when the enemy attempted an attack, but the missiles from the wall halted these attempts. For several hours the soldiers continued to pass into the city undisturbed; in fact, it began to appear that they would all be able to enter unmolested. As it was, only a few hundred of Josiah's and Nathan's soldiers remained outside when the siege engines appeared.

At first the equipment simply consisted of shields in front of the enemy army to protect the soldiers from arrows and other missiles. The army began to advance slowly, now that they were invulnerable to the ranged attacks of the city. It was almost as if they were taunting the defenders with their impending doom.

"Close the gates!"

The command came from an officer a few dozen yards down the wall from Josiah. Josiah turned and forced his way through the soldiers on the wall to where the officer was standing, giving orders to the archers around him.

"You can't close the gates!" Josiah shouted at the officer. "Those are my men down there. You close the gates, and they'll die."

"And if we don't close the gates, we will all die," the officer responded as he turned to face Josiah. "A few hundred is a small price to pay for the thousands in the city."

"More of them can get inside before the enemy gets here," Josiah argued. "Leave the gates open until you absolutely have to close them."

"If we don't close them now, it'll be too late," the officer answered.

"Well, then you have some bloody slow gates!" Josiah shouted.

"Be that as it may, they're still closing right now," the officer responded calmly and turned away from Josiah to continue giving orders to his soldiers. Josiah looked down to the gates which were starting to slowly swing shut. In that split second he made a decision and dashed down the wall stairs. Once on the ground he tore toward the gate and slid to a halt in front of it. He watched the gates continue to swing closed as some figures came to stand beside him. He turned and saw Nathan along with his bodyguard. His own guardsmen had also arrived and stood behind him.

"Are you thinking what I'm thinking?" Nathan asked.

Josiah glanced back to the closing gate and then to the soldiers behind him. He turned back to Nathan and nodded.

"Then let's do it," Nathan said and drew his sword. Josiah pulled his weapon free from its sheath and heard the scraping of swords being drawn behind him.

"You know we're dead once we step outside of those gates," Josiah stated.

"Yes, I know," Nathan answered. "But I would rather die fighting beside my men than sacrifice them to save my own miserable hide."

"Elegantly put," Josiah said with a grimace. "Well, let's get on with this."

With steady strides, the small group of soldiers passed through the slowly closing gate and stepped onto the plain outside. The soldiers parted to allow them to pass as they recognized their commanders. They continued forward until they reached the front of their army's lines. In front of them the enemy advanced, ready to crush anything in their path.

"Can your magicians do anything?" Josiah asked Nathan.

305

"I don't know how effective they will be, but I'll put them to the task," Nathan answered.

"Good," Josiah answered. "I know that we're going to die out here, but I kind of want to leave them something to remember us by," he said and gestured to the advancing army. In a much louder voice he yelled, "Form the line! We'll meet these men and give a showing for ourselves."

The soldiers formed into ranks and faced the advancing enemy horde. They were tired, near exhaustion in fact, and when the gates had begun to close they had been on the verge of surrendering. The sight of their commanders leaving the safety of the city to lead them had restored their resolve, and they would continue to fight as long as they drew breath. The gate closed with a dull thud, and the soldiers glanced over their shoulders at it.

"I suppose this is going to be one of those, 'It seemed like a good idea at the time,' moments, isn't it?" Josiah asked as he stared at the now closed gates.

"No, this *was* a good idea at the time," Nathan countered.

The two commanders turned from the city to face the enemy once more. The archers and siege engines on the wall were hurling their missiles into the advancing ranks, but the enemy's mobile shields were effectively rendering these attacks useless. Onward they continued to advance, slowly but steadily. The defenders' morale, so recently bolstered by the arrival of their commanders, was beginning to falter and fail as they stared at their impending doom.

"What are they doing?" Josiah said and cursed under his breath. "It's almost like they're trying to scare us into surrendering."

"And they may very well do that," Nathan commented with a glance at the soldiers. "This delay isn't helping our cause any."

"To heck with them," Josiah said with a meaningful glance at Nathan. The elf understood the expression perfectly, and an instant later the two commanders joined voices as they bellowed out the command to charge. Without looking back to see who was following them, they jumped forward and sprinted full speed at the attacking army.

The defenders burst into a charge an instant after the command was given and converged as one on the enemy. A slight shaking of the ground, evidence of the efforts of the elfin magicians, threw a line or two of the enemy to the ground, confusing the advance. Before they had time to recover, the charging soldiers crashed into the first line of mobile shields and pushed past them to the soldiers they were guarding. While the shields had effectively protected the soldiers from ranged attacks, they had also blocked their view of the battlefield in front of them. Consequently, they were completely unprepared when the soldiers of Magessa hit their lines. With surprise as their ally, Josiah and Nathan were able to lead their men in a devastating charge which penetrated deeply into the enemy ranks. Weapons flashing, the soldiers cut down everyone in the way of their berserk charge, and the magicians added to the confusion with small but effective acts of magic.

The primary charge was so effective, that for a while it appeared there would be no stopping the small attack force that continued to hack and bash its way through Molkekk's army. Nevertheless, the momentum of the charge gradually disappeared as the initial energy of the attackers gave way to exhaustion. And so, Josiah found himself and his men in the middle of the enemy army, surrounded on all sides and with no hope of escape. In a last desperate attempt at survival, the army formed into a defensive circle with men facing out on all fronts. Molkekk's soldiers, seeing the small army in their midst, threw themselves at it, seeking to crush it completely; however, just as a lion that is about to die becomes fearless in battle, the soldiers of Magessa fought with a ferocious effort. All around them the bodies of their enemies fell in heaps as they tried time after time to sweep aside these troublesome soldiers; however, the fearless Magessians couldn't hold out indefinitely. Something would have to give, and it would happen soon.

Josiah found himself on the front line of the defensive circle, standing shoulder to shoulder with two of his guardsmen. On his right was Brandon, wielding his massive two handed sword, and on his left was Petra. Josiah saved his comrades from death more times than he could count and had no doubt they had returned the favor many times over. As he blocked with his shield the thrust of an orc bearing a broadsword, he saw Brandon deliver a crushing, over-handed blow to a goblin. The goblin raised his shield to defend himself, but Brandon's long sword sheered the armor in two and slashed into the goblin's neck at the left shoulder. As the goblin fell to the ground, Brandon brought his weapon in an upward stroke to contact his next opponent, a dwarf. The blade caught the dwarf under the chin, killing him instantly.

Josiah jerked his attention back to his own battle and was almost too late. The orc was swinging an overhand blow at him, and he had just enough time to raise his shield. The shock from the blow drove him to his knees, and he found himself looking up at the orc, awaiting another blow. A soldier behind Josiah shoved him aside and stepped between him and the orc, taking the blow on his own shield and simultaneously driving his own weapon into the orc. Josiah scrambled away from the fighting on his hands and knees, allowing the other soldier to fill the gap his absence had created. Quickly he scrambled to his feet and tried to survey the battle, though all he could see were the heads of the people around him.

"We're falling all around," said a voice next to him. Josiah turned to see that Brandon had given his position to another soldier and was once again beside his commander.

"What's it like?" Josiah asked, recognizing that his friend's stature would provide him with a better view of the battle.

"We're killing a lot more of them than they are killing of our men, but we're dying steadily," Brandon answered. "We can't hold this for more than another ten minutes or so. After that, we'll all be dead."

"What about to the west?" Josiah asked. "If we can get back to the city, we may be able to get support from the wall again."

"No good," Brandon informed Josiah. "We're barely holding our line there as it is and we won't maintain it much longer. Dwarves are converging on that position."

"We can hold dwarves off," Josiah disagreed.

"Not these ones," Brandon said. "These ones are dwarf giants."

"Well then, let's move," Josiah shouted and began to shove his way through the crowd to the west.

******

Most of the dragons had already retired to the city of Sulmon, having caused enough damage to the enemy dragons and griffins to drive them away. Feddir and his squad had already deposited their riders in the city and were circling the area one more time to make sure no surprise attacks would be coming. It was on the last circle that Feddir's sharp eyes detected the group of soldiers deep in the lines of the army of Molkekk. With a growl he alerted the other members of his squad and dove toward the ground. The other dragons dove after him, and when they were only a hundred feet from the ground, fanned their wings to join Feddir in observing the battle.

Bodies littered the area around the stubborn pocket of soldiers that Molkekk's men were trying to exterminate. There were less than fifty of the soldiers, and as the dragons watched, more of them died. The leader of the squad gave a roar, and the dragons dropped toward the earth. At the last possible second, they extended their wings and fanned them to slow their descent. Despite this action, they still slammed into the ground with considerable force, shaking the earth and knocking people all around them to the ground. Using their wings as support, the dragons leaped over the soldiers of Magessa and landed in a circle around the remaining defenders, dousing the ground on all sides with fire.

Brandon looked up from where he was binding Josiah's wound and stared at the dragons. It took a moment for him to realize what they were there for, but once he figured it out he picked Josiah up and ran with him to the nearest beast. The remaining soldiers, less than forty in all, quickly scrambled onto the backs of the dragons, and in under a minute the squad was back in the air with its passengers. The dragons swept over the wall and deposited the soldiers inside before lifting off again for one final reconnaissance of the area.

Brandon lowered Josiah to a comfortable position and turned his attention to his commander's wound. Carefully, he unstrapped Josiah's shield from his left arm and laid the twisted metal to the side. The article of armor had been sheered in two, starting at the top and continuing for nearly half the height of the shield. One glance at the gash in Josiah's left shoulder was all it took to remind Brandon of its severity. Gently he began to unfasten Josiah's shoulder armor and work the rent metal from the wound. As he laid the torn armor aside, he felt more than saw the motion to his left and looked up to see Nathan kneeling down next to him. The elf had a busted eyebrow, a cut running down his face, and blood seeping through a bandage wrapped around his right upper arm, but the look of concern on his face was for the prone form before him.

"How is he doing?" the commander asked and looked up at Brandon. "And what in heaven's name happened to him?"

"One of those blasted dwarf giants," Brandon answered with a grim voice. "Right before the dragons arrived, he took an over-handed blow from one of their axes. He got his shield up in time, but the armor was never built to take that kind of punishment. The ax ripped right through the shield and into his shoulder armor." Brandon motioned to the ruined armor he had lain to the side. Nathan turned briefly to examine the armor and then turned back to Brandon.

"How are his vital signs?" the elf asked.

"They're still strong, at least for the moment," Brandon answered. "The shield took a lot of the force out of the blow, otherwise the ax might have cut straight through his shoulder and into his chest. As it is, I think the blade stopped at his bone, but I don't know how much damage it caused on the way there."

"Find out where there is a hospital set up," Nathan ordered one of his bodyguards. "And bring something to transport the General on."

"What do you think?" Brandon asked Nathan. "After all, you're the elf."

"I can examine him, though I must confess, my skill in such things is considerably less than the reputation of elves would indicate," Nathan responded. He began to run his hands around the shoulder wound, not touching the skin just beneath his hands. There was a crackle, and a faint blue light illuminated the skin. Moments later the light vanished, and Nathan looked back at Brandon.

"The damage isn't as bad as it looks from the wound. The shoulder bone stopped the blade before it could do serious harm. Even the harm to the bone is fairly insignificant. His blood level is rather low, however. It's a good thing you staunched the bleeding when you did, or he might have died of blood loss."

"So he'll be fine then?"

311

"Yes," Nathan answered. "He'll be fine."

Thirteen

Josiah blinked and opened his eyes. Blinding light rushed through his eyelids and flooded his skull, bringing with it a pounding headache. Josiah forced himself to sit up and swung his feet over the side of his bed. Slowly his eyes began to adjust to the light, but the headache did not subside. Instead it was slowly replaced by a duller and deeper pain in his shoulder. He craned his neck to look at the source of the pain and saw a thick, white bandage wrapped around his shoulder. His shirt and armor had been removed to allow his wound to be bandaged, but apart from that he appeared to have been plucked straight from battle and placed on the bed where he now sat.

The pounding in his head was not as intense as before, and aside from his shoulder he didn't appear to have any other bandages, so he must not have had any other serious wounds. Small cuts and bruises covered his body, but he could move all of his limbs. Slowly he pushed off of the bed with his good arm and rose to his feet, but as he did so the blood rushed from his head, leaving him dizzy and off balance. His vision went black, and he felt himself crashing back onto the bed. He lay there for several moments and waited for his vision to return to normal. When it finally did, he swung his feet back over the side of his bed and sat there with his head in his hands. He felt something pressing down on the other side of the bed and turned his head to see Petra standing to his feet, using the bed to push himself up.

"What are you doing here?" Josiah asked.

"I was supposed to be watching you for Cirro," Petra said as he straightened his uniform. "He was here all of yesterday and would only leave when I promised to stay here and tell him as soon as you woke up."

"All of yesterday?" Josiah said. "How long have I been out?"

"You were wounded in the battle yesterday and never woke up when they were tending to you," Petra explained. "About six this morning I spelled Cirro, but I guess I'm not much of a morning person. I nodded off after about half an hour and only woke up when you started banging around."

"Was it really that bad?" Josiah asked.

"Let's just say that in my subconscious, I thought it was an ogre tap dancing."

"Oh wow," Josiah muttered. "Wait, are you saying that an ogre tap dancing would be an unpleasant thing to hear?"

"Well I've never been privileged enough to witness it firsthand, but…"

"Just don't let General Levvy hear you say that," Josiah said. "I imagine he wouldn't take kindly to you implying ogres can't tap dance. Now get over here and help me stand up before I do it myself and sound like a blasted ogre again."

Petra hurried around the bed and helped Josiah stand to his feet. Josiah held onto Petra, waiting a few seconds for his dizziness to subside. He shook his head to clear his vision, but the sudden movement caused the pain to flare up in his shoulder, and he sank against Petra to prevent himself from falling over. He straightened up after the pain had passed and turned to Petra.

"Where do you suppose I could lay my hands on a shirt?" he asked.

"If you stay here, I'll be back in a second," Petra told him.

"Good. I think I can still stand, so don't worry about me," Josiah said. "If worse comes to worst, I'll just sound like a tap dancing ogre again."

Petra jogged off and returned in a few minutes with a shirt which he handed to Josiah. The garment was loose fitting, and Josiah was able to easily pull it on over the bulky bandage on his shoulder.

"Where's Nathan?" Josiah asked after the shirt was settled comfortably on his shoulders.

"Where is who?" Petra asked. "Oh, you must mean the elfin General."

"Yeah, that's who I mean," Josiah confirmed. "It just so happens that his name is Nathan."

"Yes, well I am not accustomed to people of such high rank being referred to by their first names. The last I heard was that everyone of any rank of significance was meeting in the military headquarters of the city. That was yesterday, so they may have finished their meeting, but perhaps someone there will know where we can find the General."

"Great, then we'll start there," Josiah said.

"Directly after we visit Cirro and inform him that you are up and about, I presume," Petra said.

"Do we have to?" Josiah said in a slightly whiny voice. "If we do that, he'll insist on following me around everywhere."

"Given the circumstances, I believe it would be the proper thing to do," Petra answered after a moment of evident shock.

"I was joking, Petra," Josiah said with a sigh. "You don't have much of a sense of humor, do you?"

"No sir, not given the current circumstances."

"Well, then I'll try not to make any more jokes around you," Josiah grumbled. "Now let's get moving; we're burning daylight."

******

Timothy was being slowly pulled out of sleep by stages. When he had first fallen into bed, he was so tired that he could sleep through anything, but now that he had a few hours of sleep to his credit, he couldn't ignore the stabbing pain in his side. Sleepily he rolled over to remove the pressure on his side, but he could still feel the uncomfortable object. He felt the area and found that the object was under his shirt. This turn of events didn't surprise his sleep-fogged mind; rather, he lost no time in removing the object and tossing it onto the floor beside his cot. He rolled over and was about to return to sleep when something tugged at his mind. Maybe whatever it was that he had just thrown on the floor was important. What if he needed to find it later and was not able to because he had so carelessly discarded it? Groggily, he rolled over and felt around on the floor for several moments before he was able to locate the object. It was flat like a book, he noticed; in fact, it was a book. No matter, the point was that it would lay flat under his pillow and not cause him any discomfort. After placing the book under his pillow, he lay back down and closed his eyes, waiting for blessed sleep to wash over him again.

He was just beginning to drift off when the sound of footsteps jolted him to consciousness again. He sat up immediately, but it was only three soldiers walking past him, their armor and weapons clanking together as they passed. With an angry glare at the soldiers, he lay back down and tried to let himself fall back asleep but found that to be an impossibility. Having been woken a second time, he was now fully conscious and could not go back to sleep no matter how hard he tried.

After a quarter hour of tossing and turning, Timothy resigned himself to his fate and sat up, rubbing his eyes. Swinging his feet over the side of the cot, he pulled his boots on and laced them up. He retrieved his armor from under the cot and struggled into it as quietly as possible. Finally, he grabbed the book from under his pillow and headed for the door to the barracks.

Outside the building, the first evidence of the rising sun could be seen to the east. The air was cool, and for what seemed like the first time in weeks, there was no sound of men fighting or preparing for battle. The city in no way looked deserted, as there were soldiers on every wall, but as for the streets of the city, there were only a few scattered people traveling them. Timothy knew that the relative silence would be broken all too soon, but for the moment he was content to find a bench and sit quietly. For several minutes he sat silently praying to Elohim. He alternately thanked and praised Him and finished by asking protection for all the soldiers of Magessa as well as a speedy victory over Molkekk's horde.

By the time he finished, the sun had freed itself completely from the horizon and was starting to ascend into the sky. The city, which had risen with the sun was coming to life, yet Timothy still couldn't hear evidence of fighting of any kind. He looked at the book on the bench beside him and then at the soldiers on the wall. Surely the enemy would attack as soon as he picked up the volume, he reasoned, so he delayed opening the book for several minutes. Instead he reclined comfortably on the bench and closed his eyes. He stayed that way as the moments turned into minutes, but still there was no call to arms. Finally, when he could stand it no longer, he opened his eyes and looked up at the soldiers on the wall. They did not appear alarmed in the least, which was a good sign. Apparently, the enemy was not approaching to attack.

Timothy shrugged and reached for the book. He turned it over in his hands so that the title faced him and for the first time realized exactly what it was that he held in his hands. In elaborate gold script, the solitary word *Molkekk* stared up at him from the cover of the thin volume. This was the book which Vladimir had given him in Molkekk's tower in Vollexa Temp, and which he had apparently carried with him all of the way from that evil city without opening it even once. Instantly his interest multiplied a hundred times, and he opened the book and began to read. The first few pages were rather dull, and quite frankly Timothy had a hard time understanding how they pertained to the topic, but he struggled through them nonetheless. The beginning of the third chapter was where the interesting material began, and as soon as Timothy reached that point, he was lost to the world.

******

Josiah entered the council chambers of Sulmon, drawing stares from everyone present. The doorman would not allow Cirro and Petra to enter the meeting, and they had been forced to stay in the hall. Now Josiah found himself wishing they were still behind him. He always found it easier to do things when he knew they had his back. The door closed with a bang, effectively separating him from his moral support.

"And who are you?" a man at the far end of the room asked. His position indicated that he was not the moderator of the meeting, but he was of a rather high rank.

"General Pondran, at your service," Josiah answered with a salute. "I'm sorry that I am late, but I was just informed of the meeting."

"Actually, General Pondran has been indisposed since the council convened," said Nathan from another part of the room.

"He was wounded just before we arrived and has been unconscious ever since."

"Very well. Take a seat, General," the moderator said. "When you are seated, we will proceed."

Josiah looked at Nathan again and saw the elf motioning to an empty seat beside him. Quickly Josiah made his way around the large table which dominated the room to a seat beside his friend and sat down. Immediately the conversation began again, but Nathan leaned over to Josiah.

"Welcome back to the world of the living," he whispered. "Last time I saw you, you were in pretty rough shape."

"So where's Levvy?" Josiah asked as he looked around the room. "Shouldn't he be here too?"

"Yes, but apparently the people here don't appreciate the fact that the ogres have been an indispensable help to us, and have refused to allow him into their council," Nathan answered. "Apparently the ogres have been oppressed even worse in the recent past than the elves have been, and it's carried over until now."

"That's a pity," Josiah said. "He, for one, might actually have something useful to say. Hopefully he's off doing something that *is* actually useful."

"Shh," Nathan hissed at Josiah. "I want to hear this."

"The question we come to again is, 'Why isn't the enemy attacking?'" one of the council members was saying. "They have not pressed their advantage since everyone got into the city, and we locked the gates. But why not?"

"I can answer that question," Josiah said, and every eye turned to him. "Or maybe I should say that I can address it. My response to the question is this: Why are we even asking ourselves such a question? There's no way to know the answer, leaving only speculation. And what would we do if we *did* know

319

the reason for their not attacking? Would we really be able to use that knowledge to our advantage? Maybe, but maybe not."

"Then what would you have us do, General?" one of the council members said with a sneer. "Do you really think you're smarter than a whole room full of your superiors?"

"What are you, an Admiral?" Josiah asked as he considered the man's rank insignia. "Don't patronize me on that count. I was your rank at one time, and let me tell you something; being an Admiral doesn't make you a lick smarter than anyone else. Now, what I *would* have you do is respond to the actions of the enemy, not to the supposed reason for their actions. I would have you outside doing something rather than sitting in here for extended lengths of time discussing matters that you can't possibly know."

Josiah suddenly rose to his feet, his voice rising as he continued. "I would have you take council with *all* of your allies, not just those you deem worthy of your consideration. After all, the ogre General you denied a seat in this council probably has more sense than you do!"

For a moment the room was stunned into silence by the outburst. It had taken place so suddenly that no one understood what had brought it on or what it was truly about. Finally, the admiral whom Josiah had been addressing stood up and leaned over with his hands on the table in front of him.

"Do you have any idea who you're talking to?" he yelled at Josiah.

"My apologies, sir," Josiah said in a calmer voice. "With all due respect, the ogre General you denied a seat in this council probably has more sense than you do, *sir*. With your leave, I would like to go consult with him."

Josiah gave a crisp salute, spun on his heels, and was out the door before anyone could say a word. The doorman gave him a quizzical look; apparently he was not used to seeing people leave such councils so quickly. Josiah didn't even see whether he saluted or not, but marched straight past him without a glance. Cirro and Petra fell in behind him, but he didn't acknowledge them until they were outdoors. Then he finally turned around and faced his friends.

"That didn't take long, Josiah," Cirro began tentatively. "What happened?"

"I found out that the leaders of our armies are idiots," Josiah answered. "I also realized that I need to find General Levvy."

"He shouldn't be too hard to find," Petra commented. "The ogres have been restricted to a small portion of the city, so we will most likely find him there."

"Well, let's go there posthaste," Josiah ordered. "Who knows how much time we have to save this blasted city."

******

Timothy was half way through the book in his hands and hadn't looked up from it yet. Life continued around him, and people even used the bench he occupied, but he didn't notice any of them. His entire attention was focused on the details of Molkekk's life and reign that were recorded in the book. Vladimir had read the book while Timothy was asleep, apparently the younger magician was a speed reader, and his notes in the margins, though sometimes difficult to read, were very helpful. They offered insight into the contents of the book and several times drew conclusions that Timothy would never have arrived at by himself.

The time passed quickly as Timothy rushed through the book. He was only a half dozen pages from the end when he looked up for the first time. The sun was almost at its apex in the sky meaning that several hours had gone by. Timothy rose from his seat to stretch and walk a while along the road. The book, it appeared, was practically over, and though it had told him several things of interest, it would not really help him in his current situation. Molkekk was dead, and the problem was with his remaining army, not Molkekk himself. If he had still been at large, the book would have provided information on how to kill him. As it was, the topic was moot.

Suddenly Timothy jerked to a halt, a line from the book stopping him dead in his tracks. That was it, wasn't it? Though this created more questions than it answered. Of course, he wasn't sure, so he would have to talk to someone who knew.

Josiah would probably know, Timothy thought suddenly. It had been months since he'd last seen the man, but the memories forged in battle were not easily forgotten. Yes, Josiah would be able to help him out, but where could he find such an important man as the General of Saddun's armies?

******

When Josiah and his friends crossed the city division into ogre territory, they could not immediately tell the difference. There was no significant change in look or smell. Rather, the change came simply in the size of the inhabitants. Now instead of the people surrounding them being their own size, they were nine feet tall and hairy. Finding General Levvy was not as easy as Petra had indicated it would be. Apparently many of the ogres either did not understand Josiah or simply did not want to help a human after how the humans had insulted them by confining them to a specific part of the city. Nevertheless, after asking more than a dozen of the hairy people, Josiah was able to find one who tried to point them in the right direction, though he was not entirely sure of where Levvy was. Even so, the directions were better than Josiah had received all day, and he was thankful for them.

He followed the road the ogre had indicated, and after fifteen minutes of walking came to a largish building with guards at the entrances. Approaching one of the guards, he asked of the whereabouts of the General and learned that he was inside the building. Gaining access to the building, however, was nearly impossible, even after he had convinced the guard that he was a General and needed to speak to the ogre leader. After fifteen minutes of arguing with the guard, he was finally able to persuade him to go and tell Levvy that Josiah was outside and requesting an audience with him.

Josiah, Cirro, and Petra stood outside under the glare of the other guard as the first guard disappeared inside. Another fifteen minutes passed, and Josiah was beginning to despair that his message was even being delivered, when the doors flew open, and Levvy bounced down the steps of the building.

"General, how good to see you!" he yelled as he flung his arms around Josiah and crushed him in a giant bear hug. "I trust that your visit does not herald bad news?"

"Well, that depends on what you mean by bad news," Josiah admitted. "I came to talk to you about defending this city. On the bright side, I can say you're more intelligent than all of the human officers in the city put together."

"Is the city not secure?" Levvy asked with a frown.

"For the moment it is," Josiah answered, "but only for the moment. As you probably know, Molkekk's army has ceased its attacks on us, which is enough to puzzle anyone. Nevertheless, I cannot believe that I just came from a war council in which they were discussing what the motive of the enemy might be in not attacking us."

"Wouldn't it make more sense to prepare for another attack rather than discuss that?" Levvy asked.

"There you go again, showing your ignorance," Josiah said sarcastically. "You agree with me, so you must be wrong."

"Well, what have you come to talk to me about then?" Levvy asked.

Josiah started to answer, but was interrupted by a commotion down the street. Ogres were stepping aside to allow someone to pass, though Josiah could not see who it was. He caught his first glimpse of the man running down the street when he was only thirty yards away. The man sprinted the last yards up the steps to Josiah and stopped in front of him.

"Josiah!" he greeted the soldier.

"Timothy," Josiah answered. "It's been a long time since I've seen you. How have you been?"

"As well as someone can be in a war, I suppose," Timothy answered. "Listen, I need to talk to you. Now."

"About what?" Josiah asked.

"About this," Timothy said and held out a book that Josiah had not noticed before. It was a thin volume, elaborate gold script gracing its front cover.

"What's that?" Josiah asked.

"It's a book about Molkekk," Timothy explained. "Read this part right here."

Timothy opened the book to a spot near the end and shoved it into Josiah's hands. It took Josiah's brain a few seconds to adjust to the complicated script of the book, but once he did he was able to read the passage with no trouble. When he finished, he looked up at Timothy expectantly; and suddenly it hit him.

"Is this saying what I think it is?" he asked.

"Yes," Timothy answered. "Now, look at this picture." He flipped a page and showed a sketch in the book to Josiah.

"Who is that?" Josiah asked. He looked down to the bottom of the picture. "It says it's Molkekk."

"Yes, that's what it says, but it also looks like someone else I know," Timothy said.

"I don't get it," Josiah said. "What are you getting at?"

"This is a note my friend made," Timothy said and tapped a penned scribble on the edge of the page. Josiah took a moment to decipher the note, but when he did he looked up at Timothy in alarm.

"Does that mean…?"

"Yes," Timothy interrupted him. Josiah cursed.

"Cirro," he said as he spun to face his friend. "Get the soldiers ready for battle. Levvy, you had better also get your men ready. Petra, take a message to anyone who will listen and tell them an attack is imminent."

"What is this about, Josiah?" Levvy rumbled.

"I'll tell you later," Josiah answered. "We need to act immediately, or we won't survive the day."

"What are you going to do?" Cirro asked Josiah.

Suddenly Timothy pointed a finger at a massive tower near the city wall.

"Up there?" Josiah asked. Timothy nodded.

"I'm going to take care of some unfinished business," Josiah told Cirro over his shoulder. "Make sure you get my soldiers ready." Then he and Timothy were off, running toward the tower.

Fourteen

Senndra, William, Richard, and Alyss were relaxing in a park near the center of the city. Lydia was with them, having joined them earlier that day when she had happened to encounter the soldiers and recognize Senndra from their meeting in Saddun. The extended time apart had brought about significant changes in both girls, but they recognized each other almost immediately. Moments later Senndra discovered that Lydia was not doing anything in particular and immediately invited her to join her friends for the day. And so, the five young people found themselves enjoying the sunshine and relative peace for the first time in weeks.

Senndra lay on her back in the grass. Her eyes were closed, and she was simply soaking in the sun, not thinking about the massive army camped outside the city walls. In her world, there was nothing to be afraid of, nobody to fight, and nothing to do but lay back and relax with her friends. She cracked one eye open and looked over to where Lydia and Alyss sat, talking in low voices. For the second time that day, she noticed how much Lydia had changed since they had first met in Saddun. Smiling to herself she remembered the shy girl who had talked to her on the ruined walls of that city and explored the library with her. The girl sitting before her now had matured so much since that time. She had lost her shyness, allowing her friendliness to show through. Senndra smiled as she remembered how Lydia had exchanged pleasantries with almost everyone that they met, as well as talking at length to another group of people when they reached the park.

Senndra continued to smile as she lay back and closed her eyes again. Everything about her world was perfect now, and she wished it would stay that way, at least for the rest of the day. Her mind began to wander again, and for a time she thought of nothing evil or unpleasant. She was just beginning to drift off to sleep when the pounding of footsteps caused her to jerk her eyes open. Not twenty yards from her, two figures that she knew well were running across the park at top speed. She sat up to get a better look and determined they were indeed who she thought they were.

"Timothy! Josiah!" she called, but the men must not have heard her because they continued to run at breakneck speed without hesitating even once.

How odd, she thought to herself. There didn't appear to be anyone else rushing anywhere, so it couldn't be an attack. But if it wasn't an attack, what on earth would possess someone to run that quickly anywhere? Maybe they're just exercising, she told herself as she lay back down and closed her eyes. In any case, she wasn't curious enough to find out for certain what was going on.

******

Josiah followed Timothy as quickly as he could but already was beginning to tire. Despite the magic and medicine used on his wounds, they were beginning to throb and he estimated they were only about halfway to the tower. His armor had been designed to be comfortable while marching and fighting, but the rhythmic pounding of his feet on the ground had shaken the various pieces from their intended positions. Now they were digging painfully into his body. He pushed away the pain and lengthened his stride in order to keep up with the magician in front of him. The two men dashed out of the park and onto a road only partially filled with people. Nevertheless, their pace slowed considerably as they raced around and between the city's citizens.

Timothy suddenly turned off the street and into a crack between two buildings. Josiah followed him down the alley and out onto the lawn of another building. They sprinted across the grass and up the stairs of the building. They followed the portico around the building and leaped over a small wall and down onto another road. The street was deserted except for a horse here or a carriage there; by contrast, the sidewalks had considerably more traffic. Before Josiah knew what was happening, Timothy had angled off the sidewalk onto the street and was busting down it at full speed. Josiah followed, though his lungs and muscles screamed at him for a break. Down the street loomed their destination, so Josiah ignored his body and poured on a final burst of speed.

By the time Josiah reached the tower, Timothy was already standing at the door, bending over and panting for breath. Josiah stood beside him and followed suit, sucking in long droughts of oxygen and waiting for his muscles to regain some of their strength.

"How did you figure it out?" he asked Timothy when he could talk. "I thought you said you had already taken care of this problem."

"The picture and notes in the book were the beginning, but the goblins were what tipped me off," Timothy answered between gasps.

"How so?" Josiah asked in puzzlement.

"Goblins were not descended from the original man and woman," Timothy explained. "They are not really a race in their own right but were created by Molkekk. They don't even have a will of their own, but are more of an extension of Molkekk's consciousness."

"So if Molkekk had died, then all of the goblins should have died as well?" Josiah asked.

"Exactly," Timothy confirmed. "And since they aren't dead that means…"

"That Molkekk isn't dead!" Josiah finished.

"Precisely," Timothy said. "And unless I miss my guess, which I don't think I have, he's at the top of this tower right now."

"Well, then let's go up there and finish this thing once and for all," Josiah said as he straightened and reached for the latch of the tower door.

"I'm right behind you," Timothy said, "but remember, Molkekk is a magician, and a strong one at that. Be careful when we reach him; he can probably kill you with a motion of his hand."

"On second thought, maybe you should go first," Josiah said and stepped aside to allow Timothy to pass him.

"You're probably right," Timothy replied, opening the tower door.

The interior of the tower consisted of one large room. An odd smell filled the room, a smell that was almost sickeningly sweet. A large table with twenty chairs around it filled a significant portion of the room. The table still had food upon it, as though a meal was about to be eaten, and several of the chairs were occupied. Oddly the people were not partaking of the food but instead were slumped over onto the table and appeared to be sleeping. There were what looked like several large puddles under the table, and Josiah squinted, trying to get a better look at them. Timothy walked quietly to the table and tapped one of the men on the shoulder. There was no response, and he tapped the man again. Again there was no response, so he tapped the man again, this time a bit harder.

"Hello, sir," he said in a loud voice.

"Timothy, be quiet," Josiah hissed from his spot near the door. Timothy turned to look at him, and he simply pointed to the puddles beneath the table. Timothy bent down to examine them and stood back up an instant later.

"Blood," he said, but Josiah had already guessed that much. Quickly he crossed the room to the table and began to examine each of the dead men. All of their throats had been slit. Josiah looked across the table to see Timothy looking at him. As soon as he had Josiah's attention, Timothy motioned to a staircase winding around the outer wall of the tower to the second level. Quietly both men walked to the stairs and started upward. Nineteen steps later, they were directly under a trapdoor.

"Get ready," Timothy whispered to Josiah. Slowly Josiah drew his sword and nodded to Timothy. The magician planted his hand on the trap door and threw it open in one fluid motion. In a flash he had scaled the short ladder which allowed access to the second level and disappeared from Josiah's view. Holding his sword above him, Josiah struggled up the ladder and planted his boots on the second floor. As he did so, his eyes scanned the room, and determined that it held no threats. Timothy stood in the middle of the room, sheathing his own blade, so Josiah slid his sword back into its scabbard.

This floor appeared to be the sleeping quarters for roughly a dozen men. Cots lined the wall, each with a trunk at the foot. Weapons hung on racks attached to the walls, and armor was heaped in piles around the room. Presumably this was where the people below slept.

Josiah and Timothy took the stairs in this room to the next floor which was also sleeping quarters. The floor after that was a work shop of sorts for repairing armor and weapons. Two more floors of sleeping quarters came next, and then another work shop.

The eighth floor was different from any of the lower ones. Shelves filled the room, containing thousands of books. A small partitioned area contained a bed, but Josiah and Timothy ignored all of this and walked straight to the staircase. These stairs started in the middle of the room and ascended straight up. A door at the top was ajar. Timothy drew his sword and slowly began to ascend the stairs. One of the steps creaked, and Timothy froze instantly, but no noise came from the top of the stairs, so he continued his climb with Josiah close behind. Finally, they reached the door, and Timothy paused for a moment. Taking a deep breath, he lowered his shoulder and hit the door, slamming it open. In a single leap he cleared the last step and flew several feet into the room. Josiah dashed through the door a moment later and stopped short. This was his first look at the feared Molkekk, and the magician was not exactly what he had expected.

******

Petra sprinted down the street toward the tower that Timothy had pointed at. After Levvy and Cirro had hurried off to muster as many soldiers as they could and left him standing alone, he realized that he really had nothing to do. After a moment of indecision, he had started off toward the tower, prepared to give Timothy and Josiah whatever assistance he could. He came to a park and dashed across it. As he ran, the sun dipped behind a cloud, and the temperature seemed to drop several degrees. The chill only made Petra push himself harder, and in moments he had gained the street on the other side of the park. He sprinted down the road at top speed, hoping against hope that he would arrive in time to help.

******

Senndra awoke again to the sound of running feet. She opened her eyes to see another man running across the park. What in heaven's name was going on? She glanced over at her friends,

331

but they all appeared to be asleep. Shrugging, she climbed to her feet and started off after the man who had just cut across the park. She was not running very quickly, so he continued to put distance between himself and her. Shaking the last remnants of sleep, Senndra picked up her pace and started to shorten the distance to the person she was following.

******

Nathan sat in the council chambers considering the grain of the table in front of him. The others in the room were still discussing the same thing they had been discussing half an hour ago, and they still hadn't come to any decisions at all. Nathan was more a man of action and all of the talking was making him uncomfortable. Not to mention that he agreed with what Josiah had said before; he figured there was something he could be doing that would be a better use of his time. As he traced the wood of the table with his index finger, a faint warning began at the back of his mind. At first he was not sure if he actually felt it or not, but as the seconds passed, it became more and more distinct.

Without knowing why, Nathan stood to his feet and started to work his way out of the room. The task wasn't easy since many of the council members had their chairs pressed up against the wall, blocking the path to the door. The progress was maddeningly slow to Nathan, and still the feeling of urgency continued to grow. Finally he could stand it no longer and forsook the floor. With a single bound he jumped onto the table and sprinted across it to the door. The conversation had ended by this time, but he didn't notice the silence as he vaulted the chair between him and the door. He flung open the door and dashed out past the stunned doorman. Moments later he was out of the building.

******

Brandon awoke with a start and sat straight up on his cot. He glanced around the room, but there didn't appear to be anything that would have pulled him from his slumber, so he lay back down. Only then did he feel the uneasiness stirring in his gut. He tried to shove it away, but instead it continued to grow until he felt he had to do something or he would burst. Quickly he pulled his boots on and stood to his feet, stretching a bit. He glanced down and spied his claymore sticking out from under the bed, and without knowing why, he reached down and retrieved it. He strapped the sheath onto his back as he left the building and stepped out into the sunshine. His gaze was strangely drawn to the north where a tower rose into the air near the city wall. Nothing about the tower impressed him, yet he still turned to walk toward it. His pace quickened until he was running as fast as he could toward the building.

******

The man on the other side of the room was sitting in a chair and had his boots propped up on a table in front of him. He was drinking out of a goblet in his hand. Looking over the rim of his cup as the door opened, he considered the two men before him. Slowly he placed his cup back on the table and in measured movements took his feet from the table and rested them on the ground.

"Molkekk," Josiah said in a small voice.

"Tiberius," Timothy said at the same time. "You dastardly, misbegotten, flee-bitten mongrel."

"Both of you are right," Molkekk said as he stood to his feet. "Tiberius was a form I took on for a time. In fact, I like it so much, I think I might stay this way."

"Yeah, you can stay that way for the next thirty seconds," Timothy said as he started forward. "That's about how long it'll take me to kill you."

"I don't think so," Molkekk said, and with a wave of his hand Timothy stopped moving. "You aren't nearly powerful enough to rival me, you untamed cur."

Josiah didn't say anything, but instead dashed across the room, his sword extended toward Molkekk. Molkekk motioned toward Josiah who suddenly found himself unable to move. Molkekk gave a scornful laugh at the surprised look on Josiah's face.

"Did you really think you could kill me when your magician friend couldn't?" he snorted derisively.

Josiah strained to bring his sword around, but Molkekk motioned again, and his arms bent around until they were sticking straight out from his sides.

"Let's relieve you of that weapon before you hurt someone," Molkekk said. Josiah struggled again as his fingers were forced open by an invisible force and watched helplessly as his sword clattered to the ground.

"Now, to get back to you," Molkekk growled and turned back to where he had left Timothy; but as he turned, a fist flew forward and smashed into his face. With Molkekk distracted by Josiah, Timothy had managed to work himself free of the spell holding him and was now on the offensive.

Molkekk was caught off guard by the blow and staggered backward several steps. His nose was crooked and blood streamed from it, evidence of the damage that Timothy had caused. Molkekk looked up and drew his hand back, but before he could do anything to protect himself, he was hit by a spell so powerful that it flung him across the tower and into the wall on the far side.

With a sidelong glance at his stunned enemy, Timothy turned to Josiah and quickly freed him from the spell holding him. Then he turned back to Molkekk, who was slowly rising to his feet, and blasted another spell at him.

The wizard's reflexes had been retarded from slamming into the wall, but he was able to erect a shield just as Timothy attacked him. Even in this weakened state, he was much more powerful than the magician in front of him. Molkekk dropped the shield and flung another spell at his opponent. Timothy dove to the side to avoid the attack, and a suit of armor behind him received the force of the spell. Instantly it shrank to a fraction of its normal height.

After being freed from the spell that held him, Josiah had collapsed onto the ground, unable to move for the moment. Apparently the spell did more than restrain the victim because his whole body felt numb. In a few moments, feeling began to return to his extremities, and he rose to his hands and knees. His sword lay on the ground only a few feet away, and he crawled quickly to it and retrieved the weapon. He felt almost entirely revived by now and jumped to his feet. He began to advance on Molkekk, but the wizard gave him a disdainful look.

"Let's take care of that pig sticker, shall we," he said and turned his attention to Timothy.

The blade of Josiah's sword glowed red and collapsed to the ground in a puddle. The pain hit Josiah a moment later, and he dropped the sword hilt like a hot potato. Almost as soon as it appeared, the pain was gone, and Josiah was left looking at his destroyed sword. He glanced up and saw Timothy and Molkekk engaged in some sort of duel, though what exactly they were doing he could not determine. In any case, it looked as if Timothy was losing, so Josiah sprung to his rescue. He leaped onto Molkekk's back and rabbit-punched him. The wizard was stunned by the blow, but still retaliated with a stunning blow of his own. Josiah could not tell if the blow was physical or magical, but in either case it was strong enough to break the grip he had on the wizard's neck and fling him to the side.

Timothy took advantage of the distraction and leaped forward, slamming his shoulder into the wizard's stomach. Molkekk flew backward and hit the floor with Timothy still on his chest. The magician landed a series of precise blows on the wizard's face and throat before being flung off by a smashing strike of the wizard's fist.

Molkekk rose to his feet and wiped at the blood running down his face. He looked at Timothy and muttered a few words under his breath. Instantly the magician was jerked upright by his hands and stretched out spread-eagle with his feet three or four inches from the floor.

"So now I have you, and without much effort either," Molkekk taunted Timothy. "Did you really think you could defeat me singlehandedly when many magicians much better than you have failed to do so?"

"I simply do what I can with what I am given," Timothy answered. "After that, I leave the results to Elohim. If it is His will that I defeat you, then I will; however, if His will is that I die here by your hand, then I will. In either case, I will still serve Him."

"I don't care whether you serve Him or not," Molkekk said. "Never has any magician who served Him even come close to defeating me; I have killed them all, just as I will kill you."

"Really? What about the magician Jothnial?" Timothy asked. His gaze strayed to something behind Molkekk before focusing back on the wizard's face. "We still honor him greatly because he defeated you and confined you to your tower."

"And yet, you see that I am here before you and not in the tower," Molkekk retorted. "Apparently your Jothnial did not do as thorough of a job as you thought he did."

"You say that with scorn in your voice, and yet I saw a flicker of fear in your eyes when I mentioned his name," Timothy said in a calm voice. "I would guess that he was much more of a threat than you're letting on." Molkekk didn't answer, so Timothy continued. "Would it disturb you to know that Wellter is in this city?"

"I do not know who this Wellter is, though if he is anything like you, he must be pathetic indeed," Molkekk mocked. "Why would I be disturbed to know of his presence?"

"You don't recognize his name?" Timothy asked. "Perhaps you didn't see him before that reckless, inexperienced magician Jothnial rushed you. He was on the same squad and, quite frankly, the better of the two when it came to skill with magic."

"Well, as interesting as that history lesson was, I fear that the time for your death has come," Molkekk said and started to make a motion with his hand.

"Wait," Timothy shouted, stopping the wizard in mid-motion. "If you're going to kill me, I need to know one thing." Molkekk relaxed a little, so Timothy continued. "Obviously it wasn't you we killed in the tower, so what was it?"

"An illusion," Molkekk answered. "A very good illusion, but nonetheless merely an illusion."

"That was the best illusion I have ever seen," Timothy commented, admiration shining in his eyes. "I've never seen anything so lifelike that could also fight so many magicians at once."

"It was rather difficult to create," Molkekk admitted. "Of course, when you are sitting around for so many years on end, you have time to come up with things like that. But why am I explaining all of this to you when I'm just going to kill you?"

"What if I just killed you instead?" Timothy asked. "What would you do then?"

"You're just stalling for time now," Molkekk growled. "There's no way you can kill me. You don't even have your weapons with you anymore."

Timothy looked down to his belt and saw the empty sheaths for both his sword and dagger. He looked up and fixed Molkekk with an unreadable stare.

"I must have dropped them," Timothy said simply.

The look of victory disappeared from Molkekk's face, and he gasped in surprise and pain. Turning around slowly, he found himself face-to-face with Josiah, who had just driven Timothy's dagger between the wizard's shoulders. The two men stared at each other for a moment, then Josiah grabbed the wizard by the collar and slung him across the room. Molkekk slammed into the table and fell to the ground. With his left hand he reached for the dagger buried in his back and tried to pull it out.

Before he could do so, Josiah was on him again. This time he jerked the wizard to his feet and struck a violent blow to his stomach. Molkekk doubled over and clutched his stomach. He regained his breath and straightened in time to see the large goblet he had been using earlier in Josiah's grip. Josiah swung the cup upward with all of his strength, catching the wizard under the chin and throwing him off his feet. The wizard struggled back to his feet only to be knocked down again by another blow from the goblet, this time to his left cheek.

"I guess now that the tables are turned, you know what it's like to feel helpless," Josiah snarled as Molkekk struggled back to his feet. "Now you know exactly how all those men, women, and children felt as your army destroyed their homes and killed them."

Molkekk was again reaching for the knife in his back, but Josiah hardly noticed as he continued his tirade. "Well, now it's time for vengeance!" He was shouting as he advanced on Molkekk, forcing the wizard to back away from him. "Now I will serve justice for all of the people you and your army have killed. Now I will…"

Molkekk had backed across the room until his back was pressed against a window. All the while he had been tugging on the dagger in his back, trying to dislodge it. Finally he succeeded, and as he drew out the weapon with one hand, he flung a spell at Josiah with the other. The spell froze Josiah in mid-step, surprising him so much that he stopped talking in midsentence. As he struggled uselessly against the invisible bonds, he was vaguely aware of a shout behind him. Molkekk cast a spell, and the shout was instantly silenced. Josiah twisted his head around to see Timothy slam into the ground with a sickening thud.

"Well, now that he is out of the way, I can give you my full attention," Molkekk said with an evil laugh. "I was going to be content to just kill you, but since you have caused me so much pain, I think I will return the favor. Now, what do you think I should do? Perhaps rip your fingernails off; that would be painful."

Josiah felt his right thumbnail begin to peel up and away from his thumb, but the pain only lasted for a moment.

"No, I think it should be something more painful. Maybe I'll do something like this." A stabbing pain shot through Josiah's head so suddenly that he would have staggered backward had he been able to move. The pain was gone a moment later, and Molkekk paced in front of Josiah.

"No, come to think of it, that wouldn't be painful enough either. Perhaps…" Molkekk trailed off and stared at something behind Josiah. "I think I've got it."

Molkekk motioned with his hand, and Josiah heard a grinding noise coming from behind him. A sharp cracking followed, and he sensed a large object fly over his head. He found himself looking back at his image in a large mirror, probably six feet or so in height. Its edges were slightly cracked where Molkekk had torn it from its setting, but for the most part it was unharmed. Josiah stared at his reflection and wondered exactly what Molkekk was planning. He shifted his gaze to the wizard, but Molkekk simply stared back with an evil leer.

"Do you feel fear yet, human?" Molkekk asked. "Are you frightened of what I am going to do to you?"

"Not really," Josiah admitted. "What are you doing with the mirror? I'm not as bad as all that to look at, you know. Or are you going to slam it into me? I dare say that you've done worse than that to me."

"Shut up, fool," Molkekk growled. "Your flapping tongue annoys me to no end."

Josiah was about to answer when Molkekk looked at the mirror and motioned slightly with his hand. Josiah shifted his eyes back to the mirror and saw a slight ripple run across its length. The glass appeared to be stretching, though Josiah couldn't be sure that his eyes were not deceiving him. The stretching continued, and when Josiah was finally sure he was not imagining it, the mirror shivered apart into a million tiny slivers of glass. A look of fear flashed across his face, and he could see a taunting leer on Molkekk's face out of the corner of his eye.

The glass shot toward Josiah, and he had only enough time to turn his head before it hit. His armor protected him wherever it covered his body, but at all of the joints and on the left side of his face, the glass smashed into the soft tissue, penetrating deeply. A moment later the pain seared through Josiah, driving all thoughts from his mind, and all that he could do was throw his head back and scream.

"How do you feel now?" Molkekk shouted at him. "I bet you don't feel so cocky now, do you? Not so high and mighty and ready to take on a wizard anymore, huh? You humans are so fragile. It's almost insulting to have to deal with you!"

The pain was slightly more bearable now, and Josiah dropped his head back down so that he could see Molkekk. Hate flowed from the wizard's eyes, a hate that contorted his features and gave him a demonic look.

"I bet you wish that you hadn't made the mistake of coming for me, don't you?"

"There's only one person here who made a mistake," Josiah said through gritted teeth. "You! You turned your back on Elohim, and because of that you will fall. No one can stand against Him."

"Are you finished with your useless threats, human?" Molkekk asked.

"No, there's one other mistake you made," Josiah retorted.

"And what would that be?" Molkekk growled, thrusting his face into Josiah's. "I haven't made any mistakes at all!"

"You stood too close to me," Josiah said and swung his head forward. His forehead smashed into Molkekk's face, crushing the wizard's nose and sending him staggering backward. A moment later, the spell holding Josiah in place disappeared. His damaged legs could not sustain the weight so suddenly thrust upon them, and Josiah crashed to the floor.

He rolled onto his back, ready to defend himself, but Molkekk's attention had been diverted to Timothy, who was again cascading attack after attack of magic on the wizard. The wizard had erected a shield and was currently not returning attack, but Josiah could sense that this was about to change. His brain told him that Timothy would need his help, so he forced himself to his knees and then to his feet, shunting the pain away. He staggered two steps toward Molkekk and grabbed his collar in one hand and the seat of his pants in the other. The wizard was occupied with Timothy and did not notice Josiah until it was too late. He lashed out with his fists, but Josiah ignored the blows and hurled the wizard out of the tower window. Moments later Josiah collapsed to his hands and knees.

341

******

Cirro stood in his tent, strapping on his sword belt. He glanced down at himself, quickly accounting for all of his armor and weapons. He was appropriately attired, so he reached for his sword and slid it into its sheath. The tent flap opened behind him, and he turned to see one of Josiah's men standing in the opening.

"Have you mustered the men?" Cirro asked. The man nodded. "How many besides ours are preparing for battle?"

"Everyone we can see," the man answered. "After we roused our own, we went to take the news of attack to the others, but they had already been warned and were preparing."

"Very good," Cirro said. "When the men are ready, have them assemble at the town square. The General will be there shortly."

The soldier saluted and left the tent, leaving Cirro alone again. Cirro moved his hand to the hilt of his sword and took a deep breath. Slowly he let the air escape as he reached for the tent flap and pulled it aside. He stepped out of the dimness of the tent and into the brilliant sunshine, squinting as he did so. Someone was only a few feet away, but he could not tell who it was because of the sun glinting off of their armor. The man stepped to the side, and Cirro immediately recognized the man who had spoken to Josiah on the march to Rampön. His armor was golden this time instead of silver, but Cirro was sure that it was the same man.

"Greetings, Cirro, protector of the realm of Magessa," the man said.

"Greetings," Cirro replied. "To what honor do I credit this meeting?"

"There is a war," the man replied. "The villain Molkekk must be dealt with once and for all, and today in this city is where we will meet him and his army."

"You must be mistaken," Cirro said with a smile. "Molkekk's army is still at large, but the wizard himself has been killed already."

"Unfortunately, that is not the case," the man said. "The wizard is still alive and is threatening your friends even as we speak. We must move quickly if we are to defeat him."

"Wait, you said 'we,'" Cirro said. "Does that mean you're staying to fight this time?"

"I am," the man answered. "I will lead the soldiers into battle this time. Where are your men assembling?"

"In the center of the city," Cirro answered.

"Then let us be off," the man said. "We do not have much time."

******

Brandon thought that he was running as fast as he possibly could, but as he rounded the last corner and finally had a clear view of the tower in its entirety, his pace quickened yet again. A figure was running toward him from beyond the tower, but he could not tell who it was. The distance between the two runners decreased until Brandon could finally recognize Petra running toward him.

Both men were in the shadow of the tower when a shattering noise was heard from above, and a body flew out of a window at the top of the tower. With a glance upward, Brandon sprinted the final steps to Petra and dove into him, knocking him backward. Even as they came to rest on the ground, he could feel the impact of the body slamming into the dirt directly where they had been a moment earlier. Slowly he rose to his feet and helped Petra up as well. Only when he was certain that his friend was unharmed did he turn to examine the body on the ground behind him. The body was perfectly still as he would have expected it to be, yet even as he watched, the man moved a finger.

"Are you hurt?" Brandon asked as he dropped to the man's side. He was stunned that the man had survived the fall, but that was not the most important issue at the moment. "Where are you hurt? Is there anything I can do to help?"

"Yes, there is," the man said as he sat up. "You can die."

"Brandon, watch out!" Petra yelled, but his warning came a split second too late. A bolt of magic slammed into Brandon and sent him flipping through the air. He landed on the ground several yards from Molkekk with a sickening crunch, but Petra did not have time to attend to him. Already Molkekk was rising to his feet and preparing to attack. Petra pulled his sword from its scabbard.

"Out of my way, worm, or I will kill you," Molkekk growled.

"I think you will find me harder to kill than you expect, wizard," Petra commented softly. "Do what you will, though, for I will not move out of the way."

"Then die like your friend!" Molkekk shouted and flung his hands toward Petra. Petra ducked and dodged away from where he had been standing. As his sword trailed through the air behind him, a shower of sparks formed around it.

"You are not as powerful as you think," Petra said. "Your blow hasn't killed my friend, nor will your attacks kill me."

"You think you're so high and mighty because you have a silver sword?" Molkekk laughed. "Not even it can save you from the spells I know."

"It's worked pretty well so far," Petra taunted. "So give me your best. You might be able to catch me then."

Molkekk didn't say anything but began to fling spell after spell at Petra. Petra bobbed, jumped, and spun away from the magical attacks. With every move he drew closer and closer to Molkekk, but the wizard didn't notice. The fact that the man

344

before him was able to evade all his attacks infuriated him to no end, and he was now recklessly flinging spell after spell at Petra. In his frenzy, he didn't notice his enemy's approach until he was on top of him. With a quick slash, Petra opened a deep gash in the wizard's arm but was then forced to dance away.

"Enough!" Molkekk roared, falling to one knee. He raised his fist and slammed it into the ground, forming a shockwave that spread out in all directions. The indirect attack caught Petra off guard, and he was flung into the air. The impact of his landing jarred the sword from his grip, and the weapon cartwheeled to a spot several yards away from him. Molkekk flung a spell so powerful at his fallen opponent that it should have killed him, but Petra was too quick. He was already moving from the place where he had landed; however, the spell still caught him on his leg and flung him into a lamp post.

"Very impressive, but perhaps you would like to try your hand against a more worthy opponent."

Molkekk spun around to see Timothy standing just across the road.

"I thought I was done with you!" Molkekk bellowed. "What do I have to do to kill you?"

"Well, I thought that I was done with you when I threw you out the window," Josiah said as he stepped from behind Timothy. "But look at you. I guess we shouldn't jump to conclusions."

"You little worm! I'll deal with you once and for all," Molkekk shrieked and flung a spell at Josiah.

Timothy waved his hand and threw up a shield in time to deflect the attack. Molkekk flung another spell, but this one didn't hit the shield. Instead it was directed toward the tower behind Josiah and Timothy. A large section of the wall broke loose and fell on the two men, pinning them beneath a pile of bricks and other debris.

A roar blasted from the sky, followed closely by a ball of fire which hit Molkekk, enveloping him and everything around him. Josiah could feel the heat from the fire and looked up to see a brown dragon circling back up into the air. A shout of victory formed on his lips, but died stillborn as he turned his eyes back to the flames and saw the figure of Molkekk striding from them. His clothes were singed, but other than that he appeared to be unharmed.

"You will have to do much better than that to kill me, dragon!" Molkekk shouted into the sky. As if in answer to the taunt, the dragon circled back around and came at Molkekk again. For the first time Josiah could see a figure on the back of the dragon, a figure with a drawn bow. An arrow flew toward Molkekk, but the wizard didn't move. The arrow got within a foot of him before simply shattering into a hundred pieces and falling to the ground. The dragon rider loosed two more arrows, but they met with the same fate as the first. The dragon swooped over Molkekk and wheeled sharply, dropping like a stone to land in front of the wizard. The figure slid off of the dragon's back and ran to where Josiah and Timothy lay on the ground, and Josiah was finally able to identify the rider as Senndra.

"Are you okay?" Senndra asked in a worried voice as she started to pull the debris off the two men.

"I don't know," Josiah said. "I think Timothy's unconscious."

"We need to get this off of him," Senndra said as she continued to move pieces of wall.

"Wait," Josiah said and laid a hand on Senndra's arm. "Look!"

Behind Senndra, Feddir was facing off against Molkekk. The two of them had gone several rounds with Feddir attempting to stomp on the wizard; however, Molkekk was too fast and dodged the dragon's feet every time. The next time the dragon tried to crush the wizard, Molkekk spun away from the claw and shoved with both hands toward Feddir. Feddir flipped across the road, coming to rest against a building. Another spell brought the whole wall down on the beast.

"Who will contest me?" Molkekk shouted to no one in particular. "There are none that can stand against me."

"None at all?"

Josiah could not see the newcomer, but his voice sounded familiar. Craning his neck as far as he could, he was finally able to see an elf walking down the street toward Molkekk. A moment later he recognized the figure as Nathan.

"You are powerful, magician. I can tell that already, but not even you can stand against the might of a wizard," Molkekk said.

"You are mistaken, wizard," Nathan answered. "I am not very powerful at all. In fact, I can hardly heal a flesh wound with magic. No, I believe you may be sensing the magician behind you."

"Behind me?" Molkekk spun around to see another elf advancing on him. This one he recognized from many years before. "So, this is Wellter, the magician who should have fought me instead of Jothnial. You're shorter than I expected."

Wellter didn't say anything, and silence fell as the two men stared at each other. Neither moved at all, but it soon became obvious that they were fighting for their lives, though the battle was not visible to the eye.

The air directly in front of Molkekk began to darken and slowly spread out from him; at the same time the air in front of Wellter brightened and began to spread out in front of him. The contrast was striking, darkness flowing out from one man and light from the other. Sparks showered down to the ground as light and dark smashed into each other, and the strain of both became evident as they tried to use brute force to overpower the other.

For several moments, the darkness and light pressed against each other, fighting each other, trying to push the other back, but neither made any progress. Then, so slowly that it was barely noticeable, the light began to recede. As Wellter began to show signs of weariness, Molkekk grew more vigorous and redoubled his attack. The forward progress of the darkness continued as it ate up the light until it had almost reached Wellter.

The magician made one last desperate attempt to push off the darkness and stopped its march for a moment, but then it surged forward, completely extinguishing the light and enveloping the magician. There was no explosion and no sparks; Wellter simply collapsed to the ground under the cloud of darkness.

Molkekk lifted his head to the sky and let forth a victorious cry, daring anyone to come and challenge him. Josiah couldn't tear his eyes away from the wizard who was looking around at all of his fallen enemies. Slowly Molkekk's gaze swung around until it found Josiah. Their eyes locked for a moment, and the wizard started across the ground toward him.

******

Rita's eyes flew open, and she sat straight up. She was still in the park which she and her friends had walked to that morning, and as she looked around, she could see Richard, Alyss, William, and Lydia sitting up and looking around as well. Apparently the thing that had awoken her had done the same for them. Something was wrong, but Rita's sleep-fogged mind couldn't figure out what it was. She struggled to make herself concentrate, but the effort was useless. Then it suddenly hit her; Senndra was nowhere to be seen.

Quickly Rita rose to her feet and looked at the city around her. The bright sun that had been in the sky that morning was gone, hidden behind a cover of clouds, and a chilling wind was sweeping across the city. Oddly, the clouds weren't covering the entire sky, nor were they coming from the horizon; rather it almost appeared that they were coming from the city, near a tower Rita could see above the buildings.

Without knowing why, she started walking toward the tower. Behind her she could hear her friends calling to her, but their voices were carried away on the wind, so she couldn't quite tell what they were saying. Her pace started to increase gradually until she was running across lawns and down allies. Finally, she burst out onto a street and saw the tower standing before her, but it was what was in the building's shadow that caught her eye.

Sparks flew as two men faced off and as she ran, she saw one of them fall. The other turned and started walking toward a pile of rubble. As Rita drew closer, she could see two people buried under the rubble with Senndra standing over them. As she watched, Senndra drew her sword and ran toward the advancing man, but he ducked under her blow and backhanded her in the side of the head. She fell like a stone to the pavement.

At the sight of her friend being treated in such a fashion, a rage burst into Rita's mind. Her pace increased to a sprint, and she drew the only weapon that she had, a long knife hanging on her belt. The man finally saw her when she was only a few feet away, but didn't move to protect himself in any way. Rita continued at her breakneck speed, and the distance between the man and her disappeared. She raised her knife to deliver a blow and slammed into a wall of thin air. The knife flew from her grip, and she bounced backward, stumbling over her feet. Her head contacted the pavement with a sharp crack, and pain flooded her skull.

******

Cirro led the man in golden armor to the center of the city where his men had gathered and was surprised to see that there were more than twice the number he had expected to be present.

The man in golden armor walked directly through the ranks of soldiers as they parted to allow him to pass. No words were spoken, but it was evident they would follow him into battle. Cirro stayed close behind the man as he left the city square and veered off toward the gates. His pace was brisk but not fast, and in fifteen minutes he had led the army to the city gates.

The gates were slowly opening, and beyond them the army of Molkekk was charging directly toward the city. The grappling hooks on the wall and dead soldiers at the door of the gatehouse told the story; some of the enemy had scaled the wall without being spotted and killed the guards at the gate. Now they were opening the gates to allow their army access to the city.

The man in golden armor drew his sword and held it above his head. A clamor filled the air as the soldiers behind him drew their weapons and increased their speed to match his jog. By now the gates were fully open, and the enemy soldiers were coming out of the gatehouse. Seeing the soldiers of Magessa, they drew their weapons, but they were of no use. The man in golden armor reached them first, and a blow from his sword sheered through their swords and decapitated them.

The army of Magessa reached the gates a hundred yards in front of Molkekk's men, and they formed a line while a few entered the gatehouse. Cirro retrieved one of the weapons from the dead gate guards and stood with two swords, daring the enemy to continue. He felt a tap on his shoulder and turned to see the man in golden armor.

"I must leave you now," the man said.

"What?" Cirro demanded. "There's no way we can defeat this army without you!"

"Defeating Molkekk is more important than defeating his army," the man answered. "I go now to find the wizard and kill him. You must hold this gate until I succeed."

"Yes sir, I will do my best," Cirro said. He watched as the man disappeared among the soldiers then turned back to the enemy. He raised his swords and waited.

******

Rita sat up and rubbed the back of her head. At first she thought she was dreaming, but now she knew she had to be awake. She glanced around quickly, trying to get her bearings, but nothing looked familiar. The sky overhead was red and open space rather than buildings surrounded her. Slowly she stood to her feet and realized she was on a battlefield that had been deserted for several days already. Dead bodies covered the ground around her, bodies wearing the armor of Magessa as well as bodies which wore the livery of Molkekk, but time had not taken note of whom the soldiers had paid allegiance. All of them were starting to decay, and birds were circling over the field, dropping down to feed on the dead.

The bodies of another breed of soldier were mingled among the dead, soldiers that had wings sprouting from their backs and wearing armor that was now dull, but still glowed with faint light. In an instant Rita remembered the whole battle, the army of Magessa being defeated, but an angelic host coming to their rescue. Slowly, almost afraid to look, she looked at the ground in front of her.

The man in golden armor was lying on the ground, his face deathly pale. Rita's sword was still buried in his stomach, and it was obvious that he had been dead for a long time. Dried blood covered his armor and the ground around him, but miraculously time had not ravaged his body.

The emotions that had filled Rita the last time she had seen this man, emotions she had successfully forgotten, came flooding back, and tears flowed down her cheeks. Hopelessness and sorrow filled her as she gazed at him and realized for the second time that she had killed the very person who could have given her any hope at all. Her mind told her that this was the very son of Elohim, and by killing him she had chosen her side. Who was she to try and ignore her decision? She couldn't continue to fight for Magessa, for Elohim, now that she had done this.

Slowly her tears subsided, and she rubbed them from her face. She took one last look at the man's face, and even though his features were lifeless, she could still see love on them. She vaguely remembered Senndra saying something important.

"Remember this," her friend had said. "Elohim loves you and will always take you back. All that you have to do is ask."

Hope flooded Rita. Could that possibly be true? Would Elohim forgive her even after what she had done? She looked back to where the man in golden armor was lying, but as her gaze touched him a blinding light appeared, accompanied by a loud roar. The earth under her feet shook, and she fell to the ground. She planted her hands over her ears and squeezed her eyes shut, but she could still hear the roaring, and the light still found a way to her eyes. Gradually the shaking faded away, and the roaring was close behind it. The light softened from its harsh glare, and Rita was able to open her eyes and look around. From her position on the ground, she could not see the body that had been in front of her a moment ago, so she struggled to her knees and craned her neck until she could see behind herself.

There was nothing there, so she turned back around and only then noticed her sword sticking out of the ground. Dried blood surrounded the weapon, but there was no sign of the body which had been there moments before.

Rita shook her head slowly and looked again, but the body was still gone. She crawled forward on her hands and knees until she reached her sword. Pulling it from the ground, she examined the blade and then the ground, but she could find nothing out of the ordinary, nothing to explain the disappearance of the body. Finally she stopped looking at the ground and rocked back on her heels. What was happening? The man had been here only a moment ago. He had been dead, so there was no way he could have moved. Rita's mind was a whirlwind of thoughts as she stared at the bloody ground.

"Rita."

The single word came from behind Rita and silenced all of her confusion. Slowly she turned and saw the man behind her, the one who had been lying dead on the ground. His golden armor shone as if it was giving off a light of its own, and best of all, the blood that had been caked on his breastplate was gone.

"Rita, you are forgiven if you will but accept it," the man said gently.

Tears began to run unbidden down Rita's cheeks as she looked up at the man. Love shone from his eyes, and it was more than Rita could bear. How could this man love her after what she had done to him? She bowed her head in shame. The man knelt down in front of her and gently lifted her face to look at him. With one hand he wiped the tears from her face.

"You are forgiven, Rita," he said.

An unexplainable joy exploded inside of Rita and she threw her arms around the man's neck. She was laughing through her tears now, and the man laughed along with her. He stood up and pulled her to her feet.

"You are mine now, Rita," the man said. He directed Rita's gaze to the battlefield, where she could make out movement among the mass of bodies. One by one the angels and soldiers of Magessa stood up. Their flesh and skin grew back until they were whole again.

"I have a job for you, Rita," the man said after the soldiers were all standing. "My enemy Molkekk is at large and, if he is not stopped, will destroy all of Magessa. I need you to go back and face him."

"But he's a wizard, and I'm just a person," Rita argued. "I will gladly go to fight him if you send me, but of what use will it be?"

"You are not just a person anymore, you are mine, and I will protect you," the man said. "If you will obey me, I will help you stand against all your adversaries."

"If you say so, my lord, I will do it," Rita said.

******

Josiah watched as Molkekk batted Senndra away. He strained under the load of bricks on top of him and was able to dislodge a few, but they were too heavy for him to be able to free himself. He looked up and saw a girl come bounding down the street straight toward Molkekk, but she slammed into an invisible wall before she even reached him. She fell backwards and hit the ground with a dull smack, ending in a motionless heap.

Molkekk walked purposefully toward Josiah, a murderous light glinting in his eyes. Josiah struggled with the bricks, shoving them off his chest so that he could sit up. Pain flared through his back, but he fought against it. He pulled a knife from his belt and stabbed at Molkekk as soon as he got close enough, but the wizard simply dodged the poorly aimed swipe. Releasing a laugh, he pulled his sword from its scabbard.

"Now to finally be done with you, flea," Molkekk said and swung his sword at Josiah's head. Josiah heard a whistling sound coming from behind, and the wizard's blade stopped with a ringing sound against a sword that seemed to have materialized from nowhere.

The girl, who moments before had hit the wizard's invisible wall, pushed him away from Josiah and inserted herself between the two men. She exchanged a flurry of blows with the wizard, driving him further from Josiah until she had put twenty feet between him and them. A blow from Molkekk jarred her sword from her grasp, and she stumbled backward. His next attack, one intended to finish her off, was a thrust at her chest, but she dodged to the side and moved inside his guard. Reaching with her left arm under his armpit, she planted her palm on his shoulder. With a move almost too fast for Josiah to see, she twisted and pushed Molkekk forward. With her other hand, she stabbed a dagger Josiah had not seen until now upward with her other hand, burying it in the wizard's throat.

Molkekk staggered backwards, clutching at his throat, and Rita looked on in victory. The shocked look on Molkekk's face, however, changed to a smile, and he raised an eyebrow. He grabbed the dagger, jerked it out of his throat, and tossed it at Rita's feet.

Rita took an involuntary step backward as Molkekk stood up. Slowly he lifted his hands and pointed at her, and darkness began to flow from his fingertips toward her. It reached her quickly and enveloped her. She clutched her throat and fell to her knees as the darkness choked the life out of her. Her vision began to dim, and she knew consciousness would leave her at any moment.

"Leave the girl alone, or I'll tear you apart."

Molkekk turned toward the weak threat and saw Timothy clawing his way out from under the rubble that covered him. He knocked aside what he could with his hands and dislodged the larger pieces with magic.

"Are you not vanquished yet?" Molkekk growled. "I've seen ogres killed easier than you."

"You lied about my family," Timothy said as he staggered to his feet. "You killed the people I care most about, but I will not allow you to do it to this girl."

"Wait a moment," Molkekk said. He tossed Rita to the side and walked toward Timothy. "I know who you are."

355

"That's very clever of you," Timothy said sarcastically. "It didn't take the illusion in your tower nearly as long."

"Yes, well, there's so much more going on up here than in the head of an illusion," Molkekk said, tapping a finger to his forehead. "All that's irrelevant, however. Your service is to me, so why are we fighting?"

"I don't serve you anymore," Timothy said. "My master is Elohim, and Him alone."

"That's too bad," Molkekk commented in an offhanded fashion. "I might have let you live, but now I will kill you like a bug."

"For all your talk, that has yet to happen," Timothy said. "If you want my life, come and take it."

"I knew someone like you once," Molkekk said. He made a fist and magic started to crackle around it. "He resisted me as well. I offered a gift, but he did not want to take it. In the end he submitted to my will; everyone does."

"I will not," Timothy grated. He threw a ward together just in time to deflect the spell Molkekk flung at him.

"Have you not seen me dispatch everyone who has stood against me?" Molkekk asked. "I will overcome you. Surrender now, and I will kill you quickly."

"I surrendered to you once before and have hated myself for doing so ever since," Timothy said. "It will not happen again."

"Then you have chosen the more painful death," Molkekk said coldly. He blasted a beam of magic at Timothy. The young magician tried to deflect the blow, but he didn't have the strength. His ward crumpled under the attack. The force of Molkekk's spell threw him onto his back where he lay trying to catch his breath. An unseen hand gripped his chest and began to squeeze. His lungs labored to draw breath, and his ribs creaked dangerously. In moments they would begin to snap like twigs.

356

"Molkekk, leave that man alone." The command carried so much power with it that Molkekk stopped. Timothy, able to inhale once more, drew a ragged breath. He turned his head and saw a single man walking down the street toward Molkekk.

The man was covered with golden armor from head to toe, and a golden shield hung on his left arm. He drew a sword with his right hand and held it out in front of him as he advanced. Timothy couldn't pull his gaze away from the man as he moved forward; something about him was irresistible. From deep inside himself, Timothy realized this was a man who could defeat Molkekk once and for all.

Fear crossed Molkekk's face as he watched the man's progress, but it lasted for only a moment. He clenched his fists and hunched his shoulders. Instantly he was surrounded in a cloud of red mist which dissipated quickly to reveal the wizard clothed in a hideous suit of armor. He had no shield, but held a massive claymore in both hands. All of his armor was tinted red, as if it were covered with a fine layer of rust.

"Let us fight," Molkekk called as he moved toward the man. "Not even you are powerful enough to match me, and you are the most powerful magician I have ever met."

The man in golden armor said nothing as he continued to walk down the street at a measured pace. As he neared Molkekk, he reached up with his sword hand and pulled his visor down to cover his face. Molkekk did the same, and an instant later the two men were at each other's throats.

******

Cirro and the soldiers with him at the gate watched as Molkekk's army rushed toward them and braced themselves for the attack. The gates should have been inching closed by now, but they remained steadfastly open to the enemy charge. Most likely the enemy soldiers had sabotaged the gate after they had opened it so that it could not be closed. Cirro knew this would make the

357

battle much harder since the soldiers of Magessa would have to hold the city entrance rather than being able to hide behind their wall. The rest of the soldiers realized this as well, but rather than be cowed by it, they rallied together. They raised their shields and locked them, forming a wall the enemy would be hard pressed to break.

Molkekk's soldiers flooded toward the small army of defenders at the gate with battle cries and shouts of victory. The gates to the city stood open to them like waiting arms, and it seemed to them as though they had already won. With the force of a million soldiers, they slammed into the defenders, but to their surprise and anger they were unable to break through the line. The defenders put up such a fight that Molkekk's soldiers were forced back away from the city. Molkekk's men were not to be deterred, however, and they rallied for another attack.

The defenders held their position with a grim determination, knowing that if the enemy gained entrance to the city, the battle would be lost. Standing behind their wall of shields, they slashed and stabbed at the disorderly attacks of the enemy. Four times Molkekk's soldiers attacked and four times they were driven back.

They attacked a fifth time, but their attack was different this time. Ogres led the attack with their massive clubs and axes, causing the line of defenders to bow greatly in the middle until it seemed on the verge of breaking. At the last second, the defenders rallied together and drove the attackers back away from the city. The city was still secure, but the defenders were tiring from the force of the enemy's attacks. Many more of them, and the gate would fall for certain.

******

Timothy had seen skilled warriors fight before, but the fiercest battle he had ever witnessed was nothing compared to this. A ferocity words could not describe was in the movements of both men as they traded blows. They fought up and down the

358

street, neither having any clear advantage that Josiah could see. There was one difference between the two, however. The man in gold was always driving Molkekk before him as they moved. Then, all at once, the tone of the fight changed.

Never once had Molkekk been in control of the fight, but he had at least held his own against his opponent. Now, however, his offensive strokes became fewer until he was simply fighting for his life, blocking what he could but also receiving many wounds. Then, with a stroke so fast that his sword seemed to blur, the golden man simultaneously batted Molkekk's sword from his hands and drove him to his knees.

"Will you yield?" the golden man asked. "This is my only offer of quarter."

"I will never yield!" Molkekk shouted and, jerking a knife from his belt, stabbed at his enemy. The man in golden armor blocked the clumsy blow with his shield and ran his own blade directly into Molkekk's breastplate. The wizard looked down in disbelief at his wound as blood seeped around the blade. He looked up at his opponent, but saw only the unyielding visor of his helmet. The golden knight jerked his blade free from Molkekk's body and swung hard, slashing through Molkekk's neck.

******

Cirro overlapped his shield with that of the soldier beside him and waited for the charging soldiers to reach him. He was slightly winded, but the men to either side of him were showing signs of extreme fatigue which seemed to be a trend all along the defending line. The enemy had rotated their soldiers so that a new batch was attacking the gate, and as Cirro raised his sword, he knew this would be the final charge. There was no way he and the other defenders could hold off this attack, not given the condition that they were in.

Sensing victory was finally within their grasp, the enemy soldiers charged forward with all the speed that they could muster. Cirro watched as they flooded over the ground toward him, and for the first time in a long time, he felt fear. He had always known he might die in battle, but that knowledge had not been complete. In every battle in which he had ever participated, there had been a place to retreat to in case of defeat, but this time there was no place to run.

In that moment, Cirro knew with startling certainty that he was going to die. The faces of the soldiers rushing toward him came into focus, and he saw that they were almost exclusively goblins. Well, he would dispatch as many of the filthy creatures as he could before succumbing to their weapons.

The distance between the defenders and the attackers dwindled from fifty feet to forty, then to thirty. In a moment they were twenty feet away, then only ten. Cirro raised his sword, but just as the soldiers came within striking distance, they began to buckle and fall as if they had been struck down by arrows. Cirro saw that only the goblins were falling, leaving the dwarves, orcs, and ogres for the defenders to deal with, but even so the enemy army was left in shambles. The soldiers who managed to reach the gate were cut down amidst a roar of victory from the defenders, and the rest, seeing the bulk of their army destroyed in an instant, turned and fled.

The defenders raised a deafening shout of triumph as a squad of dragons finally entered the battle. They chased after the fleeing soldiers, killing them in scores. The dragons of Molkekk were nowhere to be seen, and Cirro surmised that they had fled along with the rest of the army. With a yell, Cirro raised his sword and led the soldiers of Magessa after their enemies.

******

Senndra watched in stunned silence as the decapitated body of Molkekk toppled forward at the golden knight's feet. She had begun to think the wizard was unbeatable, yet this knight had easily defeated him. The golden knight crouched beside his fallen opponent whose armor had disappeared as soon as he had been dispatched. Carefully he wiped his soiled blade on the wizard's clothes before sheathing his weapon. Then he stood to his feet and removed his helmet.

Senndra tried to focus on the man's face, but her vision started to blur. She tried to force herself to a sitting position, but the world swam in front of her eyes. She fell backward and felt her head connect painfully with something. Her mouth felt dry, and no words came out when she tried to speak. She saw two faces appear and look down at her, but by now she was fighting just to keep her eyes open. Blackness flooded across her vision. She pushed it back, and for a moment she saw the face of the golden knight clearly before the blackness flooded back, this time for good.

******

As the golden knight pulled the rubble off of Josiah, Timothy turned his attention to Senndra. She had passed out by now, but was muttering to herself as she slept. He rushed to her and knelt by her side. A wound just above the knee on the inside of her left leg gushed blood, and it was evident that if it was not dealt with quickly, she would bleed out.

Timothy unbuckled the armor from Senndra's leg and slit the leg of her pants to a point above the gash. Next he ripped a strip from the bottom of his shirt and pressed it against the wound. The blood saturated the cloth almost instantly and stained both of his hands. A cold fear began to build up inside of him, and he started to rip another strip from his shirt, but before he could, more cloth was shoved into his hands. He didn't look back to see who had given him the cloth, but instead placed it over the wound and applied pressure.

Blood soaked the cloth in less than a minute, and Timothy's fear increased at the sight of Senndra bleeding out in front of him. He turned to find more cloth when Nathan knelt down opposite him. The elf motioned for Timothy to take his hands off of Senndra, so he rocked back on his heels, clenching and unclenching his hands. The elf closed his eyes and ran his hand over the wound. Finally he sat back and shook his head slowly.

"If she weren't hurt so badly, I could probably help her," he said softly. "If I were a better magician, I might be able to help her, but as it is, she's lost so much blood already that there's nothing I can do."

"You have to be able to do something," Timothy said, almost angrily.

Nathan shook his head sadly and stood to his feet. He watched as Timothy clasped Senndra's pale hand and let his tears drip onto her. Nathan wished he could do something to help, and for the hundredth time cursed his lack of skill with magic. He could no longer bear the scene and averted his eyes, but as he turned away, his gaze fell on the golden knight. He was standing a dozen feet away, watching the events unfold. Suddenly Nathan remembered how the man had defeated Molkekk, and he began to hope. Perhaps this man could do something to help Senndra.

"Can you help her?" Nathan asked simply. "Please."

The man appeared to have been only waiting for the request and strode the few steps to Senndra. Easily lifting her limp body in his arms, he carried the fallen heroine away from the battle scene.

Fifteen

"She's awake!"

Senndra rubbed her eyes and tried to sit up, but found herself smothered by someone hugging her. The situation was awkward, and Senndra was glad when the person finally let go. She looked up to see the smiling face of Rita. Despite the pain in her leg, she was able to force herself up into a sitting position.

"Well, look who's back among the living."

Senndra turned and saw a small crowd standing by the other side of her bed. She could see Petra, Lydia, and Rita, but it was Cirro who had spoken. He was dirty, and a multitude of bruises and cuts adorned his body, but something else struck Senndra. He had worn armor almost the entire time since Molkekk's army attacked Magessa, but now he was without it. Neither did he have a sword at his hip; it had been replaced with a small dagger.

"What's up? Is the war over?" Senndra asked jokingly.

"As a matter of fact, yes, it is," Cirro answered with a light tone Senndra had not heard in the last several months. "Most of Molkekk's army was composed of goblins, and as soon as he died, they died as well. Seeing the bulk of their force perish before their eyes, the rest of the soldiers turned tail and ran. Our dragons are out tracking them down now, but most of them have fled Magessa already."

"It's really over?" Senndra asked. The statement hardly seemed possible. "Molkekk is dead?"

"Yes, he is really dead," Rita said. "I still find it hard to believe myself, though I saw it with my own eyes."

"What about everyone who challenged him?" Senndra asked as she craned her neck to see everyone who was crowded around her bed. "I don't see everyone, though I guess it wouldn't make sense for them to come see me. They're fine though, right?"

"Josiah escaped with his life even though he was fairly beat up," Petra explained. "Nathan is fine, though heaven knows where he is. Sadly, Wellter didn't make it. He was dead when we found him; we think he died instantly when Molkekk's darkness overcame him."

"That's too bad," Senndra said after a long moment of silence. "He was a good man and a talented magician. It was only because of him that any of us are here today, I think."

"That's the truth," Cirro affirmed. "From what I hear, if he hadn't confronted Molkekk when he did, you would have all been history by the time the golden knight showed up."

"Where is the golden knight?" Senndra asked. "I would like to thank him. I'm not certain, but I think I owe him my life."

"You do," Rita said. "You have a nasty wound on your leg from your bout with Molkekk, and nobody could do anything about it. You were bleeding so much that you almost died. I don't know what the man did, but what I do know is that you would be dead by now if it weren't for him. We don't know what happened to him; he disappeared shortly after he killed Molkekk."

Slowly Senndra shook her head at the sudden deluge of news. It was almost too much to take in all at once. Strangely, though, she had the feeling that she was forgetting something.

"Timothy!" she blurted out suddenly.

"He's alright," Lydia assured her. "He's been at your side since the battle. He just slipped out to get some food."

"Tell me again that the war is over," Senndra said to no one in particular. "After that, pinch me to make sure I'm awake."

"The war is over, Senndra," Cirro said and pinched her as hard as he could.

"You didn't have to pinch me that hard, you brute," Senndra complained and playfully shoved him.

"Just wanted to make sure you were actually awake," Cirro shot back. "It would suck if you weren't because that would make me a figment of your imagination."

Senndra was about to spout off a comeback when a familiar figure pushed through the crowd. Timothy looked worn out, but he still held his head high and his eyes were still bright. He held a steaming mug in one hand and a pastry in the other. Evidently he had not noticed Senndra.

"She's awake, idiot," Petra said.

"What?" Timothy asked. He caught sight of Senndra at the same moment and was so startled that he spilled his mug all over himself. With a yelp and a curse, he dropped the pastry and mug and swiped the hot liquid off of himself. The smell engulfed Senndra.

"I didn't think you drank coffee," she said.

"I don't, but it does wonders for keeping a person awake," Timothy said. "I'm pretty much running on fumes right now."

"Well, don't make it a habit," Senndra said. "It'll stain your teeth funny colors."

"I'm a magician," Timothy shot back. "If my teeth get stained, I'll just turn them white again."

"With your affinity for destruction magic, I'd be worried about losing a few of them in the process. Besides, that's a frivolous use of magic," Senndra teased. "Couldn't that turn you into an evil wizard like Molkekk?"

Her face suddenly darkened as her own words jogged her memory.

"But you already work for him, don't you?" she said.

The laughter which the witty banter had aroused in the others was cut off suddenly. Timothy's expression said this was a subject he wanted to avoid, yet he knew it would come up eventually.

"Can you give us some time alone?" he said to the others. They nodded and quickly left the make-shift hospital. It wasn't quite as private as Timothy had hoped, with all of the other patients around, but it would have to do. He sat down on the bed next to Senndra's.

"This wasn't the way I wanted you to find out..." he began, but Senndra cut him off.

"You weren't ever going to tell me, were you?" she accused.

"I was going to, I just didn't know how," Timothy said. "How do you tell someone you really like that you've been working for the bad guy all along? Worse, how do you tell her you've been working for the man who killed her father?"

"There's no good way to tell someone that because it's unthinkable," Senndra retorted.

"It's not what you think," Timothy explained. "There's a lot more to this situation than you know."

"I know you work for Molkekk," Senndra said. "What more is there to explain?"

"I *used* to work for him," Timothy said. "And then, two days ago, I helped defeat him for good. I don't expect you to like me after this or even to forgive me, but I want to explain so you understand."

"If you really think you have an explanation good enough, go ahead," Senndra said and crossed her arms.

"Six months ago, when you found out I was a magician, I told you that if you wanted to be my friend you had to realize I still had secrets. These are the secrets I was referring to; I now have nothing left to hide.

"Do you remember the story I told you? About my early years as a magician? Well, what I told you was completely true, minus a few details. Gillian pulled strings to get me into the academy at Belvárd and sent me there. The trip was long, and I was alone. My family happened to live on the way, so I made a detour to visit them. When Gillian had rescued me, I was unsure how my actions would affect my family, so I never told him about them. Consequently, he didn't anticipate the detour, but I figured that it couldn't hurt. I was wrong.

"My activities as a young magician had attracted a lot of attention and not the good kind. It turns out that Molkekk had been looking for a person with my particular talents to perform a task for him. Evidently I fit the bill perfectly. By the time he got to me, I had turned to Elohim, and an attempt to entice me with power would have failed. Consequently, he was forced to try a different tact. His agents followed me and invaded my family's home. They took my family into captivity and threatened them with bodily injury if I didn't obey Molkekk's orders."

"If that's true, how did you end up at the academy?" Senndra asked.

"As it turned out, my entrance into the academy played to Molkekk's advantage," Timothy answered. "The task he had in mind was going to take me there anyway, and the fact that I was already enrolled would keep suspicion off of me. I hated myself for being under Molkekk's thumb, but I didn't have a choice. My family was locked away in Vollexa Temp, and there was nothing I could do about it. By doing Molkekk's biding, I was able to keep them safe, so that's what I did.

"After we invaded the evil city, I searched for my family. I didn't expect to find them alive, but even seeing their bodies would have given me a sense of closure. I found nothing and can only guess that they're buried in one of the countless unmarked graves outside the city. Anyway, their absence marked the end of Molkekk's hold over me. I was finally free."

"And then you helped to kill the wizard," Senndra said softly. There was clearly much more to this young man than met the eye. "I'm sorry about your family."

"They are in Elohim's hands now," Timothy said. "I only regret that Molkekk was able to use them to bend me to his will."

Silence fell between the two young people. Senndra did not say anything, but her heart burned for Timothy. She forgave him, of course. Because her father had died while she was still young, she understood the pain the loss of a family member produced. Had she been in Timothy's situation, she would also have done whatever was necessary to protect the ones she loved.

"Well, that's the story of why I served Molkekk," Timothy said. "Like I said, I don't expect you to forgive me, but I just hope you understand why I did what I did."

He started to rise, but Senndra stopped him with a hand on his knee.

"If we're going to make this work," she said, motioning to the two of them, "you have to promise me that there won't be any more secrets."

"I promise," Timothy said, sitting back down and taking Senndra's hand in both of his. "No more secrets. If I think of any, I'll blurt them right out."

"Well, you can start with this," Senndra said. "What exactly did you do for Molkekk?"

"You won't believe me if I tell you," Timothy said. Senndra gave him a look, and he added, "But I'll tell you. As I said before, I have nothing to hide anymore. The solitary task Molkekk assigned me was to protect, at all costs, the lives of Lemin and Vladimir."

"Protect them?" Senndra asked in surprise. "Why would he want you to do that?"

"I don't know," Timothy answered. "I didn't know who they were at the time the task was given to me, but now I wonder what his interest in them might have been."

"Well, whatever the case, it doesn't matter," Senndra said. "All three of them are dead."

"Molkekk might be dead, but not the other two," Timothy said with a smile.

"Not dead?!" Senndra exclaimed and suddenly sat upright. "But they were in the tower. They were destroyed with it."

"My dear lady, when I'm given a task, I do not fail, especially when it has to do with protecting my friends," Timothy said. "When we finally confronted Molkekk's illusion in his tower, I saw first-hand how powerful and cunning he was and knew that might alone would not bring about his downfall. I needed to be as cunning as he was to throw him out of stride. The only thing I had to my advantage was the information that he wanted Lemin and Vladimir alive for some reason, and I reasoned that destroying them would arrest his ability to fight, at least momentarily." Timothy dropped his eyes to avoid Senndra's before resuming his explanation. "To my shame, I must also admit I wanted nothing more than to thumb my nose at him, and killing his prized magicians was the easiest way I could think of doing it. I do regret some of the motivation for my actions, though not the actions themselves. The result was spectacular, and we were able to destroy Molkekk. Well, at least the illusion of him."

"I'm not following you," Senndra said, holding up a hand to stop Timothy's explanation. "You said Lemin and Vladimir are not dead, and yet you killed them to distract the illusion."

"I haven't given you all the details quite yet," Timothy answered the unspoken question. "I created a portal and tricked Molkekk into thinking it led to hell, the place of eternal death. Then I shoved Lemin and Vladimir through it. Of course, the portal didn't actually lead to hell."

"Where, then?" Senndra asked.

"That's the embarrassing part," Timothy said with a dry laugh. "I have a penchant for destruction magic, and portals don't come easily to me. The design wasn't my own but something I learned from Lemin. He was just introducing the concept of portals and never told me where it led, but I was able to remember the construction of it. I'm not saying the decision was a good one, and my pride and anger were certainly what drove me to it. But I take comfort in the knowledge that at least they're someplace Lemin will recognize."

"That's true, and the two of them are resourceful magicians," Senndra commented. "No matter the case, it's out of our hands now. The only thing we can do it send up a prayer for them to Elohim."

"Agreed," Timothy said. His thoughts and prayers had been with Lemin and Vladimir since he had sent them through the portal, but it wouldn't hurt to do it again, especially to ease Senndra's mind.

Epilogue

Consciousness is a fickle thing, the man thought. When there's a particularly bad situation or memory that someone wants to forget, consciousness seems to never leave, hanging on by the slightest thread to torment you with thought or action. On the other hand, no matter how much someone wants, no, *needs* to remain cognizant of their surroundings, a good smack to the head will send consciousness running. And then there was the whole situation of being partially conscious, aware of surroundings but unable to do anything.

That was where he found himself now. Just moments ago, he could feel the heat of flames and gagged at the smell of burning sulfur. He had the strangest feeling, and then it was all gone. For one blessed moment there was nothing to sense, nothing to feel, until gravity yanked him toward the ground that he was clearly not on anymore. Branches slapped his face and arms as he plummeted downward, slamming to a stop in the relatively soft earth below. Something landed heavily on top of him, driving the breath from his lungs.

For a moment he lay on the ground, assessing the pounding in his head and gathering his breath. Finally he rolled the object off of himself, noticing that it was a boy. He checked the boy to assure himself that he was alive before sitting on the ground beside him.

It was raining, he realized, and the ground he sat on was soaking wet. It occurred to him that he was still wearing his armor and weapons, though the information meant nothing in his current situation. If he had some flint and steel or some food, that would be something, but he was fairly certain he did not. No matter, he would just have to tough it out.

The body beside him moved, and he helped him sit up. At first the boy did not know where he was, but he recognized the man.

"Where are we?" Vladimir rasped."

"I don't know," Lemin answered as he looked at the dripping trees around him. "But if you can get up, we can go and find out."

About the Author

Peter Last was very nearly born in an elevator and has continued to be unconventional ever since. He is the sixth child in a large family and has had a conservative upbringing by Yankee parents living in the south. Despite having been homeschooled from kindergarten until twelfth grade, Peter has an expansive social life and has never been locked in a closet. He began writing his first novel, *Guardians of Magessa*, at the age of eleven, receiving great encouragement from his family in the form of compliments such as "Your book is actually not that bad!" He is currently slogging his way through his fifth and final year in college, doggedly working toward a degree in Civil Engineering and promising himself he will have more time when he graduates. In the little spare time he has, Peter writes a blog (www.peterlast.com) where he posts short stories, reviews books and movies, and addresses a mixture of serious and absurd topics, from global warming to pencil sharpeners. Peter's other hobbies include drawing, dabbling in amateur film directing, and discharging powerful firearms at shooting ranges. Between school, his social life, and his hobbies, Peter has been forced to cut back on unnecessary activities such as sleeping. At present, he is busy with yet another series, *Shadow for Hire*. Book one, *The Wages of Death*, will be released in the spring.

 The Archives of Magessa contains exclusive members' only content. Members have access to the forum, some of the concept art for my book series, and more. Join the club today to receive access!